THE DAY IS DARK

THE DAY IS DARK

Translated from the Icelandic by
Philip Roughton

Yrsa Sigurdardóttir

**WINDSOR
PARAGON**

First published 2011
by Hodder & Stoughton
This Large Print edition published 2012
by AudioGO Ltd
by arrangement with
Hodder & Stoughton Ltd

Hardcover   ISBN: 978 1 445 87801 0
Softcover   ISBN: 978 1 445 87802 7

British Library Cataloguing in Publication Data available

Printed and bound in Great Britain by
MPG Books Group Limited

This book is dedicated to my sister,

Laufey Ýr Sigurdardóttir.

Acknowledgements

Many people assisted in the writing of this book, but special thanks go to Jenný Einarsdóttir of Ístak, Jóhann Kröyer and Arnbjörg Jóhannsdóttir, and Arvid Thastum, a resident of Kulusuk.

It should be mentioned that although some of the characters in the book have the same names as some of my friends and family members, their names are the only thing they have in common.

—*Yrsa*

Prologue

31 October 2007

Oddný Hildur looked away from the computer screen, took the headphones from her ears and listened. The wind moaned outside; the wooden walls creaked in the strongest gusts, but otherwise she couldn't hear anything. Strange. She'd had the feeling that there was someone else in the building. She relaxed her shoulders slightly and looked at the clock. A few minutes to midnight. Was it really so late? It was highly unlikely that anyone had come over; most of the others were either asleep or well on their way to dreamland. It must have been her imagination. Who could be up and about so late? Oddný Hildur sighed. She had been working non-stop since coming over to her office after supper. The weather had done a complete about-face, the beautiful, ice-cold calm turning into a noisy gale that whipped up the snow from the morning. The changeable weather here no longer surprised her, although she would never get used to it. Now she regretted not having followed the safety regulations and given notice of her plans; she had avoided doing so out of fear that someone would want to join her. Arnar had talked about doing some more work, but luckily he hadn't shown up. She had very much wanted to be alone with the work she'd been putting off, work that now really needed to be done. There was never any peace and quiet when the others were there too, especially in the evenings after a long day at work.

1

Suddenly she regretted having slunk over here on her own. Instead of feeling good about her solitude, she was overwhelmed by an odd sensation of discomfort. It was unlike her; she was known to have anything but a fertile imagination, and usually stared blankly at whoever had told the joke while others roared with laughter. It's not like there was even a chance that she would get the joke later; generally speaking, anything other than pure fact went over her head. This had worked to her advantage in geology, but it was a hindrance when it came to human interaction.

She yawned and shook off her uneasiness. Before shutting her laptop she checked whether her husband Stebbi was on MSN chat, but of course he'd long since gone to bed. The time difference made it midnight for him, and he was supposed to start work at Ártúnshofði at 8 a.m. The morning traffic meant he had to give himself plenty of time to make it all the way from Hafnarfjörður, where they'd bought their first apartment. It was this investment in real estate that had forced her to accept this difficult job, which paid much better than comparable positions in town—partly thanks to the extra allowance included to offset the long absences from her family. They had waited too long to buy, deciding to do so only after the prices had been driven sky-high, and now they had their hands full trying to pay it off. Fortunately they hadn't taken a loan in foreign currency for the purchase, as so many who now bore the consequences of the falling rate of the Icelandic króna had done, but the payments had increased nevertheless and they were eating into their income. When Oddný Hildur saw the advertisement for the Berg Technology job on the east coast of Greenland, common sense had told her to apply. Her husband was not as keen, since it meant she would be away for four weeks at a time. Why live together if we sleep in different countries? he'd argued. She tried to look on the bright side, however: high wages and two weeks off work in between tours. Afterwards they would be able to think about having children, which they'd put off doing due to their financial struggles. But until that day came, Oddný Hildur had to make the best of hanging around in a work camp in a godforsaken place far from civilization.

She gazed disconsolately at the MSN chat window on her laptop. Occasionally when Stebbi was unable to sleep he signed in on the off-chance, but that was not the case tonight. The unpleasant sensation crept over her again. Now she had a strong feeling that someone was staring at the back of her neck. Of course she knew that was impossible, but she still needed to gather the courage to turn around to make sure. She only had two more days left on this tour and knew she was suffering from fatigue. To make matters worse, the weather forecast was bad and she had been worrying about having to travel home in bad weather, or getting stuck here. Some harsh words she'd used during an argument earlier were also niggling at her, and she regretted having reacted so brusquely.

She stiffened.

Either she was going mad or someone was watching her. Could somebody be outside the window? Whoever it was would have a clear view of her in the brightly lit office. She turned in her chair very slowly and peered out into the black night, but

3

saw only her own reflection in the window. Her face seemed to belong to someone much younger than herself; her wide, fearful eyes gave her a childish look she hadn't seen for many years. What was wrong with her, anyway? She was alone in the office, because Arnar would certainly have looked in on her if he'd come as planned. And of course there was nobody outside. Her co-workers would hardly be spying on her in this perilous weather, nor was she irresistible enough for any man to go to such trouble. But what about the residents of the village? Was one of the locals out there? She cursed herself again for having failed to lock the door. What was wrong with her? Of course no one had struggled against the gale all the way from the village; the only ones who would even have considered such a thing were the alcoholics, and she knew they'd all have fallen into bed long ago, dead drunk. The fact that it was Tuesday changed nothing; to those poor wretches, every day was the same. It was out of the question that any of them was up and about so late in the evening, and no one else was likely to hang around outside the window. Although the locals took a dim view of Berg Technology, she thought it unlikely that their antipathy ran so deep that they would seek revenge.

Contrary to all logic, her apprehension would not leave her. She rolled her chair towards the wall and turned off the light, but was in no rush to go back to the window and look out. Finally she plucked up the courage.

A strong gust of wind shook the building, then died down. Oddný Hildur gasped when she saw what was outside. A large, bedraggled husky sat in the parking area, staring at her. Its ears moved

4

in the wind, but otherwise it was like a statue. Their eyes met and the dog stared at her without blinking. She gazed back as if hypnotized, her heart hammering in her chest. One of the first things she'd been told was not to approach the huskies, neither to pet them nor to feed them. They were working dogs, and did not associate with people in the same way that pets did back home. She had learned this second-hand when travelling on an emergency medical flight to Reykjavík, shortly after starting work in Greenland. It was the first and last time she would take such a flight. A little girl had wandered into a group of huskies, and her face had been mauled. The sound of her crying, which hadn't stopped all the way to Iceland, still echoed in Oddný Hildur's ears, as did the desperate attempts of the girl's mother to soothe the child. Oddný Hildur's stomach tightened as she recalled how the girl had looked when she saw her several months later, on one of her few trips into the village, playing with an old doll by the side of the road. It was entirely possible that the dog outside was one of those that had attacked the girl. None of them had been put to sleep. She wondered whether she should swallow her pride and call Gísli, who was in charge of security for the area. He would accompany her to her apartment without a grumble, even though he was probably already asleep. He took his job very seriously, performed it devotedly and was incredibly obliging. On the other hand, she didn't want to have to endure the ribbing of her co-workers for dragging people out of bed in the middle of the night to walk her the short distance home. She was unpopular enough at the moment. No, she would be fine by herself.

5

She had heard that dogs did not attack people unprovoked; there was no risk if they were left in peace. She would walk the short distance home briskly, and the dog would stay where it was and then disappear into the night. Before she knew it she would be in bed. Oddný Hildur turned off her computer and prepared to leave. Before she went into the corridor she looked once more through the window and saw the dog still staring at her. Suddenly it tilted its head, as if it were wondering why she had stood up. She regretted having given in to curiosity; now the dog knew that she was on her way out and would lie in wait for her at the door. However, it did not appear to be that cunning—it just sat there, still as stone. Oddný Hildur tugged at the curtain intending to block the dog's view, but when it emitted a howl she was so shaken that she dropped it. Then she heard a muffled bark, but what startled her most was the creature's sudden movement. She left the curtain as it was and hurried out. This was getting ridiculous. She turned off the light in Arnar's office on the way out, but most of the other rooms were already dark. Their electricity came from a diesel-powered generator and she'd had to get accustomed to using it sparingly, which to her was a completely alien idea.

In the vestibule she put on a thick eiderdown jacket that had proven invaluable in this stormy place, and with the damaged face of the little girl in mind she took a scarf from one of the hooks and wound it tightly around her head, leaving only her eyes uncovered. Finally she put on mittens and pulled on the warmest boots she could find. Her shoes were wet, since she had once again forgotten to turn them upside down. The snow on them had melted as she worked, and made them soggy and cold. The same went for her hat, which had fallen off its hook onto the wet floor, so she also grabbed a fur hat to keep the wind and cold out of her ears. No one would miss it, or the scarf and boots, if she came to work early enough the next day. She pushed her trouser bottoms into the boots and stood up stiffly. She was so warmly dressed that she could barely move, and it would be no easier when she got outside, with the wind in her face. She drew a deep breath and opened the front door. Suddenly it struck her that perhaps the dog had been warning her, not menacing her—was there something else she should be afraid of?

The cold invigorated her and she pushed this thought aside. Her unease was probably all due to the video recording she'd just been puzzling over. Just before supper a clip had been e-mailed to her and her co-workers, showing Bjarki and Dóri, the two drillers, mucking around in the smokers' room. Oddný Hildur didn't know who had shot the video; maybe they'd set up the camera themselves, since there were few others besides the two of them who could bear the little smoke-saturated room for any length of time. However, what had caught her attention was not their stupid antics, but something that shot past the window behind them without their realizing it. Since she had little interest in this kind of foolishness she hadn't opened the e-mail before supper, when she could have asked her colleagues about it. Maybe the apparition behind them was part of the joke? She had tried unsuccessfully to pause the clip and get a better view of it, but the movement was so swift that she never managed to stop it in the right place.

7

It looked to her like a person wearing some kind of mask or strange headdress, and after it disappeared a red streak was left behind on the windowpane. The person—or whatever it was—had been holding something red, which must have bumped into the window or been dragged across it on purpose. But what was it? The rapid movement and dark red, irregular streak formed something of a gruesome backdrop to the drillers' pranks, and her failure to figure it out unsettled her. Maybe she would laugh it off in the morning, but right now she wished she had an explanation. For some reason she couldn't imagine stopping by the smokers' room to see if any marks were still there. Deep inside she knew that it was out of fear that the dark red streak was blood.

Oddný Hildur exhaled in the doorway and put her hands in her pockets. The dog was nowhere to be seen. She walked out into the drifting snow and darkness for the last time.

8

Chapter 1

18 March 2008

Thóra Gudmundsdóttir put down the overview of her last month's work schedule at the legal firm. It was hardly what she would call encouraging reading: the cases taken by her and Bragi, her business partner, along with two paralegals, were numerous, but mostly small-scale and quickly processed. That was certainly good for the firm's clients, but it didn't put much in the till. Nor was it all about the money. The most exciting cases demanded a great deal of work and were more complex than the smaller ones, which were usually run-of-the-mill and monotonous. Thóra groaned inwardly. She didn't dare groan audibly for fear that one of the young lawyers would hear her. If he sensed that she were worried about the firm's workload, he might start thinking of moving on, and they could not afford that. She and Bragi could never run the firm and everything belonging to it—not least their dreadful secretary, Bella—alone. Although it would be difficult to imagine how it could be possible to do her job any worse than Bella herself did it, Thóra had no interest in stepping in for the girl, and Bragi would do whatever was necessary to avoid having to sit and take phone calls. So they would just have to accept this arrangement: these two young lawyers who appeared more interested in YouTube than Supreme Court judgements, and Bella, who also spent more time than was healthy on the Internet.

Thóra turned back to the list of clients and

cases. Divorces, bankruptcies and other financial entanglements were the most prominent types of case by far. There were some involving inheritances, paternity suits and sporadic minor cases. It was probably not appropriate to think so, but Thóra longed for more criminal cases. They were much more demanding than divorces, which Bragi had been specializing in recently. He had built up a good reputation in this area, which meant that more and more people turned to the firm for help when their marriages were on the rocks.

Such cases, however, could often be quite colourful. One of her current clients was a man named Trausti, who wanted to change his name following his divorce since his wife had left him for another man with the same name. Of course it was no trouble to obtain permission to name oneself something other than what was recorded on the church register. But things became complicated when this was not enough for Trausti; he also insisted that their children's patronymics be changed accordingly. He wanted to make it clear to everyone that he and not his wife's new partner was the father of his children. Although the laws on namegiving allowed for changes in children's surnames under special circumstances, the legislation had not foreseen this possibility, thus there was no easy resolution to the case. Thóra thought it highly unlikely that a Trausti who did not want to be named Trausti would be permitted to change his children's surname, especially in light of the children's mother being totally opposed to the change. Her protestations only made her husband more determined to have his way, and in the end Thóra gave in and sent a letter describing the matter to the Minister of Justice. By then Thóra would actually have been completely willing to change her *own* name rather than sign such an unprecedented letter. Over a month had passed since she had sent it, and still no word had been received. She took that to mean that the authorities were wondering if this were some sort of joke.

At the time, her own divorce had certainly brought out less than the best in her and Hannes, her ex-husband. However, they hadn't had the imagination for anything much beyond quarrelling over worldly possessions—which of them would get the flat-screen TV, and so on. Name changes would have been inconceivable. It was probably this experience that distinguished her from Bragi, who enjoyed working on such cases. He had been happily married to the same woman for three decades, and thus had no personal experience of marital failure. Thóra, on the other hand, could easily identify with her clients and what they were going through. As a result, what she always wanted most was to tell her clients to face the fact that lying ahead of them were difficult times in which the spouse who was previously so dear to them would radically transform into the Devil himself and that no one, not even their mothers, would feel like listening to the dramatic stories of the other's cruelty. Enough time had passed since Thóra's own divorce for her to realize how unbearable she must have been; she had taken every opportunity she could in her conversations with others to complain about how impossible Hannes was. She had clearly been extremely unreasonable towards him—and vice versa. In any case, divorce had been the only sensible option in their situation, since they both

11

agreed that they'd had enough.

Now things looked different. Thóra was in a stable relationship with Matthew Reich, who had accepted a job as head of security for Kaupthing Bank. But they hadn't yet gone so far as to move in together. Not for lack of willingness on his part—it was Thóra who wasn't quite ready. She was in over her head at the moment: her two children, Sóley and Gylfi, made sure her hands were always full, not to mention her grandson Orri, who was almost two. Thóra was much more involved in Orri's life than most grandmothers; her son had only been a child himself when he and his girlfriend, Sigga, had rushed rather heedlessly into their biological experiment. As a result, they would never be named Parents of the Year; with their son they behaved almost more like his siblings, and didn't fully shoulder the responsibilities that come with a small child. Thóra realized this was partly her own fault, along with Sigga's parents. It was too easy to take over and do things herself; easier than following from a distance the teenagers' unorthodox attempts at childcare. When Orri was with her, it was as if the child was Thóra's own. She felt happiest when the boy was at home, but when she took him and his young parents into town she must have looked like a dubious mother, to put it mildly. Orri was barely talking and he already called Thóra 'mama', meaning that those who didn't know their situation must have thought she was a bit strange, letting her older children look after the youngest and not seeming to care when Orri cried or called for his mother. But that was the life of a young grandmother.

So it wasn't because she didn't want to live with

Matthew that she had responded to his suggestion unenthusiastically. She just found it so comforting to be able to switch to a different life now and then; a life in which everything was clean and tidy; no dirty nappies, no sandwiches to make or piles of clothes to wash. In that other life Thóra could go out to eat at a café, or do whatever else she wanted. That life revolved only around her and Matthew, adults with no obligation to wake up at the crack of dawn on weekends and watch cartoons. Thóra enjoyed that parallel life only on alternate weekends, when the whole gang abandoned her home and went to Hannes and his new wife. Few things cheered Thóra more than the pretend look of happiness on Weekend Daddy's face when she drove up to his house with the youngsters. His smile had grown even stiffer after Sigga fell out with her mother and moved in with Thóra. She reluctantly went along with the others to Hannes' and as soon as he tried to object, Gylfi said simply that if Sigga were made to feel unwelcome in any way he wouldn't come either. His father quickly held his tongue and never complained again about the lack of space. Gylfi was now eighteen years old, which meant that he wasn't obliged to spend time with his father every other weekend; in fact he could have refused to do so from the age of sixteen. Thóra doubted Gylfi realized this, but she had decided not to mention it so that he and his father would remain in touch. And also so that she herself would continue to have some space.

Thóra tried to direct her attention back to her work—a draft of a prenuptial agreement. Part of it concerned a two-storey single-family home which was to be divided into two separate apartments to save the owner (the prospective bridegroom) from the black hole of the currency basket loan that he had taken at the wrong time, during a fit of great optimism.

Before she could get stuck in again, Matthew called. It was rather unusual for him to call her during working hours—unlike Thóra, he was quite formal and took everything very seriously. For example, he had enrolled in a course in Icelandic for foreigners—he was German—and worked on it very diligently. At first she had helped him out with the homework and had been unable to resist the temptation to slip in a few words at an inappropriately high level. Matthew wasn't at all amused when this came to light, and he stopped asking for her help. Thóra's daughter Sóley had then taken over as teacher's aide. She was only eight years old and thus still bore an almost unlimited respect for every sort of schooling. As a result the two of them had become good friends and Matthew started making quick progress in the language, even though he and Thóra still spoke German together.

'How would you like to take on a little project for the bank?' asked Matthew, after apologizing for calling her at work.

'The bank?' repeated Thóra. She was surprised, since the banks had armies of specialists and lawyers at their fingertips. 'What kind of project?' She stared at the prenup awaiting her on the computer screen. Did they need a contract of this sort? Had their own army of lawyers refused to come anywhere near such trivialities?

'It has to do with a performance bond,' replied Matthew. 'The bank has guaranteed a contractor

14

called Berg Technology, which apparently is not going to fulfil a contract it signed with a British mining company. It looks as if the British want to claim insurance, meaning the bank will take the hit. It really is a lot of money, even more in the current financial situation, since the guarantee is in Euros.'

'And what's my job?' asked Thóra. 'Get the mining company to drop their claim to the money?'

Matthew laughed curtly. 'No, neither you nor anyone else would be able to do that. I understand they're really hard to deal with, since they're not in the business of giving money away. Even if they get the insurance money out of the bank, they still lose out on the work contract. They're simply cutting their losses.'

'What am I supposed to do?' asked Thóra. 'See to it that the Euros change hands, or maybe try to file a complaint?' This was sounding potentially even duller than prenups, so it might be better not to take the job.

'Neither,' replied Matthew. 'As things have gone, Berg Technology is way behind schedule and unlikely to be able to make up for the delays that have already occurred. On top of that, their work has come to a complete stop, and it looks as if that situation won't be remedied any time soon. Their employees refuse to return to the site, and the work is so specialized that replacements can't be picked up off the street. The plan is to send a team there to assess things and decide whether the bank should hire another contractor if the situation is irretrievable.'

'Can they do that?' she asked. Although her work had focused on contract law for some time now, an actual construction contract had never found its way onto her desk. She was not that familiar with them, but knew enough to understand what they involved, and to realise that they were considerably different from other, more traditional contracts.

'Yes,' said Matthew. 'I'd like to send you the construction contract and the details of the performance bond if you're interested, but I hope you understand that I can't do so unless you've accepted the project.'

Thóra thought it over for a moment. 'Am I to understand that the work is being done overseas?' She was quite prepared to get out of Iceland for a few days. The winter had been the hardest she could remember for a while, and although it was March it was still one storm after another.

'Yes, you would have to go abroad,' he said, without elaborating.

The tone of his voice suggested someplace rather unexciting. She was fairly sure there were no Icelandic contractors working in Gaza, Iraq, Afghanistan or any other war zone, so it couldn't be too bad. 'What type of work is this precisely, and where?' she asked, crossing her fingers in the hope that it involved building a hotel in the Caribbean. She had a great bikini that she hadn't had the chance to saunter around in since God knows when, and it was conceivable that the mining company wanted to branch out and try its luck in the tourist industry.

'They're doing preliminary studies and constructing infrastructure facilities on behalf of Arctic Mining for a mining operation in Greenland. Berg Technology made the lowest bid for the project and has had workers there for nearly a year. Until now everything has gone without a hitch,

16

though the results haven't been exemplary. But now something has happened to unsettle the workers.'

Thóra's mind had begun to wander when she heard the name. Greenland. One of the few countries that was colder and more unbearable at this time of year than Iceland. Her bikini would be of no use if she took this job—what she'd need would be sealskin trousers. She swallowed her disappointment. 'Are the workers in Greenland?'

'No, they're in Iceland. All but two people who are probably still on site. The others came home during their allotted leave, but now refuse to return.'

'What do you mean when you say that the two who remained behind are *probably* still on site?'

'Nothing's been heard from them for around ten days, and they can't get hold of anyone there to go and find out what's happening. It's possible that the camp's communication system has simply failed, but apparently the only way to find out is to go there. If a logical explanation is found for their silence, it's conceivable that the other employees can be persuaded to return. That of course would be the best solution for the bank.'

'Could something have happened to them? Could they have been trapped outside, or something along those lines?'

'That's one possible explanation,' said Matthew. 'It's happened before. About six months ago a geologist there disappeared from the camp, a young woman, now presumed dead. She was never found, but it's most likely that she got lost in a storm and froze to death.'

'She was out taking a walk in a *snowstorm*?'

'Nobody knows,' he replied. 'She disappeared,

17

so she could have committed suicide. People tend to get depressed in that kind of isolation.' Thóra was silent, not knowing how to respond. Matthew was quick to add: 'That incident has nothing to do with your task, nor with the disappearance of the two others. In the best-case scenario, they're still alive; the camp's transmitter has failed and they simply haven't been able to get it working again. Other explanations for their fate are rather more gloomy: the weather there has been like it's been here recently, only worse. They wouldn't have been able to survive it if they were anywhere but indoors. In any case, things have become serious, both with regard to these men and to the interests of Berg Technology—and, by association, the bank.'

'Isn't it simpler to call on a Greenlandic emergency rescue team, or the police there?' she asked. 'This all sounds rather frightening, and if something *has* happened, it'll be up to law enforcement there to investigate it.'

'The site is in the wilderness on the east coast. Of course there's a small village nearby, but it doesn't have a regular police force, and the locals can't be persuaded to go and investigate either for us or for Arctic Mining. If the men have suffered food poisoning or become ill in some other way, every day makes a difference and we can't waste any time trying to get the Greenlanders to help.'

'I'm not going to be of much help if this is about a disease,' said Thóra. 'And I'm not sure I want to go if I'm going to find people who are seriously ill—or even dying.'

'You wouldn't be going alone,' said Matthew. 'A doctor has already joined the team, as well as a highly experienced rescuer and a former employee

18

of Berg Technology who knows her way around the place. The team will also include an information systems technician, to get the connection working again.' He paused. 'And me.'

'Ahh,' said Thóra. That was certainly a plus. The location was a minus, at least in winter. 'When is the team leaving, and for how long?' Judging by the number of people involved, this would be no overnight camping trip.

'We're scheduled to leave tomorrow morning,' he told her. 'The forecast is favourable—for once. We aim to be there for as short a time as possible, but that'll become clearer when we get there. The weather will have a lot to do with it, of course.'

'Where would we be staying?' she asked, suspecting she knew what the answer would be. It was unlikely that a five-star hotel of the kind you might see in the Caribbean was to be found in those parts.

Matthew cleared his throat. 'At the work camp. If it's considered safe. If not, then we have to negotiate with the villagers for accommodation.'

Thóra looked at her computer screen and the boring document glowing back at her. She'd just been offered a little adventure, barely five minutes after she'd mentally complained about her unexciting work. She could easily leave the office for several days if the young lawyers took up the slack. They'd just have to spend less time on the Internet during her absence. 'I'll go with you,' she said, but hurriedly added: 'Actually, I need to see about getting Hannes or my mother to look after the kids before I can give you a definite answer, but I don't expect it to be a problem.'

'Fantastic,' said Matthew, and the satisfaction

in his voice was plain to hear. 'We can get it all arranged if you drop in here and speak to the person responsible. You'll be well paid for it, that I can guarantee.'

'Why aren't any of your lawyers going?' asked Thóra.

'Their hands are full at the moment, and anyway they're not that interested. It doesn't suit them. You, on the other hand, are perfect for the job.'

Thóra couldn't understand why. She was no good at skiing or hiking, and didn't care much for outdoor activities beyond short walks in good weather. However, the reason was irrelevant. Matthew saw the world differently to her, and as close as they were, he might very well be under the impression that Thóra dreamed of being the first grandma under forty to reach the North Pole with a grandchild in her arms, for all she knew. 'Those men,' she said, adding what was pressing most heavily on her mind: 'Do you think they're dead?'

Matthew inhaled sharply. 'One of them has probably died, but hopefully not both.'

'What do you mean?' asked Thóra, startled. It was unlike Matthew to be so vague.

'One of the employees of Berg Technology here in Iceland made repeated attempts to gain remote access to the system and seems to have got in, although attempts by others since then haven't produced any result. So there was a computer connection for a time, even though it was patchy, but now it appears to have been lost for good. In any case, the man managed to look up the latest files and among them he found a particularly interesting one that was created after the rest of the group left the site. The man saved it and then sent it to others in the group, and it seems the e-mail is the main reason why the staff refuse to return.'

'What did this file contain, then?' asked Thóra.

'Everything in it suggests that one of the men is alive, or at least that someone is still at the work site. It's what caused the matter to be put on highest priority.'

'What was in the file?' insisted Thóra .

'I'll just send it to you. Some of it is actually impossible to put into words,' he said. 'Are you sure you want to see it? I'm warning you, the contents are not for the faint-hearted.'

Naturally Thóra had to see the file, and as quickly as possible. They said goodbye and hung up, and she waited impatiently for the e-mail and clicked on it immediately when it appeared. The attachment was a wmp. file, its name made up of an indecipherable sequence of numbers. The numbers could not refer to the date, and must have been made up by the video camera itself. Thóra right-clicked on the file and saw that it had been created four days ago, just before midnight on 13 March. She couldn't determine whether this information had been added by the camera, or the computer onto which the file had been transferred. A wrongly set clock or different time zone could of course have confused this information. She shut the window and opened the attachment itself.

Chapter 2

18 March 2008

The video was short but powerful. It took Thóra a few moments to figure out what was being filmed; the quality was poor and the image appeared in an impractically small window on the screen. When Thóra tried to enlarge it the image became grainy and even less distinguishable as a result. The sound was also of rather poor quality, characterized by a continual low buzz. It would have been little problem for the characters in an episode of *CSI* to clean it up, but since the legal firm had no research lab at its disposal Thóra had to make do with the unclear sound. That was unfortunate, because it was what could be heard through the buzzing that affected her most. The clip was shot indoors, but it was difficult to determine in what sort of building the camera's operator was located, since his or her hands were extremely unsteady. Thóra caught a glimpse of a bookshelf and chair at the start of the clip, but then the camera was pointed almost immediately down towards the speckled linoleum. That was pretty much the perspective until the end of the clip. Apart from the linoleum, nothing else could be seen but two feet and legs up to the knees. The owner of the legs was lying or sitting on the floor, which in itself was peculiar. Whoever it was also appeared to be completely immobile, which made the scene even stranger. Thóra hadn't seen anyone lying so still since her days of going out on the town when she was younger. Sometimes a guest or two at a late-night post-club party would be lying in the same position, but judging by the footwear this hadn't been any sort of party. The feet were in thick, probably woollen, socks and open slippers that had never been and would never be in style; hardly appropriate for a social get-together. The person in the video sat or lay flat on the floor in jeans, his or her legs splayed in either direction. Thóra had the feeling that it was a man, without being able to explain why, since it was impossible to determine the size of the feet or shoes.

In the three minutes and twenty-two seconds that the video played, the legs jerked weirdly four times. Just before each time a whistling sound momentarily rose above the buzzing, ending with a muffled thud. Then the legs would jerk, and a dark liquid sprayed across the middle of the frame. Over the years Thóra had found herself forced to watch numerous horror films with her son Gylfi, which is probably why she imagined the worst possible scenario. To her it seemed as if a body were being dismembered, or someone was being killed with an axe or a heavy club. But it couldn't be the latter, since there was no screaming or any other sound of anguish. There was only the whistling, a thump— and what sounded like the strange crooning of a child. Thóra could distinguish a melody, but could make nothing of the words. Either the child was babbling nonsense or its language was totally alien to her. She reached for her phone and rang Bragi's extension. 'Come here for a second,' she said, squinting as she watched the video for the third time. 'I need to get your opinion on something.' She stopped the video and leaned back in her chair, thinking it over. It had clearly been a mistake

23

to say that she would go along, even though she could always change her mind. She looked askance at the paperwork on her desk and glanced at the documents for the name-change case at the top of a thick stack of other papers. She looked back at the computer screen. Judging from the video, this Greenlandic case would certainly be different.

'What's going on?' asked Bragi curiously as he appeared in the doorway. He was a large man with a teddy bear-ish manner who wore his age well. He was wearing a dark suit with a tie, since he was one of the generation of lawyers who thought it brought shame to the profession to dress in comfortable clothes. His orthodoxy, however, was not strong enough to prevent him from loosening the knot of his tie and leaving the top button of his shirt undone, which slightly diminished his respectability.

'Take a look at this,' said Thóra, pointing to the screen. 'And tell me what you think is going on there.' She started the video and pushed the desk chair aside to allow him to come closer for a better view. Bragi enjoyed anything strange, so this should be right up his alley. She waited until it was over and the peculiar chanting had stopped. 'Well,' she said, 'let's hear it.'

Bragi's eyes flashed. 'If this is related to a divorce, then I have dibs on the case, as the kids say.' He fumbled for the mouse to replay the video. 'This is great.'

Thóra interrupted him and told him the basics about Matthew's offer and the origin of the video. She watched his smile fade as he realized this probably had nothing to do with a marriage at death's door. 'But what do you think this is?' she asked.

24

'Best case scenario, assault. Worst, murder,' replied Bragi, making no attempt to hide his disappointment that this wasn't a divorce case.

'That's what I thought,' said Thóra, exhaling. 'I don't know, maybe I should pull out of this one. It's more than a little bit strange, and much more serious than a loss of insurance money.'

'Well, that depends on how high the insurance is,' said Bragi. 'There are tables showing individuals' monetary worth, so if the poor fellow has been called from this life, we could certainly set the nominal value placed on loss of life against the amount of insurance lost, and measure which is considered more severe.' He thought for a moment and then added: 'We would certainly need additional information, like gender, age and education, to make more precise calculations.'

Thóra grimaced. 'I know that,' she said, irritated at Bragi's bad taste. 'I'm mainly wondering now whether it would be safe for me to make this trip. What if the video was shot at the camp?'

'I wouldn't read too much into it,' said Bragi, patting her shoulder. 'This could have been anything, and shot anywhere. Even at a fitness centre.'

'I doubt many people wear woolly socks at the gym,' said Thóra. 'And what kind of exercise do you call that?'

'God only knows,' said Bragi. 'From what I know, all sorts of things go on at those places. I have a divorce case that all started at a fitness centre. The husband became obsessed with his body and completely forgot about his wife and children. It wouldn't surprise me if this loser put up with that treatment in the hope of increasing his muscle quantity.'

'Muscle mass,' corrected Thóra, without thinking.

'That's what I mean,' said Bragi. He looked Thóra in the eye. 'I'm getting mixed up with all these digressions. The main point of all this is that for us it opens a door to the banks. Up until now they've had their own lawyers, or looked to the big firms. This could be the start of some excellent business opportunities for us. Not to mention the changes that you're longing for so much.'

Thóra nodded thoughtfully. Naturally, this could be of advantage to the firm and the bank could possibly become a great source of income for them in the future, but she thought it more probable that the bank had simply opted out of the Greenland trip and that this would be a one-off. When it came to other cases that could be handled at a normal pace, there would be no reason for the bank to seek their assistance. On the other hand, clouds had been gathering over the nation's economy, and even though Thóra didn't follow the financial sector that closely she hadn't missed hearing about the attacks of foreign hedge funds on the Icelandic króna and the dubious position of various large Icelandic enterprises. Concepts no one had understood, much less used, a month ago were now on everyone's lips, most noticeably terms like 'short selling' and 'cross-ownership'. Thóra suspected that her eight-year-old daughter could explain these concepts now. This trend also suggested strongly that more hardship lay ahead, which often meant increased work for lawyers, particularly in debt collection. No matter how dismal she found collecting, it was more than likely that they would happily accept such cases if the economy froze. Chances were that this video was just some nonsense from the Internet, completely irrelevant to the employees of Berg Technology. 'I'll think about it,' said Thóra. 'It's best if I look into this a little further, and if this video turns out to be showing what we both think it might, then this is definitely out of my sphere. We'd need to call the police.'

'The Greenlandic police?' said Bragi. 'You might as well ask your neighbourhood sports' association to undertake research on fundraising.'

'What do you mean?' Thóra exclaimed. 'Is something wrong with them?' She interrupted herself. 'And anyway, what would you know about the police, or anything else in Greenland? You've never even been there.'

'No, maybe not, but everyone knows the situation there is absolutely dreadful. The police aren't immune to it, no more than anyone.'

'Dreadful' was a word Thóra's mother used frequently when she was fretting over something, and Thóra couldn't help but smile. 'In any case the police here in Iceland need to be informed about this. Then they can put themselves in touch with their colleagues over in that dreadful Greenland.'

Suddenly Bragi's eyes widened. 'Listen,' he said heartily, 'you should take Bella with you! She'll look after you, and besides, she's completely expendable for that short amount of time. There are a lot of different traditions and customs in Greenland and I'm sure it will be good to have her along under those circumstances.'

Bella was more likely to trip Thóra up straight into the jaws of a polar bear than come to her rescue. 'Matthew will be there, so I'm sure I'll be safe. I don't need her,' said Thóra, grinning. Then she hurriedly added: 'If in fact I go.'

'Yes, my dear, you should go, and it won't do you any harm to take Bella along,' said Bragi, clearly enthralled with his own idea. 'It would even help me out if she weren't here for the next few days, since I have to take care of so many cases. It would be a great relief to be free of her.'

'There's no room for Bella on the plane,' Thóra lied. 'Just do what you were thinking the other day, and put up a partition so you don't have to see or hear her.' She stood up. 'I'm going to go and talk to the head of the bank about this,' she said, to put an end to the conversation about Bella. 'I'll make my final decision afterwards.'

*   *   *

'And?' asked Matthew curiously as he followed her out of the bank. 'What are you going to do?'

'I'm inclined to take the job. But still . . . oh, I don't know,' replied Thóra. The head of the bank had turned out to have several years, if not decades, to go before he could live up to his job title. He was in fact a slender young man who smelled so strongly of aftershave that it had taken all Thóra's willpower not to pinch her nose shut as they spoke. She suspected the overapplication was deliberate; his palms were sweaty and he appeared nervous. It was easy to read between the lines and guess that his future at the bank hung on the same thread as the insurance. If the bank had to pay the insurance, he would be handed his marching orders. It seemed there was much more to this case than just the insurance money; there were great expectations for the mine in Greenland, even though there hadn't been much public discussion about it. It was hoped that it would be serviced from Iceland, since the closest town with an airport was Ísafjörður. This could lead to more jobs that would both directly and indirectly serve the mine, but these teething troubles had not inspired the locals to put their trust in this big company. It could also be the case that political interests were threatening the young man's position. However, he wasn't all bad; Thóra was quite pleased with much of what she heard, especially the fact that he had informed the police about the situation and requested that they do what they could to persuade the Greenlandic authorities to intervene. The bank's interests were not high on the police department's list of priorities. The idea behind the group's expedition was to survey the situation and try as hard as possible to minimize the damage if everything had gone completely awry, so that Berg Technology would be released from its contract. The equipment and tools belonging to the contractors needed to be inspected and the status of the research evaluated so that the bank could either get another contractor to take over, or persuade the employees to return to the site. According to the young man this was not out of the question; the group had been gripped by mass hysteria but, more often than not, these things passed when common sense returned. If, on the other hand, there really was something unusual about the situation at the site, information pertaining to it would have to be gathered. This would help the bank to demonstrate that conditions were extraordinary and therefore outside the company's control: in short, they could invoke force majeure.

This term kindled Thóra's interest in the case. Force majeure meant that the parties to the contract could be freed from their obligations if they were unable to fulfil them due to circumstances beyond their control. This included war, workers' strikes and earthquakes, or anything else that the parties to the contract could not influence. Thóra was well aware that no war was being fought in Greenland, and nor had she heard of any natural disasters or strikes there, either recently or in the past. This was what pricked her curiosity: there was a definite challenge involved in evaluating a situation in search of what could be considered uncontrollable. Crimes could be categorized under force majeure, and considering the video it was possible that might be the case here; however, that was not at all a given, making this an even more exciting legal issue. And there were other factors involved: whoever did not fulfil his obligations had to demonstrate that he had tried everything within his power to minimize the impact of external factors. In this case, determining such a thing could prove to be more challenging than pinpointing the actual phenomenon that had prevented the party from fulfilling its contract. Was this not precisely what she had craved so much—that very morning, in fact? A challenging case that wouldn't make her yearn to throw her pen at her client's head in fury?

'I'll come,' she told him, without considering the matter any further. As soon as she said it she felt a definite sense of relief and anticipation. She actually also felt troubled, but pushed that feeling aside.

Matthew stopped for a moment in the elegant

lobby of the bank's headquarters. He hurriedly stepped away when he realized that he was standing in the middle of the entrance and that the large automatic glass plate doors were about to close on him. 'Really?' Now it was his turn to have doubts. 'You realize it's going to be a difficult trip—it's a real wilderness of ice and snow there.'

Thóra was certainly aware of the snow. It was what was *not* there that attracted her most. Boring, routine cases. This would be different; that was for sure.

*   *   *

'What colour are Greenlanders?' asked Sóley, yawning. She was lying in bed and should have been asleep long ago, but in the light of her impending trip, Thóra had decided to ignore her daughter's normal bedtime. She kissed the girl's blonde head.

'They're just like us, darling. Not green, if that's what you think.'

'Mummy,' said her daughter indignantly, 'I know that. I meant whether they were yellow like Chinese people or something like that.'

'Chinese people aren't yellow any more than the Independents are blue,' said Thóra, smoothing down the pink duvet cover.

'What?' asked Sóley, who knew as much about politics as any other eight-year-old child.

Thóra merely smiled at her. 'You'll behave yourself at Daddy's while I'm gone, won't you?'

'Yes, if you bring back a nice present for me,' replied Sóley, smiling. 'Sweeties, too.'

There must be sweets in Greenland. 'I'll buy something,' answered Thóra. 'Maybe a polar bear cub.'

'Oh, yes,' said Sóley, excitedly. 'A real one.'

'Well, I meant a teddy bear,' said Thóra, patting one of the many soft toys lying on the bed. She prepared to stand up. 'It's much too late. Try to sleep now.'

'A dog?' implored Sóley, taking her mother's hand, and Thóra shook her head out of old habit. Sóley piped up at least once a day about getting a pet. More often on weekends. 'Why not? Gylfi got to have a baby—why can't I have a puppy or kitten?'

'Good night,' said Thóra, standing up from the bedside. 'We'll wake up at the same time in the morning, you'll go to school and Mummy will go to the airport. I'll try to call you when you've got to Daddy's, but I can't promise that it will work.' She responded in advance to the question that would inevitably follow: 'There are phones in Greenland, but I don't know if they work where I'll be. They might be broken.'

After switching off the light in the pink room and staring for a few moments at the numerous glittering teddy bear eyes, Thóra went out to the garage. She had no rucksack, as Matthew had recommended she bring—a suitcase would have to do. Things became more complicated, however, when it came to what she should pack. No one knew how long she would be there or what the conditions would be like; it was best just to take a bloody big pile of clothes. The doorbell rang, forcing Thóra to put aside any further thoughts on packing. Her friend Gugga was standing in front of the house, smiling from ear to ear and waving two bottles of white wine. 'You've got to let me in,' she said as Thóra opened the door, as though Thóra

32

were in the habit of slamming the door in visitors' faces. 'I just bought a new car and really want to celebrate it with someone.' Thóra could think of a number of ways to celebrate the purchase of a new car without alcohol being involved, but she smiled nonetheless. She was well aware that the car had probably been bought with the highest loan Gugga could get, and that after six months her friend would show up at her door, again with bottles in hand, to drown her sorrows over the sea of debt she was in and her repossessed car. Sometimes one had to live in the here and now and indulge oneself in the spirit of Louis XIV. He would probably have taken advantage of a car loan if such things had existed in his day.

So there was to be no packing until later, when Gugga finally left in a taxi. Around that time Thóra was starting to see double, and when she dozed off, exhausted from the effort of trying to shut the overstuffed suitcase, it was impossible for her to recall what she'd thrown into it.

Chapter 3

19 March 2008

The coffee at Reykjavík City Airport was quite good, even though it was simply called 'coffee' and came not from a gleaming chrome machine that spouted steam like a locomotive as it brewed one cup at a time, but an old coffeepot standing on a hot plate, reflecting the style of the tired old terminal. You'd have to go a long way to find such an old-fashioned brewing method in town, where the fancy machines had taken over everywhere. Thóra had even received one of the newfangled contraptions as a Christmas present from her parents. On Christmas Eve she had gulped down immoderate amounts of coffee without realizing that the new coffee was much stronger than the weak liquid she was used to. All that night she lay stiffly with her eyes wide open, barely able to blink, much less sleep. Since then the coffeemaker had been collecting dust. However, now Thóra would not have objected to a double espresso from her machine to perk her up; her head was throbbing and her mental abilities were a wreck. An overly large dose of coffee would probably help.

'You should have brought a rucksack,' muttered Matthew as he sat down next to her in the waiting area. He was still agitated about the suitcase Thóra had turned up with. 'I told you specifically.'

'Oh, come on, sweetheart,' she replied, putting down her coffee cup. 'It's on wheels. There are even four of them.' She had been careful to select the suitcase that would be easiest to pull behind her, and it most resembled a well-trained dog, following almost automatically at her heels. Luckily she had chosen the bag before gulping down all that wine.

'Thank goodness they all work,' said Matthew, just as unimpressed as he'd been when he picked her up half an hour ago. Thóra hadn't been able to disguise how sleep-deprived and hungover she was, which was not at all to his liking. She felt too poorly for that to make any difference to her, which seemed to irritate him even more. 'Winters are rough out there.' Matthew had clearly gone

34

and bought himself a new rucksack. Thóra came to this conclusion partly because she did not believe that he would have already owned one, but also because his huge backpack was so brilliantly clean that it could have come straight from the shop that very morning. Apparently that hadn't been his only new purchase, because, for once, he was wearing a proper coat. Beneath this, though, he was wearing pressed, neatly creased trousers and a shirt that was actually quite casual for him. At least he'd had the sense to skip the tie. But Thóra was pretty sure he had one or two in his backpack, just in case.

'I know,' said Thóra, trying not to let his grumbling about the suitcase get on her nerves. One of their fellow travellers, whom they had met at the check-in counter, had confined himself to a quick, dubious glance at the bright green lump of plastic. He had introduced himself as Dr Finnbogi Kolbeinsson; he looked to be approaching fifty, with a slender build, and his battered hiking boots suggested that he was quite the outdoorsman. On the large rucksack that he swung as if it were empty were the remains of all types of stickers and patches from distant lands. Thóra had the feeling that Matthew's new and shiny rucksack inspired the same indignation in the doctor as her suitcase did— possibly even more. At least she wasn't putting on pretences.

Thóra couldn't wait to show off to Matthew everything she'd thought to put into her big bag. She had no idea precisely what was in it, but hoped some sensible garments were hidden therein. She was actually pretty certain that Matthew had packed without knowing anything about cold weather conditions and camping, and although

35

she of course could personally be considered no expert in either, she was quite familiar with sudden weather changes and winter conditions, a familiarity that had hopefully survived her intoxication. When Matthew tore everything out of his rucksack at their destination in search of woollen socks, and his ties and shirts were flung around the room, she could get back at him for all his grumbling. Still, she decided to change the subject, since his nagging and her headache were not a good combination. 'I'm trying to memorize who's who,' said Thóra, looking over the group, which had spread out around the little airport, each member armed with a mobile phone. Theirs was the only flight scheduled at this hour—the bank had made arrangements with Air Iceland to fly them to Kulusuk, where the company made regularly scheduled flights in the summer. From there they were to be transported north by helicopter, to a small village near the work camp. It wasn't yet clear how they would travel the final stretch of their journey, but it was considered likely that they would find one or two cars from Berg Technology in the hangar by the helicopter pad, where they would usually have been stored. The employees who had gone home had left them behind, so unless they had been stolen the vehicles should be there. Thóra prayed to God that that was not the case; if they had to walk, she would be in trouble. Her luggage was hardly designed for long hikes.

'I can't say that I know all the names, but I know who does what,' said Matthew, apparently willing to abandon the suitcase discussion. 'There aren't that many on the team, and you'll get to know them quite quickly in our isolation.'

'Of course, of course,' said Thóra. 'Everyone looks okay to me.' She watched as the youngest member of the group by far, Eyjólfur Þorsteinsson, stuck a coin into the gumball machine standing near one wall. The machine swallowed the coin but refused to deliver the gum, and after trying peacefully to get his money back, the young man pounded energetically on the machine's large plastic bowl, tossing the gumballs around inside it. This produced no result and he walked away angrily. Thóra hoped that this wasn't representative of Eyjólfur's technical skills, because Matthew had said he was responsible for everything connected with the site's computer system. In fact it was he who had first set it up, and thus knew all of its ins and outs. He looked to be about twenty-five years old, slim with a dark complexion, and probably popular among the women, handsome as he was. In that regard he was the absolute opposite of Alvar Pálsson. Alvar was fortyish, and had been enlisted for the expedition because of his experience on rescue teams that had connections with Greenland—he had been among the Icelanders recruited to assist the Greenlanders in the organization of a rescue-team system there. Thóra didn't know what his main occupation was, but guessed that he was probably a lighthouse keeper or had a similar job that involved little human interaction. His face was fiery red, and he had barely responded when Matthew tried introducing Thóra to him; he had simply snorted something and carried on trying to attach his walking stick to his rucksack. If Thóra had been forced to describe him, the word 'bad' would have featured frequently; the poor man had bad teeth, smelled bad, looked in

37

bad shape, and to make matters worse, was badly shaven.

'Where did the geologist go?' asked Thóra. 'The woman?' Of the team's six members there was one other woman besides Thóra, Friðrikka Jónsdóttir. She had worked on this project during its early days but had resigned and gone to work for Reykjavík Energy. Matthew told Thóra that a decent sum of money had persuaded her to take some days off to come with them, since she knew the project so well and was likely to be able to assess the status of the drilling without needing to first familiarize herself with everything.

'She must be here somewhere. At least, she'd already checked in by the time we did. Maybe she's just out having a cigarette, or on the phone?'

'Did she see the video?' asked Thóra.

'No,' he replied, setting his briefcase down on the table between them. 'There was no time for that, and perhaps it wouldn't have been appropriate either. If she'd backed out, there was no need to have bothered her with unnecessary details.' He opened the briefcase and took out a hefty stack of spiral bound notebooks. 'I wanted to give you these. It's probably good for you to have them on the plane if you want to use the time to read through them. They're all about the construction contract.'

Thóra took the entire pile, which was far thicker than the contracts she was used to. 'But this Friðrikka might still have been able to say whether the video was taken at the site, and maybe even have recognized the feet by the slippers,' she said.

'Yes, of course,' said Matthew. 'Still, we decided not to show this to anyone but you and the doctor. We'll see how it goes once we get there. Maybe then it'll be time to let the others watch it. The IT guy could also possibly identify the feet, since he knows the group even though he didn't actually belong to it.' He shut the briefcase. 'But I'm hoping that we won't need to do that.' Looking around, he added: 'We're actually missing one passenger.'

'Oh?' asked Thóra. 'Who's that?'

'Bella,' he replied, not meeting her eye.

'Ha ha,' said Thóra sarcastically. Her hangover felt even worse at the thought of her secretary. She stared piercingly at Matthew, who was still avoiding her gaze. 'Don't even joke about it—is that meant to be funny?'

'No,' said Matthew hesitantly. 'Your partner Bragi called me last night and fobbed her off on me, saying we didn't even need to pay her. It'll help to have someone who can take care of typing everything up on the computer. I called the bank this morning and they gave it the green light—they were ecstatic, even, since it's not often they're offered something for free.' He was gabbling now, and added even more rapidly: 'She'll be helping the group out before you know it, and you won't even know she's there. There's a lot of information that needs to be entered on the computer, so her skills will undoubtedly be of great use to us.'

'You're kidding!' said Thóra. 'I have a hunch that the seal hunters in Greenland would be better at typing up information than Bella, and they'd certainly move faster.'

Matthew made no attempt to argue this point. 'I couldn't say no,' he hissed. 'You've always said how pushy Bragi can be, and he gave me no other choice than to accept the help.' He smiled sheepishly. 'Believe me, I tried many times to decline it.'

Thóra was speechless. She was both frustrated with Matthew and furious at Bragi, and couldn't decide which of them she would rather lock inside a cupboard with Bella for a week. But her hangover prevented her from arguing about this any further. The entrance to the airport was not visible from where they sat, but she could see the check-in counter, where all was quiet. 'Maybe she'll miss the plane,' said Thóra, looking at the clock on the wall. 'I bet she misses the plane.' Then she started thumbing through the documents in the hope that her anger would dissipate.

'Yes, maybe,' said Matthew, awkwardly. 'But we won't make a fuss about it if she turns up too late. It was only this morning that I received final confirmation that she could come, but I don't know when Bragi delivered the message to her.'

Thóra ground her teeth and continued to read. There was a total of five volumes of various thicknesses and she could see immediately that only two of them mattered: the contract terms and letters sent between Berg Technology and Arctic Mining during the negotiation process. The other three volumes contained information about geological studies of the area, the climate and drawings that had been scaled down so small that Thóra was unable to make out the tiny print. One of the notebooks was labelled 'Job Description', and its contents covered the details of each of Berg Technology's tasks and how they would be paid for. Thóra knew that she would have to read over the last volume, especially if everything on site had gone to pot. 'Why is no one from the contractors joining us?' she asked without looking up. 'This is a rather large contract and I doubt that everyone from the company was working on site. At least not the management.'

'It's not a big company,' replied Matthew, clearly relieved that Thóra was talking about something other than his having given in to Bragi. 'It's very specialized and has managed to make a name for itself in geological research and related feasibility studies, though mainly in the field of geothermal heat. Berg Technology's main man and founder is now involved in another project in the Azores, along with five employees. The company has no other staff apart from the twelve who went to Greenland, and ten of them refuse to go back there, while the other two . . .' He cleared his throat before continuing. 'The company had planned greatly to expand its workforce this summer, when it was supposed to start major construction projects like laying an airport runway, but whether that will actually happen depends on whether Berg Technology manages to stay afloat. The kind of workers they need are much easier to find than the ones working at the site now, and it shouldn't be any trouble to hire them if an agreement can be reached with the mining company. As far as the owner is concerned, we've been in constant contact with him by telephone and e-mail, but he can't get away for the time being. They're about to complete an important stage of their project in the Azores and he's afraid that if he leaves now, the company that hired them will start having doubts. The last thing Berg needs now is for that project to be put at risk as well. We're not going to press him, because he could become an albatross around our necks. His company is naturally far more important to him than the financial standing of the bank, so you never know what he might do. Berg has three board members, including the owner, but the other two have never come to Greenland, so it's not really worthwhile dragging them along.'

Thóra nodded. The voice on the tannoy announced that the charter flight to Greenland was ready for departure. Thóra stuck the documents back into the briefcase. She smiled as she stood up. It looked as if Bella would not make the plane. Sometimes you got lucky. They walked along with the others towards the gate and Thóra noticed that a woman in her early thirties had joined the group. This must be the geologist Friðrikka. She was tall like Thóra, but otherwise they were quite different. Thóra was blonde, but Friðrikka had curly bright red hair that she was obviously trying to keep under control with an elastic band. She was also a little plump, while Thóra was quite skinny. Matthew stopped when he saw her approaching and as he introduced her to Thóra, Friðrikka extended a calloused hand. The woman seemed rather shy, but her grip was firm nevertheless and her low-key greeting sincere.

Thóra hadn't thought about the fact that there was a little duty-free shop at the airport, but she didn't really want anything. Some of the group went to the tills with cartons of cigarettes, but the only one who seemed to want to take advantage of the inexpensive alcohol was the rescuer Alvar Pálsson. He stood in line at the register with a bottle of rum and another of Campari, still just as red-faced as when Thóra had seen him first. Considering the amount he was buying for such a short trip, he was either a lush or preparing himself for a longer stay in Greenland than planned.

'Are you going to buy something?' asked Matthew, who appeared rather unimpressed by the little shop.

'No,' replied Thóra. 'I don't think I need anything they sell.' Headache tablets would have been useful, but there were none to be seen. They started walking out of the shop, but Thóra stopped abruptly in the doorway when she heard a familiar voice coming from the security gate.

'If I can take one lighter on board, then why can't I take two?' thundered Bella. 'What can I do with two lighters that I can't do with one?'

Thóra went back into the shop and headed towards the spirits section.

*　　　*　　　*

The flight only took two hours and Thóra used the time to read the contract, in search of anything that might be useful if it came to a breach of agreement. She found nothing other than the clause about force majeure. Everything else was nailed down pretty tightly. Special emphasis had even been put on local conditions and difficulties connected with transportation and climate. The bank clearly wanted to ensure as far as possible that Berg Technology could not request additional payments or postponements due to the area turning out to be more difficult than anticipated at first, or the costs higher. She also noted that any contractual disputes were to be settled in a British court, which meant the bank would no longer have need of her services at the conclusion of this trip. It might take her a few days to process whatever data they gathered, then her part in the matter would be finished. So Thóra's prediction had turned out to be right: as soon as the case was straightened out, others would take over. Although she was naturally a bit miffed about this, it was comforting to imagine Bragi's disappointment. Her longing to tell him about it only intensified when she heard Bella jabbering away to herself at the back of the plane.

The eight passengers on board the charter had plenty of room. Thóra and Matthew sat at the front, so she couldn't see her fellow travellers, but the sound of snoring suggested that some of them had decided to nap on the way. That was understandable; although it was light outside, there was nothing to see but sky and sea. It wasn't until they reached the coast of Greenland that the view was worth waking up for. The country looked very unwelcoming. It was covered with snow except in a few places where the mountainsides were too steep for it to settle, and on a slender strip near the coast where the encroaching sea had melted it. Icebergs were floating everywhere off the coast and the overriding impression was that the land was being ground into pieces and driven out into the sea. The jaggedness of the coastline did nothing to diminish this effect. The same went for the interior: there were no level areas, and the mountain peaks were innumerable. There were no visible signs of human habitation.

'Has the pilot got confused and taken us to the North Pole?' Thóra asked Matthew, after turning away from the glacier's glare. 'No one could possibly be living down there.'

He leaned towards the window and looked slightly shaken when he turned back to her. 'It looks worse from such a great height,' he said.

44

'Also, maybe we're still too far north. I'm sure it will look better when we land.' He appeared to be trying to convince himself as much as Thóra.

'I hope you're right,' said Thóra. 'Erik the Red must have been colour-blind when he named the country. Everything down there is white. I don't know how we're going to avoid polar bears—if they close their eyes they'll be invisible.'

'There won't be any polar bears,' said Matthew, although he was still peering out nervously. 'The trip itself is the only problem we're going to have.'

'I hope so,' she replied, smiling. 'But one thing's for certain—there was no polar bear swinging an axe or a club in the video.' She leaned in and whispered, 'Did you notice that Bella is the only other person awake?' Stealthily, she turned to check whether this was still the case. 'If she weren't here I could invite you to the toilet and initiate you into the mile high club.' She looked Matthew in the eye and grinned. 'Damn it, what a shame she had to come.' She turned back to the window, pleased with herself.

Shortly afterwards the aircraft landed gently. The travellers disembarked, full of expectation tempered with anxiety. All except one. That passenger had promised never to come here again. Terrible memories lingered here, memories that were impossible to push away.

It was incredible that this passenger had returned, in fact. A blue-black crow screeched on the roof of the airport, rose into the air and flew off into the wilderness.

Chapter 4

19 March 2008

Thóra wasn't as excited about the helicopter as Matthew was. What the others in the group thought, she couldn't guess, but most were at least trying to look as if they found it totally commonplace. Matthew did what he could to enthuse Thóra, saying that it was none other than a Huey, the type that was used in the Vietnam War. She was not impressed, however—even when he added that as soon as the blades started whirring, she would recognize the sound from the movies. She smiled reluctantly. 'Couldn't they have added a few more blades? It only has two.' She hoped that this shortage of propellers wouldn't cause the helicopter to fly unsteadily, because her stomach was hardly in any condition for that. The Vietnam atmosphere would be dampened somewhat if she started vomiting in the back of the helicopter.

Matthew wrinkled his nose. 'Two is quite enough.'

They watched the airport personnel load provisions and luggage onto a vehicle. Thóra's green suitcase appeared and she noticed that the loaders took the time to check whether it was marked with the correct destination tag, since it stuck out so obviously from the other bags. 'I just hope we have enough food and drink,' muttered Matthew. 'I've never needed to order provisions for so many, let alone a group making a long expedition to the North Pole in winter.' Thóra hoped he had consulted with someone else, otherwise they could

46

expect nothing from the boxes but nuts and raisins and maybe some energy drinks. Before she could ask the question he continued uneasily: 'Aren't we going to take off? At this pace we won't get to the camp before dark.'

'You've never been to Greenland before?' came a voice from behind them. It was the doctor, Finnbogi Kolbeinsson. 'Here, Murphy's Law always applies—if something can go wrong, it will.'

Thóra smiled at the man. 'Do you know all the ins and outs here?'

'I've come here several times,' replied the doctor, managing not to sound like he was trying to show off. 'I'm a devoted outdoors man. As you might have seen from the plane, it's all wide open spaces here. I've taken part in several trips around the country on behalf of a group whose goal is to reduce food poisoning, which is pretty common here in the isolated settlements. The conditions are completely different to what we're used to, since provisions can only be delivered when the weather permits, which means most deliveries stop in the winter. Because of that, people rely a great deal on canned food, which considerably increases the risk of susceptibility to various types of pathogens if the packaging is damaged, as sometimes happens.'

'Have you been to this work site before?' asked Thóra, curious.

'Actually, no,' replied Finnbogi. 'I do know where it is, and some years ago I was knocking about those parts, but the project hadn't started then. That was in the summer, so unfortunately I probably won't recognize anything.'

'That shouldn't be a problem,' said Matthew. 'If everything works out according to plan, we won't be

47

here long.'

'It won't,' said Finnbogi, calmly. He shrugged. 'That's one thing I like so much about this country. You never know what to expect once you're here.'

'At least we're lucky with the weather,' said Thóra, to help lower Matthew's blood pressure. 'It's much better than I expected.' She had imagined them stuck in a snowstorm from the time they landed until they went back to Iceland. 'I've probably brought too many hats with me.' She crossed her fingers and hoped she'd packed at least one hat.

'Don't worry,' said Finnbogi. 'They'll come in handy. Although the weather is good right now, the forecast is rather gloomy. The helicopter pilots are worried they won't make it back.'

The sky was clear, but there could very well be heavy clouds hiding behind the mountains. 'Then they must be in a hurry,' said Thóra. 'Or is there maybe time to take a quick look at Kulusuk?' Perhaps she could find something there for Sóley. The airport had a small shop that sold local handicrafts, among other things, but it was closed.

'No,' said Matthew brusquely. 'There's no way.'

'You can do that on the way home,' said Finnbogi before Matthew had the opportunity to express any further displeasure at the notion. 'It's fun to visit the town, but you don't want to risk missing the helicopter.' Just then one of the loaders appeared and asked them to prepare for departure. Sóley's present would have to wait; perhaps something could be found in the village near the work site. Still, she didn't hold out much hope that she would find a shop there. Matthew had told her that the little village of Kaanneq was a long way from any

48

traditional tourist areas, and ordinary tourists didn't pay for hour-long helicopter flights to the north just to go shopping. The bank had insisted that they all be transported at once so that it wouldn't have to pay for two helicopter trips. The village was not connected by road to other settlements, and the sea route was only open over the summer and early autumn. At other times of the year a helicopter was the only choice.

Thóra had butterflies in her stomach when the helicopter lifted off, carrying eight passengers, two pilots, baggage and supplies. She crossed her fingers instinctively for the second time.

* * *

It was actually an understatement to call the village of Kaanneq small—tiny was more like it. On steep, flat rocks that extended down to a small, ice-covered bay stood wooden houses, painted in bright colours which made them stand out from their snow-white surroundings. The houses seemed well maintained and the gardens neat, though there was no way to guess what lay beneath the snow. The helicopter had landed just above the settlement, on a level area that served as a helicopter pad. The pilots had chosen the more energetic members of the group to help them unload the helicopter at record speed and as soon as the last cardboard box was out they jumped back in and started the propellers. Matthew had arranged for them to return at noon five days later if they hadn't heard from the group by then.

'We shouldn't hold out much hope that they'll be back here at the right time,' said Eyjólfur Þorsteinsson, the young IT technician, as the helicopter vanished from their sight.

'What do you mean?' asked Matthew crossly. 'The forecast for that time is fine. The storm that's supposed to hit should be over by then.'

'It's not the weather that worries me.' The young man grinned. 'You know those are the same pilots who took the tourists up to Greenland Glacier and then forgot to pick them up at the appointed time. They remembered them several days later and it was sheer luck that the whole lot of them hadn't frozen to death.'

Matthew didn't seem amused by this story and Thóra had to suppress a giggle when she saw his expression. 'They must have learned from the experience and started writing everything down,' she said brightly, smiling at Eyjólfur. She looked back at Matthew. 'Don't you think?'

Matthew's expression was unchanged, except that he was a tiny bit paler. 'Undoubtedly,' he said. 'I'll still get in touch with them after we've arrived and remind them of it, just in case.'

Thóra did not ask about the telephone connection at the camp, which was not necessarily in working order. All would be revealed soon. Matthew had actually told her that there was no GSM connection at the work site, and the same appeared to apply to this isolated settlement. But of course they could always call from one of the villagers' phones if necessary. If in fact there were any villagers—there was no one out and about.

'Shouldn't we get going?' called Matthew to the group. It was starting to grow dark. The hangar where Berg Technology's cars were supposed to be was a short distance away, and the path there led along the edge of the village. 'If it turns out we have no means of transportation, it's better that we give ourselves enough time.' The group set out immediately, except for Bella, who eked out her long-awaited cigarette as long as she could. The only sound apart from the high-pitched creaking of the snow beneath the shoes of the expedition members was the panting of the secretary as she tried to catch up with the rest of them.

*   *   *

For the final stretch they walked past the unfenced back lot of a house where numerous huskies were curled up asleep. The dogs were chained to posts that had been driven into the ground here and there throughout the yard. They jerked awake from their peaceful dozing as the group approached. Asleep, they looked quite adorable, but awake they were rather frightening; they immediately rose to their feet and bared their gleaming white teeth. The hairs on their shoulders rose, as did a stripe down their spines. Several of them leaped forward, growling, as far as their chains permitted, jerking the wooden posts. The red-haired geologist Friðrikka whimpered and reddened. 'I hate those dogs,' she muttered, quickening her pace. None of the others spoke, but most of them sped up too, until the menacing barking of the dogs was behind them. Thóra turned around once they'd travelled a safe distance and saw that now the dogs had started to threaten each other, although their chains held them back. There was no sign of human activity. Either no one lived in the blue-painted house or the people there were used to the dogs raising a ruckus now and then.

Dr Finnbogi walked alongside Thóra the final metres to the large, corrugated-iron hangar. The rusty iron creaked in the breeze, which seemed to be picking up. 'What do we do if the cars aren't here? I don't get the feeling that the villagers are overjoyed about our being here.'

'If they haven't been stolen, then they're here,' said Thóra, watching Friðrikka and Matthew bending over a large combination lock on the hangar door. 'At least that's what the contractor says.' She looked back at the little crowd of houses. 'I doubt anyone would steal a car around here. It would take the police half an hour at most to find him.'

'There are no police here!' exclaimed Friðrikka. Between them, she and Matthew had managed to open the lock. 'The nearest police station is in Angmagssalik. It takes more than car theft to get them on a helicopter this far north.'

Bella lit a fresh cigarette. 'Like what?' she asked.

'I don't know, murder, maybe,' replied the geologist drily. 'You shouldn't imagine that things here are like what you're used to. Far from it. If you get lost, no one will search for you. If you fall into the sea, no one will fish you out. Here you're not much better off than an animal.' Friðrikka pursed her lips and said nothing more.

The others in the group smiled uncomfortably and tried in vain to think of something clever to say in response. Matthew—who wasn't yet fluent enough in Icelandic to fully understand his fellow traveller's statement—had continued trying to open the door, but ice around the catch was making his task difficult. He broke the embarrassed silence. 'Well,' he said contentedly, pulling forcefully at the door. The hinges creaked loudly and the door swung out towards the group.

Inside were two white raised pickup trucks and only Thóra knew Matthew well enough to read on his face how happy he was. In addition, there was one well-equipped Ford Econoline, which Eyjólfur told them belonged to the Greenland authorities so that the police or others on public business would have a vehicle available whenever it was needed. 'Who wants to drive?'

*   *   *

Thóra stared out of the window as they drove through the village, in the hope of seeing anyone out and about. She was troubled and could not avoid the thought that perhaps a dangerous epidemic or food poisoning had swept over the area and killed the villagers and employees of Berg Technology. Suddenly two little girls appeared, walking between the houses. They stopped abruptly when they saw the cars and fixed their dark eyes on them. They looked to Thóra to be a bit younger than Sóley, perhaps five and six years old. Yet it was difficult to be sure, since they were dressed warmly in thick hooded coats and windproof trousers that were tucked into snow boots. Their blue-black hair splayed out from beneath their hats and blew in the wind. Thóra waved to them and smiled her warmest smile but the girls stood stock-still and watched her dispassionately. The taller one grabbed her companion's mittened hand. If there had been an epidemic, it appeared that at least some of them had escaped. A third girl was sitting on a landing at the top of the stairs in front of a house at the end of the village, and down at the harbour were two adults. Thóra turned in her seat to get a better view of the girls, but they had disappeared. 'Should we try talking to the people here?' she asked. 'I saw a couple of them down at the harbour.'

'No, let's keep going,' said Matthew. 'We can come back down here tomorrow if we want. Hopefully all this will be explained when we get to the work camp, and then talking to the villagers will be unnecessary. They want to be left in peace, so it wouldn't pay to trouble them unnecessarily.'

Thóra looked around again. Just as she'd suspected, she would find no souvenir shop here. 'How far is it?' she asked. As if her hangover weren't enough, now the muscles in her bottom were killing her after a day in transit, due mainly to the helicopter seat. The helicopter's manufacturer had saved its pennies on more than just the number of propeller blades.

'It's not too far,' replied the unlovely Alvar, who was driving. 'According to the GPS, we've got only ten kilometres to go.' Twenty minutes later the work camp appeared. The low, dark green buildings were difficult to see in the encroaching darkness. The car plodded at a snail's pace over one more snowdrift, and while they waited they regarded the buildings.

'Shouldn't there be lights on if anyone is here?' asked Eyjólfur. 'That's how it was every time I came here. I don't recall ever seeing the camp so dark.'

No one said anything, but clearly they had all been thinking the same thing. Not a single light was lit in the camp.

Chapter 5

19 March 2008

There is something about abandoned places; something unpleasant but difficult to put your finger on. In an abstract way, it was clear to everyone that those who had vanished from there would not be coming back. Several times Thóra had visited the home of a deceased person to take care of the division of their estate, and had experienced this same discomfort. Perhaps it was the ornaments that would never again be admired, or the open newspaper on the table that no one would finish reading. Although the camps held neither ornaments nor newspapers, Thóra was gripped by the same feeling; they were empty of people but full of signs of human activity. Above all, it reminded Thóra of a documentary on Chernobyl that she had seen several years ago, which gave a good view of how it looked when an entire town's population has to abandon its homes and workplaces without warning. The difference was in the people. In Chernobyl, the residents had fled from something. Here it looked as though the earth had swallowed the two employees.

In the camp's main office building computers whirred; desks bore signs that the workers had had no suspicion that they would never return. Half-empty coffee mugs were left here and there and fleece jackets hung on the backs of chairs. Everything was silent, except for the faint buzzing of the computers and the occasional beeping of the fire alarm system. When they looked at it, it seemed to be flagging up a fire in the smokers' room, which they found near the main entrance with Friðrikka's assistance. There was no fire there, but the window had been left ajar, which had let in enough snow to cover the floor. The men's disappearance couldn't be attributed to a fire. The geologist informed them that the security system was sensitive and could have been set off by the unexpected ingression of snow into the building. Likewise, the smoke detectors were very sensitive to cigar and pipe smoke. On the other hand, Friðrikka thought it strange that no one had shut off that intolerable beeping—resetting the system could not be that difficult. Most likely, the alarm had gone off after the two men disappeared from the camp. According to Friðrikka they both smoked, and thus could have left the window open after their final cigarettes in there. Bella was furious at the snow-filled room since it was now impossible to smoke inside the office building, but her anger was largely appeased when Friðrikka told her that there was another little lounge for smokers in the cafeteria and residential wing. However, Bella was prohibited from going there alone until everything had been checked out, which made her grumpy again. 'Then I'll just have to smoke outside on this fucking tundra,' she muttered, putting on her coat to go out and do just that.

'I don't know how advisable it is for you to go out alone,' said the doctor gravely. 'We have no idea what occurred here, and there could well have been a polar bear outside that attacked the men.' This warning seemed to give Bella no pause, and she continued wrapping herself up for her trip outside.

56

'Not to mention how unhealthy smoking is,' added the doctor, in the hope of a better reception.

Bella stiffened as she zipped up her coat. Her expression was not one of panic, but anger. She looked straight at the doctor, resentfully. 'I can't smoke in here?' she asked. When she received no answer she bent down once more and pulled on her other boot. 'I didn't think so. Either I smoke in here or I go out.' She finished getting ready as Thóra, Matthew, Friðrikka and the doctor watched in silence, and then stormed out after flinging them one last grumpy look.

'I'm more worried about the polar bear, if they do cross paths,' said Thóra as the door closed.

They continued inspecting the office building, and after looking into all the rooms Friðrikka declared that everything but the smokers' room appeared normal. One thing struck Thóra as they rambled through the building—as far as she could see, the speckled linoleum was exactly like that visible in the video clip. She exchanged glances with Matthew and he nodded his head to indicate that he had also noticed this. On the other hand, there appeared to be no traces of blood in the rooms; although the group had only done a cursory inspection, it didn't pay to arouse the suspicion of the geologist by inspecting the walls for signs of blood spatter. It could wait.

Although everything appeared normal in the office building, it was a different story in the employees' quarters and the cafeteria. These were, respectively, little green buildings that most resembled container units and a larger building that had been put together from similar units. The larger building contained the staff's communal facilities: kitchen, cafeteria, lounge, gym and laundry room. Attached to the large building was a long wing of rooms with simple sleeping accommodation. Friðrikka told them that the buildings with separate entrances were effectively apartments. Those who stayed here for longer periods lived in them; they had a bedroom, a bathroom with a shower, a little sitting room and a kitchenette. The rooms on the wing were more modest: a bed and a locker, with a shared shower and toilet at the end of the wing.

These rooms were occupied by those who stayed for shorter periods, and occasionally regular staff when storms raged and it was inadvisable to go outside, even to get from the cafeteria to the apartments. Thóra said nothing when she heard this, but was quite surprised, since the small apartments were only a few dozen metres away. If people couldn't make it safely such a short distance in bad weather, she hoped that the impending storm would pass over quickly. She frowned when Friðrikka added that sometimes these storms could last for days. They decided to stay in the rooms on the wing, so as not to tamper with the apartments of the people who might conceivably return to work there. If they weren't able to restore power to the sleeping wing they would set themselves up in the office building, since without power it was twenty degrees below inside as well as outside. The most probable explanation for the lack of heat in the employees' quarters was that the generator supplying power was either broken or out of fuel, and Matthew, Dr Finnbogi and Alvar went to try to get it working again. Thóra, Friðrikka and Eyjólfur remained behind in the office, along with Bella, who had returned safely from her fag break.

The four of them stood in the little coffee room that had been set up in a nook in a corridor of the office building. The large coffeemaker was turned on and there was nothing preventing them from pressing a button and making coffee except that the doctor had explicitly prohibited them from doing so. He considered it unwise to consume anything in the camp while the fate of the two employees was still unclear. Thóra thought this unnecessarily dramatic; all of the rooms and living quarters had been inspected and had revealed no signs of the missing men. People did not simply evaporate from food poisoning or sickness, she thought privately; but she didn't dare make herself a coffee, even though she was parched and knew that her hangover, which was finally decreasing in intensity, would disappear almost entirely if she had a coffee or something stronger.

'The system was actually divided into two to ensure that the entire area would not lose power all at once,' said Friðrikka, breaking the silence. 'There is a separate generator for the office and another for the apartments and cafeteria. Everything here is heated with electric radiators, and even though the houses are well insulated, it gets cold quickly when the electricity goes off. But electrical failures don't matter; we have a huge oil tank that is supposed to be enough to supply both generators through the winter, but if spring arrives late we have to shut one of them down until a ship can bring more supplies.'

'Did that happen often while you were here?' asked Thóra. 'The electricity going off?'

'No, no,' replied Friðrikka. 'At first there was some trouble with the exhaust pipe of one of the

59

generators and the electricity went out when wind blew into the pipe, but that was repaired quickly. The system worked fine after that but I don't know how things went after I quit. Maybe something was already going wrong then.'

'No, I don't think so,' interjected Eyjólfur. 'I was here two weeks ago and no one mentioned anything like that.'

'Could the generator have run out of oil?' asked Thóra, directing her question at Friðrikka. 'And that's why it shut down?' She wanted to look outside, satisfy herself that the storm hadn't hit yet.

'No, that's impossible,' the other woman replied. 'Spring's still a long way off and there should be plenty of oil, unless someone badly miscalculated.'

It must have been odd not to be able to count on regular shipments except over the summer. The residents had to make arrangements for the winter at the end of that season. Thóra would have liked to see her own shopping list if she'd lived under these conditions. The hut that housed the generator was in view, but she did not see any of the men that had gone there armed with torches and a toolkit. The wind was starting to stir up the snow and Thóra shivered at the thought of having to go outside. She turned around.

'How did it all work here, then?' she asked. 'It's an unusual set-up, to say the least.'

'I actually just made short trips here,' replied Eyjólfur off-handedly. 'I wouldn't have stuck it out if I'd had to be here longer than a week.' The answer hardly came as a surprise, since the computer expert was young and doubtless had a decent social life outside of work. Everything here must have centred on daily work tasks.

60

Friðrikka shrugged and looked down at her toes. 'It was all right. You had to get used to it, but on the whole it was fine.' She drew a breath through her nose. 'Naturally it's not easy living where you work and associating only with your co-workers, but once you've got used to it it's no problem. The salary was good and made up for the isolation. I'm single and childless, so it was okay really.'

'But still, you gave it up.' said Thóra. 'May I ask why?' Eyjólfur suddenly became very interested in a little refrigerator and bent down to inspect it.

'The atmosphere changed, you might say,' replied the woman, pushing a red lock of hair that had fallen onto her cheek back behind her ear. 'When we came here about a year ago everything was done professionally and all of our interactions were normal, but the group's spirits deteriorated quickly. In the end I couldn't bear the idea of being here any longer.' She flushed, but then stuck out her chin and continued, focused: 'I wasn't even surprised when I was contacted and told that something had come up here. It was inevitable.' She looked away from Thóra. 'There was—and probably still is—a curse on this place.' She added quickly, 'And I'm not alone in that view, if that's what you think.'

'It must be okay to have a Coke,' said Eyjólfur loudly, standing up with a can in his hand. 'I'm dying of thirst and this fridge is full of drinks. The Coke can hardly be poisoned.' Thóra wasn't going to let him get away with changing the subject.

'Do you agree?' she asked, as he flicked open the can and swigged from it. 'Do you think there's a curse on this place?' She choked down her own overwhelming desire for a Coke. They needn't both become ill; it was better to wait and see

61

whether he lost consciousness before she yielded to the temptation. She wondered whether a Coke could be counted as one of the doctor's potentially contaminated canned goods.

Eyjólfur took another gulp and sighed happily before replying. 'No, I wouldn't say that.' He looked at Friðrikka as he spoke. '*Places* aren't good or bad. At most, you can only describe the people who live in them that way.' He tipped the can as if toasting the geologist. 'Don't you think so?'

Friðrikka did not reply immediately, but looked disdainfully away from the grinning man and stared at the wall. 'Doesn't matter, because in the end it's all the same. Maybe it was just all of you and what went on here that made the place bad.'

'Could you be a little clearer?' asked Thóra. She was in no condition to read between the lines. Maybe what had happened here was unconnected with recent events; perhaps it had simply been typical work stuff, like an extramarital affair or some other gossip, but it still wouldn't hurt to know what they were talking about.

'For God's sake, it was a lot of fuss over nothing,' replied Eyjólfur. 'Friðrikka simply gave up and quit. She didn't have the nerve for it, or the sense of humour you need under these conditions. There's nothing wrong with the place itself, although the work arrangements were pretty fucked-up. This kind of workplace isn't for everyone.'

He was hardly one to talk. By his own account he had only come here for a week at a time while others stayed for lengthy periods. However, Thóra decided to say nothing, to protect Friðrikka. The geologist might turn out to be a crybaby who had convinced herself everything was intolerable in order to justify her leaving. Thóra could find this out later if necessary. She looked outside once more. 'There's smoke coming from the chimney on the roof,' she said. 'That must be a good thing.'

Friðrikka peered out and nodded. 'It looks like the generator is running again,' she said. 'Unfortunately it's probably too late for the showers and water, but who knows. Hopefully it was shut off intentionally and the water drained from the system. Either way, it'll be nice not to have to sleep in here on the floor.'

'Why shouldn't the showers be working? They don't run on electricity,' said Thóra grumpily. It was bad enough not being able to have a coffee or an ice-cold Coke. Bella's expression suggested that she felt the same.

'If the camp has been without heat long enough for the water to freeze in the pipes, most of the lines are probably broken,' said Friðrikka. 'Unless they left the taps trickling, but I didn't notice that when we had our look around.' Thóra said nothing, hoping they had simply overlooked this during their inspection of the site. But she didn't hold out much hope. They would probably have heard the water running in the oppressive silence.

'Fuck,' said Eyjólfur, seemingly just as pissed off as Thóra. He didn't elaborate, but took another huge gulp of Coke. He reached for the tap on the sink next to the coffeemaker and sighed in relief when water ran out of it in a dense jet. 'Well, at least we can flush the toilet in this building.'

'I guess I should go out and help them turn the lights on and get everything working,' said Friðrikka. 'I know where everything is, so we'd get it done faster.' Thóra wondered for a moment

63

whether she should be lazy and lag behind, but she pushed away the thought. They would all have to contribute.

*   *   *

The hunter Igimaq watched the four people emerge from the big building. Three females and one male, all dressed in colourful outdoor clothing that contrasted with the environment. Despite their thick clothing and their distance from him, the man realized at the same moment that all the women were too tall for his taste, and two of them too thin. The man was no good either: he was scrawny and weak-looking, though he was not exactly a runt. It was like that with all Westerners. Their worship of skinny physiques was the best example of how they had broken all ties with nature. Despite their winter clothing, those three women would freeze to death in no time if they were forced to fend for themselves without the food and shelter they took for granted. They probably ate meat, but would puke if he took them hunting and showed them how such food was acquired. That was in the unlikely event that he would manage to catch anything with them or their ilk tagging along. They couldn't even see him right now, even though he did nothing to conceal himself. He simply stood still and allowed the blowing snow to play about his warmly dressed body. His hood shielded his eyes, but he still had to squint from time to time in the strongest gusts. He watched them walk over to the other big building, where others were standing, from the look of them two men and a woman. They spoke together briefly, but he could not make out the words and would not

64

have understood them anyway. He did understand Danish, although he had difficulty expressing himself in that language; not because he didn't know the words, but rather because they were not sufficiently descriptive for what lay in his heart. It was a language that had developed under different circumstances than Greenlandic, based on an easier struggle for life and different values. The faint sound of the people's conversation died out and he watched the group enter the building. Shortly afterwards, one light after another went on inside it. He continued to stand there, expressionless, though he felt uneasy. This couldn't end well.

Igimaq turned and walked away. It was useless to stand here any longer; he had heard the helicopter and wanted to find out whether those it carried were on their way to this area. It was bad, but following every single movement of the newcomers wouldn't help. Although they were defenceless out in the open, they were on their home field indoors. In any case he could change nothing, any more than he could anything else in this life; things went their own way and providence was often unreadable and illogical. No one knew that better than him. More than ever it seemed to him that trying to grasp what mattered most to human beings was like grabbing at sunbeams; they disappeared at the same time as one was still enjoying them, and one could never get a grip on them. Similarly, whatever a man loved always disappeared; he would come to possess something only to lose it later. The hunter had hardened his heart regarding all the things that had disappeared from his life over the years, and thankfully he had largely succeeded; he was even starting to feel the same about the family he'd lost. Perhaps he had already succeeded there, too. Igimaq could not be sure, because the thought of his family's fate was so difficult for him to bear that he had refused to allow himself to think about anything since the time just before it happened. Had he been left in peace, this would have worked; until just recently, his mind had never turned to the woman he had loved and lost, and very rarely had he given a thought to the daughter and son who had also gone from him.

The hunter grimaced at the broad expanse of ice and snow. These outsiders and those who had come before had torn open an old wound. Triggered memories of a son who had awakened in him such great hope, a hope that had felt so sublime that it was bound to fail. He still recalled the little feet sticking out from beneath the blanket when he saw him newborn; the thick, broad soles that suggested he would make his mark on the world. Nothing had come of this, any more than his wife consistently seeing to his needs following each good hunt, as she had promised. Yet he had fulfilled his obligation, had given her two children who appeared healthy and had seen to it that there was always enough food on the family's table. He had doted on the boy, but without him being aware of it. A good hunter, a real man, had to learn certain lessons on his own and build his own character through difficult experience; otherwise he would never learn the interplay between land and animals. But none of this mattered in the end. His wife and their two children were lost to him. His daughter was dead, and the same could be said for his wife and son. They would never break free from the fetters of alcohol and although it would be no trouble to visit

66

them, he knew he never would. To him they were as dead as his daughter.

He approached the snowdrift behind which he had hidden his sled and heard the regular breathing of the dogs. They were tired after their strenuous day, but when he appeared only one of them continued sleeping. That dog lay curled up with its tail over its nose to protect its respiratory system from the cold. The other dogs had cocked their heads and now watched the hunter with attentive eyes. They stood up, one after another, until finally the sleeping dog stirred. It immediately sprang up and growled, softly but deeply. The growl was not directed at the hunter; that much was certain. Perhaps it was to remind the other dogs that it was still their leader. It could also be that by growling, the animal was making clear its irritation at the fatigue it had exhibited. With good reason; its days would soon be numbered. It tired too quickly, and even though it was not particularly old, its behaviour was showing ever increasing signs of its age. The hunter did not know what caused this any more than he knew what had caused his son's life to ebb away. Maybe the dog was simply one of those whose legs failed them early, or else the battles it had fought to become the leader of the pack were starting to take their toll. After its death another such conflict would begin, in which the dogs would fight each other until the strongest and cunningest assumed power with the taste of its fellows' blood in its mouth. The hunter just hoped those fights would not cost him more dogs, as sometimes happened.

The hunter stood and looked at the lead dog and saw in the creature's intelligent eyes that it knew what lay ahead. He saw questions glittering in its speckled pupils: had it done a good job? Had it not led the team diligently through the dangers that accompanied the thinning of the ice? Had it not always made sure that the rest of the team behaved and obeyed his commands? If this creature could have spoken, they could have discussed its situation and he could explain to the dog why he was going to dispose of it. It was better to die as a lead dog than let the team force you out. But the connection between the hunter and the dog was not strong enough for such debate: the man understood the dog and the dog understood the man, but some things they could never express to each other. The dog would never understand this decision, even though it was more difficult for the man than the animal, which felt nothing. He had seldom or never had a better lead dog; this was the animal he had waited for ever since his grandfather had told him in his childhood that somewhere he would find a creature to whom he could speak without words. A beast that would understand him and help him through his greatest trials. That would follow Igimaq into the jaws of death without any hesitation.

There was something in the dog's eyes that encouraged him to wait a while before implementing his decision. It was not the creature's instinctive will to live, but something different. The moment that his grandfather had spoken of had likely not yet come, despite everything that had already happened. He should put off the inevitable just a bit longer, that would scarcely change anything. Spring was around the corner, and perhaps the dog would be refreshed by the warm winds. Or it might gain strength if he upped its food ration. The hunter could surely spare more meat. There was no shortage of it at the moment. The dog seemed almost to follow the hunter's train of thought, and it perked up proudly and glared at the other dogs. They cowered in submission, and the dog looked towards the hunter to check the man had observed its dominance over the team. The hunter smiled at the animal, his teeth gleaming whitely against his dark face, then turned and looked back at the green buildings in the distance. It was not his job to rescue full-grown children who came here on a fool's errand. He would concentrate on saving the dog; it was far more important to him.

Chapter 6

20 March 2008

Thóra woke up exhausted, having repeatedly jolted awake in alarm during the night. She didn't know why; the stillness had been absolute. Perhaps that was precisely the reason, perhaps she was unused to such overwhelming silence. This explanation was more to her liking than the idea that she had been woken by a noise or movement from someone—or something—that had fallen silent when she stirred. She felt tired and stiff after a night on the lumpy mattress of the single bed she'd shared with Matthew, although at least her hangover was gone, leaving her with a clear head and a tongue no longer puffy and fuzzy. She vaguely recalled Matthew nudging her and saying he was going to get an early start. It was probably an hour since he had left the room and it was still only seven o'clock. By Thóra's criteria, even that was too early—to get up at six in the morning she considered madness, only excusable if one had to catch a morning flight. She threw on yesterday's clothes; although her hangover was gone, she did not want to start the day by opening her suitcase and discovering what she had packed. That could wait.

The weather had not got up to much overnight, and the murmur of the wind outside now did not suggest that the much-anticipated storm had arrived. She hoped it would stay like this, since hardly anyone in the group wished to be here any longer than necessary. Thóra shuddered at the thought of being in close confinement with these people for days and days. She actually had nothing against her fellow travellers—except perhaps Bella—but being isolated with strangers was a recipe for trouble. Especially if the doctor's ban on drinking the coffee wasn't lifted. Matthew had, understandably, not had the brainwave of bringing any bottled water to Greenland. When the doctor asked him about water supplies he replied shamefacedly that he had assumed they could melt snow if they ran out. He then added that he had brought a considerable supply of milk, fruit juice and other soft drinks. Shortly afterwards Thóra had made her own contribution to the reduction of those supplies, and this morning she was dying for a coffee rather than a Coke. Hope flickered in her heart when she encountered the aroma of coffee as she approached the kitchen, but her joy was tempered somewhat when she saw Bella sitting in the cafeteria. Thóra engaged in a brief internal struggle about whether to turn around and eat a handful of snow on the way out of the office building or break the doctor's ban and have a cup of coffee in Bella's company. Her craving for caffeine had the upper hand.

'It's impossible to sleep here,' muttered Bella after Thóra bade her good morning on her way to the coffeemaker. 'My bed is completely knackered and it's fucking freezing.'

'I was wondering how you could be out of bed so early when you have so much trouble making it to work for nine,' said Thóra, reaching for a cup. 'You may want to consider getting a similar bed at home, and installing air conditioning.'

'Or enlarging a photo of you and hanging it on my wall,' replied Bella, her mouth full of cornflakes. 'It's all the same.'

Thóra refrained from responding to this, mainly because she couldn't come up with anything clever to say. 'Do you know what you're supposed to do later?' she asked instead.

'Type some stuff up. Something like that, anyway,' drawled the secretary. She was thumbing through a worn-out old book lying on the table before her and looked up as Thóra sat down with a steaming cup. 'I just hope it's warmer in the office—I can't type much wearing gloves.'

'It's much better there,' replied Thóra. 'It's only so cold here because it takes time to heat up the building. The heating never went off in the offices.' She sipped her coffee. 'What are you reading?'

'Some crap about Greenland,' said Bella, flipping a page. 'I found this on the table along with all the papers here and although it's not exactly exciting reading, it's a bit better than an out-of-date newspaper or magazine.' Looking at the book,

71

Thóra had her doubts. Judging by the hue of the colour photos on its pages the book was a few decades old, and it was incredible how quickly guidebooks passed their sell-by date. 'Do you know, for example, what the name of that miserable little town over there means?' asked Bella, finally looking up from the book.

'Kaanneq?' said Thóra in an inquisitive tone. 'I would hazard a guess at *the ends of the earth* or something along those lines. It would at least be fitting.'

'No, it means *hunger*,' said Bella, as she reached for the packet of cornflakes. 'The story goes that the first settlers there all starved to death. Maybe that's what happened here?'

'I doubt that the employees of Berg Technology starved to death, if indeed they *are* dead,' replied Thóra. 'There's enough food in the kitchen, even though we'll have to make do with our own supplies.' The doctor had not only banned them from drinking the coffee, but also from eating anything except what they had brought with them to the camp. Thóra had made sure to mark all of the food and drink that came out of the boxes so that no one would become confused and consume anything that had been there before their arrival. It wasn't just helpfulness that inspired her to label everything, but also her desire to be close to the soft drinks, as well as to see what Matthew had purchased. She had to hand it to him, it seemed the most sensible of inventories.

'In any case, something happened to the residents,' said Bella, turning the book towards Thóra. She had turned it to the relevant page, with the heading *Kaanneq* appearing over several

72

photographs and a short text. The photos were all black and white except for one that was clearly much newer, and in it the village looked similar to how it was today, a collection of colourful wooden houses. The other, older photos showed far fewer houses. They were taken from the same angle and the village looked pretty much the same; both the cold and barren landscape in the background, as well as the modest harbour in the narrow fjord, looked roughly unchanged. All the images had been taken in winter and showed the area covered in snow. The villagers had not always been so reluctant to be seen outside; in the old photographs people were out and about, dressed warmly in traditional protective garments made of sealskin. However, none of the photos dated back further than 1940, so the book did not show the original settlement that Bella had mentioned.

Thóra skimmed over the text. It didn't surprise her that it was thought that those who first settled in Eastern Greenland around two thousand years ago had all died out. One migration and settlement followed another, but it always ended the same way: no one managed to survive for long in this harsh region. It wasn't until the eighteenth century that settlements started to thrive on the east coast, but in the nineteenth century the population started to decrease. One village after another fell to ruin after the villagers died from hunger or other hardships, or found themselves forced to move to the west coast, where conditions were better. First the northernmost villages disintegrated, then one settlement after another southwards along the coast. Eventually Angmagssalik had been the only settlement remaining on the entire east coast.

Thóra shuddered involuntarily at the thought of all the people that had lived and died there. Of all the troubles that they had had to endure, it hurt her most to think of the women who had raised children there, suffering bitter cold and extreme hunger on top of everything else.

The struggle for existence there had been enormously hard. When a Danish explorer came to Angmagssalik in 1830, only around four hundred people lived there. Sixty years later, another explorer calculated that the population had dropped to three hundred, and he speculated that if nothing changed, the area would eventually become uninhabited. Subsequently, the Danes decided to set up a colony in East Greenland, in spite of the difficult land and sea connections. Angmagssalik was chosen and a missionary and trading colony established there in 1894, leading to a sharp decline in infant mortality and malnutrition. Twenty years later the population had doubled, and from the First World War onwards the settlement's population grew larger and larger, until it could no longer accommodate itself. The decision was then made to build a new town, Scoresbysund, nearly a thousand kilometres to the north, and to encourage a percentage of the residents to move there. Shortly before this organized resettlement occurred, ten families gave up on the dwindling supply of game for hunting in the Angmagssalik region and decided to pack up and move north. Why they decided to go north instead of south was never explained. This was the start of the story of the little village of Kaanneq.

Ten families set off in the summer of 1918 and little was heard of them until the autumn. They

74

were doing fine, the hunting was good and they had constructed shelter. A Danish physician who visited the tiny settlement recorded in his report that the residents were fit, the children and adults were healthy, and two women were pregnant—one about to give birth, the other more than five months along. The doctor saw no reason for particular concern but nevertheless recommended that the group be checked on twice during the winter. The same physician and a native guide made the first trip by dogsled. They stayed for two days in the new settlement and the doctor reported that everything was still fine with the people there, although they had somewhat lower food supplies than he had reckoned on in the autumn. One of the babies, a boy, had been born and was doing quite well. The other woman was due shortly. How that child would fare would come to light in the second trip.

However, this never came to pass. Three months later, in mid-February, an assistant physician set out to visit the village, accompanied by the same guide. They were never heard from again. It wasn't known whether they'd met their fate on the way to or from the new settlement, and hence whether they had made it there at all. Neither hide nor hair of the men or dogs was ever found. Admittedly, a search for them was never conducted, as there was no point; no one could survive there without shelter in midwinter.

A group of hunters from Angmagssalik said they had seen two men from Kaanneq fishing out on the ice in an area midway between the village and the new settlement, but the men from the north retreated from the group, who made no contact with them. It was their opinion that the men had fled from them and wished to avoid associating with their former neighbours. Apart from this incident, none of the residents of Kaanneq was ever seen alive again. In the spring three men went there to buy sealskins, but found all of the residents dead from hardship and hunger, or so it seemed. Some of the bodies were found in large tents, but upon closer inspection a number were found to be missing and were thought to have been buried before the famine crippled everyone and everything. However, their graves were never discovered, despite extensive searches. The majority of those lying dead around the village were women and children, suggesting that the men had gone out farther and farther to hunt as their prey became scarcer, and one after another had perished in the unforgiving wilderness. Then, when the women and children were left almost entirely alone, starvation set in. Stories of the ugly sight awakened dread and lived on in the memories of the natives, not least due to the photographs that were taken to document the horror. The natives' explanation of events was completely different to the Danes', in that the Inuits believed that something called a Tupilak had killed them all. A definition for this word was not provided, but Thóra thought it might be a storm or something else related to violent weather. In addition, the book mentioned stories circulating among the natives about the spirits of people that roamed the area, hungry, and ate anyone they met. The one constant in the history of the region was fear of starvation, and when a new village arose on the same site, the effects of the old events were still being felt and the village was named Kaanneq, or *Hunger*.

'Well, now,' muttered Thóra, feeling somewhat depressed after what she had read. 'Is there anywhere harder to survive than here?'

Bella shrugged and stood up. 'Maybe in a burning desert. But at least you can get a bit of a suntan there.' She took her plate and stood up from the table. 'I just hope we get out of here as soon as possible.'

Thóra was unable to agree with Bella out loud and further destroy her morale. It was better to roll up their sleeves and get to work—then they could go home all the faster. She closed the book and found herself face-to-face with a young Greenlander, staring at her from the cover. The man smiled sincerely at the photographer and deep laughter lines framed his slanted eyes. He was a splendid sight to behold, and from his expression the circumstances described in the book certainly didn't seem to have diminished his happiness. She finished her coffee and listened to the wind growing stronger outside.

*   *   *

It was only a short distance to the office building, but Thóra was glad when she shut the door behind her. Outside gusts had stirred up the snow, in the worst moments making it seem as if she and Bella were in a sandstorm. As they put on their coats the weather had deteriorated instantaneously. Naturally, the wind was against them, and Thóra would have bet everything she owned that when she went back over to her sleeping quarters the wind would have completely changed direction and would again be blowing in her face. She had come

77

to know the vagaries of the winds well, living on the peninsula of Seltjarnarnes just outside of Reykjavík. However, it had never been this cold there, and she had never needed to protect her face against stinging frost and biting horizontal snow.

It sounded like Matthew was alone in the office. Finnbogi, Friðrikka, Alvar and Eyjólfur were probably still sleeping, or else had gone out either to try to find the men or check on the status of the project. Given the weather, Thóra hoped this was not the case. She was not happy about the thought of having to form an ad hoc rescue team with Matthew and Bella. She took off her shoes and hung up her coat. 'Matthew,' she called into the corridor. 'We're here.'

'Who's with you?' he called back from one of the office's rooms.

'Bella,' replied Thóra, following his voice. What a funny question, she thought. 'Are you naked or something?' She smiled.

'Do you know where the doctor is?' called Matthew, ignoring her joke. He spoke unnecessarily loudly, given that Thóra was standing in the doorway.

'No.' Thóra leaned against the doorpost. 'He's either sleeping or he's gone out. But you would have noticed it if he had driven away. He could hardly have walked away.' Matthew said nothing and continued to stoop over one of the desk drawers. 'Why are you asking about him? Did you find something?'

Matthew straightened up. 'I'm no expert on bones but these are clearly from a person,' he said, pointing down into the deep drawer. 'Whether this is connected in any way with the two men who

78

disappeared I couldn't say, but hopefully the doctor can tell us.'

Thóra drew closer out of curiosity. 'I see,' she said when she saw what was in the drawer, and turned quickly from the desk. 'I guess we'd better wake him.'

Chapter 7

20 March 2008

'The bones aren't from either man.' The doctor took off his glasses and straightened up. He had examined the skull as Thóra and Matthew watched. 'In fact, they're probably female.'

'Why do you say that?' asked Thóra. There didn't seem much that looked female about the skull and jawbone. 'Are our heads smaller?'

'Yes, but without knowing what race this individual belonged to it's impossible to determine anything from its size.' He put his glasses back on and showed them the jaw. 'I base my opinion on the fact that women's jawbones are much rounder than men's. If this had been a male, the front element, or the chin, would be squarer than this.' He put down the jawbone and picked up the skull, running his index finger above the eye sockets. The skull creaked slightly when his latex gloves touched it. 'The brow bone is not protrusive enough for it to be a man's. It's more pointed, so more likely to have been a woman.' He put the skull down carefully and took his glasses back off. 'Of course, bones are not my speciality; I'm simply recalling what I learned at medical school. An expert might come to an entirely different conclusion.' He smiled and added: 'Although I doubt it. I was first in my graduating class.'

That was good enough for Thóra. Until more evidence proved otherwise, she would consider this skull to have belonged to a female. 'Then aren't these the bones of the woman who disappeared from the camp? The geologist?'

The doctor looked surprised, so it was obviously the first he'd heard of her. 'Well, I don't know about that. Who was she, and when did she disappear?'

'She was here working for Berg Technology,' said Thóra. 'It's thought that she wandered off, got lost and died in a storm. That was about six months ago, and since she was never found it just occurred to me that these bones might be hers.' Thóra stared into the lifeless shadows of the eye sockets. 'Of course, now I'm wondering how her skull made its way into one of her co-worker's desk drawers.'

'You don't have to wonder about that,' said the doctor confidently. 'This skull can't belong to someone who died of exposure six months ago. Under these conditions the bones wouldn't have been stripped clean in such a short time, and the woman's co-workers would hardly have gone to the trouble of cleaning the skull. That would be pretty cold. I also think the bones would be whiter if they were from someone who died recently.'

'Where did the skull come from, then?' asked Matthew. He was regarding the remains warily, and Thóra noticed that his lips were pursed.

'Well, I think it could have come from a grave, or from open ground. The surface is covered with little scratches and impurities that couldn't have occurred while the individual was alive. They could be marks made by the teeth or claws of small animals.' The doctor shrugged. 'I don't know whether whoever left it here found the skull outside somewhere or simply bought it on the Internet. As unbelievable as it sounds, there's a market for such things. The first theory is somewhat negated by the fact that the jawbone is here as well. If the corpse had been lying somewhere out in the wilderness, large animals would have got to it and scattered the bones. I would guess that the skull was either exhumed or purchased online.'

'You mean they might have accidentally disturbed someone's grave?' asked Thóra sceptically. 'I highly doubt there was a cemetery in this area, and if there was it would have been a very long way from the beaten path. There was nothing here before the project started, and the documents that I've looked at say nothing about the company doing anything in the vicinity of the village, where you'd expect there to be a graveyard. Who would want to be buried here, far from everything?'

'In these parts people aren't actually buried in the ground, even in the graveyards—there's no soil.' The doctor crossed his arms and nodded at the skull. 'Here they bury their dead under cairns; I don't know how they prepare the bodies, although I imagine they're either wrapped in something or placed in coffins. If they'd been wrapped in cloth, the bones would show more damage, which means that this skull probably wasn't directly beneath a pile of rocks. It's possible that it was in a coffin.'

'It also seems doubtful that Berg employees dug this up accidentally,' said Matthew. 'Cairns must

81

stand out in this landscape.'

The doctor shrugged. 'Maybe they needed to dig in the area where it was buried and didn't realize what it was until after they'd started removing the stones.'

'Could these bones date back to 1918?' asked Thóra. Maybe the workers had found the remains of the people that disappeared from the original settlement.

'No, I don't think so.' Finnbogi stroked the skull's crown. 'This doesn't look that old.' He looked at her in surprise. 'Why do you ask?'

'I read in a book over in the cafeteria that there was a settlement here, but that everyone died of famine and exposure. I thought this might be one of those poor sods.'

'That wouldn't fit at all.' The doctor heaved a sigh. 'Shame, because it would be an incredibly convenient explanation.'

'What about the tag?' Thóra asked, pointing to a scrap of paper that had been lying beneath the skull in the drawer. The code G-57—nothing else—had been written on it with a broad black felt-tip pen.

'Do you think it's related?' asked Matthew. 'Maybe it was in the drawer before the skull was put there.' He looked at the name-plate on the door of the office. 'It'll all come to light, because the person whose desk this was is one of the ones who refuses to come back here. Maybe Eyjólfur and Friðrikka also know something about this. Maybe the skull was even found when one of them was here.' He turned to the doctor. 'I know this is a ridiculous question, but is it possible to know whether this person died of natural causes?'

The doctor did not seem to find this ridiculous.

82

'Well, she didn't die from a head injury, that much is certain. The bones are whole and uncracked. The teeth suggest that she was a young person, so it wasn't old age. The teeth are also in decent condition, so the individual took good care of them. However, it's impossible to say whether she died through illness, injury or human intervention. Hopefully it'll be explained when we know more about the origin of the skull. The fact that it's here definitely points to her death occurring under unusual circumstances. In the normal way of things, the bones would have been interred in a graveyard, because they're found in most, if not all of the settlements in this country, as they are elsewhere.'

Thóra heard familiar footsteps approaching in the corridor. Bella appeared in the doorway, an unfathomable look on her face. 'There are bones in all of the desks except for five,' she said, not appearing overly surprised. Matthew had assigned her the task of exploring the other rooms in the office building in the unlikely event that more skulls could be found, or the rest of the skeleton. None of them had thought that anything would come of it. 'The drawers were all locked, but Friðrikka told me that they all had the same lock—she gave me a key that she found in one of the rooms and it worked for all of them. I didn't want to touch the bones, so you'll have to come with me if you want to see them for yourselves.'

*   *   *

'It appears to be a complete skeleton.' The doctor clearly had no idea how to deal with this new discovery. 'It's possible, of course, that it's missing something, but all the main bones are certainly here. Closer examination will reveal whether they are all from the same individual, but I would consider it likely.'

'It will have to wait,' Matthew said firmly. 'We're not going to touch the bones, and we will leave this to the police.' He shut the drawer of the last of the desks that Bella had pointed out. 'Actually, we should have left the skull alone, but we can't undo that now.' He watched the doctor place it carefully back in the desk and close the drawer.

The wind blew something against the side of the building and its foundations creaked. Thóra shuddered; the storm was about to hit—that was certain. The windows on the side of the office building facing into the wind shuddered at regular intervals, and each time Thóra was convinced that a shower of glass would rain over them. She realized she was, discreetly, keeping as far away from the windows as possible. Accompanying the whine of the wind was a regular knocking sound from the roof, which the doctor had thought was probably a loose piece of roofing. Thóra found the sound unpleasant and its regularity and pitch grated more and more on her nerves. She would rather the piece flew off and let a little snow in than have this sound constantly in her ears.

Friðrikka and Eyjólfur had come over to the office building while Finnbogi was in the middle of examining the bones, but both of them denied knowing anything about them. They both seemed convincing and sincere in their amazement as they stood in the little vestibule and brushed most of the snow from their clothing. When Matthew had quizzed them about the discovery without finding out anything new, and they had been allowed to see the remains for themselves, it was decided that Eyjólfur should inspect the computer system and try to establish contact with the outside world. Friðrikka, in the meantime, would assess the status of the project. The bones' discovery did not change the purpose of the trip.

'Does anyone know how long the storm is supposed to last?' asked Thóra, looking out into the heavy blizzard. It was starting to grow light, although visibility was still poor because of the snow. 'We can't investigate the area much if it keeps coming down like this.' Just that moment another gust struck the window, making it wobble.

'I think it's supposed to subside tonight,' said Matthew. 'It can hardly continue much longer than that.'

The doctor snorted loudly. 'Storms here can last much longer than half a day. You might as well resign yourselves to this one lasting for days. Hopefully it won't—but you never know.'

Thóra scowled. 'Oh, that's just *great*.' She put down her camera. Data collection had begun, and although it wasn't entirely clear to her how photos of the bones in the drawers could help the bank and Berg Technology in their negotiations with Arctic Mining, it might. Admittedly, it could affect the status of the negotiations if the employees of the Icelandic company appeared at worst to be connected to a possible crime, and at best guilty of unseemly conduct with a corpse. 'I think I'll go through the office of one of the missing drillers,' said Thóra to Matthew. 'Shouldn't we start with them, just in case there's something there that could possibly help us find them? You can take the

85

other one.'

They both looked at the doctor. What should he do? Each of them was clearly reluctant to trust a stranger with their own project. The doctor, seeming to sense this, straightened up ceremoniously. 'Well, I need to collect samples from the taps and elsewhere. We may very well find *Legionella pneumophila* in the pipes.' Thóra and Matthew stared at him blankly. 'Legionnaires' disease,' he explained. 'The bacteria thrives well in little-used plumbing systems and may even have infected the men. The conditions here are ideal for it.'

'And then they evaporated as a result?' asked Thóra.

'No, but they might have tried to seek help and then become too exhausted to reach their destination. Legionnaires' is a dangerous disease and can even be fatal if left untreated. Or perhaps they made it to a hospital somewhere and couldn't get in touch with anyone due to their illness.'

Thóra didn't fancy coffee any more, even if the water came from melted snow rather than the camp's plumbing system. She and Matthew went to search the offices of the two drillers and discovered quickly that they had shared one room. On the way they passed Eyjólfur, who was sitting in the corridor in a kind of makeshift computer lab. On the screen before him was an indecipherable menu and the young man's fingers flew over the keyboard. 'Is everything all right with the system?' asked Thóra. 'We're going to have a look at some of the employees' computers and we don't want to damage anything.'

The young man looked up from the screen and

smiled at her. 'You can't do any harm,' he said. 'The system is all right, except that there's no Internet connection. The servers were turned off, but they're undamaged and working properly. You can get into them just fine and that's where all the data relating to the project should be saved.' He reached for a pen and paper lying next to the keyboard. Something was scrawled on the paper but he tore off a blank strip. 'Which computers are you thinking of looking at?'

'The drillers', to start with,' she replied. 'We'll probably end up looking at all of them but we want to start there.'

'Then you need passwords.' He clicked on the mouse to bring up another menu with the names of the system's users. 'I have no idea what passwords everyone had but I'll change them all to the same one.' He wrote 1234 on the piece of paper and handed it to Thóra. 'Just use this; the username should pop up after you boot the computer but give me a shout if that doesn't happen. This should get you into everything. Except the Internet, which is totally down. I'm starting to think the dish has malfunctioned.'

'The dish?' Thóra wasn't particularly familiar with computer systems.

'We connect to the Internet via satellite dish, but everything suggests it's kaput. It's up on the roof, but no one's going up there in this weather. Hopefully there's not much wrong with it, then I should be able to fix this. The phones are dead as well, which means the dish they're connected to is probably also buggered. Bad weather might have damaged both of them, even though they were probably set up to withstand quite a lot.'

87

The door of the drillers' office was decorated with a printed-out photo of a fiery red Formula One car. One corner of it was torn and the paper was starting to turn yellow. Two dark stains had appeared on it from the Blu-Tack used to stick it up. Above it was a plate with the names of the two men, Halldór Grétarsson and Bjarki Elíasson. There was something strange about seeing their names there and knowing that things had probably ended badly for them. Thóra and Matthew went into the office, which was quite large and held two desks. The walls were covered with printed-out jokes and photographs of the two drillers grinning at the camera. As Thóra sat down at one of the computers the thought crept into her mind that the men weren't laughing now, wherever they were. She booted up the computer.

Chapter 8

20 March 2008

Arnar Jóhannesson bowed his head, and his neck cracked. He was starting to feel a bit better. The clearer the image had become in his mind, the worse he had felt. It suddenly occurred to him that he could put an end to this misery once and for all. It wasn't the first time he'd had the idea, but it had become clear to him that he lacked the courage to do so, even though he knew that his reward would be eternal atonement. It was probably fear of failure that stopped him; the idea of waking up at the hospital paralysed or with brain damage was so unbearable that even the hell that was his life was better. He didn't always feel this bad. He knew the discomfort would pass; the inevitable result of falling, of giving in to the temptation of alcohol that seduced him, promised to alleviate his suffering and dispel the unpleasant thoughts that plagued him. It wouldn't really matter. The pain was still there, as well as the terrible thoughts, and now self-loathing had been added to the mix. He had given in like a miserable wretch, and for a while he had rejoiced in being a loser.

He stood up and pulled the belt of his bathrobe tighter. He had lost a lot of weight on this days long binge and he felt like a weakling. All his effort in recent months, weightlifting and running, had come to nothing. Why wasn't it as difficult to get out of shape as into it? He had put a lot of energy into looking good and being in good condition, and it was no walk in the park. That was probably the greatest indicator of the influence of this disease that he had inherited from his mother. When he drank, he became completely apathetic about the things that mattered to him; the only thing that mattered was the next drink—maintaining the high and ensuring that it never diminished. It had been incredibly easy for him to take the first step in the Twelve-Step Programme: *'We admitted we were powerless over alcohol—that our lives had become unmanageable.'* The second step had proven much more difficult. He could thank his lucky stars for having been helped into treatment this time, before he did more damage to himself than excessive weight loss. Usually when he succumbed to temptation, more and more time would pass until he got back on the right track. It had actually been a good long time since he had last stumbled; he had been dry for four hundred and eighty-three days before letting himself be tempted again.

He vaguely recalled having rung the Alcoholics Anonymous emergency helpline, but he had no idea what had inspired him to do so. He had been a slave to alcohol since he took his first sip as a teenager, and could only ever recall flashes of what happened while he drank—and those scraps of memory generally caused him hellish torment. What little he remembered was always utterly humiliating. He tried to forget about why he might have called and content himself with being grateful that he had. Who knew where he would have been at this moment if he had never made the call—and he didn't want to know. Every drink pushed him further and further into a dark corner of society, and the space between drinks had been reduced to almost nothing by the time he picked up the phone. He looked around the Spartan room. He had sworn never to have to visit such a room again, but that vow had been washed away with his first sip of beer, along with his self-respect. There was nothing else to do but renew the vow. One day at a time, go to the meetings, listen to the others and eventually open up. However, he would not, for the time being, speak up. Right now his self-esteem was too low for that. The last thing he wanted was to start bawling like a little girl in front of others who were in the same boat. That would be just ridiculous. He could not feel sorry for himself; he had managed to make a mess of things entirely unaided. He had held his life in his own two hands, but instead of nurturing it he'd decided to squeeze his fists and crush it. He would settle for listening to stories of families falling apart, missed opportunities and junkies' hard-luck stories.

Arnar was dying for one sweet little drink. Just one glass. One fucking glass. This was costing him enough as it was and one glass now and then could hardly make a difference. What a fucking idiot he was, calling AA. If he'd skipped it, he'd be sinking a cool one right now. Detox and rehab were maybe not the way to go. There were probably other types of treatment, aimed at teaching compulsives like him how to get to grips with drinking less. It wasn't the first glass that caused the problem, but the many more that inevitably followed. As this thought subsided, he recalled what had inspired him to pick up the phone. He had done something unforgivable. His business with the AA people had not been a cry for help, but rather a chance to talk to someone about the interpretation of Steps 8 and 9: *'Made a list of all persons we had harmed, and became willing to make amends to them all...Made direct amends to such people whenever possible, except when to do so would injure them or others.'* Too late. It was far too late for that. A chill crept through his heart and it seemed as if the blood in his veins had thickened. He waited until it was totally frozen and he felt like he had when he was in Greenland. Then he left his room to join the meeting, with its flickering promise of redemption.

*   *   *

Thóra had been at the computer for hours and felt no closer to discovering anything. Like any other IT system, it was characterized by numerous files that were impossible for strangers to figure out;

91

it didn't help that most of them existed in many different versions. So she had called on Eyjólfur to help get her going, and he had willingly granted her a little insight into how the system was arranged. It was broadly divided into four areas: photographs, journals—which everyone was required to keep—records related to the project, and finally employees' personal documents.

Thóra decided to start with the journals, which were most likely to contain decipherable information. She thought it best to wait with the project and work files, as well as the personal documents. Eyjólfur had told her the latter category had caused system problems, since the music and video files the staff liked to download took up so much disk space. Out of curiosity Thóra opened one folder entitled 'Doddi' and in return got a dauntingly long list of files of various kinds. Before he left her, Eyjólfur informed her that the staff had been discouraged from saving non-essential files onto the hard drives of their computers. They wouldn't make a backup of all the files from each machine—only from the central server.

Thóra pored over the files, promptly copied what she considered important and sent it to the printer that Eyjólfur said was located in the corridor. He promised to make sure that no one took the pages, and even regularly brought her the printouts. After rushing through the journals, she nosed around a bit in the other categories and found a file or two that also appeared meaningful, so she would have something to show Matthew when he came back. He had gone to inspect the offices for traces of blood, leaving her alone in the drillers' room. 'I found one office that I'm almost sure is the one in

92

the video. When you look at it closely you can tell someone has tried to clean up after an absolute bloodbath. There are splotches on the folders and signs that the walls and floor have been wiped down with a rag or something. Obviously I don't have any ultraviolet equipment to illuminate biological material, but I don't think there's any doubt what the stains are. There's a video camera on the desk, still connected to the computer. I didn't dare mess with the camera, but it's fairly obvious that it's the one that took the video.'

'What does this mean?' Thóra stretched her back out. She'd been sitting bent over for too long.

'I don't quite understand it, but I've locked the room and we'll simply leave it to the police to investigate as they see fit. We are neither equipped to conduct a police investigation, nor is it our responsibility. They've simply got to come out here. We can't solve a case like this, so we should simply focus on the aspects of it that affect the progress and survival of the project. As soon as we get in touch with the police I'll demand that they send a team here.' Matthew looked at the screen in front of Thóra. 'But how's it been going for you?'

'I don't quite get all of this but I think I've found some documents that could make a difference,' said Thóra, proudly tapping the small stack of papers on the table. 'To go over all the files with a magnifying glass would take much longer than we have. I didn't really look at anything in detail apart from the journals and part of the drillers' files, and even that was rather haphazard. Of course I also checked some of the files belonging to Gísli Pálsson, who was responsible for security on site. I found his name on an organization chart in a folder

93

of general files.'

'Don't worry,' said Matthew, 'Eyjólfur is copying all the files for us, so it doesn't matter if we overlook something now.'

Thóra was rather relieved to hear this. 'Fine. I haven't quite got my bearings but I decided to focus on the disappearance of the three employees while I'm learning the system. I didn't actually find anything out yet, but I'm a little bit closer.' She handed him a printout from the driller Bjarki's journal. 'Eyjólfur told me the geologist disappeared on the 31st of October last year, so I looked carefully at that month and November. I also went carefully over the preceding two months in the hope of discovering something that could explain the disappearance of the two men, but I didn't find much. I also looked over the security guard's journals for the same period because I thought it was odd that there wasn't much in the drillers' journals about the woman going missing. I don't know whether her disappearance is at all related to theirs, but if it's one of the reasons that the staff can't be persuaded to return, it would be well worth spending some time exploring what actually happened to her. Who knows, maybe the staff can be convinced to return if we can find an explanation. Then the bank would be saved.' She looked at Matthew. 'The woman who disappeared was named Oddný Hildur.'

He looked up from the journal. 'What else did you find out about her?' He put down the papers. 'This is all so complicated.'

'Not much. The drillers only noted down the number of hours spent searching for her. Judging from what I read, they didn't take part in the search

94

out of the kindness of their hearts, but because the security guard ordered them to. One of them, this Bjarki, wrote something suggesting that they called a halt to the search after a week—the weather had deteriorated so sharply that it had become hopeless. Then I tried looking at the same month in Gísli, the security guard's journal.'

'And?' asked Matthew. 'Did it reveal anything?'

'His account is more detailed, at least. He says that the woman was last seen at supper on the evening of October 31st, and no one knew her movements after she left the cafeteria. No one saw where she went, and she didn't let anyone know her plans. According to him, the documents she was working on were last modified just before midnight that evening, so she was most likely in her office.'

'Almost certainly, surely, if her computer record said so?' said Matthew. 'Could someone else have worked on the documents?'

'No,' she replied. 'The text notes that she could also have been in her apartment, since there's a wireless connection set up to enable the staff to work if they're trapped in the residential wing by the weather. Eyjólfur confirmed that that could have been the case, although he can't tell from the file whether she was connected remotely, or if she was actually in the office. He also said that he should have been able to see whether she'd been working at the desktop or her laptop, but unfortunately the security guard saved the files after opening them and in doing so deleted the information about their previous use.'

'Damn, that was stupid,' muttered Matthew.

'From what I read in Gísli's journal,' continued Thóra, 'she didn't seem very outdoorsy, but she was

95

accustomed enough to the area not to rush outside without good reason.'

'Is he suggesting that she *intended* to die of exposure?'

'No, that's not how I understood it,' she replied. 'Quite the reverse; he mentions that this Oddný Hildur had been looking forward to going home to her husband and hadn't been behaving at all unusually. He thought it more likely that there had been an accident. He writes that the measurements from the weather monitor showed that the weather had been quite bad that night, and if the woman had gone out after it worsened she could easily have lost her way among the buildings and wandered farther and farther out into the wilderness.' Thóra couldn't help but glance towards the window to check on the weather. 'He had the other staff members search the area in groups of four, without any luck. After a week the search was called off entirely for fear that other people would get lost in the storm, which had got even worse.'

'And there was no mention of bones or anything like that?' asked Matthew. 'I was wondering whether they might have come across any other human remains during their search.'

'Not a word. This Gísli would have recorded it in his diary—he appears to have been very thorough in his entries and in his responses to situations. Among other things, he went to Kaanneq to see if the woman might have wandered down there, and he also phoned to request the assistance of the authorities, although understandably they couldn't do much apart from take down the information.'

'So there's nothing more to learn from this?' Matthew said. 'Actually, this is just a slightly more detailed description of everything we already knew. The geologist vanished from the camp and no one knows what became of her.'

'Well, actually there's a little bit more that could possibly make a difference,' she corrected him. 'On 1st November the security guard claims to have found a patch of blood or some other substance on one of the outside walls of the residential wing, where Oddný Hildur's apartment was. He writes that he has no idea whether it was blood from a person or an animal, or how long the stain had been there, but he does say that he took a sample and was planning to bring it with him to Reykjavík for a DNA test. After that, he forbade the staff from going outside alone—he was afraid a polar bear might be in the area, and that Oddný Hildur had fallen prey to it.'

'Did he tell the others about this?' asked Matthew. 'That's the first I've heard of it.'

'No. He considered the group's situation to be so bad that he didn't want to cause any more unnecessary trouble and risk things boiling over.'

'He was worried that people would start panicking?'

'No, he doesn't say that. His wording is rather odd. I don't understand why he talks about "causing any more trouble" or things "boiling over" in a group that was out searching for a lost colleague. At least, I would have worded it differently. It's as if he's referring to a situation that existed before the woman went missing.' Thóra clicked on the mouse to bring the screen back up. 'I searched for the word "DNA" in the months that passed from the woman's disappearance until the day the group returned home for the last time, and I found one

97

entry in which Gísli calls the results of the test "disappointing". The sample appears to have been contaminated during transport and no conclusion could be reached other than that it was blood—whether that of an animal or a human being isn't known. I also searched for the words "polar bear" without result. If it was a polar bear attack, it must have been extremely unlucky, since the security guard's journal never mentions that such a beast had been seen around here, and surely he would have recorded it if it had.'

'Hopefully we'll have a chance to speak to this Gísli when we get back to Iceland. He may very well have information that didn't make it into that journal.' Matthew picked up the papers again and thumbed through them. 'What else did you find?'

'The drillers' last entries were rather curt.' She took the stack of papers from Matthew and flipped through them. 'Here's a normal day, with the entries filling two whole pages and containing reports on geology, the weather, the equipment, etc. Here we have the days just before everyone left, with only three sentences: *Weather good. Drilling rig on the south slope, L-3. No progress, need advice on an unusual find*. Other entries up until the date they stopped filling in the journals are similar. *No output, worked on the find*.' Thóra looked at Matthew. 'It isn't clear whether this find was geological or something entirely different.'

'Such as?' Matthew read over the journal entry.

'Maybe the body of Oddný Hildur?' replied Thóra calmly.

'Isn't that stretching things a bit?' He gave her a sceptical look.

'Yes, if I'd only had these daily reports to go on,'

98

she said. 'However, I found something else that supports this theory.' She didn't waste any time describing what she meant, but instead turned to the screen and brought up an image file labelled *D & G*. Eyjólfur had assured her that it did not stand for Dolce & Gabbana, but Drilling and Grouting. She pointed out one of the images to Matthew. At first it looked like nothing but ice on the screen, but if you looked closer you could see clenched fingers in a block of ice. Before he could say anything Thóra hurriedly brought up the list of file names for the photographs taken that day. 'Look here. Based on the file numbers, it seems as though the next twenty images have been erased.' She looked at Matthew. 'I don't have a clue who would have done that or why, but one thing is certain—it's a human hand, and whoever it belonged to is not alive.'

Chapter 9

20 March 2008

Eyjólfur agreed with Thóra's theory about the photos that appeared to be missing from the folder. However, he couldn't tell whether the images had been deleted from the camera or the computer system. That actually didn't matter, since the images were gone and there was no way of knowing what was in them, although it was safe to assume they showed the same ice-bound hand and perhaps other body parts belonging to this unfortunate person. He turned to Thóra and Matthew. 'Of course I could go over the backup files to check whether the images are in there. If they were deleted the day after they were uploaded it's possible that they are.' He smiled resignedly. 'If in fact the photos made it onto the system.'

Matthew agreed to Eyjólfur's plan and Eyjólfur went off to find the tapes. As he left he said that this work would be time-consuming, although there was little else for him to do for the time being; at least he wouldn't be climbing up on the roof to fix the satellite dishes in this weather. 'We could go and visit this place,' said Thóra after he'd gone. 'The journal described it quite oddly, and I'm sure Friðrikka will know what it means.' Before they could go anywhere, however, the weather would have to improve.

Matthew pointed at the image on the screen. 'Do you think that's the owner of the bones lying here in all the drawers?'

'I doubt it,' said Thóra. 'It looks like there's flesh on this hand and the photos are only just over a week old. Besides, there aren't any bones in the desk drawers of the drillers, who are probably the ones who took the photos.'

Bella stuck her head through the doorway. 'It's twelve thirty now and I'm ravenous. Is there anything to eat here, or did the trip include both starving and freezing to death?' Thóra did not reply, but her own stomach was starting to rumble.

'Yes, I guess it's best to round everyone up and go over to the cafeteria,' said Matthew. 'Since the weather is so bad we ought to stick together.' They went and found the others: Eyjólfur was working on the Internet servers, Friðrikka sat absorbed at a computer in one of the geologists' offices, and the doctor was busily marking little plastic cups

100

half full of water in the coffee room. They found Alvar in the security guard's office, bent over a pile of ropes. Alvar saw the surprise on Eyjólfur's face and his cheeks grew even redder as he muttered something about making a line between the houses that they could follow during blizzards. They put on their outerwear and walked in single file over to the cafeteria, without the safety line. Naturally, the wind had turned and it blew in their faces.

'It looks to me as if everything fell apart after I quit,' said Friðrikka, putting down her fork. They were sitting in the cafeteria, having just munched their way through grilled ham and cheese sandwiches. It was certainly no feast, but the sandwiches were quick and easy to prepare and left little to wash up afterwards. 'I went over a chart they used to keep track of the progress of the project and that they sent weekly to Arctic Mining, but little seems to have happened. The work schedule is completely messed up and I totally understand why the mining company got worried. They were very insistent that we follow it.'

'Do you know what caused the disruption?' asked Thóra, considering whether she should have a third sandwich. There was only one left, and Bella was quicker to grab it.

'I went over some of the journals and it looked to me as if there were a lot of possibilities.' Friðrikka became a bit bashful when all eyes focused on her and she appeared to regret having said anything. 'It seems as though they experienced significant mechanical failures, besides the havoc wreaked by the weather. This winter was much more severe than last year's, when I was here.'

'Didn't those bastard Greenlanders just sabotage

the equipment?' asked Eyjólfur immediately. 'They'd certainly be capable of it.'

'What the hell are you talking about, boy?' snapped the doctor. 'Why would they want to sabotage anything here? I'm certain I know more about the natives in this country than you do, and I can tell you for sure that they're the kindest of people and wish no one ill.'

'Except for their women,' interrupted Friðrikka. 'They're not particularly kind to *them*.' Again she seemed to regret having spoken, and pressed her lips shut.

The doctor harrumphed, then said. 'The way that a particular people or race handles alcohol says nothing about its disposition. Alcohol doesn't really bring out the best in Icelanders either. What if we were deprived of our sustenance, like these people have been because of bleeding-heart liberal Westerners banning the hunting they depend upon?' He paused for a moment. 'These people are innately good but they have suffered badly. I also think that conditions here on the east coast are the worst of anywhere in Greenland. The society on the west coast is more like what we're used to.'

Finally Thóra joined in. 'Why do you think that the natives had something to do with the machinery?' she asked Eyjólfur. 'Were you here when any of this happened? That kind of thing could matter as far as the insurance is concerned.'

Eyjólfur seemed to have calmed down a bit. 'Yeah, I'm not making it up; I know a bit about what happened,' he answered, happy to have the opportunity to defend himself. 'I'm not prejudiced or anything.' No one bothered to contest this feeble excuse. 'But I was here once when the

102

drilling rig failed, and the drillers said someone had contaminated its fuel, poured sugar into it or something. It took them a long time to fix it and I can promise you that none of our people would have done such a thing. We all knew what was at stake.'

'Is it possible that this Oddný Hildur, the one who disappeared, might have been involved?' asked Matthew. 'Maybe she was mentally unbalanced, and upset with the workplace or with Berg Technology.'

Friðrikka cleared her throat, her face red with anger. 'The equipment failed after she disappeared. And besides, the very idea is ridiculous. Oddný Hildur was my friend; she was quiet and reserved by nature and I can guarantee you that she didn't sabotage the equipment or anything else. And I won't listen to this nonsense about her mental condition; she simply died of exposure, it was an accident and any talk about anything else is fucking bullshit. I was here when she vanished and there was nothing wrong with her. I found the insinuations that she committed suicide tasteless, and they were only made to cover the fact that those who were supposed to be taking care of us did not deal with the matter appropriately.'

'What do you mean?' asked Thóra. 'I read through the journals and it looked to me as if your security guard, Gísli, was completely on the case. Are they not to be trusted?' She had already decided to go back over his data, making note of the time period when the vandalism to the drilling rig had taken place, in order to get a clearer view of the bigger picture. If the man had been making things up in his journals, she might not need to spend much time on them.

'I don't know,' replied Friðrikka. 'Gísli tried a bit but he called off the search too early, and he could have done more in my opinion. And there were others who could also have done better as far as the search is concerned. The owner of the company seemed not to take her disappearance particularly badly and didn't even make the trip out here. The same goes for the police in Greenland; they never came. Oddný Hildur might even have still been alive somewhere, maybe with a broken leg, and unable to make it back to camp. If we had searched better, we might have been able to save her.' She looked close to tears.

'What are you on about?' said Eyjólfur angrily. 'I was here too. We did everything we could. You'd do better to take a good look at yourself. Fat lot of use you were, with all your hysterics. You were little better than that ponce Arnar. Oddný Hildur would never have survived in the kind of blizzard we experienced that week, with or without a broken leg. Things could have gone badly wrong if we had kept looking. You and Arnar were the ones who messed up in the search, if memory serves.' At this, Friðrikka's face turned so red that Alvar looked pale in comparison.

'Who is this Arnar?' asked Matthew. 'Did he work here?' Thóra recognized the name from the organizational chart but didn't recall what the man's job was.

'He's an engineer. I think he's still working for the company.' It was Friðrikka who answered. 'It's not fair to compare me to him as far as the search for Oddný Hildur is concerned. I put just as much effort into it as the others, even though I

104

was chosen to investigate the area closest to camp so I wasn't out all over the place. I highly doubt that Arnar took it as seriously as I did, though he might have tried to help a bit. When Oddný Hildur disappeared I was the one who suffered the most.'

'You?' shot back Eyjólfur. 'In the end she and Arnar were pretty close, in this whole mess.' He took a drink of the apple juice that had been served with the sandwiches.

Thóra looked at him curiously. 'What do you mean by "close"? Were they having an affair?' Oddný Hildur had been married, and probably this Arnar was as well.

Eyjólfur choked slightly on his drink. 'Far from it. He bats for the other side. That's why I called him a ponce. Couldn't stand him.' He stopped, clearly realizing from the looks on the others' faces that he'd now revealed his homophobia as well as his racism. 'That's not what I meant. He wasn't intolerable because he's gay; that has nothing to do with it. He'd stopped drinking and was obsessed with his sobriety.' Thóra recalled having seen a card listing the Twelve Steps hanging in one of the offices. 'Nobody was bothered that he was gay. It wasn't like that.'

'Rubbish,' bristled Friðrikka. 'You had a massive problem with him being at the camp, just because he's gay. All his AA crap was nothing to do with it.' She turned to the others. 'Most of the guys here are real "men's men". They talk non-stop about football and other equally fascinating topics. When Arnar came out of the closet after he stopped drinking they all turned their backs on him, and Eyjólfur was no exception. It was as if they thought it was infectious.'

105

'Bullshit,' muttered Eyjólfur. 'I don't know what he was like when he was drinking, but sober he was a boring, narrow-minded bastard.'

'Did you resign because of what happened to your friend Oddný Hildur?' asked Thóra, regarding Friðrikka steadily. Again she had found it necessary to intervene to ease the tension. What would things at the work camp have been like, she wondered, if it had always been this volatile in the cafeteria?

'Yes.' Friðrikka let this answer suffice. She pursed her lips, picked up her fork and started drawing it through the ketchup on her plate. Thóra thought it best not to irritate her, since she was hoping the other woman would help them locate the place the photo had been taken. She seemed a stubborn sort, and was probably more than capable of refusing to help them. Matthew was clearly thinking along the same lines, because he also said nothing.

'Still, it was definitely the Greenlanders,' muttered Eyjólfur, breaking the silence. He was obviously the type who had to have the last word. 'They've been a problem since the project started.' Rather than keeping silent when no one protested, the young man went on. This did not bode well for whatever woman married him in the future. 'They stole stuff no one in their right mind would want, and everyone knew that they didn't give a shit about this project.'

'What did they steal?' asked Matthew. Thóra's ears pricked up.

'Just some minor stuff. I don't remember in detail but it was some stuff lying around that had been left behind. Pieces of wood, jackets, petrol cans. Things like that.' Eyjólfur thought for a moment. 'Boots, too. And probably other things I don't remember or

106

never heard about.'

So much for Thóra's hope that theft or vandalism might be the key to saving the bank's insurance money.

*   *   *

It had been a long day, and for Thóra the happiest part of it was the moment she finally crawled into bed. There was no sign that the storm was slackening, so the team had decided to work late to avoid having to return to the office building after supper. They said little over the meal and quickly disappeared one by one into their own rooms. Warm showers would have lightened their moods but all the pipes in this part of the camp had frozen, making that a distant dream. It was imperative that they finish the job here and get home, or somewhere else where the plumbing was in order. But the weather would dictate when that would happen. They hoped the storm would subside in the night so they could go to the work site the next day, or even down to Kaanneq to check whether anyone there knew about the men.

As Thóra drifted off, with Matthew snoring next to her, she ran over what she had learned that day. She felt particularly bad about not having a good enough understanding of the work done on site. In the contractual documents Matthew had given her she was able to read up on the main purpose of the project; namely, to prepare the area for the proposed mining of molybdenum, a metal that Thóra had never heard of but that was apparently used to temper steel. The exact details of how these preparations were accomplished were much fuzzier

107

in her mind, meaning there was no way to work out what mattered and what didn't while going over the data. Of course only a tiny proportion of the material stored in the computer system was of any actual use, and the trick was to fish up what mattered out of the digital soup. Her mind's eye was filled with the hundreds of photographs she'd glanced over; endless pictures of the machinery, the core samples and other things that all had the common factor of being surrounded by every conceivable form of snow and ice. By the time she stopped to go to bed, she'd been struck snow-blind simply from staring at the computer screen. Some of the photos had been taken in Kaanneq and showed the same empty streets and colourful houses as they had seen on their way from the helicopter pad. However, she still hadn't found the twenty photos that had been deleted from the file made the day that the drillers recorded finding something unusual—photos presumably showing, from various angles, a hand covered in ice.

She had spent quite some time examining the drillers' private files in the hope of getting to know them and gaining a better idea of what they could have got themselves into; perhaps even discovering what might have led to their disappearance. It didn't take her long to come to the conclusion that they were a pair of jokers who were always sending round gags and funny stories on e-mail. Thóra knew they were both unmarried, and after reading the e-mails it looked to her as if they didn't have girlfriends either. Nowhere did she find a message to a girl expressing how much they missed her or arranging a date. They were much better at inviting friends and acquaintances to parties and getting themselves invited to dinner by others.

In any case, Thóra found it made for depressing reading; Halldór Grétarsson and Bjarki Elíasson had undoubtedly met a sad end and there was something tragic about thinking that no spouse would be weeping over her husband's disappearance—no matter how twisted it might be for Thóra to imagine it. Halldór, known as Dóri, had been interested in Greenland; among other things, his computer had links to websites about the country and its history. Thóra could not look at these sites since the Internet connection was still down, but the names of the links suggested the nature of their content. Dóri had even saved screengrabs from some of them, and those Thóra could see. In one of them she had discovered photos from when all the original inhabitants of the settlement had been found dead. Women and children lay as if asleep, except for the way their eyes stared vacuously into the lens. The images were black and white, but Thóra thought she could see bloodstains on the beds of the dead, although she wasn't sure. The book in the cafeteria had said nothing about them dying violently, so that could hardly be right. The stains even appeared to form the same pattern on most of the beds. Almost like a kind of roughly drawn face, so there must have been another explanation for them.

The other driller, Bjarki, seemed to have been something of a hypochondriac, since most of the web pages he had bookmarked were related to diseases. Thóra had asked Eyjólfur whether Bjarki had been ill at all, but Eyjólfur had shaken his head and said it had never come up in conversation. Bjarki had always appeared to be in good shape.

Maybe he was obsessed with his health, thought Thóra, but maybe he also just had dandruff or something and wanted to get rid of it. She could not get onto any of his bookmarked pages to find out what had been troubling him.

The data thus came from all directions and there was no one particular thing that appeared potentially useful for extricating the bank from its predicament. On the contrary, Thóra was making no progress: there was no evidence that any kind of criminal activity had stopped work here, and it looked unlikely that they would be able to explain the disappearance of either the drillers or the geologist. Gísli's journal entries had been non-committal regarding whether he personally suspected vandalism, though at one point he expressed doubt that the residents of Kaanneq would have had anything to do with any potential sabotage, and elsewhere he wondered whether it might have been the work of protestors. Thóra realized that that would certainly strengthen the bank's position. But in any case, what was lacking was a definite conclusion; speculation was of little use.

All she had to show for the day's labours were the bones in the desk drawers and the photograph of the frozen hand. Thóra drifted off to sleep wondering how long a corpse could stay suspended in ice.

Around midnight she woke to the creaking of the floor slats out in the corridor. Someone seemed to be trying to walk down it as carefully as possible. Thóra shuddered. Instead of checking who it was, she turned on her side and in a short time fell back asleep. In the morning she was unsure of whether it

110

had actually happened or whether it had been part of the dream she'd been having: a dream about the people who settled this country a long time ago in the hope of a better life, but who had reaped only hunger, hardship and a sad death.

Chapter 10

21 March 2008

Thóra did not get out of bed until Matthew was gone. She wanted to lie in a little longer, and didn't want to give him the chance to peek into her suitcase when she looked in it for clean clothes. She had been shocked the night before when she finally saw what was in it. On top were high-heeled shoes and other equally inspired choices: capri pants that she'd probably thrown in because they looked good on her, skirts, dresses and a glittery pashmina shawl her parents had given her after one of their numerous trips to the Canary Islands. She had never worn the pashmina and never would, least of all here. After a long search she finally managed to find her jeans and a thick jumper that she could wear without embarrassment. Under the jumper she wore a silk blouse. The weather appeared to have calmed down, so luckily they weren't in too much danger. Even if a wild storm hit they would still be inside, and then Thóra could saunter over to the cafeteria in her high heels and glittery shawl.

She brushed her teeth with the water they'd boiled in one of the sinks in the shared bathroom. She stared at the showerhead hanging there provocatively, the steel bone-dry and shiny. She was met in the mirror by an ugly sight: her hair was greasy at the roots and she had black mascara circles under her eyes. She covertly used a few splashes of the boiled water to wash her face and, after smearing on cream that supposedly guaranteed eternal youth and applying mascara, she finally looked presentable. As she stepped into the corridor she met Eyjólfur, who had a toothbrush in his hand. He looked almost as bad as she had just now. Nevertheless he smiled and stopped her as they crossed paths. 'I forgot to mention one thing yesterday,' he said. 'I actually noticed that Bjarki's jacket and boots are in the vestibule of the office building. That seems ominous, unless he's wearing someone else's jacket.'

Thóra tried to recall which garments had been hanging in the vestibule. She remembered two identical down jackets hanging on a hook and several dirty work coveralls. The floor was covered with shoes, mainly insulated work boots with steel toes. 'Are the clothes labelled?' she asked. 'I mean, how do you know his clothes from the others'?'

'Yes, they're labelled,' said Eyjólfur, smoothing down his hair in a fruitless attempt to make it look better. 'Berg provided us all with outerwear and protective clothing. Of course I didn't need a coverall, but the jacket and cold-weather boots have come in handy. Since we all had exactly the same kind of outerwear we had to label every garment, and one of the jackets hanging on the coat rack is marked "Bjarki". His boots are there too.'

Thóra nodded thoughtfully. 'And it's not possible that he took someone else's jacket by mistake?'

'No, definitely not. The ones who went on leave

112

took their jackets with them so they wouldn't freeze to death on the way back, and the only extra jacket in camp is still hanging on the coat rack. It was left behind when an employee resigned shortly after the work started.' He saw from Thóra's expression that she wanted to know more about this person and hurriedly added: 'He was an old man who'd simply had enough of the weather. No great mystery there. In fact, it's incredible how low the staff turnover has been here. It's my understanding that people rarely last long in this kind of workplace.' He smiled at Thóra again. 'Despite what Friðrikka said, Berg Technology is an exceptionally fair employer and that's why its employees are so loyal. It would have been impossible for the owner to rush out here to take part in the search for a lost person, so it's no reflection on him or how he treats his staff.'

'Still, they all quit.' Thóra was watching him carefully. 'Except for you, no?'

Eyjólfur's smile evaporated. 'I'm sure they regret it,' he said. 'Of course, I don't work directly for the company; I was just hired through an employment agency. My employer is the company responsible for Berg's computers.'

'Did you notice the jacket or boots of the other driller, Halldór?' asked Thóra, keen to get off to breakfast.

'No. They weren't in the office, and I didn't find them in the vestibule.' Eyjólfur bit his lip. 'Hopefully it means Dóri made it out of here alive, but I didn't check his apartment, so we'll probably find them there.'

'Hopefully he's wearing them.' It didn't take a genius to conclude that without protective clothing the man had little hope. Eyjólfur didn't respond,

113

but his expression brightened abruptly. 'Had you heard about the tracks?'

'Tracks?' Thóra was speechless.

'Yes, I met Alvar here earlier and this morning he found tracks leading from here out to Oddný Hildur's building. Someone dug the snow from around the walls of her building and it looks like they removed something from beneath the house.'

'Like what?'

'No idea. It happened in the night or early this morning, since Alvar was apparently the first one up and the first to go out and see them.'

Thóra recalled the noise in the corridor the night before. 'Could he tell from the tracks what shoes were worn? We're all wearing different types of footwear, so it might be possible to compare the tracks with the soles of our shoes.'

'It's my understanding that the wind has blown so much snow into them that that would be impossible. All you can see is that someone went over there and did something around the crawlspace under the hut. Who it was, or why, nobody knows.'

'Isn't it possible to see whether something was there beneath the building, and what it was?'

'No, as far as I understand from Alvar, it looked as if there was nothing there. A thin layer of snow had blown under the building and it appeared untouched, so this is all really strange. All I know for sure is that it wasn't me out there.'

*   *   *

The tyres on the jeeps were so big and over-inflated that they reminded Thóra of Donald Duck's car. She hadn't noticed this when they arrived, since she hadn't been in any condition to do so. It had taken everything she'd had just to squirm into the back seat. Now her attention was more focused and she took careful notice of everything she saw along the way. The scenery was indescribably beautiful, but at the same time it awakened dread in her heart. Alvar was at the wheel, and he, Thóra and Matthew had been joined by Friðrikka. She had recognized the description of the place immediately, *south slope, L-3*, and said that she could certainly take them there to look for signs of anything unusual. 'It's not much further,' she said, pointing Alvar to a crag that could be seen vaguely, rising from the snow. 'Turn left here. The trail runs in the direction of that mountain ahead.'

'I located the spot too, on the GPS, so I know exactly where I'm going,' muttered Alvar. 'Someone took the trouble to input a lot of information into it, which is wise.' He looked from the road to the device. 'We're just about there.' Suddenly they saw something flash orange in the sheer white surroundings. The closer they drew the better their view of the drilling rig, which was unlike any piece of machinery Thóra had seen before. It was a large oblong house on tracks. Lying across the rig was an arm and on this a vertical steel mast that Friðrikka said was the drill. Next to it stood a little ramshackle hut. It must have been stronger than it looked since it had withstood yesterday's storm, and doubtless others much worse. Friðrikka told them it was a moveable work shed for the drillers. Thóra saw no evidence of construction, but when she asked her the geologist replied that that wasn't surprising; the snow covered all disturbances of the earth immediately, so signs of construction could very well lie directly beneath them. They would have to dig down if they were interested in seeing that. At that Alvar cheered up; he had just loaded the platform with all sorts of hand tools and ropes.

The cold bit right through them when they stepped out of the jeep. They were standing near a low peak in the shadow of taller mountains surrounding the area. Thóra was wearing a fur hat that was much too large, which she had borrowed from the coat rack in the cafeteria; it was constantly dropping down over her eyes. She had got her thick mittens from the same place and they fit her about as well as the hat did. They all stood silently for a moment as they adjusted to the cold, which attacked their lungs with each breath. Staring at the shed, they must have all been thinking the same thing: Were the men in there? If that was the case, the oppressive silence gave no indication that they were alive. 'Who wants to go in first?' asked Thóra, staring at the dented door.

'I'll go,' said Matthew, and off he went. His hat and gloves fitted him perfectly, and were both as new-looking as his rucksack. 'Is it locked?' he asked Friðrikka, who was standing in stiff silence, her eyes glued to the little house.

'Oh! Yes,' she said, starting from her thoughts. 'I know where the key is.' She went with him to the drilling rig and opened a little hatch on its side, which emitted a low screech that echoed for a long time in the desolation around them. She stuck in her hand and pulled out a clunky-looking key. 'There you are.' She walked back to Alvar and Thóra and contented herself with watching from a distance as Matthew tried to put the key in the lock. First he had to move a covering that prevented

116

fine snow from filling the lock when the wind blew outside. 'I don't know whether I should hope they're in there or not.'

It wasn't clear to Thóra whether Friðrikka was talking to herself, or to her and Alvar. 'You knew them, I assume?'

Friðrikka simply nodded. A silence followed, which was interrupted when Matthew dramatically opened the door to the shed. He stuck his head in and then looked out again immediately. 'No one here,' he called out unnecessarily loudly.

The others relaxed visibly and walked over to the shed. It was larger inside than it appeared from the exterior and they all fitted in there easily. There was a little kitchen with two chairs and shelves fixed up along all the walls. On these were wooden boxes that Friðrikka said were designed specially to store core samples, to prevent them from being broken, damaged or mixed up.

Although Thóra thought she'd gone over the data in the case quite well, it wasn't entirely clear to her why these samples were so important.

'They show what the ground beneath us contains,' explained Friðrikka patiently, when Thóra voiced her puzzlement. 'The purpose of this project is to determine whether there is molybdenum here in any usable quantity. The more we exploit accessible areas of the earth, the more expensive the metals and other precious material in the ground become. So it starts to pay off to get it from remote places like this.' She pointed at the boxes. 'There is much less known about the bedrock here on the east coast than on the west coast, so we basically have to start from scratch. We drill boreholes in the ground and extract core samples that show a full breakdown of

117

what's to be found here. It's all documented and if a sufficient quantity of precious material is found in the samples, then it's possible that it would pay to establish a mine somewhere in the vicinity. We prepare maps that show the strata and estimate how they are situated between the boreholes, and after that's done we can pinpoint the most suitable place for the mine. Mining sites aren't just chosen by sticking a pin in a map or throwing dice.'

'But isn't it hopeless trying to drill through all this snow?' asked Thóra. She would have thought such work would have been much easier during the summer, when the ground was bare.

'No, absolutely not. The drill goes through the snow like a knife through butter, and the snow protects the ground and covers over disturbances caused by the machinery or the transport of people, worksheds, and other things like that. We need to cover a lot of ground in the search and it wouldn't be a pretty sight if the snow weren't so thick. We try to keep our impact here to a minimum. It's an expensive process, and in some instances we also need to restore the area after a project, which can also be costly.' She shrugged. 'Since the snow cover melts so quickly every year, we actually have to work fast in our studies. In a few years things will be much more difficult, and we'll make tracks all over the place.'

Thóra frowned. 'Is the snow thinning and the ice melting?' The hand in the photograph had appeared to be enclosed in ice, and if the ice were retreating rather than advancing it seemed doubtful that it was Oddný Hildur's hand. 'Do you mean, then, that more ice melts in the summer than is formed in the winter?'

118

Friðrikka gave her a puzzled look. 'Yes, I suppose so. I'm not always so good at the small details of these things, but I would think so. And of course the geological conditions from place to place, as well as the wind, probably play a part. Even though it appears white everywhere you look, the layers are thinning and more melts away each summer.' She looked out of the shed's tiny window and raised her hand to shield her eyes from the glare of the snow cover outside. But shouldn't we get going to Borehole L-3 and investigate whether the photo was taken there?'

'And what if we do find a hand in the ice?' exclaimed Alvar.

None of them knew the answer to that.

*   *   *

The people in Kaanneq treated Igimaq coldly, as usual. The women gave him the evil eye and the men greeted him only by lifting their chins slightly. One of them actually called out to him and asked whether it wasn't too late for him to move back in with his wife, now that all the men had used her. The hunter ground his teeth but did not turn around, acting as if nothing were out of the ordinary. Whoever said it was a coward; no one with a trace of self-respect would say such a thing to a man whose back was turned. A real man either spoke his mind to your face, or kept quiet and let the womenfolk gossip. Igimaq recognized the voice and knew perfectly well who the man was. It was one of those sheep, a man who had allowed himself to be debauched by alcohol and now let the system provide for him. Like Naruana, his son.

Still, their fates were not comparable, nor was the man's as tragic. He had had nothing to offer, had been a poor hunter with the stamina of a little boy. He'd been skinny his whole life and conditions here weren't suited to that build, as you could see from the creatures that thrived in this place.

His son, however, had been blessed with all the qualities a good man needed. He was sturdily built, tenacious and unflappable. He had done the hunter's ancestors proud, until he started to slip down the slope of misfortune. The boy had lost everything that drives a man: pride, enthusiasm and perseverance. From being self-sufficient and having enough to spare, he became like that wretch who shouted insults at people. Hopefully Naruana had not yet sunk so low—still, he had fallen far enough. Igimaq hoped he would not run into his son. He wouldn't be able to bear it and he feared losing his self-control and hitting him so hard that the young man's remaining teeth would be knocked out. But realistically there was no danger of seeing him. It was still too early in the day for his son to be on his feet. His time was the night; his behaviour that of the scavengers that hung around the heels of superior and more resourceful animals. Memories of the lessons when the hunter had held his son's soft hand in his rough palms piled up. The stump where his index finger had been ached.

The hunter's finger had been frostbitten. At the start of a seal-hunting expedition out on the ice he had clumsily cut a hole in one of his gloves with a small knife inherited from his father, and instead of turning back and waiting until the next morning he had allowed himself to be lured by the great catch the day promised. The ice had been thick

120

and uncracked and the weather the best it could be for hunting. When he returned home that evening with a sledful of seals, his finger was useless. He cut it off before he went to sleep and asked his son to take his place on a sled trip he had promised to lead with a group of Westerners. He wanted to repair the glove before he went back out into the cold, and that's how his son became acquainted with brennivín; he sat drinking with the group at the end of the trip and never looked back. The loss of his finger had cost the hunter much more than the effort it took to train his middle finger to pull the trigger of his rifle easily and securely. Naturally it took several months for the young man to plunge to the bottom, but all the signs of what was to come appeared immediately after he returned from the trip. He stared at the beer cans in the hands of people they met in a way that was embarrassing to see. Then he started disappearing night after night and always returned home late, until the day came when he did not return. The hunter's wife went the same way soon afterwards, and that's when he left. Now he lived in a tent, like his forefathers, far enough from the village to ensure that no one would disturb him. The only ones who visited him were the old men, who appreciated the ancient values and understood his decision and the pattern of his life.

No, the hunter had other things to attend to than meeting up with the disgrace that was his family. He had come to speak to the man considered to hold the most power in the village, a childhood friend of his who had been involved in casting his son and wife to ruin. The hunter did not look forward to it, but their conversation had to take place nonetheless. This former friend of his had to listen to him—he owed him that, having cost him his daughter. He took no pleasure in watching his friend grovel and count the minutes until their conversation ended. Far from it. However, the hunter had to warn people, and this was the way that he felt would be most effective. He wasn't about to start going from house to house to tell people that hanging over them was the same fate met by the first residents of the town. No one would listen to him that way. Besides, it was only this former friend of his who knew the story and so would hopefully understand the gravity of the situation immediately. Unless he had lost his connection with his roots.

Two little girls with tightly plaited hair walked past and quickened their pace when they saw him. Their mothers had doubtless warned them about him, told them that the man in the tent would take them and eat them if they didn't behave themselves. He never saw any boys here any more, which hurt him more than the loss of his own son. Perhaps this conversation wouldn't matter. The town was marked for death anyway if there were no men left in it to hunt.

*　　　*　　　*

Thóra felt terribly sunburned on the tiny bit of her face that was exposed. The snow magnified the weak winter sun, which had risen slowly as they drove to the site. She felt relieved when they put down their shovels and went back into the shed. Still, their efforts had been successful; beneath the heavy snow they had found an irregular hole in the

122

apparently bottomless ice layer, but Friðrikka said that it did not fit with any procedure the drillers were supposed to carry out. It was the correct location for their drilling, but according to her the drill had been applied in an extremely unusual manner, and there were peculiar marks left by ice axes and shovels. If the proper procedures had been followed, facing them now should have been a single black borehole the same diameter as the drill shaft, but instead there were many holes scattered about, none of which penetrated deep enough into the ice to be useful for gathering core samples. All of these peculiar holes had been made in one larger pit that appeared to have been dug with a shovel, but when they cleared it of snow it turned out to be empty. The pit was up against a cliff wall at the foot of a mountain rising high above them a bit further north. Directly behind the pit appeared an arched line of stone in the cliff, which rose up through the ice and formed a sort of halo. At the edge of the pit Matthew had caught a glimpse of something in the ice, and they decided to try to get whatever it was out in the hope of gaining some idea of what the ice might have contained before the drillers started working. With great difficulty they managed to scrape out an extremely unusual object, the likes of which neither Thóra nor Matthew had ever seen before. After removing most of the ice from it, it turned out to be a bone that had been polished, with holes drilled in two places in the middle. A leather strap had been tied to it at both ends, meaning that above all, it resembled a giant's armband.

'Does anyone know what this is?' Matthew passed around the object.

'No idea,' said Friðrikka. 'It's something

123

Greenlandic, but what it's for I don't know.' Alvar took the bone and looked it over, but he was equally unable to provide an explanation for it and gave up trying to guess what it was. He handed the object back to Matthew with a shrug.

'Maybe the villagers can provide us with an answer,' said Matthew, grabbing a dirty tea towel from the back of one of the chairs in the shed. He wrapped it around the bone and stuck it in his pocket. They were hungry and ready to head back to the camp. Thóra hoped that someone had had the sense to put together lunch for the group, but she doubted it. Neither the doctor nor Eyjólfur appeared likely to be very domestically minded, and she knew Bella well enough to recognize that she would be the last person to have prepared them a meal.

On the way to the car Friðrikka opened the door to the drilling rig's cab. They could see through the window that no one was inside it, either alive or dead. Nevertheless, she wanted to have a look inside in case the drillers had left behind a notebook or any other clues that could explain what they were doing. She said that they'd all been careful to record things as they went along, because it was difficult to rely on memory alone when it came to writing it all up in their journals in the evenings. Matthew followed Friðrikka and Thóra saw him climb into the cab after they seemed to have spotted something.

'Did you find anything?' called out Thóra to Friðrikka, who was still standing outside the cab.

'Yes,' replied the geologist. 'Now I'm completely at a loss.'

124

Chapter 11

21 March 2008

The therapist was too experienced to have much sympathy for Arnar's story, which perhaps was not strange, considering how short this binge had been. He simply had little to say. The man appeared almost disappointed, as though he had expected something more exciting. It occurred to Arnar to indulge his need for ingratiating himself with others and come up with something to ignite a spark in the therapist's eyes. He had enough to draw on from the past few years and it would be no problem to recount something juicy. But that's not what he did. In the self-examination that he'd undergone during his last treatment he had discovered that life was much simpler when you realized that you couldn't please everyone—and that there was no reason to do so. His own well-being was just as important as anyone else's. He needed to keep that firmly in mind until the day dawned when his first thought was not how good it would feel to have a drink.

'I know you're aware that every time you lapse, you pick up where you left off last time. The past few weeks have shown you that in black and white.' The therapist held Arnar's gaze as if to emphasize the importance of what he was saying. The effect was lessened somewhat by the way his eyes kept flickering up to the clock. It was never good to hold a session just before lunch.

The therapist's eyes were slightly protruding and Arnar had the discomfiting thought that all the

125

tales of sorrow and misfortune he'd had to listen to had filled his entire skull and now pressed against the backs of his eyes. After a few years his tongue and ears might also pop out. Arnar wondered whether he was experiencing delirium tremens, so vivid was this mental image. He shook himself slightly to get rid of it. 'I know,' he said, unsure what else to say. 'This is pathetic.' He could not concentrate and it was the best he could come up with.

'Yes, it's pathetic,' echoed the therapist, equally uninspired. 'You'll have to start from scratch, and now it's clear that you'll have to be more diligent about attending meetings than you have been in the past few years.' He rubbed his forehead, trying to appear serious and intelligent and concerned about Arnar's recovery. But he just looked like a hungry man with bulging eyes.

'It was hard to find a meeting in the middle of a glacier.' Arnar had investigated whether there were any AA meetings anywhere near the work site but the nearest had been in Angmagssalik, and it was far too much trouble to go there. So he had used CD recordings of American meetings, which had helped considerably, even though it wasn't the same as attending a meeting with other addicts. Defeated people had more powers of dissuasion than mere words—as did the joy in the eyes of those who had overcome their problems, at least for the time being.

'A glacier?' The therapist had apparently forgotten Arnar's story, or had not heard a single word of it. Perhaps the overcrowding in his skull made it impossible for him to absorb new information.

126

'I was working in Greenland.' Arnar couldn't care less about the therapist's lack of interest, which made this even more awkward. 'But I didn't fall off the wagon there.'

'No, that's right.' The therapist's expression was completely blank. 'Are you aware of what it was that led you back to the bottle?'

'Yes.' Arnar did not want to share that story with the man. He had had enough and was starting to look forward to lunch himself. He didn't know if it was his imagination, but it seemed as though the smell of food was being carried all the way to them from the cafeteria. 'But I don't care to discuss it.' No doubt the therapist would quickly lose his appetite if Arnar started to describe the events leading to his fall. Terrible, mindless vengeance and violence—and not from someone who kills for survival but from him, a supposedly civilized human being. And towards his colleagues, too . . . He felt sick when he recalled the reasons behind his actions. But though the others' behaviour towards him had been disgraceful, he alone was responsible for what had happened. And for that, he couldn't blame alcohol. Drunkenness did not get the ball rolling; that happened when in his ignorance he let himself be overwhelmed by hatred and ignore everything but his own lust for revenge.

*   *   *

Bella was the only one who was not impressed by Thóra's expedition with the others. She curled her lip so that no one could doubt how boring she found their story. But Thóra could sense something else behind Bella's contempt: she envied their little

127

field trip. She had been left behind with Eyjólfur to make a list of all the computers and other technical equipment at the camp, which was the first step in trying to determine the monetary value of it all. The two of them had gone from room to room; he had announced what was there and she had written it down, no doubt with a face like thunder. The doctor had continued to make his sample collection, which he alone controlled and understood fully.

'So you think that the corpse of the geologist who disappeared had been where they were planning to drill?' asked the doctor in a rather sceptical tone. 'That would mean this photo could be of a work glove.' He put down the poor-quality printout of the photo: the colours were odd and the image itself grainy.

Eyjólfur snorted. 'Yes, precisely. I think that you should look at the image on the screen; this printout is shitty. Onscreen you can see the nails in better resolution—albeit vaguely, but still.'

'Yes, no doubt,' said the doctor, although his tone didn't suggest that he believed it. 'This is all just too incredible. What are the chances of boring one little hole in that place and hitting exactly upon the spot where the woman died of exposure?'

'Little to none.' Friðrikka still looked worn out from the trip. 'Actually, they drilled more than one hole, and in more than one place. But it would certainly be a huge coincidence.'

'Could your friend, Oddný Hildur, have got lost in the storm but then realized she was in the vicinity of the shed? Could she have been searching for it to use as shelter?' Thóra knew as soon as she said this that such a scenario was beyond absurd. The distance was far too great for one person to make it

128

safe and sound through a storm.

Friðrikka shook her head. Her red hair was dirty—as was all their hair, in fact. 'No. When Oddný Hildur disappeared the shed was located elsewhere. It gets moved after every drilling. I'm not sure when it was put where it is now but it was after I quit. When I left the drilling rig the shed had been a bit further north for several months, in a place where drilling was coming to an end.'

'Then couldn't she have been heading there?' asked Matthew. 'And simply given up at the point where the shed is now?'

'If so, then she strayed a long way from the camp,' exclaimed Eyjólfur. 'That's too far to go on foot. I can't imagine how she could have made it that far; the weather was absolutely abominable.' 'And by car?' asked Matthew. 'Could she have driven or got a lift?'

Both Eyjólfur and Friðrikka were silent. The former was the first to speak up. 'She didn't go by car because they were all in their places the next day, and as far as getting a lift goes, that doesn't add up. Who would she have gone with? No one saw her after dinner that night, and no one would lie about that.' He looked at Matthew, bewildered. 'I don't know why any one of us would have kept it quiet. We were searching high and low for a whole week.'

'Five days,' interjected Friðrikka. 'You only searched for five days.' She said nothing for a moment and looked down, staring as if entranced at the pattern on the linoleum. 'Maybe whoever gave her a lift wanted to hurt her. And left her there intentionally.'

Eyjólfur glared at Friðrikka, then exhaled deeply.

It looked to Thóra as if he were counting to ten. He appeared to regain his composure. 'If anyone drove her, then it was one of those weirdo villagers. None of *us* did, since the weather made it impossible to be driving around out there. If she didn't walk, she must have gone by dogsled.'

Another argument was brewing, and Bella perked up. 'Maybe it doesn't matter at this moment how the woman got there,' said Matthew drily. 'I think it's more important to try to find out what happened to the body—if it was in fact a body in the ice.' He looked at the objects they had found in the hole. They lay on the table, menacing in their strangeness and irritating in the light of how poorly they fitted into the theory that Oddný Hildur had been found frozen in the ice. As if it weren't enough to think about where the drillers had taken her body and what had then become of them.

'Were they into drugs?' asked Bella, pointing at a large and rather battered-looking glass syringe. It had no needle. 'These drillers or the missing woman?'

'Fat chance,' said Eyjólfur flatly; characteristically, hardly leaping to his colleagues' defence. 'No junkie could work here. Where would you buy dope if you were running out?' His argument was fairly sound; drug addicts kept mainly to the cities and avoided the wilderness. And they wouldn't be likely to carry around any of what was lying beside the syringe. All of it was in rather poor condition: snowshoes and a leather jacket that was scratched and tattered, and so black with grease and filth that it was impossible to determine what animal the leather had come from; a newish-looking ice axe and a little bone statue

130

that Matthew had wrapped in a scarf for protection. The other objects hadn't been handled as carefully, since they weren't as delicate. Next to these things lay the bone with the holes in it, on top of the tea towel that Matthew had taken from the shed.

'I have a feeling this is probably some kind of Tupilak,' said Friðrikka, pointing at the figurine. At first Thóra had found the figurine resembled a banana upon which something had been scratched, but when she looked more closely she saw that it was an intricately carved bone to which had been tied some strange-looking odds and ends: hair, some kind of leather and a bird's claw. The craftsman appeared to have tried to make the bone itself resemble an ogre, and indeed the figurine looked quite monstrous. It had a large face with open jaws and numerous sharp teeth. Little hands with claws were carved onto its belly but otherwise the monster was covered with a pattern that they couldn't understand, but that possibly symbolized something. On the figurine's back a tail could be distinguished.

'What is a Tupilak, if I might ask?' Thóra was dying to hold the object, but considering how carefully Matthew had held it before he wrapped it in the scarf, it was unlikely that she would be granted the opportunity to do so. 'I read in a book here in the cafeteria that the natives blame it, whatever it is, for what happened to the original inhabitants of the area. Maybe it's related to those people somehow.'

'I must confess that I don't know exactly what its role is,' said Friðrikka. 'It's connected somehow to Greenlandic folk beliefs, and these kinds of bones are sold in all the tourist spots.' She stared at the

131

one in Matthew's hand. 'I don't think that any two are alike, and they don't follow any specific form. However, they do all have scary faces like that. Still, I don't recall seeing a version like this one. For example, there isn't usually anything tied to the figure.'

'So this could be some sort of tourist knick-knack?' Matthew peered doubtfully at its snarling face. 'Who would want to own a souvenir like that?'

'I have no idea where it came from. At least, I've never seen it before.' Friðrikka looked across the table. 'Nor the other things.'

'I don't know where that syringe comes from, but it's very different to the ones I'm used to.' Finnbogi bent down to examine it more closely. 'It might be used for veterinary medicine. It's big enough.' He straightened up. 'It's not a drug addict's, that's for certain.'

'The jacket is definitely Greenlandic,' said Alvar, who had kept to himself until now. 'The other junk I know nothing about.'

Eyjólfur looked triumphant. 'So my theory that Oddný Hildur got a ride on a dogsled is maybe not so far-fetched after all. Maybe this jacket and these snowshoes are from whoever drove the sled.'

'And why should he have left them behind? Was there a sudden heatwave?' Friðrikka spoke like a primary school kid, with the same sing-song contempt that can be heard in every school playground at break-time.

Matthew let go of the back of the chair that he'd been holding on to and it hit the edge of the table hard, shifting the objects slightly. 'This is all just conjecture. We don't know what was out there in

132

the ice and we don't know anything about these things, which—according to Friðrikka—shouldn't have been in the drilling rig.' He nudged the ice axe. 'The only logical explanation is that this was used to free whatever was in the ice. Anything else is so far from being feasible that it's pointless to wonder about it.'

'One other thing is certain. If this was Oddný Hildur, then she didn't die of exposure,' said Friðrikka, now speaking in her normal, slightly husky voice. 'It's been about six months since she disappeared and it's impossible that she was buried beneath two metres of ice and snow during that time. Maybe snow, but not ice. It was a deep hole and it would have been necessary to use a shovel for her to have been buried that deep.'

'Would she have been able to dig herself down to take shelter from the weather?' asked Thóra, directing her question at Alvar. As a rescuer, he must know this.

'Dig herself into the ice?' He shook his head slowly. 'I can't imagine it. People generally find themselves a snowdrift or thick sheets of snow. I've never heard of someone digging himself or herself several metres down into ice.' He looked at his toes, embarrassed at his own stream of words. Thóra had never met a man so shy. 'Of course I don't know how conditions have changed these past six months.'

They all stared at the table, each struggling to come up with a sensible explanation. Surprisingly, it was Bella who broke the silence with a theory that seemed fairly reasonable. 'Couldn't someone have murdered this geologist lady and buried her, and then when the drillers found the body by accident,

133

the same person murdered them too?'

They nodded thoughtfully, all except the doctor who stood with his arms crossed and an unhappy look on his sunburned face. 'I don't see why this mysterious murderer should have wanted to kill this woman in the first place, let alone any men who might have found the body. What would be the point?' Bella had managed to offend the doctor that morning, when he had tried again to point out to her the hazards of smoking. She had told him to mind his own business, and added that she wasn't constantly pointing out to him that he was losing his hair, which was just as obvious as the fact that smoking was dangerous. 'That I don't know,' she now replied airily. 'Maybe they found something on the body that pointed to the killer? Maybe one of these things is a clue to the identity of the murderer.'

'Bloody nonsense.' The doctor turned to Matthew. 'This is ludicrous, completely fantastical. We don't even know for certain that a body was there, still less the body of this particular woman.'

'Oh yes,' said Bella sarcastically. 'That would make the case *much* simpler, if it involved yet another dead body.'

Thóra cleared her throat. As if it weren't bad enough having to continually try to make peace between Friðrikka and Eyjólfur. 'This case certainly isn't simple. Don't forget the bones in the desk drawers. They're yet another unexplained phenomenon in this peculiar place.' She forced out a smile that was supposed to be encouraging. 'But hopefully we'll find an explanation for all of it. As things stand, I can't say that we're on the right track but you never know, things might become

134

clear later.'

'That's right.' Matthew tried to smile along with Thóra, but his smile came out even less convincing than hers. 'Let's not waste time arguing about this; it's of little use.' He unwrapped the scarf from the little drilled bone. It was still moist from the ice that had melted off it. Then he lifted the idol gently. Tupilak. It stared back at them with its teeth bared; the figurine may not have been very big, but it was impressively hideous. 'I think we should go down to the village and find someone who can help us sort this out. Maybe this little statue has a rational meaning? Maybe the villagers knew about the drillers and can explain the jacket and snowshoes, as well as the bone?' He abruptly changed gears. 'But it may well be that these things have no connection with the body in the ice. In any case, our only hope at the moment is that the villagers can explain some of it. We should visit them straight away.'

'They'll never help you,' muttered Friðrikka. 'The villagers turned their backs on us when we went to them for assistance after Oddný Hildur's disappearance. They won't tell us anything.'

'We'll just have to see about that,' said Thóra. 'We have to try.' She recalled the empty streets and the baleful stares of the girls they had seen from a distance. She felt goosebumps on her forearms but did not know whether they were caused by the cooling temperature or the thought of a hostile reception in a village at the end of earth. She thought of the girls' piercing black eyes again and realized that she was afraid to go to the village. The trip, however, could not be avoided.

135

Chapter 12

21 March 2008

The village turned out to be just as Thóra had been expecting—gloomy and hostile. It was as if the inhabitants were not of this world and feared coming out into the open air. The streets were still nearly deserted and a thin fog contributed to the unreal atmosphere. They had watched the fog cover the colourful village as they drove down the hill that separated it from the work site. It seemed as though the residents had ordered it to block the sight of these outsiders—with the assistance of nature, they were concealing what strangers were only intended to see hazily. The light was also peculiar: even though the sun hung in the sky it only gave off a dim glow, and was already preparing itself to sink back down into slumber. Three of them had come on this trip: Thóra, Matthew and Dr Finnbogi. Eyjólfur had decided to try to repair the satellite dishes in the hope of re-establishing a connection with the outside world, and Alvar had offered to help him. Bella had been asked to put her handwritten inventory of the camp's technical equipment onto the computer and Friðrikka continued to assess the status of the project. They all appeared to be happy not to have to go down to the village, and Thóra felt that Friðrikka and Eyjólfur in particular were breathing more easily as a result. This did nothing to diminish Thóra's conviction that things were not quite right in the village; the only ones in the group who were familiar with it did not want to go back there.

The doctor turned and looked at Thóra. 'Where should we start?' He had stopped the car on the slope while they silently watched the fog cover the area. 'No one place seems better than another.'

Matthew pointed out of the front window. 'There were two or three people down at the pier. Should we take the chance that they're still there?' A thick fog bank now covered both the pier and the foreshore.

They drove through the village to the little harbour, seeing not a single soul along the way. 'I don't know whether they're avoiding us or whether the villagers generally remain indoors, but I find this very odd.' The doctor drove slowly, thereby allowing himself the leisure to lean over the steering wheel and have a good look around. 'I've been to lots of villages like this in Greenland and generally people are very friendly and sociable. If everything were as it should be, they would all be coming out to meet us instead of avoiding us.' Neither Thóra nor Matthew said anything, contenting themselves with looking at the lonely street as it passed slowly by. Colourful curtains were drawn across all the windows. All the doors were shut.

'Maybe they start the day very early and then take a kind of siesta,' said Thóra, more to herself than to her colleagues in the car.

'I've never heard of that.' The doctor sped up a bit after they'd driven past the last house. 'They're not about to waste what little daylight they have at this time of year by napping.' He suddenly slowed down as the fog became denser. 'I don't want to drive into the sea,' he muttered. 'You can't see more than two metres in front of the car.' When they caught sight of the pier's woodwork at the end of the gravel path he parked off to the side. The slamming of the car doors broke the silence, then the only sound was the low lapping of the waves and a thump now and then when a loose ice floe bumped against a pier pillar. They looked at each other as if they were all waiting for one of them to take the initiative and lead them out onto the pier. 'Just so it's clear, I've never heard of Greenlanders attacking tourists,' said Finnbogi, looking down the pier, which vanished before them in the fog. 'We'll just talk as we go so that we don't catch anyone off-guard.'

'If they're still there.' Matthew listened carefully and announced that he thought he heard some activity in the fog. 'We got lucky,' he said, but Thóra couldn't tell if he was being ironic or serious. He walked out onto the pier and Thóra and Finnbogi followed him closely.

There was barely enough room for them to walk side by side down the jetty. It was built straight out into the sea, making it possible to dock on both sides. The villagers' fleet appeared neither large nor elegant; it included three small, unsightly motorized fishing boats and several open motorboats tied to dock rings. There was not a kayak in sight. It was unclear how far the structure extended, because they did not need to walk far before they saw the indistinct shapes of two men. Both of them had stopped what they were doing and stood motionless, watching the party approach. Their expressions revealed neither anger nor enmity; they only appeared surprised at the visit and neither of them answered Finnbogi's greeting.

138

The man in the boat put down a battered knife that was covered in blood and his companion on the pier raised a gloved hand to his forehead and stroked back the hair from his eyes.

'Good day,' said Finnbogi in Danish with a strong Icelandic accent, bowing his head curtly. 'Are you from here?' Thóra had to make an effort not to burst out laughing at this absurd question. The men were dressed in sealskin clothing, had dark skin, black hair, and slanted eyes—they were as Greenlandic as could be. There was even a dead seal, its belly cut open, lying on the pier, just to complete the picture. The men said nothing and just stared, as silent as before. The smile inside Thóra withered as quickly as it had bloomed. Perhaps the men were offended by such a ridiculous question. She stared at the large knife held by the man in front of them. He was covered in blood from working on the seal. The doctor tried again. 'We are visiting the work site to the north and we're in a bit of trouble.' The doctor's Danish was decent, in Thóra's opinion, but that wasn't saying much as she had never been very good at it herself. She still had enough high-school Danish to be able to follow the conversation—if the Greenlanders wanted to converse with them. On the other hand, Matthew understood nothing; he had enough trouble comprehending Icelandic without having to compound his difficulties by tackling another language. However, no language skills were necessary to understand that the hunters weren't happy to see them. Yet Finnbogi was unperturbed and kept on as if the men had happily acquiesced to his request for help. 'We're missing two men who were at the work camp just

139

over a week ago, and we wanted to check whether you knew anything about them.' He paused for a moment, but then continued when their only response was to stare at him. 'Have you seen these men at all? They could possibly have come here in the hope of finding transportation by land or sea.'

Thóra held out a printed photo of the two drillers, which they had made especially for this visit to the village. In the photo the men sat side by side in the camp's cafeteria, wearing thick woollen jumpers, their faces red. In front of them on the table were two heaped-up plates of food. The hunters made no move to take the photo, so Thóra turned it towards them. 'These two,' she said, pointing with one finger above the heads of the men in the photo.

The two Greenlanders looked at the photo with what at least appeared to be sincere interest. The one standing in the boat even moved closer to get a better look. Thóra extended the photo to him carefully until he took it. He looked over the photo without a word, nodded calmly and said something to his friend in Greenlandic. The friend took the picture and regarded it for a moment before returning it to Thóra. The image was now covered in blood but Thóra acted as if she didn't notice, taking it back without any hint of hesitation. She suspected that the little sign of interest that the men had shown would disappear quickly if she frowned.

The men looked at each other and then at them. Both shook their heads. 'Not here,' replied the one on the pier. His Danish seemed as good as Thóra's high-school Danish.

Finnbogi smiled from ear to ear over what he

clearly considered an outstanding step in the right direction in their relations with the natives. 'Can you refer us to someone in the village who might be able to assist us? Is there a police station here, municipal offices or a health clinic?'

The men shook their heads again. 'Not here,' repeated the man on the pier.

Thóra wasn't sure whether the man still meant the drillers in the photo or whether he was saying that there were no public services in the village. She nudged Matthew with her elbow and asked him to show the men the objects that they'd brought with them: the drilled bone with the leather strap and the Tupilak figure. He pulled them out and showed them to the men—without handing them over. The men did nothing to hide their reactions. They started in surprise upon seeing the drilled bone and could not conceal their amazement. The Tupilak appeared not to surprise them at all, until they came nearer to get a better look at it. The man in the boat even clambered up onto the pier to get closer still, incredibly agile despite his thick clothing. Then they looked at each other inquisitively and exchanged a few incomprehensible words. The man who'd been on the pier at first then turned to Matthew and asked: 'Where did you get this?'

Since Matthew did not understand a word, the doctor interrupted. 'What is it?' he asked. 'Do you recognize this object?'

'Where did you get this?' repeated the hunter. His tone was determined and he continued to look stiffly at Matthew. 'Where did you get it?' He held out his hand, palm up. He wanted to hold the object. It was clear to all of them that if they gave it

141

to him, they would not get it back. Thóra suddenly felt happy that the man who'd been standing in the boat was now on the pier, because there he was far from the knife that he'd set down.

'I don't think we're going to get any help here,' said the doctor suddenly but calmly in Icelandic, smiling at the men. 'They don't want to do anything for us and it's unclear whether they speak any more Danish than what we've already heard.'

Although Thóra had no desire whatsoever to stand there on the pier surrounded by cold fog any longer than necessary, she didn't want to give up so easily. 'On the ice. We found it on the ice.'

The men stared at her. 'Where? Where on the ice?' asked the same man as before. He pointed up along the pier. 'On land? On the sea?' Thóra had so entirely lost her sense of direction that it took a great effort for her not to point out to sea. In her mind she tried to recall the position of the pier in relation to the foreshore and imagined the lie of the land on both sides of the hill when she had looked over both the work site and the village. 'There,' she said, pointing in what she thought was the right direction. 'By the mountains.' Her Danish didn't allow her to provide a better description of the landscape around the drilling rig.

At first the hunters said nothing and instead looked again at the objects, apparently frightened. They both took one step back. 'Leave,' said the one who spoke for both of them. 'We are working.' He waved both his hands to indicate that they should clear off. 'Leave.' The red flesh of the seal lying at his feet on the pier gleamed, and for the first time Thóra caught the body's iron-like smell of blood, which overwhelmed the suddenly mild scent of

142

the sea. He didn't have to tell her twice, and she walked away. Matthew and Finnbogi followed and the doctor didn't bother to say goodbye to the men, since it would have been a waste of time.

As they walked back to land they heard the men speaking to each other, quickly and very animatedly. Their language was unlike any other that Thóra had heard and she had difficulty distinguishing where each word ended and the next began. There was no way to understand what they said to each other but she was relieved nonetheless that they did not simply watch silently as the three of them walked away, because if she could hear their distant voices she knew they weren't running after them up the pier, brandishing their knives. She was enormously grateful when she got back into the car.

'Greenlanders aren't often like that, I can tell you.' Finnbogi started the engine and turned the pickup truck around. 'Generally, they're extremely nice and can't do enough for you. I'm starting to sound like a broken record, but I'm just so surprised at all of this.'

Matthew listened attentively, his expression revealing nothing other than that he highly doubted the doctor. 'Hopefully we'll meet someone friendlier in this strange village,' he said. 'We'd better go and see, although I don't expect we'll find anyone who can help us. Obviously, Friðrikka was right.'

Thóra's desire to suggest that they simply go back to camp and continue to investigate the computers was overwhelming, but instead she stared silently out of the window. She watched how the fog cleared almost completely the farther it drew from their sight. It was a short trip and soon the houses reappeared, lonely and abandoned, or so it seemed. Her attention was drawn particularly towards one of the houses, rather ugly and ramshackle. It looked to her as if something had moved in the window.

*   *   *

Naruana let go of the curtain, closing the little gap through which he'd been watching the car drive through the village. He stood motionless, staring at the worn-out, mottled fabric on the curtain rod that was starting to come loose. It wouldn't be long before it fell off, and he knew it would be left to lie there; no one, least of all him, would put it back up again. His life was in the same state as the house, and he was glad he'd come to live here; here nothing gave him any trouble. When he went to a place where everything was clean and beautiful on the surface he stuck out, and the ruin that he had become was even more obvious. He had tried to avoid this scenario, which is why he lived here, in the home of a woman who was only slightly behind him on the road to perdition, and if he left the house it was to be around people in the same boat as him. He did not love this woman; he didn't even feel particularly fond of her. But neither did he hate or even dislike her. She was just there; she had inherited her mother's house and could therefore provide him with both shelter and company in his drinking. Her feelings were just as absent. There was no affection, only practicality and loneliness.

He had nowhere else to turn. He couldn't imagine living with his mother, even though he fitted perfectly into the environment there. No,

144

he couldn't stand the sight of her, and the feeling was mutual. They had two things in common: they were both slaves to alcohol and they despised each other. Neither of them reminded the other of how life was before the alcohol took over completely, when it was still possible for them to enjoy pleasant moments without being drunk. Nor could he go and live with his father, who would kill him; there was no question about that. Fortunately, Naruana had seldom run into him in recent years, but when it happened, he found the old man's overwhelming indifference suffocating. He looked down at his toes and saw that they were dirty, which came as no surprise. They had looked like that since he could remember; the only difference was the nature of the dirt. The dirtiness of his youth had been natural dirt that had gathered on him outdoors. The grubbiness he saw now came from the filth that filled every corner of the house.

So it was a strange coincidence that that morning he had spotted both his father and these outsiders, who until that point he had heard of but not seen. At least not that he recalled. He could very well have seen the group drive through the town before, but he would have been drunk and therefore unable to recall it. However, he thought this unlikely. He would have remembered it; not to have done so was impossible. This visit was such bad news that no amount of alcohol would have been able to erase it from his mind. He stared at the curtains and breathed deeply, suddenly seized with the desire to go out; find his old, worn-out work coverall, load his rifle and go hunting. For a moment he was filled with a sense of joy that he didn't know he could still feel; his headache disappeared and the cut on the back of his hand stopped hurting, although it had been bothering him for days. Then he remembered that he had traded his treasured rifle for a case of beer, and as a result was no more on his way to a hunt than a weaponless girl. It was no wonder his father hated him so much—he had given him the rifle as a gift when Naruana turned sixteen, and the weapon had cost his father a considerable portion of his summer wages. Naruana hoped his father was unaware of the fate of the firearm, but part of him realized that the old man seemed to know everything and see everything even though he was nowhere near. Naruana could only hope that Igimaq didn't know what his son had done, how low he had stooped. Hope that he hadn't seen him as he stood there, his hands stained with the blood of a prey no hunter would boast about.

His headache returned and his hand hurt even more than before.

Chapter 13

21 March 2008

Thóra watched as Matthew and Dr Finnbogi walked up to yet another house, knocked on the door and waited patiently for someone to answer. No house had looked more like a public building than the others, so they had had to resort to simply going door to door. There was no one out on the streets to ask for information. At first Thóra had accompanied Matthew and Finnbogi, but when it seemed clear that their efforts would provide little or no result she decided instead to wait in the car and make an attempt to warm herself up. The humidity in the air as a result of the fog made it considerably colder. She was chilled to the bone and cursed herself for the stupidity of her packing as she sat there in her borrowed gloves and hat in the car's back seat. She watched Matthew and Finnbogi fidget on the doorstep and make another attempt to get someone to answer. Then they knocked on the door so loudly that the noise carried all the way into the car. They waited a moment before moving on to the next house. A mist had started to form on the windows and Thóra reached out over the seat to wipe it off, so that she could keep better track of the two men's movements. When she leaned back in her seat again she gripped her chest with both hands and let out a low cry. Someone was standing right next to the car, staring at her.

She was an apparently young woman, although it was difficult to discern her age due to the fog on the window as well as her thick clothing. Her face was expressionless as she stared straight at Thóra, who fought to regulate her heart rate. The woman stood that way for several seconds, and when Thóra got sufficient hold of herself to roll down the window she continued to stand there like a statue. The only thing differentiating her from a shop-window mannequin was the occasional blink of her dark eyes. More than anything else Thóra wanted her to leave, but if she drove the woman away Matthew and Finnbogi would kill her, after they'd trudged through the village from end to end in search of residents to speak to.

'Good day,' said Thóra in Danish. 'Can I help you?' Her voice sounded shrill and she spoke

147

unnecessarily loudly.

At first the woman just stared back at her, causing Thóra to think that perhaps she did not speak Danish. Before Thóra could give English a try the woman opened her mouth and spoke. What could be seen of her face suggested that she was young, between twenty and thirty. Her face was strong and her high cheekbones were further emphasized by the redness of her cheeks. Her eyes were dark and clear, but the yellowish tinge to their whites ruined her otherwise healthy appearance. 'You shouldn't be here,' said the woman. A dull odour of alcohol was carried into the car on her breath, which formed thin white clouds in the cold air.

'In the village?' asked Thóra. 'We just wanted to ask a few questions. There are two men lost, and they might possibly have come here.'

'You should go home,' said the woman, still staring at Thóra expressionlessly. 'Back to your home. Wherever that is.'

'We're leaving soon.' Thóra wished that she understood what was going on. Now her Danish would really be put to the test. She started speaking and although her vocabulary was childish she hoped that the gist of what she wanted to say came across. 'Are you opposed to the project or did the employees of the Icelandic company do something to you?'

The woman gave Thóra an inquisitive look, not unlike the one Thóra had just given her. 'You're staying in a bad place. No one should be there. Go home.'

'How is it bad?' Thóra pressed the button to roll the window all the way down. She did this without thinking, as if it were the windowpane separating

148

them that made her unable to understand what the woman was talking about.

'Bad.' The woman appeared impatient, showing a reaction at last. 'You don't need to understand why. Just believe me. Take your friends and leave and don't come back.'

'Why are you telling me this?' Thóra wondered whether this strange conversation would be any easier if she stepped out of the car and they stood side by side.

'You'll have to pay me for more information.' The woman had become stony faced again. Thóra did not know how she should answer. She had no money with her, apart from several hundred nearly worthless Icelandic krónur, which was probably fitting as she didn't expect the information she was buying to be worth much. 'I need to know more than that if I'm supposed to pay you.' Hopefully Matthew or the doctor had some money with them. Matthew must have taken out some Danish currency, just in case. In most things he was the perfect opposite of Thóra, who trusted more often than not in God and luck.

'You won't get anyone else to talk to you. The people here don't want anything to do with you.' The woman's eyes narrowed and she appeared lost in thought. 'It's not a good time for me—otherwise I wouldn't be talking to you. How much do I get for talking to you?'

'That depends on what you can tell me.' Thóra hoped that Matthew and the doctor wouldn't come rushing up and scare the woman away. She had something to say and Thóra guessed that now she was trying to put a value on the information. 'I'm mainly trying to find out about two men who

149

disappeared from here recently.'

The woman exhaled, once again emitting a sour odour of alcohol. 'I know which men you're talking about.'

Thóra tried to conceal the excitement that gripped her. Was it conceivable that the men were here in the village? 'Have you met them recently?' The woman shook her head energetically. 'Did they come here after the others went home?'

'One of them,' replied the woman. 'The fat one. He came alone.'

'When was that and what did he want?' After blurting this out, Thóra went silent; she had to keep control of her questions even though others were springing to mind. Matthew and Finnbogi had the photo of the drillers, so she couldn't ask the woman to point out the one she meant. If Thóra remembered correctly, Bjarki was much bigger than Dóri, but that was a moot point if only one of them had come to the village.

The woman shrugged, causing her light blue jacket to lift slightly. It was so thick and stiff that it took a moment for the garment to sink back to its place. Until it did, the woman looked neckless. 'I don't know exactly when he arrived. It was more than a week ago. Maybe two. He wanted to make a call.'

'A call?' Thóra could not remember having read or heard of a phone call during the period the woman was talking about. The camp's telephone connection had supposedly been cut off several days after the two drillers were left behind alone, and no one had mentioned that they'd made contact since then. 'Do you know who he wanted to call?'

150

The woman looked with pursed lips at Thóra. 'You're definitely going to pay me?' Thóra nodded and the woman continued, although the words seemed to come out reluctantly. 'I don't know. Probably the police or a doctor. He was looking for someone like that.'

'And was he able to make a call?' asked Thóra, hoping that the answer would be yes. Maybe the men had been arrested and because of some red tape had been stuck in a Greenlandic prison without the knowledge of the Icelandic authorities. The arrest could even have been connected with the body they found in the ice.

'No,' replied the woman. 'No one would let him in. He was very strange and I know it never crossed my mind to open my door. He would have been better off going home, as I tried to tell him through the door. He didn't listen.'

'How do you know that he didn't go home?'

'Well, he left when it became clear that he wouldn't be able to use a phone, and he couldn't have gone anywhere else other than back to the camp. The only clear way from here to other towns is by helicopter, and no one else came here between the time that the big group left and you arrived. There are no roads leading here, and the man didn't have access to a boat, not that he would have been able to sail it through the ice anyway.'

'What about a dogsled or a snowmobile?' Thóra hadn't seen a snowmobile at the work site, though it was unthinkable that Berg Technology wouldn't have provided such a thing. Perhaps the men had tried to make it to a more southerly settlement by snowmobile, and died of exposure on the way.

'He didn't go by dogsled, that's for sure,' replied

the woman emphatically. 'There's no one here who would have taken him, and he didn't steal dogs or a sled. I would have heard about it. And I didn't notice any snowmobiles. They're loud and the dogs always bark at them.' She stuck her hands in her pockets and shrugged her shoulders, her jacket rising again and making her neck disappear once more. 'They know that they're a threat to them. They can sometimes replace the dogs. But not always.' She realized that she'd got off the subject and went back to it. 'No one would have taken the man on a dogsled or a snowmobile.'

'Why would no one have wanted to take him if he needed help?' Thóra suspected that the woman wasn't quite as all-knowing about what happened in the village as she pretended to be. 'Do you dislike outsiders so much?' Thóra's sentences had become practically all English since her Danish vocabulary could no longer handle the conversation. But it didn't seem to do any harm.

The woman frowned. 'We're not bad to outsiders. We don't like the place you choose to live in. No one should be there; you are disturbing the evil that dwells there and by doing so you're putting us all in danger. We just want you to go somewhere else.'

In a way, Thóra was slightly relieved, as it was conceivable that the natives' prejudices against the work site could be used to justify the delays on the project. There was nothing in the contract to protect Berg against this, even though it could be argued that it should have been included. The villagers had possibly done more than just nag the staff to go home. 'What's wrong with that area?'

The woman looked panicked. 'Nothing that you would understand,' she said. 'I want my money.'

152

'You've got to tell me,' replied Thóra. 'Is the area considered bad because of a particular occurrence, or is something else wrong with it? Something palpable such as polar bears or other dangers?'

The woman had grown irritated. Her eyes narrowed as she stood there shuffling her feet and looking around as if to see how many people were witness to the conversation. Although there was no one else to be seen, there were doubtless people watching from behind the curtains of the nearby houses. 'I don't know. It's just something that everyone knows. The area is bad and it's dangerous to be there. We never go there and if you had listened to us then you wouldn't be looking for this man.' She stopped her hopeless search for invisible observers and looked at Thóra head-on. Her pitch-black pupils gleamed in the yellow whites of her eyes. 'You'll never find him.'

Before Thóra could reply to this assertion, Matthew and Finnbogi started heading back over to the car. The woman appeared startled. 'Those are my friends,' said Thóra, to try to calm her down. She had a certain sympathy for the woman's sense of self-preservation, to agree to speak to a stranger in the hope of payment—there were hardly many opportunities to make money in the village. The boats in the harbour were of the sort used for small, personal catches; larger fishing vessels could not enter the harbour, which was surrounded by sea ice. The villagers should actually have celebrated the project as a source of increased opportunities for work that it surely brought. Instead, their complete lack of interest in attempting to profit from the project clearly revealed their deep-rooted fear of the afflicted place. Thóra pointed at Matthew as he

153

approached with Finnbogi. 'He's got the money.' The woman nodded worriedly. While Thóra explained things to the two men, the Greenlander stood there looking as if she expected the three of them to do her in.

None of them had any idea how much they should pay the woman. Finnbogi was convinced that if they paid her too much, they would soon be beset by people who would invent stories simply for the money. In the end they gave her five hundred Danish crowns and she took them without any indication as to whether it was more or less than she'd expected. She thanked them in a soft voice as she stuffed the bills into her pocket. 'Where do you live?' asked Thóra.

'Why?' The woman's voice was suspicious and she frowned instinctively.

'I might need to speak to you again,' Thóra replied. 'If the phones at the camp can't be reconnected we might need to make a call from your phone. Of course we'll pay if it should come to that. I'd also like to know more about what you were saying about the work site. You could maybe try to find out from some of the older people here what the explanation is for the area's bad reputation.'

The woman shook her head. 'I don't want to talk to them for you. You'll just have to do that yourselves.' She appeared to be somewhat undecided, however, and it was perhaps in the hope of receiving more cash that she didn't leave. She looked away from Thóra and began to scan the windows of the nearby houses again.

'We can't get anyone else to speak to us and you know that,' said Thóra. 'You're the only person who's offered to help at all. I promise that we'll pay you for all the assistance you give us.'

The woman looked around her one last time and finally turned to Thóra and pointed discreetly in the direction of the harbour. 'See that house standing at the end of the village? It's blue.' Thóra saw that it was the house she'd noticed as they drove through the village. From this angle it didn't appear any more attractive than it had earlier. Bright orange skis stood stuck in the snow against the house's gable but otherwise there was little there that called to mind sports or a healthy lifestyle. Thóra assumed that the woman had been behind the curtains that moved as they passed by. 'I live there.' She peered furtively at the men. 'You can make calls from there if you want. Not them. Just you.' She turned away without saying goodbye.

'What about the information?' called out Thóra after the woman had turned her back on them. 'Can you try to find out for me about the history of the area?'

The woman replied without looking back. 'No. You could try talking to Igimaq. He should know the story.'

'Who is Igimaq?' The doctor was the first to ask and Thóra tried as best she could to hide her irritation. The woman clearly would not answer him—only Thóra.

The woman looked back angrily and stared hard at Thóra, acting as if the two men were not standing there. Finnbogi had the good sense to say nothing. 'He's an old hunter and he knows this area well. He's even experienced first hand what it costs to spend time in those parts. He lost his daughter there.'

155

'What do you mean?' Thóra started thinking about the polar bear again. 'Did she die of exposure?'

'Ask Igimaq yourself. He lives west of town. If you head towards the black cliff you can see in front of the glacier, you'll come across his tent.' She looked from Thóra to the car. 'You won't make it there in that. You've got to find yourselves dogsleds or snowmobiles.' She turned away from them once more and walked away. 'Good luck finding it.'

They watched her as she strode off, proud and upright, and Thóra admired the way the young woman managed to keep her back so straight. It was as if they were watching one of the most illustrious women in the village. Despite her yellowed eyes and the odour of alcohol, they could still sense her proud spirit, which must have been based on her coming from much sturdier stock than them. It was as if she were two different people, a front and a back, where the front had stumbled on the road of life but the back was still proud and victorious.

'Okay. Igimaq.' Finnbogi looked to the sky in the hope of seeing where the sun was in its short working day. He had forgotten about the fog, which made it impossible for him to determine the source of the grey light that slipped through. 'Perhaps we should check whether we can find even one snowmobile.' He sighed loudly. 'We forgot to show her the bone and the Tupilak.' He tapped lightly at his jacket pocket.

'It doesn't matter,' said Matthew. 'I suspect this Igimaq knows more about these things than the girl, anyway.'

'If he wants to talk to us about them at all,' said

156

Thóra, rolling up the window. There was no need to breathe in more cold air when warmer air was available. It wasn't always possible to make such a choice. On a snowmobile, for instance.

Chapter 14

21 March 2008

In the end they were unable to meet Igimaq. There was a snowmobile at the camp, as Thóra had expected, but it wasn't in working order. Alvar spent the rest of the day trying to repair it, with no luck. They'd found it inside a storage unit behind the camp on a tip-off from Friðrikka and Eyjólfur, the latter of whom went with Matthew and Alvar to the unit, happy to stop working on the satellite dishes for a while. He had made no progress, and the dishes appeared to have suffered some rather unusual damage. The one on the roof of the office building was on its side, but the roof and the cables, which still connected it to strong fastenings, had prevented it from falling off. The banging they had heard during the storm had most likely come from the dish. Eyjólfur had fixed it back in its place but hadn't got it to work properly, even though he considered it possible that the Internet connection could go on and off as it appeared to have done while the dish was swinging on the roof at the mercy of the wind. It was a different story with the dish on the roof of the cafeteria, to which the phones were connected. It was in a worse state, having presumably been subjected to more damage before

157

it came loose, and in the end Eyjólfur came to the conclusion that its receiving equipment was so badly broken that phone calls were out of the question.

It was difficult to gauge the reasons why the dishes had suffered so much damage outside. Eyjólfur thought it doubtful that the weather was to blame, and tended towards the opinion that someone had hammered at the devices with a crowbar or other heavy object until they came loose. There could be no other explanation for the dents on them, he thought.

Eyjólfur must have still been thinking about the satellite dishes when he arrived at the storage unit, since the first thing that crossed his mind was that it had been broken into. The unit was unlocked and the paint was scraped away in several dented spots around the lock bracket. Inside was the snowmobile, surrounded by tyres of all shapes and sizes, spare car parts and various other supplies. Eyjólfur didn't notice anything missing, so the team did not set much store by his conclusion that it was a case of breaking and entering. There could have been other reasons for the dents on the rusted bracket, and it was also possible that the hanging lock on the unit had disappeared long ago. Eyjólfur pointed out that he wasn't particularly interested in cars or their maintenance and had only been in the unit once before, so he couldn't say for sure what it had contained. However, he was certain that the unit's door had always been securely locked. Friðrikka had never been in the unit either, but she remembered that she had once walked past it when its door stood open. She recalled nothing about what had been in it. Of course it was possible that someone had broken into it to damage the

158

snowmobile, although on what impulse she had no idea. The only motive they could think of was that someone had intended to hinder the drillers' movements, although no one could contribute anything when Matthew sought an explanation for the possible reasons for wanting to do this. It was clear that the damage—if there was actually any damage—was not of the kind suffered by the satellite dishes, since there were no marks or dents visible on the snowmobile.

As the discussion about possible vandalism reached its peak, Friðrikka pointed out that the drillers had also had the use of two cars, so damaging the snowmobile to immobilize the men would have been a fairly pointless exercise. The cars had been parked outside when they arrived and it hadn't crossed anyone's mind to check their condition. When they went to do so, they discovered that the cars wouldn't start, and it looked very likely that one of the engines had burned out.

Now, Thóra was sitting at the computer in the office that Friðrikka said had been used by Oddný Hildur. She was planning to upload the photos that Eyjólfur had taken of the damage to the satellite dishes on the roof. Later, she would transfer the images to her laptop, but it was easier to view them on a good screen that wasn't covered with the fingerprints of small children. Everything now suggested that the drillers' disappearance, and consequently the cessation of the project, could be attributed to human intervention, and hence the photos could be useful to the bank in its dispute with the mining company. However, it was impossible to say who was behind this or why. Of

159

course it was not out of the question that nature had been asserting itself, that a violent wind had blown over the satellite dishes, but Thóra doubted that a polar bear or other wild animal had been involved; the roof was too high for that. Nor did the damage to the dishes appear to have been caused by claws or teeth. The dents in the thick metal shield were huge, and there were no scratches or scrapes to be seen. The marks could hardly have been made by anything but a tool. After her conversation with the Greenlandic woman she found it not entirely absurd to suppose that one of the villagers might bear the responsibility for it. There was a thin line between denying assistance to those in need and causing them wilful damage through acts of vandalism. Perhaps the villagers had been offended when their warnings hadn't been heeded and had taken action in this way, which then raised the question of whether they had also played a part in the disappearance and death of Oddný Hildur. Thóra had deliberately chosen to use the computer the missing woman had used, on the off-chance that something was hidden there that might shed light on her disappearance. So after uploading the photographs, Thóra focused on combing through the computer's files, and quickly became lost in that jungle.

By the time she had more or less finished viewing everything that she considered to be of any worth, the rumbling in her belly was driving her crazy. She looked at the clock on the screen and saw that time had flown. She didn't feel any better informed. Oddný Hildur appeared to have been rather reticent and did not leave any clues about herself on her computer. Her e-mails were

160

incredibly unexciting and centred mostly on work; there were numerous short messages with attached reports about the progress of the project and strata that Thóra did not understand at all. Still, several messages to the owner of the company roused Thóra's interest. In them Oddný Hildur appeared to be complaining about the atmosphere at the workplace and the harassment she said the engineer Arnar was suffering. Thóra searched for and found the man's reply, in which he seemed to disregard all of Oddný Hildur's concerns and make little of her request for him to intervene. His message contained rather feeble advice such as, '*It sounds like it's just good-natured teasing that shouldn't be taken seriously,*' and '*I'm sure it doesn't matter to him, he has a thick skin,*' and Thóra could not help but admire the geologist's determination not to give up. She had sent her final message on this subject two days before she disappeared. The message hadn't been answered. In it she had said that it was now no longer possible to turn a blind eye to the matter; the man was having a bad time of it and the cruelty of his co-workers clearly 'did matter to him'; the harassment was becoming more serious and was heading towards something that could not be taken back. Thóra recalled the tiff between Friðrikka and Eyjólfur over the homosexual engineer. Although she was unable to be completely certain, it all looked as if the poor man had been made an outsider by the prejudices of his co-workers. At least that's what she had understood from the conversation, even though she also vaguely recalled Eyjólfur's argument that it was the man's alcoholism that had made him unpopular—or rather the fact that he had managed

161

to gain control over the disease, which had made him boringly holier-than-thou. It wasn't possible to determine, either from Oddný Hildur's messages or from her boss's reply, whether it was the man's sexual preference or his sobriety that had provoked the harassment.

Besides this, Thóra found an exchange of emails between Oddný Hildur and Arnar himself. It wasn't clear from these either what had caused the harassment or how Arnar felt about it. Thóra's interpretation was that he had tried to tough it out, and didn't feel comfortable complaining even though his co-workers' behaviour hurt him. Of course it must have. If Oddný Hildur's insinuations were anything to go by, it would have been bad enough to have had to endure it eight to ten hours a day, five days a week, but in this case workplace and home were merged into one for a huge portion of the year, with no refuge to be had anywhere. Thus, statements such as, *'It doesn't matter, I'm not going to let them affect me,'* and *'Luckily I don't care what others think of me,'* could not have been made with complete sincerity. Arnar had written them more to convince himself than Oddný Hildur; he had tried to build an invisible shield that protected him from all of it. However, one sentence clearly showed that if there were such a shield, it was not solid. Arnar had invited Oddný Hildur to coffee at his apartment one evening to discuss this and that; he had been thinking about quitting since *'this isn't working any more'*. This message was the last that Thóra found from him to Oddný Hildur, and it had been sent two days before the geologist disappeared. If she had answered him, her message had been deleted. It was certainly possible that

162

Oddný Hildur had accepted the invitation verbally; they worked in the same building and ate all their meals at the same table. It was actually strange that they should have e-mailed each other at all, although Thóra knew that she herself sent her colleagues e-mails when she didn't feel like getting up and speaking to them face to face. It was often just quicker that way. In any case, she would have to speak to this Arnar when they returned to Iceland.

The woman appeared to have had few friends to whom she sent e-mails, but that might not be the whole story. Thóra personally chose to keep her work e-mail separate from her personal e-mail, other than in exceptional circumstances. She used a different address for the personal mail and it was generally full to the brim with silly pictures, jokes and stories that one was supposed to forward to at least ten others, who doubtless cared as little for such rubbish as Thóra herself did. It could well be that Oddný Hildur had been drowning in e-mails from her friends and acquaintances but that that mailbox was located elsewhere in cyberspace. With things as they were, it would be of little use for Thóra to try to investigate the main e-mail applications in the hope that the geologist had let the computer save her password. It was fairly clear that Oddný Hildur's friends and relatives were not connected with her disappearance, but it was conceivable that the woman had sent them more comprehensive descriptions of the situation in the camp.

Suddenly Thóra missed her family terribly. Never before had she been out of touch with her children for so long. She longed to know what they were doing, how Orri's potty training was going and

163

whether Sóley was practising her violin, which she had recently started learning at her father's request. Thóra suspected that Hannes would be much less enthusiastic about the idea when the shrill notes started sounding through his house than he had been when he asked Thóra to encourage their daughter to practise. She hoped that everything was going well, and was especially concerned about Gylfi's relationship with his father. They had probably ended up arguing a bit while Thóra was away. Her little family was fragile and without her it lacked the padding that generally absorbed the worst knocks of daily life. She had to hold on to her chair to prevent herself from running out to the car and rushing over to the house of the woman in the village to phone home. Her hunger must be starting to affect her brain function; it was high time she had something to eat.

Matthew walked in. 'How's it going? I'm absolutely famished, and Bella's probably finished putting dinner together.'

'Bella? Is she cooking?' At that news Thóra's hunger disappeared like dew under the sun. 'What's on the menu? Barbecued seal fins and cigarette pudding?' She turned off the monitor in front of her.

'She didn't have anything to do so I thought it was the perfect assignment.' Matthew smiled at her. 'I would ask you out to eat but it's probably not that easy to get a table at such short notice at the restaurants round here.' He wrapped his arms around her shoulders. 'We're almost done here. The helicopter's coming not tomorrow, not the day after, but the day after that, so we actually only have two days left.'

164

Thóra smiled back at him. 'I'll never talk to you again if the weather prevents it.' She stood up and stretched. Her vertebrae cracked. 'The worst thing is that I feel we're making so little progress. I'm no closer to understanding what happened here, and every new piece of information we discover just complicates things.'

'At least we know how things look now, and Friðrikka says that she's advanced quite a long way with her assessment of the project. She can't see anything that would prevent her from finishing before we leave.' He pointed at a multi-coloured organizational chart that had been taped to the wall. 'You never know, we might just get to the bottom of this when we talk to the employees in Iceland.'

'If they want to talk to us,' said Thóra. 'It's entirely up to them.' She pulled herself together and pushed aside her pessimism. 'That would be interesting, actually. I found various things in Oddný Hildur's e-mail to confirm the harassment that Friðrikka mentioned. Maybe it played some part in this.'

'How?' asked Matthew. 'Did Oddný Hildur suffer because of it? Or the drillers?' His expression was one giant question mark. 'Do you think that all these people committed suicide?' Before Thóra could reply he interrupted himself: 'I wonder if that would be sufficient grounds to absolve Berg of responsibility for what's happened with the project?'

'No, probably not. It's up to the contractor to ensure that the atmosphere at the workplace is not harmful to the workers, either mentally or physically. No, I didn't mean that. These three

165

don't appear to have been affected by the bullying. Oddný Hildur was concerned about one of the engineers and didn't mention the drillers in this context, though I think they were more perpetrators than victims.'

'What do you base that on?'

'Nothing special. I scrutinized their computers and got the feeling that they were funny guys, the class clowns. I'm not saying they were the main perpetrators, but I can well imagine that they didn't hold back, although they might not have realized it was harassment.' Thóra rubbed her face. 'Actually, I don't know what I'm talking about. This probably had nothing to do with harassment. I'm just trying to fit what I came across with what we're investigating. This was probably an incredibly normal workplace, at least given the circumstances. It makes more sense to focus on the natives' stories about this place. At least they might shed some light on the question of the insurance, although they hardly explain everything.'

'We'll try to find the hunter,' said Matthew. 'Hopefully the snowmobile can be repaired. If not, then maybe that woman can find someone to take us by dogsled.'

'Or maybe we'll just wake up with wings and fly there.' Thóra went to the window and drew the curtain. She didn't know why she chose to do so—there was nothing but darkness outside. 'How's it been going otherwise?'

Matthew and the doctor had gone through the apartments of all the full-time employees one by one, in the hope of spotting something that hadn't come to light before. They had originally investigated with torches, before the electricity was

166

restored. 'We found two strange things,' replied Matthew. 'I'll show them to you on the way over to the cafeteria if you can bear to wait a few minutes before tasting Bella's delicacies.'

They put on their jackets and boots and went out into the darkness outside. The cold was refreshing and the air so still that their frozen breath did not rise into the air, but rather hung there before their faces for a moment before evaporating. The sky was bright with stars, so much more numerous and so much brighter than those Thóra was used to that it seemed like Greenland was closer to outer space than to any other earthly country. The Milky Way itself could be seen clearly as it lay in a dense, broad streak across the heavens. Thóra held on to Matthew and let him lead her so that she could stare into the sky. She hoped that if there were life on other planets, it was gentler than what Mother Nature had created on Earth. And not as cold.

'Careful, there's a platform ahead.' Matthew slowed his pace and Thóra looked down. They had arrived at one of the green units containing the workers' apartments. They were built in a straight line, in two sets of four. In front of each was a platform, and they stepped onto the one before them and stood there as Matthew took out a key and stuck it in the lock. He jiggled it for a moment, then opened the door. 'This is the apartment of one of the drillers, Halldór Grétarsson,' Matthew said. 'Be careful not to touch anything.'

They walked into the tiny vestibule, where they found a small coat rack upon which hung a yellow work coverall with wide reflective stripes and a fleece jacket, side by side. There wasn't a single down jacket to be seen. On the frame above it lay

167

a helmet that was both scratched and dirty. Next to the vestibule was a small bathroom with a shower. A shelf above the sink held a little electric razor, inexpensive-looking aftershave lotion, a toothbrush, hairbrush, deodorant and several cotton buds. Dental floss trailed from a white plastic box onto the shelf and halfway down to the sink. The apartment had a small kitchen that opened onto a rather austere sitting room with a two-seater sofa that looked extremely uncomfortable, a modern chair, a coffee table with a half-full ashtray and a shelving unit with a television and DVD player.

There were several books on the shelf above the DVD player and they appeared to Thóra to be all foreign crime novels. On one kitchen chair hung a down jacket, so the chances that the man had somehow made it out of the area looked rather slim. Off the sitting room was the bedroom, which was what Matthew had wanted to show her. Everything in there was a mess. There were towels and dirty clothes on the floor, along with a bucket that had been placed at the side of the bed. 'Well, now,' said Thóra. 'Not exactly the tidiest person.' In the poor man's defence, he probably hadn't expected anyone else to come into his apartment.

'But look here,' said Matthew, pointing at the bed. 'It looks to me like this might be blood.'

Thóra drew nearer. Matthew was right: on the pillow she could see what were clearly bloodstains. They weren't terribly large, but they were obviously more than dots from the man's last shave. There were four in total they seemed to form a kind of face: two eyes, a nose and a wide smirking mouth. 'Do you think the man was hit on the head as he slept?' Thóra bent down to take a better look at

168

the marks. There was something about them that bothered her. 'Was there something similar in the other man's room?'

'No,' said Matthew. 'There were several small stains on the floor, but nothing like this. Maybe we can get the police to come now.' He shook his head. 'It may well be that the other driller killed the man who lived here, got rid of the body and ran off. The blood in the other apartment might have dripped off him after he did the dirty deed.'

'You know what?' said Thóra, standing up straight. 'I need to show you something that's just as frightening as this is.' She pointed at the bloody pillow. 'Either I've finally gone completely crazy or these stains are exactly the same as those on one of the beds of the first residents of the area that I saw in those old photographs. One of the original inhabitants who was supposed to have died of hunger.'

Chapter 15

21 March 2008

Arnar's hands trembled. He sat on the bed and stared at the blank wall. It suited him just fine not to have anything else to look at. The uncontrollable movements of his hands bothered him only because the jerking prevented him from emptying his mind, from focusing only on the paint and the rough plaster behind it. As he concentrated on staring at the coarse surface he could push other, more difficult thoughts away. He changed from a man

169

tormented by distress and pain into a body that only performed the most basic of functions. He stared angrily at his fingers, which had shaken more than ever in the cold in Greenland and had deprived him of the peace of mind that he'd desired so much. He had considered asking the doctor for pills that would reduce the trembling, but he couldn't bring himself to do it. He doubtless needed to go through this, to meet the purifying fire completely exposed and without any assistance from the pharmaceutical industry. And there was no guarantee that he would get anything for it even if he asked.

It struck him just how unfair all of this was. The town was full of people who could drink without going down the same path as he did whenever he permitted himself to take a sip. Still, he had enough on his shoulders. Poor me, poor me, pour me a drink, he thought. Arnar looked from his trembling hands to the wall again, in the hope of rediscovering his calm place. He had to stop this whining. He had spent enough time in therapy to know he needed to abandon this self-pity and accept responsibility for his own behaviour. Yes, he was unlucky not to be able to resist alcohol, but no one had forced him into it. He raised the glass to his lips himself, knowing that he would be giving up his self-respect and common sense shortly afterwards. He needed to keep this fixed in his mind. He alone could keep the problem in check, lock the addiction behind imaginary bars where it would hiss and growl in his mind but be unable to bite him. He had long ago accepted that he would have to live with the craving; there was no magic solution that would take it away. The trick was just to accept it; not let the mind go to the moment when the first sip would trickle down his throat, bringing the promise that everything would be fine and one more drink wouldn't do him any harm. The problem wasn't how he felt when he stopped keeping tabs on his drinking; he would never even consider drinking if he felt that way after the first sip. When he was drunk the short-lived sense of well-being vanished, although he did not feel bad, exactly. He simply went numb, and his existence revolved around ensuring the next drink was within reach. No, it was the first mouthfuls that were dangerous, so dangerously good that he let himself be tempted time and time again, always just as convinced that this time he could put the cork back in after two—at the most three—glasses. Such bottomless stupidity and self-deception. Arnar stared at the paint and forced himself to concentrate on its texture. Maybe he should just commit himself to this place forever. He could sit here on the edge of the bed and look at the wall while his life went on and the years passed by outside. The world would go on turning even if he weren't around.

There was a light knock at the door and Arnar was forced to tear his eyes from the wall. He neither stood up nor invited the person standing outside to come in. After a moment the door opened and in peeked a woman he had seen in the corridor the day before. She was on the staff but didn't need her uniform to distinguish her from the patients. Her expression was too cheerful for her to be in treatment. Arnar looked at her and waited for her to state her business.

'How are you feeling?' she asked, smiling. Arnar wondered how often she had asked that same question with precisely that expression. He said nothing. 'We were hoping that you'd feel up to coming to the meeting, but you haven't come.' Arnar had no recollection of being told about this meeting. Of course he had little reason to attend; others' exaggerated tales of their own drinking were not of interest right now. 'It would do you good to meet other people, plus you also have to take an active role in the programme if you want it to produce results.'

Arnar turned his back to the wall. 'What do you think about killing animals?' he asked.

'Me?' asked the young woman, as if he could have meant someone else. 'I don't find it pleasant to think about, but it's okay if the animals are meant to be eaten.'

'And people?' asked Arnar, without changing his expression or his tone of voice. 'Is that all right?'

The silence in the doorway suggested that the young woman had never before discussed such a topic, even though she must have heard a thing or two in her career.

'No,' she finally answered, tentatively. 'I wouldn't say that.'

Arnar looked at her. She was beautiful, but the ridiculous blonde streaks in her long hair, the sunbed tan and the gaudy earrings did little for her. She could have been one of the endless stream of girls like that filling the streets downtown on the weekends, when they strutted around in little groups and hoped to be noticed. No doubt he judged her too harshly; she was unlikely to be a drinker and she might have become that tanned and her hair been bleached by spending a lot of time outdoors. He sensed that she was uncomfortable about the way he was staring at her.

'Sometimes I think it's okay.'

'I see.' The young woman looked a bit queasy. She had come to persuade him to go to a meeting, not to consider moral questions about whether or when a man should kill another. Arnar didn't know what her job was: nurse, psychologist, therapist or something entirely different. She couldn't be a doctor, she was too young for that, unless he underestimated her age. With each year that passed it became more difficult for him to guess young people's ages; he drew further and further away from youth, much to his dismay.

'But do you think there's good reason to punish those who have murdered someone?' He could see that she understood none of what he was saying. 'The damage is already done; what purpose does it serve?'

The woman looked at the clock and glanced nervously down the corridor. 'It's not my department, but I do think people should be punished for the crimes they commit. It doesn't do any good to act as if nothing happened and not avenge the person who died.'

'Avenge them?' said Arnar thoughtfully, looking away from the woman. 'But what if the person who committed murder was in fact avenging another death? Wouldn't that just be a vicious circle?' He closed his eyes and wished for the millionth time that he were religious. Then he would find it much easier to separate things into black and white.

'Is there any particular reason you're thinking about this?' The smile she had bestowed upon him when she'd first knocked at his door had vanished.

'No.' Arnar couldn't put her through a confession of his problems. She probably had enough of

173

her own—like everyone else, in fact. 'I was just thinking.'

'I would like to suggest that you set up an appointment with the psychiatrist.' The girl appeared to be having trouble deciding whether she should insist that Arnar attend the meeting or whether his condition and behaviour suggested that it would be better if he were allowed to continue to rest. 'These kinds of thoughts don't do any good and I'm sure you'd feel better after speaking to someone. But I'm not the right person.'

Arnar nodded. 'No, probably not.' He thought for a moment and realized that he shouldn't discuss this with this woman or anyone else. He was not so stupid as to think that blathering about it would change anything. Some things were simply impossible to change. The dead don't come back to life. He tried to compensate for this oversight.

'Don't worry. I don't need to talk to anyone, I'm just a little distracted at the moment.' He stood up. 'I'd better come to this meeting.' His hands were trembling more than ever before. 'Would you mind checking whether I could have something for this?' He held out his hands and they both watched his fingers quiver, almost as if he were doing it on purpose, exaggerating his condition like the people now spilling their guts at the meeting. But he was not. His nervous system was perfectly capable of making his fingers shake on their own. Perhaps it was a consequence of the chill in his wretched heart, from which no warmth in this world could free him. Pills would change nothing; he regretted having asked for them and hoped that the woman would forget his request. He didn't want to see a doctor; he didn't want to see anyone. He only

174

wished to be left alone, to allow his discomfort to root itself so deeply in his body that it would branch out into his bone marrow. He did not deserve to feel any better than he did now; if he suffered hellishly enough, perhaps over time he could cleanse himself of the guilt and try to start a new life.

*   *   *

Igimaq had nothing against waiting, and his old friend Sikki must have known that he wouldn't give up and leave. He knew Igimaq too well for that. Sikki should have tried to find another way to get rid of him, because there was no hunter better at sitting motionless and letting time pass. He spent days and days out on the ice, patiently awaiting his prey. His father had taught him the best way to do this: free oneself almost completely from one's thoughts, allow them to wander as if in a daydream. He could induce this state of mind without closing his eyes, and, more importantly, without shifting his attention from the environment and what was in his line of vision. After Sikki's wife had slammed the door in his face, declaring that her husband was not at home and was not expected in the near future, he had taken a seat on the steps outside the house and started his wait. This was his third attempt to meet the man, and this time he had been careful to approach the house unseen, so that Sikki would not be aware of him. He had also chosen to come a bit later in the day, when it was likely that Sikki would be at home.

Sikki's wife looked out now and then in the hope that he had gone away, but apart from that, little

175

disturbed the hunter. A teenage girl had walked past and looked askance at him before quickening her pace and disappearing down the street. There was no one left in town who dressed like him, so she did not need great powers of deduction to work out who was sitting there on the steps. Her gait reminded him of his daughter Usinna when she was the same age; he'd always been enamoured by the way every step she took appeared to have a purpose, to bring her closer to the unexpected adventures that she was convinced awaited her around the corner. He hadn't been surprised when she pressed hard to be allowed to go and study in Denmark several years later, and he hadn't opposed her, which would have been useless. Usinna would have gone anyway. Even so, he regretted not having tried to forbid her leaving, to demand that she take care of her family, find herself a husband and sustain the circle of life. Maybe everything would have turned out differently if he'd done that.

He heard the door creak behind him and looked round. Sikki stood in the doorway frowning down at him. 'Look who's here. You clearly haven't changed much, Igimaq. Except your appearance, because you look as decrepit as I do.'

The hunter stood up and stared into the eyes of his childhood friend. 'I need to talk to you.' There was no reason to reproach Sikki for making him sit out in the cold. 'I choose to do so where we will be left alone.' He suspected that Sikki would prefer not to let him in and although he had nothing against continuing to sit outside, the subject matter was sensitive and not appropriate for discussing in public.

Sikki frowned again but signalled to him to

come inside. He showed him to a small and rather unattractive room that was lit by a single floor lamp. 'I need to replace the bulb in the ceiling light,' muttered Sikki as he sat down. He had an undeniable air of authority, although he wasn't like his father, who would never have showed such weakness as to allow his gaze to budge from Igimaq's face. He would have stared the hunter down, and easily. 'I'm tired, Igimaq. What's so urgent?'

'More people have come to the work camp.' Igimaq felt uncomfortable in the chair in which he sat. Sikki hadn't offered to take his jacket and he was boiling hot in his thick winter clothing.

'I'm aware of that.' Sikki shifted in his chair and reached out to turn up the heat on the radiator.

'Don't you remember what we were taught, Sikki?' The hunter stared at his friend. 'We are responsible for this area.' He recalled as if it were yesterday how the two of them had been entrusted with this task; Igimaq because he was a direct descendant of the greatest hunters in the village on his father's side, and Sikki because he was in line to become the next angekokk, or shaman, as his father and grandfather had been before him. Sikki was supposed to be able to heal the sick and communicate with the dead, although Igimaq had never seen any sign of such abilities in his friend. When the two of them were entrusted with this great responsibility they were a full sixteen years old and it was clear that they would follow the path intended for them, the trail that their ancestors had already blazed, although Sikki probably did not possess the powers that his ancestors had been endowed with at birth.

177

Sikki narrowed his eyes and breathed through his nose, as though to make himself appear tougher. It did not work, and he seemed to sense it. He adopted a more normal expression and began. 'The world has changed, Igimaq. What we were taught no longer applies, and the fact that you are trying to uphold the old way of life doesn't change the fact that it's on the way out. Take us, for example. I don't have a son and yours is hardly following in your footsteps, as I understand it.'

'That has nothing to do with it, Sikki.' Igimaq felt a bead of sweat run down his back. 'You know that very well. This isn't about old times.'

'I know, I know,' muttered Sikki. 'What do you suggest I do? Drive the people away?' He snorted. 'This mine is the best thing that has happened here in years. Maybe we'll finally have work for the young folk. You have no idea how badly they want respectable jobs. It's not healthy for anyone to live on what comes in an envelope once a month for doing nothing at all. They've got to have something to do and it should be as clear to you as it is to me that they can't make a living in the old ways. That time has passed. No one wants to buy what we have to sell. These days we're lucky to get three hundred Danish crowns per sealskin, if we find someone to buy them. You know more than anyone how much work goes into tanning the skins.'

The hunter shrugged, causing several more drops of sweat to run down his spine. All the trades that had previously kept the village alive had been prohibited. It would be easier for them to try selling snow than sealskins or whale products. 'You swore to your ancestors that you would ensure the area wouldn't be built on or disturbed. The mine can be

178

dug elsewhere.'

Sikki stared at Igimaq, no longer foolishly trying to assert his authority. Instead he wore a look of sadness, as if he felt more sorry for his friend than he could put into words. 'It doesn't work like that. Either the mine will be there or in some other place entirely, so far away that it may as well be one of the stars in the sky.' He shook his head very slowly as if he wished that they were sixteen again and ready and able for anything, not two old men who had lost their grip on what mattered. 'There's nothing we can do.'

'What has changed since my Usinna was there?' Igimaq felt his heart skip a beat and for a second the oppressive heat didn't matter to him. 'Tell me.'

A large drop of sweat formed at Sikki's hairline and ran down his forehead. 'Don't blame me for that.'

'I'm not, Sikki. I'm simply asking you what has changed. You took your responsibilities very seriously back then.' He was unable to continue. The gait of the young girl he had watched walk down the street had ripped open old wounds he had thought healed.

Sikki rubbed the arm of his chair with his thick, strong hands. 'I've just explained it to you. These days everything is at stake. If there is no mine there will be no village. Everyone here will go. Most of them are still scared of the mine but that will change, and then our young folk might be able to finally hold their heads higher. I'm telling you, if nothing becomes of the mine, everyone will leave. Maybe not tomorrow, but over time.'

'What does it matter?' Igimaq spat, displaying more anger than he had intended. 'If our people

179

want to live their lives in the same way as those in the cities then there is no reason for them to keep living here. There's enough work to be had in Nuuk for everyone who lives here.'

Sikki had no answer for this. 'It will be all right. Trust me.'

'Like I trusted you with Usinna?' said Igimaq softly. 'It cost her her life. How many more people need to die before the price of these mining jobs of yours will be considered too high?'

'That's enough for now.' Sikki stood up, his cheeks red. 'It's impossible to discuss this with you. You don't understand.'

Igimaq followed the example of his former friend and stood up as well. 'I understand perfectly. It's you who understands nothing.' He walked out of the room, refusing to greet Sikki's wife who stood wide-eyed in the hallway. She had probably been listening in but he couldn't care less about that now. Sikki followed him to the vestibule, which could hardly be crossed for the pairs of shoes covering the little floor. As Igimaq opened the door Sikki spoke again, wanting to get in the last word.

'It was in your power to save her, Igimaq,' he said slowly, without much emotion. 'She even thought right until the end that you would, but you chose your honour and your dusty old obligations to our ancestors over her. Don't forget that when you condemn me.'

As if the hunter would ever forget.

Chapter 16

21 March 2008

'The snowmobile and the cars didn't break down by themselves. Who could have tampered with them?' Alvar directed his words at a flower pot on a windowsill in the lounge. The plant had certainly seen better days and it now lay on its side, brown and withered. All minds now focused on the theory that something had been added to the petrol tanks: sugar, or something else that had damaged the engines when they were started. 'Wasn't there also a suspicion that the drilling equipment had been tampered with?' Alvar turned to the team, looked at them without meeting any of their eyes, then started examining his hands. 'That's what I thought, anyway.'

'I need you to come with me and photograph this, Alvar,' said Thóra as cheerfully as she could without sounding idiotic. 'It would also be good if you could prepare a short report on what you've found out.' She turned to Matthew. 'We're even wondering whether we should make arrangements to transport the vehicles to Iceland to have them looked over by mechanics, or get someone to come here.'

Matthew nodded and made an unsuccessful attempt to suppress a yawn. He had been silent since the end of supper. It looked as though the lack of sleep the last few nights had started to take its toll. The simple food had scarcely increased his stamina: pasta with tinned sauce that had so little flavour that they might as well have used milk. He wasn't alone in being tired: Dr Finnbogi had found it difficult to swallow his food between yawns, and it looked to Thóra as if Friðrikka had dozed off. Eyjólfur had gone straight to his room to sleep after supper, while the others had gathered in the lounge, with the exception of Bella, who had been assigned the task of washing up. Perhaps this strange herd mentality could be attributed to fatigue; Thóra didn't know about the others, but she always felt sleepy after being out in the open for a long time and breathing in too much oxygen. 'Can't we move the return journey forward?' Friðrikka appeared more than just tired; her face was grey and she had dark circles under her eyes. 'It was a mistake to come here.'

'It won't be long now,' muttered the doctor. He looked back towards the window where the potted plant stood, and stared at the pitch-black glass. 'That is, if the weather stays decent.'

'I'm sure it will,' said Thóra, with false optimism. She ignored the vague whistling of the wind that carried in from outside. 'In any case, won't you be able to finish all your work?'

Friðrikka nodded miserably. 'Of course, of course. I'll be finished with most of it tomorrow, and then I'll make copies of what I can't go over and look at it back in Iceland.' Talking about work seemed to cheer her up a bit. 'It hasn't been that much work; they didn't accomplish much after I left, so going over the data has been relatively easy. They should never have tried to work here beyond the New Year.' She added, smugly: 'As I actually pointed out more than once.'

Thóra vaguely recalled seeing it mentioned

in the documents accompanying the contract that conditions at the work site made it almost impossible to work there during the first four months of the year. It had been left to Berg Technology to decide when the work would be done, but this had been pointed out to ensure the company realized that it could not aim for full-capacity production all year round. 'Why did they keep working after the New Year?' she asked. 'Was it because of the delays?'

'Yes, I suppose so,' said Friðrikka. 'This came up before I resigned and understandably the idea of carrying on was not very popular. Part of the reason the employees were willing to take on this job was the long winter break. That was the last straw for me; after Oddný Hildur's disappearance there was no way I was going to take on extra responsibilities for such a crappy employer.'

Alvar stood up dramatically. It was as if he had been insulted by Friðrikka's negativity and could not bear any more of this dreariness. 'I'm going to bed,' he said.

'Oh, hell,' exclaimed the doctor. 'I was going to offer you a nightcap.' He slapped the arm of his chair with both hands. 'Is everyone going to bed?'

Alvar stopped awkwardly in his tracks. It was abundantly clear that he was dying for a drink and would happily have taken back his previous announcement. 'Well, I guess bed-time could wait a bit,' he said, sitting down again gently. 'I'm not in that big a rush.'

Thóra tried not to smile at the poor man, mindful of his purchases at the duty free shop. 'Good idea.' She smiled at the doctor. 'I have a bottle of Opal liquorice schnapps if anyone is interested.' Matthew

183

frowned, but stood up nevertheless to go and get the drink, which Thóra knew he could only have found less appealing if it were popcorn-flavoured. The doctor followed him and Thóra hoped that while walking down the corridor they would take the opportunity to discuss the bloodstains on Dóri's pillow.

After examining them thoroughly Thóra had dragged Matthew back over to the office building to show him the old photographs and convince him of how oddly similar they were to the stains on the beds of the unfortunate first settlers. Matthew had had to admit that the similarities were striking, and before they sat down at the supper table they had got the doctor to examine the evidence as well as the photos. Finnbogi couldn't actually say anything about the stains or why they appeared to have doppelgangers from the past, but he felt that it was probably coincidence. Thóra found this rather unlikely and tried to convince him that for unknown reasons someone had tried to imitate the ugly scene in the tents. However, he and Matthew both seemed adamant that this did not prove the original inhabitants had died of anything other than starvation, let alone been murdered—their main reasoning being that no one would have had any incentive to want these people dead. They could hardly have been engaged in disputes with others and they were certainly not in conflict with neighbouring settlements, since there were none around. The men relented a bit when Thóra asked whether death by starvation caused bleeding from the head, but they warmed to their theme again when the doctor said that the stains in the photographs were likely to be something other than blood; shadows, or some sort of dirt that could be explained by something other than violence. If they were bloodstains, they would be both larger and more widespread. However, although it was difficult to reach any conclusion about the old photographs, it seemed pretty clear to Thóra that the stains on the driller's pillow could only be blood, although it wasn't clear how it had got there.

Bella walked into the lounge and they could see from her expression that doing the washing up hadn't been her idea of a good time. Thóra found that understandable: the water was obtained by melting snow, so it took a long time to wash the few dishes and pots that they used. 'I'm not doing that again,' she thundered. 'I don't care how busy you lot pretend to be.' She looked contemptuously at Thóra, Alvar and Friðrikka as they sat there relaxing.

'My dear, sit down and unwind. It's not as if we haven't all had to do the dishes at some point.' Friðrikka's expression was no more friendly than Bella's. Thóra felt as if she were at a gathering of people with social disorders. 'We were just going to sit here and chat a bit. Hopefully about anything other than this work site.' As she said this, Friðrikka looked right at Thóra.

Thóra smiled back in the hope of lightening the mood. If Friðrikka always acted like this, she had nothing but sympathy for her co-workers in this isolated place. 'I'm up for that,' she said. 'There are countless other topics. You get the ball rolling, and I won't hold back.'

No one said anything and while Bella took her seat the other three sat silently, staring straight ahead. The only topics that Thóra could think of

185

were connected to their project and she suspected that the same went for Alvar and Friðrikka. She hoped Matthew and the doctor would get back soon with the drinks. That would certainly loosen their tongues, and even Alvar would talk the hind legs off a donkey after tossing back a few shots of Opal. Maybe things would get so lively that she would slip on some of her party clothes, since she had brought such a splendid variety. The floor of the corridor outside the lounge creaked and everyone cheered up.

'Well,' said Thóra, looking around. 'Are there any wine glasses here?'

'No,' replied Friðrikka. 'The camp's regulations prohibit drinking, so the only glasses are the ones in the kitchen.'

She prepared to stand up to go and get them, but Thóra beat her to it. 'Did you all really follow the rules?' she asked on her way out.

'No,' Friðrikka said again. 'It's impossible to forbid adults to drink unless it interferes with their work. Arnar was strongly opposed to people drinking here, but no one listened to him. It wasn't that much really, we stayed here for months at a time and never brought anything more than the amount allowed by customs, and maybe a case of beer we bought in Kulusuk if we had time before continuing on our way here. Arnar just made himself scarce the few times that we drank here in the lounge. Now and then, on special occasions, the company served wine with dinner and invited us to drinks in the evening—when we were here over the holidays, for instance.' She pointed at a printed poster on the wall next to the doorway, announcing a Midwinter Feast that was to have been held on

186

Saturday 16 February. For such a small workforce, a lot of effort had clearly been put into the event: a banquet director had been nominated and the evening's entertainment included everything from bingo to a karaoke contest. 'I expect there would have been alcohol at that,' she declared.

Thóra met Matthew and Finnbogi at the door. Matthew was holding a plastic bottle with the colourful Opal label, and the doctor a bottle of cognac. She hoped he wouldn't mind drinking from a milk glass. The only glasses she could see in the cabinets were the same as the ones they used for their suppers, clumsy cafeteria glasses that stood upside down among the small white coffee cups and a few larger and more colourful mugs. These looked like they belonged to particular employees, and Thóra started looking through them automatically. When she picked up a mug decorated with blue flowers and inscribed *Oddný Hildur*, the good mood that had slowly been overcoming her physical fatigue disappeared again. She hurriedly put the mug back in its place, surprised that the woman's co-workers hadn't removed it so as not to be constantly reminded of her disappearance. Perhaps they thought that would be a symbolic defeat: by getting rid of the mug they would be admitting she was dead. Thóra hurriedly gathered seven glasses in her arms, one extra in case Eyjólfur showed up.

The refrigerator started up unexpectedly and noisily, and Thóra was so startled she thanked her stars that she didn't drop the glasses. Adrenaline rushed through her veins and her heart beat wildly; it calmed down quickly, but she hastened out of the lonely cafeteria nonetheless.

187

Shortly after they had filled their glasses Eyjólfur appeared, looking dishevelled. 'Is this where you all are?' he snorted. 'I fell asleep.' He plonked himself down next to the door. 'Did anything happen while I was sleeping?' He smiled sarcastically, clearly convinced that they were no closer to getting to the bottom of things as they'd been earlier in the evening. When no one answered, he looked indifferently at the window. 'The weather's getting worse. My window woke me up shaking and rattling.' He laughed mirthlessly. 'I was so confused when I woke up that I thought for a moment there was someone outside knocking on my window.' He yawned again. 'I even thought it was Bjarki.'

'Ugh, Eyjólfur.' Friðrikka put down her glass. 'We're trying to forget what happened here. I don't know about the others but I don't want Bjarki to appear in front of me out there, like the living dead.' She fell silent.

Suddenly the ceiling light dimmed. They heard a loud bang and saw a sudden bright light outside. 'What the hell?' Alvar, who was sitting near the window, stood up and shaded his eyes. Friðrikka let out a low moan and Eyjólfur grabbed the arms of his chair with both hands and squeezed until his knuckles whitened. Although they were all startled, the light did not induce such extreme reactions in Thóra, Matthew, Bella and Dr Finnbogi.

'What was that?' asked Thóra, when it became clear no one else was about to say anything. 'Did a car go past?' Maybe the helicopter pilots had come to fetch them by land.

Friðrikka was breathing rapidly. 'Those are the floodlights that were set up after Oddný Hildur disappeared. The security guard suggested them.'

188

'And?' The doctor seemed just as puzzled as Thóra.

'And they come on if movement is detected by the sensors attached to posts around the camp. The idea was to scare away any polar bears or other unwelcome visitors.'

'Is there a polar bear out there?' The Opal had definitely started to make itself felt and Thóra felt quite exhilarated at the thought of seeing one. Standing up, she went to the window, pressed her face against it and peered out. The lights, mounted on two tall towers, made the white snow even brighter. She hadn't noticed them earlier.

'Get away from the window.' Eyjólfur's tone was stern. 'It's probably not a bear.'

'How do you know?' asked the doctor, who had followed Thóra's example and looked out. There was no answer.

Thóra moved away from the cold glass. 'What is it then?' If she'd been tipsy before, the feeling had left her abruptly. She imagined the bloodstains on the driller's pillow and wondered whether the floodlights had gone on just before he had started to bleed.

'It's not an animal.' Friðrikka ran her hand through her red hair. It was so dirty that it stood up on its own. 'The system hasn't been working since we arrived. I'd even forgotten about it. It has to be turned on, and a polar bear can't do that.'

Now they all understood why Friðrikka and Eyjólfur had reacted as they did. 'Where does one turn on the system?' Now Matthew had stood up and come over to the window, despite Eyjólfur's warnings. He peered out but saw no more than Thóra had. 'And where are the sensors?'

189

'The sensors are located between the towers, and they're turned on from the office building. It's rather complicated, meaning no one can do it by accident. The equipment is under the steps.' Eyjólfur looked at Friðrikka. 'Did you turn on the system?'

'No, of course not.' Friðrikka seemed even more alarmed. 'I hadn't even remembered it.' Their old mutual animosity was stirring again. 'And are you going to say next that I set off the floodlights? I was sitting here, in case you've forgotten. Just like you.'

Matthew interrupted. 'None of us did this.' He turned back to the window. 'Probably some animal wandered through the sensor beam and ran off when the lights went on.' He looked around at everyone. 'Did anyone mess with the equipment at the office building?' No one spoke up. Matthew looked out one last time and stared at the lifeless environment until the floodlights suddenly flicked off, leaving him looking only at his own reflection in dark glass. 'It must have been caused by a power outage. It was probably on the whole time but someone connected the electricity this evening, which brought power back to the system.'

Everyone was happy with this conjecture. This was one of those moments when it was good to have some sort of explanation, however unlikely. The healing power of words destroyed doubt, and everyone contributed by murmuring 'of course' and 'that must be it'.

They sat down again shamefacedly and tried to revive the cheerful mood that had developed earlier. The bottles were quick to empty and it wasn't long before Alvar started fidgeting in his seat. Friðrikka, who also appeared to want more,

190

stood and announced that she was going to check whether the wine kept there for celebrations was still in its place. 'Was there any alcohol left after the Midwinter Feast, Eyjólfur?'

'No idea. I wasn't here.'

At that Friðrikka left, and Thóra drank the remainder of the Opal from her glass. She wasn't sure that she'd want any more when Friðrikka returned; the alcohol would just make her sleepier. It looked as if Matthew was in the same state, but all the others appeared to have been refreshed by the drinks; the frown had even vanished from Bella's face, though she was still several glasses away from smiling. So fatigue was probably the reason why Thóra and Matthew were the last to react when Friðrikka's screams carried into the lounge.

Chapter 17

21 March 2008

Arnar's hands had stopped trembling, but instead of relief, he only felt regret. That in itself didn't really matter; he didn't expect to feel better any time soon, and the regret wasn't the worst of it. What bothered him was that he didn't know what he regretted, what he was missing. It wasn't the trembling of his fingers, but something else, something he could not grasp. There was enough to choose from: mistakes from the past that he would never have the chance to mend; money that was gone and the debts it had left behind; friendships that would never be revived.

191

No one thing stood out.

He had started from a dreamless sleep from which he felt he had derived no rest, because he was just as exhausted as when he had laid his head on the pillow. It was possible that he'd only slept for a short time; he had lost his watch and since he wasn't allowed a mobile phone in therapy he couldn't use that to see how much time had passed. It was pitch-black outside, but that meant nothing; the sun didn't come up until around nine in the morning at this time of year. He could always wander into the hallway and ask the night guard what time it was, but he didn't feel like it, knowing that if he got out of bed it would be even harder to get back to sleep. He tried in vain to think of something positive. All that came to mind other than the hopelessness of his life was the empty bed facing him. It had previously contained his roommate, an alcoholic who had suffered arrhythmia and been taken to hospital. The man had snored terribly and would occasionally talk in his sleep. This should have made it easier to sleep soundly without him, but that wasn't the case. In fact, Arnar wouldn't have long to wait before another person took the man's place; in fact, it was a little strange that the gap had not been filled the next day. Arnar suspected it was because of his sexual orientation, which he had admitted to the group early on, during his second day of therapy. He had decided to come out with it immediately to prevent the men from talking to him about 'chicks' and picking up women. The story had spread like wildfire throughout the treatment centre. He couldn't care less; everyone here shared a problem with alcohol, first and foremost, and no doubt welcomed having something else to talk about. By revealing this information he also ensured himself a certain privacy, because it meant the men generally avoided him; but on the flip side, the women, who were in the minority, paid him more attention than before. Arnar didn't believe that the men avoided him because of any antipathy toward homosexuals; they simply had enough to contend with, without complicating life by spending time with a fellow addict who might also be eyeing them up. As it happened, Arnar had no interest in anyone at the centre, either as a sexual partner or as a friend; it would be a long time before his desire for sex or companionship reawakened. Luckily, others couldn't possibly know that.

Maybe his former roommate, the old snorer, had invented his heart ailment for fear that Arnar might try to take him by force in his sleep. Arnar smiled for the first time since being admitted. The man was in his sixties and slept wearing his false teeth, that produced a wet clack at the start and end of every snore. Arnar would never have dreamed of it.

His smile vanished as abruptly as it had appeared. He didn't deserve to regain his happiness, any more than anyone else who had selfishly and stupidly extinguished the light in the eyes of a fellow human being. He recalled the words of a woman he had sat next to at lunch. This young woman had sat hunched over her plate, looking completely broken. Under normal circumstances she would probably have been good-looking, but now she resembled a zombie. She had nodded at Arnar when she sat down next to him but hadn't followed it up with any polite chatter. After picking at her food for a long time without taking so much as a single bite, the woman had suddenly turned to Arnar and told

193

him that pasta had always been her favourite food. She said it mechanically, as if reading from a sheet of paper. When she opened her mouth, a sore on her upper lip tore open. A thick, dark red bead of blood formed in one corner of her mouth and fell to the brown plate, whence it ran slowly down into her pile of tortellini. The woman did nothing to try to stop the bleeding and instead continued to talk, announcing to Arnar that she would never again have a favourite food nor take pleasure in anything whatsoever. She would never smile again. Then she picked up her plate in her frail-looking hands and left without saying goodbye. Arnar didn't need to be psychic to notice the pale mark on the ring finger of her left hand. It was easy to imagine what had happened. More often than not, the patients who had it toughest at Vogur Hospital were young women who had lost the love of their husband or children on their way to the bottom. He lost his own appetite at the thought of children sitting with their father at the supper table, wondering why their mother couldn't be like other mothers. It was a blessing that he himself had no offspring to offend with his drinking.

He turned onto his side and wished he could have brought his iPod. Music usually helped when he wanted to focus on something other than his own wretchedness. He had to content himself with thinking about which songs he would play if he had access to it. After putting together a list in his mind he let the songs play from memory, and although he didn't get the lyrics right he managed to stick to the melody in more or less most of them. When he was halfway through the fifth song he realized that the singers were all rather gloomy and perfect for kindling the self-pity that simmered inside him as it had done before. He abandoned his interior playlist. Why couldn't they watch TV here? That was good sleeping medicine, given how boring it had been the few times he'd watched it. Even the snorer was better than nothing; Arnar could look at him and try to imagine that he was watching a live feed from some reality series. That was far better than wondering what had caused the sadness that engulfed him.

Arnar pulled the bedclothes down over his toes. His room was cold, since he'd left the window wide open to make sure that he wouldn't wake with a headache, as he'd done the day before. Greenland came to mind, cold and lonely, just like him. His robe hung on a hook on the wall at the end of his bed and he considered putting it on to make himself warmer beneath the covers. He decided not to, since it was unbearable enough having to put it on and take it off, day in day out, without doing so at night as well. He had had a wonderful duvet in Greenland, which he had splurged on after his first work tour. The quilt he'd received from Berg Technology had been similar to the one he lay under now, filled with polyester or some other artificial material that crumpled stiffly over him with each movement. He hoped no one would take the duvet before he could make arrangements to send for his belongings. If someone broke into his place there wasn't anything else to steal, except perhaps the old laptop he'd used mainly to watch movies. He couldn't imagine anyone would want that old piece of junk, but one never knew. What had disappeared from the camp hadn't exactly all been important or valuable. He'd lost a pair of snow boots, and a hat that he couldn't imagine a thief would be able to resell. He had owned the boots for many years, and the only reason he hadn't thrown them away was that he felt it was useful to have a worn-out pair of boots for walking between the buildings at the work camp. When they were stolen, he thought at first that it was yet another practical joke played by his co-workers at his expense and thus didn't ask around for them until it became clear that that was not the case. Thieves who found a reason to steal worn-out old moon boots and a matching hat were just as likely to nab a laptop. And the bedspread. It was also possible that his co-workers had taken it and damaged it, just to make life miserable for him. That would have been typical.

He found it unpleasant to let his mind wander to his old workplace, even though he'd managed to avoid thinking about what caused him the most pain. It was bad enough to be reminded of the endless teasing that had got worse and worse the longer it went on. At the recollection of it he felt a stabbing pain in his chest, and a familiar ache as though they actually had punched him. The only difference was that if he had been subjected to physical violence the pain would have disappeared long ago, along with the bruises. Worst of all, he could neither discuss this in the group nor with the psychiatrist or therapist. It would probably ease his mind to speak to a professional, but it might not and it wasn't worth the risk. He wanted people to like him, but that wouldn't happen if he told the whole story as it had really occurred. They would think him an idiot who deserved everything he got. The staff had already started regarding him askance, clearly sensing that something more than his alcoholism was troubling him. It had been a mistake to speak to the girl the night before, about good and evil. She had probably told his therapist about their conversation. At least his sponsor had paid Arnar more attention today than on previous days and had called in on him repeatedly to find out how he was doing.

For example, the therapist had asked Arnar why he never called his friends or relatives. The man apparently kept tabs on him, because when Arnar lied that he'd made several phone calls that morning, the man shook his head and said that that wasn't strictly true, was it; he knew Arnar hadn't called anyone since he had been admitted, when he'd asked to be allowed to call his employer to inform them that he was in rehab. Arnar dropped the subject, finding it easier than telling the truth— that he had no one to call. His mother was dead, and his relationship with his father so fragile that it would certainly be shattered if he called him— again—from Vogur. His two brothers had had more than enough of him and the same went for the small group of people he had once considered his friends. If he wanted to have a comforting phone conversation with someone he would have to call the Red Cross helpline, and he hadn't sunk that low yet. Tomorrow he would go and ask if he could have some money from the pocket of the jacket he'd been made to leave behind along with his other belongings on admission. Then he would call directory enquiries and ask for some random addresses and phone numbers. If he were lucky this would get noticed and they would think he was calling someone close to him. Maybe then they would look at him like any other patient.

Arnar heard footsteps out in the corridor. This was either the night guard on his rounds or someone on the day shift just starting work. He didn't know which would be worse, that the night was young or the morning close at hand; he didn't like either option. He determined to try to sleep. To stop thinking about what was past, since it meant little when all was said and done. He could change none of it. It was equally useless to wonder about the future, since it wasn't in his hands. The moment was the only thing that he could control; try to rest, and not worry about everything under the sun. Arnar squeezed his eyes shut again and started counting in his head. It didn't have the intended effect. One—lost employee; two—also lost; three—dead. One—lost employee; two—also lost; three—dead. One—lost employee; two—also lost; three—dead. He wanted a drink desperately, despite having resolved to stop. Surprisingly enough, it wasn't the effect of being drunk that tugged at him; instead he missed the dreamless sleep, the ability to drink away his consciousness and turn off his brain, allowing it to rest. Even his bad conscience could not hold out against the alcohol. It always won.

*   *   *

Friðrikka had been bursting into tears at regular intervals, and her puffy face glistened with tears and mucus. Thóra took care not to reveal how little she wanted to look at this but tried to stay cheerful and comfort her. She was unused to soothing the tears of grown-ups and didn't know where to begin.

In the end she just sighed and laid her hand gently on Friðrikka's shoulder. The men, who had been standing around awkwardly, seemed relieved. They had all looked to Thóra in unison in the hope that she would do something. Although no one said a word it was clear that she had to take care of this, as the only other woman there besides Friðrikka and Bella. 'It'll be all right.' Thóra couldn't think of anything better to say. 'We'll let the police know, and now they'll have to come.'

'There's red wine on my socks,' snivelled the geologist, starting to pull off the offending items. 'It looks like blood.' She wasn't the only one; she'd dropped two bottles of the stuff on the ground and they'd all stepped in it as they rushed to get to her.

'What were you doing inside the freezer?' It was perhaps better to speak normally to the woman rather than encourage more tears by being overly compassionate. 'Surely you didn't find the bottles of wine in there?'

'What?' Friðrikka looked up and stared dully at Thóra. She was holding one of her socks. Suddenly she seemed to pull herself together. She spoke slowly, and once or twice a hiccup interrupted what she was saying. 'The wine is stored in the cook's office and I went there first. I only found three bottles and I thought that wouldn't be enough, so I decided to check and see whether there was any brennivín.' Out of the corner of her eye Thóra noticed Matthew shudder. 'They served some at the Midwinter Feast when I was here and it didn't get finished, and it occurred to me that it had probably also been served the previous February and there might be some left over. It was stored in the freezer last year, so I went in there.' The walk-in freezer was rather large. There were shelves along the walls and although several of them were empty some of them still held packaged meat, frozen bread and bags of vegetables. The freezer had a heavy steel door that now stood halfway open, allowing air to stream into the kitchen in cold gusts. A red alarm light spun in circles on the wall to warn that the door was open.

'But why did you lift the plastic sheet?' asked Thóra. 'Wasn't the brennivín kept on a shelf?'

Friðrikka closed her eyes and tears squeezed out of them. She stifled a sob; she was apparently reliving her moment of terror. 'I thought that the cook might have hidden the bottle so that no one could sneak a drink from it. I saw the pile at the back of the freezer and peeked under the plastic to see if the bottle might be there.' She opened her eyes. 'I didn't expect *this*.'

'Hasn't anyone looked there since we arrived?' asked Eyjólfur. 'When we were looking for Dóri and Bjarki, for instance?' They all shook their heads.

'It didn't occur to us that we might find someone inside the freezer,' said the doctor apologetically. 'I looked in the kitchen, and completely overlooked that possibility.'

'I think we should shut the freezer and go back,' said Matthew. 'The police will have to take over and it's important that we disturb the scene as little as possible, things being as they are.' They had all pushed into the freezer to see what had caused Friðrikka such agitation. 'It was a mistake to go in there in the first place, and it's best not to make a bad thing worse.'

'Was it Oddný Hildur?' Friðrikka looked

200

inquisitively at Matthew. 'I didn't look. I couldn't.'

Matthew shook his head. 'No, it was a man, as far as I could see.' Friðrikka let out a sigh of relief, then her expression became mournful again. 'Dóri or Bjarki?'

'No.' Eyjólfur shook his head. 'It was neither of them.'

'What *happened* here?' None of this had seemed to have any particular effect on Bella until now, but suddenly she seemed just as stunned as the others. 'Three people missing, and when we finally find someone, it's a completely different person.'

Thóra got goosebumps. What the hell was in the freezer? Who had taken the trouble to put the disgusting frozen corpse of this unknown man there? 'Could this have been there the whole time?' she asked. 'Maybe it was put there before when the floodlights went on, and whoever did it might still be in here somewhere.' She looked around instinctively as if she expected a madman to jump out of the large dishwasher.

Friðrikka screamed again, the scream of someone driven mad with fear.

Chapter 18

21 March 2008

Friðrikka had stopped crying. It was as if her tear ducts had finally dried up. She let out several sobs, and then appeared to have recovered. She said nothing for a long time, but then announced that she would not sleep in this building while there was a body in the freezer. Attempts were made to persuade her otherwise, without success. In the end it was decided that Thóra and Bella would sleep with her in the office building, since it wasn't an option to let her stay there alone in the state she was in, especially while it was unclear what had happened there. They lugged their mattresses through the snow to the office building and although it was relatively calm outside, the breeze pushed hard against the thin foam pads. Their duvets were easier to carry through the wind and eventually everything was transferred and three beds set up on the floor of the meeting room.

Thóra tried and failed to imagine less exciting accommodation. She could feel the floor through the worn-out foam, and Bella's heavy breathing reminded her constantly of the company she was in. Although it didn't feel that cold in the building when they were standing up, it was quite chilly down on the floor. In addition, Friðrikka had demanded that the lights be left on, and the glare from the fluorescent bulb was so bright that you could still sense it with your eyes shut. One tube blinked, softly clicking, over and over again.

'Are you awake?' Thóra replied that she was— she and Friðrikka were clearly in the same boat. 'Who could it be?' The geologist's voice was hoarse after all her crying.

'I don't know,' replied Thóra. 'It was so hard to see him, and I didn't know any of the people here anyway. It could have been anyone.' Nonetheless, Thóra tried to recall what she had seen. 'It was definitely a man, and it looked to me as if he might have been a Greenlander. At least, he was wearing a jacket made of skins, though I only saw him

202

from the shoulders up. We didn't want to disturb anything unnecessarily.' Thóra raised herself up on one elbow to see Friðrikka. She felt uncomfortable staring at the ceiling while Friðrikka spoke. 'No locals worked here, did they?'

Friðrikka shook her head on the pillow. 'No. They tried to persuade some to work here but as I recall no one was interested. The villagers have always been wary of the employees here. They had absolutely no reason to be, since we were nothing but kind to them, and they never used the land that was being taken over for the mine for anything. So it wasn't resentment over the loss of the land that caused them to be suspicious of us. They simply believed the area to be evil, it seems.'

'Maybe the locals don't like outsiders very much? There can't be many tourists here. Is there anywhere to stay in this area?'

'No, I don't think so,' replied Friðrikka, who seemed to be regaining her composure a little. Apparently it was doing her good to talk calmly like this. 'Of course there are huts here and there where the hunters stay, but I can't imagine they'd be good enough for tourists.' She grimaced. 'I've actually seen inside one of them and I won't even try to describe the mess. I'd rather sleep in a snowdrift.'

'Or on the floor of an office building?' Thóra smiled at the woman, who looked over and smiled back.

'Thanks for staying here with me. I couldn't have slept over there.' Friðrikka said nothing for a few moments. 'Isn't it strange what people will do for money? When I left here I swore never to return, but here I am. Just because the pay was tempting. I actually accepted the original job here for the

203

same reason, so you can't say I'm not consistent. I started at Berg several years before this project began but I never planned to go into exile like this. When I heard how high the salary was, things looked different. I won't let myself be controlled by greed again, that's for certain. You'd think I'd have learned my lesson by now, but apparently not. My job here cost me my marriage, for example, but I still came back.'

'Oh, that must have hurt.' Thóra looked compassionately at her. 'I'm divorced myself and I know it's not easy. Still, I don't regret it now, and as time goes on you'll probably be happy to have made the decision.'

'I didn't make it. My husband left me. Saw his chance while I was spending a lot of time away from home, and hid behind the pretext that distance had come between us. Complete bullshit.'

'Oh.' By now Thóra knew most of the reasons for divorce and in this instance it sounded as if the husband might have tried his luck elsewhere. 'Did he leave you for another woman?'

'No.' Friðrikka flushed. 'For a man.'

'O-kay.' *That* kind of divorce was yet to come across Thóra's desk. 'I imagine that was pretty painful.'

'Horribly painful. Not to mention humiliating.' Friðrikka held her head a little higher, perhaps to remind herself and Thóra that she still had her pride. 'Oddný Hildur's disappearance was the last straw, but I was quite depressed and not prepared to be the only woman in the group after she vanished. The money had lost its allure, but as I said, I seem to be able to push my principles aside if I'm offered enough of it. I actually find that fact the

204

most depressing of all the things we've encountered on this trip.'

'People need to live,' Thóra replied. 'That's a fact of life, there's not much point fighting against it. I can imagine plenty of worse things than surrendering that kind of principle.' Thóra's own wages would have to be increased significantly before she could be compelled to come back here. 'Quite apart from the fact that no one could have foreseen what awaited us here—I have to say, I didn't expect anything like this. The worst I imagined was that we'd find the two men frozen in a snowdrift. I doubt you would have considered returning here if you could have seen the future.'

'No, that's for sure,' said Friðrikka fervently. 'Actually, I always had a bad feeling about this place, so maybe deep down I knew how this would turn out.' She turned her head abruptly to the side to look directly at Thóra. 'I don't believe in the supernatural or anything like that. I just mean that I've had a feeling simmering inside me without fully realizing what it was. When I think back, I know I never felt good about it, to say the least.'

'So how did you feel, exactly?'

'I don't know, maybe it was the atmosphere of the group—something wasn't quite right. Most of the men had worked out here, together in isolation, for years, and it was like their moods were collective. It can be unhealthy living and working so close together. It's also a disadvantage to be a woman in this kind of group, it never feels cosy like a proper community. And it's not just the lack of women, there are no older people or children, either. I don't know what it's like to be at sea but I can imagine that it's similar.'

'Are you talking about how Arnar was treated?'

'That was part of it, but it's certainly not the whole story. Although it pains me to admit it, Eyjólfur was right about him to a certain extent. He was too single-minded in his sobriety and quite hard on us, since we weren't as virtuous. But that doesn't really justify how they treated him. As I said, it's difficult to describe the atmosphere. It was subtle stuff, talking behind the guy's back, that sort of thing.' She paused for a moment. 'I know it sounds strange but that's how it was. I can't explain it more clearly, unfortunately. The actual harassment was almost better, because at least it was out in the open. Most people didn't like him and made it obvious. They made fun of everything he said. If they went anywhere in their free time, there was never any room for him. Taking more cars was out of the question, and the few times that Arnar settled for driving on his own behind the others, they ignored him completely. So he started going off by himself on his days off.'

'That sounds pretty cold.' Thóra had heard many ugly stories of bullying by children, but fewer involving adults. 'Was it like that from day one?'

'No; he was never exactly popular, but it wasn't too bad at first. But isolation didn't have a good effect on anyone and it got progressively worse. At first it was just dirty looks when Arnar said or did something the others disliked, but in the end the persecution was obvious to everyone. He always ate alone in the cafeteria. If he sat down with the group who couldn't stand him, they moved to another table. The rest of us didn't want to end up in the same situation, so we did what cowards do and avoided sitting near him too. Oddný Hildur was the only one who seemed not to care. She actively chose to sit with him, if only because she couldn't bear to see what was going on. I wasn't so kind and I only thought about myself, although I tried to be as friendly to him as I could. I never took part in any of the bullying, but I was a silent witness, which is hardly better. I deeply regret it now but it's too late to say sorry, as is so often the way.'

'She informed the managing director about it,' said Thóra. 'Just before she disappeared, she got in contact with him and asked him to do something about it. Did that have anything to do with what happened later?'

'Not while I was there. I resigned just over a month after Oddný Hildur went missing and nothing was done during that time. Actually the group was quite despondent after that, as you can imagine, so the harassment came down a notch or two.'

'Could Oddný Hildur have been harmed because she let the MD know about it?' Thóra tried to put this gently so as not to upset Friðrikka. Although she appeared calm at the moment, she clearly didn't have her emotions completely under control. 'Could some of the perpetrators have found out about the e-mails and wanted to play a nasty trick on her? Maybe not intending to make her disappear, but somehow it accidentally turned out that way?'

'What do you mean?' Friðrikka's pale cheeks turned red. 'That she was killed?'

'No, that's not really what I'm saying.' Thóra deeply regretted her last remark. 'More like whether this might have been a prank that got out of control.'

Friðrikka took her time responding. 'No. That can't be what happened. I remember it as if it were yesterday, and they were all just as stunned as I was. None of them was a good enough actor to feign ignorance if they were involved.' She was quiet again. 'I did wonder if someone from the village might have harmed her. You know that violence against women is relatively common in Greenland.'

Thóra didn't know what to say to this. It could very well be that locals had played a part in Oddný Hildur's disappearance; however, it was more likely that the woman had simply got lost in a snowstorm or been killed by someone closer to her. There was just something implausible about the idea of people journeying from the village to the camp in the hope of meeting a woman who was out alone. There would have been a much higher chance of them coming across a man. 'Isn't it the same here as elsewhere, that it's mainly wives and girlfriends who are being abused?' Thóra looked enquiringly at Friðrikka. 'Did you know that Oddný Hildur had complained to the director?'

'Yes, she told me about it. We were friends. I doubt anyone else knew, though. She obviously didn't broadcast it, and I doubt the MD told anyone about it without her knowledge.'

'How did she take it when he did nothing in response to her reports?'

'She was angry, clearly, but she didn't let it get to her too much.'

'Do you know why she didn't do anything about it earlier? You'd been here for over a year before she reported it.'

'The harassment got worse, as I said; and another factor was that we were facing a longer winter residency than we'd originally expected. Instead of going home for several months for the Christmas holiday, we suddenly had to return in mid-January and be here at the worst time of the year. She thought that made matters worse, and she was probably right. I actually believed at the time that the decision would be revoked but that's not what happened, unfortunately.'

Thóra lay her head back onto her pillow. She was finally feeling sleepy and the cold that came up from the floor had become bearable, since it had grown quite warm beneath the covers. 'I'm sure this will all be explained,' she declared, thought it wasn't what she actually believed, 'and then we'll be home before we know it.' She said good night and waited, in the hope that Friðrikka would suggest they turn off the light. Her wish was not granted.

'How did that man end up in the freezer?' Friðrikka's voice was shaky again.

'I have no idea, any more than I know how human bones could have ended up in the desk drawers. Maybe he wandered in there by accident and died of the cold. That would be a bit weird, though, since it's easy to open the door from the inside.'

'Yes, maybe.' Friðrikka sounded sceptical. 'You know, I read somewhere that in the old days the Greenlanders never had any actual religion. In place of faith they lived with fear.' Friðrikka's breathing was regular, as if she were drifting off and speaking almost in her sleep. 'That's how I feel. I'm not religious but I feel a persistent fear of something, though I don't know what.'

Thóra said nothing. She lay with her eyes closed, looking at the illuminated pink inside of her eyelid. She was too tired to try to contradict her, and in a way she knew exactly how Friðrikka felt.

*   *   *

'I believe this man has been dead for a long time.' Finnbogi sat with his hands on the kitchen table, having just put down a saltcellar he'd been rolling back and forth in the palm of his hand. 'Of course I didn't examine him carefully, but despite having seen him only from the shoulders up, I think it is out of the question that this man died recently.'

Matthew nodded. 'Do you have some idea of how he might have died?'

The doctor smiled grimly. 'I can't say, since I only saw him for a minute or two. There were no visible injuries to his head, and he doesn't appear to have suffocated—if he had, he would have been blue around the mouth. Nor did I see any evidence of frostbite on his nose or ears, which would certainly be present if he had died of hypothermia. However, this excludes only three things. People can die of many other causes, and it will require an autopsy to find out what caused his death. I have no idea who handles such things in these parts but I expect there are facilities for it in one of the hospitals on the west coast. I'm sure it would take a long time. I could go back in and examine the man in a bit more detail, but I doubt I would come any closer to an answer. I'm not worried about infection, since it's below zero in there.'

'No one is going back in there before the police arrive.' Matthew was resolute on this point. He could see that the doctor was itching to go back into the freezer, since he was unlikely ever again to be witness to such a thing. The other two men

210

had returned to the lounge, although Matthew had had to insist that they get out of the kitchen. They were so interested in the corpse that he was afraid they would sneak back in to take photos. It was extremely unfortunate that this should come to light when so many people were in the camp, to put it mildly. 'In fact we should get out of here, but I really don't know where we'd go, so we'll just have to stay until either the police or the helicopter arrive.'

'Where are you planning to go to call the police?' asked Finnbogi. 'To that woman's place, in the village?'

'Is there any other choice?' said Matthew. 'We'll just have to hope she lets us in. It would be best to go there immediately, but, well . . .'

'Are you thinking of the alcohol we've been drinking?' The doctor sounded surprised. 'It wasn't so much that it would matter under these circumstances.'

Finnbogi's interruption got on Matthew's nerves. He was weary of all this and dreamed of going home to his shower. 'No, I'm thinking more about not leaving the others behind. I don't know what Alvar and his friend Eyjólfur could get up to, and I really don't like the idea of leaving the women behind.'

'It's good that they can't hear you,' joked the doctor. 'I imagine that Bella thinks she can look after herself, at least.'

'Well, the drillers were hardly weaklings, judging by the photos, but they're still gone.' Matthew pointed behind the doctor in the direction of the kitchen. 'And our frozen friend appears to have been quite hefty, judging by the size of the body

211

beneath the plastic. Anyway, we can't go tonight, since we need to take Thóra with us. The woman seemed to trust her and I'm not sure that she would open the door to just us. I suppose Thóra could come with us now, but I don't know how Friðrikka would react if she were left behind with only Bella to lean on. I can't bear any more tears this evening.'

'Same here. How would she have reacted if it *had* been her friend?'

Matthew sighed at the thought. 'It's almost enough to make you hope she stays lost.'

Barely had he said this when the floodlights came on again outside.

Chapter 19

21 March 2008

Thóra was extremely relieved that Friðrikka was asleep when the intense light lit up the meeting room where they lay on the floor. She slipped carefully out from under the duvet and tiptoed to the one window on which the lights appeared to fall directly. Bella had closed the curtains at Friðrikka's request, and now Thóra lifted one corner and looked out. Outside was a man. She was so startled that she dropped the curtain and stepped back from the window. She knew he hadn't seen her because he was turned away, looking towards the cafeteria. Still, Thóra was alarmed and could not shake off the feeling that he had seen her. She made a desperate attempt to remember whether the front door had been locked but couldn't recall at all which of them had shut it behind the men when they left. She looked at her companions, who were sleeping quietly, and wondered whether she should wake them. The answer was easy enough as far as Friðrikka was concerned, but Bella would probably remain calm and could even chase the man away. 'Bella, Bella.' Thóra whispered her secretary's name as she shook her shoulder, first gently but then more forcefully. 'Wake up! There's someone outside.' Bella only opened one eye, but she managed to give Thóra a look that conveyed her intense displeasure at being woken. 'Get up. But be careful not to wake Friðrikka,' Thóra said, still whispering.

The lights outside went off, and Bella appeared galvanized into movement. She raised herself on one elbow and got to her feet. They both looked ridiculous. Bella was wearing flannel pyjamas, while Thóra was wearing an evening dress made from quite a soft material, which had made her think it might work very well as a nightgown. 'Who's out there?' asked Bella hoarsely. She went to the window and peeked out. 'I don't see anyone.' Now that the floodlights were off, it was more difficult to see into the darkness from the well-lit room. Bella pulled the curtain a bit higher to get a better view, but then turned around quickly. 'I saw him. He's on his way out to the kitchen,' she said, short of breath.

Thóra was completely taken aback. Under normal circumstances she could have called Matthew and warned him, but there was no mobile phone signal here. 'Shouldn't we let them know?' She tried to remember whether the office building had a back door, but couldn't. 'We could go out through the back window and run over without him noticing us.'

Bella arched an eyebrow. 'Are you *mental*?'

213

'What if they're asleep and this is the man in the clip?' Thóra shuffled her feet on the cold floor in agitation.

'What clip? What exactly do you mean by "clip"?' Bella was starting to raise her voice a bit too much and Friðrikka shifted on the floor at their feet.

In the excitement Thóra had forgotten that the others in the group had no idea there was a video showing the lower half of a man as he lay on the floor, apparently being decapitated or beaten, with blood flying everywhere. 'Nothing,' she replied hurriedly. 'Doesn't matter. We just need to let them know so that the man doesn't catch them off-guard.'

'Then it's best that you go,' muttered Bella. 'One of us needs to stay with Friðrikka anyway. We can't leave her behind alone.'

Thóra couldn't waste time arguing with Bella. 'Then I'll go, but you have to promise to watch me through the window.' She narrowed her eyes at her secretary. 'You're not to take your eyes off me, or go out for a smoke.'

Bella agreed, and Thóra hurried to the vestibule and pulled a coverall over her dress. She didn't have time to choose carefully and the one she ended up with was too large. Then she put on snow boots that were also too big, but at least this meant they were quicker to pull on than her walking shoes. She called back to Bella to let her know she was on her way out, and although she received no reply she had to move quickly. She would never fit through the window in this get-up, so she decided to use the door and hope for the best. If it came to the worst and the man attacked her, she would scream with all her might. She pushed aside the thought that

214

this was a ridiculous plan—no one could come to her assistance in time—and opened the door.

It was freezing outside, but for the first time since arriving in Greenland she didn't think about the cold; the strip of land between the office building and the cafeteria occupied her thoughts entirely. The man was nowhere to be seen. Thóra's heart hammered in her chest. She had not expected this. She had assumed that the man was on his way over and would now have his back turned towards her so that she could sneak unseen between the houses. She tried to spot any new tracks but more or less all of the snow seemed to be tramped down on the way over to the cafeteria, making it impossible to discern which of the tracks belonged to the intruder. All she could do was keep going and hope he wasn't lying in wait for her. She walked faster, heading straight for the entrance instead of going behind the building as she had originally intended. Since the intruder was nowhere to be seen it was just as likely that he was there. The large, awkward coverall made it difficult for her and the back cuffs of the legs dragged through the snow, meaning she didn't go as quietly as she'd intended. Intent on the rustling noise the coverall was making, she didn't notice the tracks that turned off from the path towards the rubbish bin and got a terrible shock when she walked past the large steel box: in its shadow stood the man. Thóra gasped.

He was wearing an animal-skin jacket and furry white trousers that looked to Thóra to be made from a polar bear pelt. The man could have been very well-built or quite puny; his clothes were so bulky that it was impossible to tell. His eyes were deep brown, almost black. Yet he was not

215

cruel-looking, his face giving more of an impression of sorrow than evil. Thóra stood frozen, in an agony of indecision. Her original plan to scream for help was forgotten and fear was scrambling her common sense, so all she could think of to do was wish him good evening. As soon as she had said the words she could not recall what language she'd said them in. She'd probably spoken Icelandic, since the man stared at her, clearly understanding nothing. She repeated her greeting in Danish, just to be sure.

'You must leave this place.' The man spoke Danish, which even Thóra could hear was not his mother-tongue.

'Why?' asked Thóra. Although she didn't really expect a reply, the man could hardly expect her simply to say yes, go inside and start packing.

'Your friends are not coming back. Go home.' The man's voice gave no hint of whether he was threatening or advising her.

'How do you know that?' Thóra suddenly felt the cold that she hadn't noticed during her initial adrenaline rush. 'What happened to them?'

'They're gone.' The man stared at her without blinking. 'This is an evil place.' Maybe this was the old hunter the woman in the village had mentioned. He was dressed strangely enough to be living rough in the wilderness.

Thóra remembered his name and decided to ask him straight out. 'Are you Igimaq?' The man appeared surprised by the question, but he nodded. 'I was told you could tell me about this area.'

'I *have* told you. This is an evil place. Leave immediately.' He didn't ask who had told Thóra about him. 'You don't understand and you don't belong here. Go and tell the others to leave. This

216

place is evil.'

Here was Thóra's opportunity to squeeze some information out of him about what was wrong with the place. It would be nigh on impossible to find this peculiar man again if he didn't want to be found, and if he had had anything to do with the disappearance of the drillers or Oddný Hildur he would be just as likely to go into hiding when the police arrived. 'You've got to explain this to me better. Maybe we'll leave when we understand why this is necessary.'

The man stared at her. He appeared to be growing angry. 'People died here.'

'The people who first moved here?' Thóra remembered the chapter about the settlement in which everyone had died of hunger. 'Is that what you mean?' The book hadn't mentioned a direct link, but it seemed likely to her that the legend of a curse on the area had arisen in consequence of those long-ago deaths. She wasn't sure whether this would help the bank's case, but one never knew.

'The people who died have no descendants, because they also died. Therefore their souls could not be reborn in their children and grandchildren and they are still here, even though this occurred many years ago. They will be here forever. This is not a good place and those who come here might never leave again.'

Thóra had grown colder than could be explained by the frost alone. Although she wasn't religious and didn't believe in ghosts, she felt very moved by the idea of the poor original inhabitants, who would never be free from cold and poverty even after their deaths. 'So the souls of those who starved to death here are to blame for the disappearances?'

217

'The ice preserves many things, and destroys nothing. In the end it returns what it has swallowed.' The man took off one of his leather gloves. His hand was missing its index finger. He showed Thóra his palm, in which nestled a little square made of tiny coloured beads. 'My wife was making this thirty years ago. She never finished it, because she lost it. Yesterday I found it in a place where I often go at this time of year. The ice is melting and revealing what it's been keeping. It's bad to be here, now more than ever.'

It seemed a simple *yes* or *no* was too much to ask of him. 'I understand that you know this area better than anyone. Are you willing to tell me what's wrong with this place? Are there often polar bears here?'

'I *was* telling you. You do not listen.' The man had become angry again.

'Yes, I was listening but I have trouble understanding what you're saying. We speak and think in a different way where I live. For example, our souls don't move around after we die.' Thóra knew she had a limited time to ask the man what she wanted to know. His eyes were starting to dart around as if to determine which way he should leave. To Thóra it was all one endless ice sheet that led either to the mountains or out to sea, but for him the landscape must look much more diverse. 'We are missing two men and one woman from our camp. You said that our friends would not return. Do you mean these people, and are you implying that they are dead?' The man did not reply, gazing into the distance. 'Are they dead?' For the first time since stopping in her tracks Thóra moved, stepping directly into the man's line of sight. 'I've

218

got to know.'

'Leave this place and tell the others to keep away.' He stared into her eyes. 'You will regret it if you do not.'

The man clearly didn't intend to explain any further, so Thóra tried a different tactic. 'What happened to your daughter? I was told that she died here in this place.'

Igimaq squinted at her. The corners of his mouth turned down. 'My daughter is none of your business. She is no longer here.'

Precisely. 'Did the same thing happen to her as to the people we're looking for?'

'You will certainly find that out if you do not leave. Then it will all be too late.'

He put the piece of beadwork in his pocket and put his glove back on. 'When you see the marks you will understand what I am talking about.' He moved past her. 'But then it will be too late.'

'What?' Now it was Thóra's turn to be angry. 'Marks? Can't you just explain properly? What marks do you mean?' The man walked away without looking back. 'Why did you come here?' she called out after him, hoping to delay him.

'I have done what I came to do. I came to ask you to leave.' The man turned around, and now his face was framed by the fur hood he had thrown over his head as he left. 'But you do not listen, any more than those who came here before you.'

'Did you damage the satellite dishes and snowmobile?' Thóra's limited language skills prevented her from knowing what these things were called in Danish, but she hoped that the Danes had taken the English names unchanged, as they usually did with technical terms. The man looked back one

219

last time at this, but his expression showed that he understood none of it.

Thóra watched him walk into the night, annoyed at herself. He had a long stride but walked in complete silence. It was as if he had made a deal with the snow not to crunch beneath his feet. When he walked between the floodlight towers they went on again, but he appeared not to be startled by the intense light. It wasn't until he disappeared entirely from her sight that Thóra got moving herself. I doubt Bella is even watching, she thought as she tore open the cafeteria door. The man could have killed and eaten her during the time she had been gone, and there was no sign of her chain-smoking guardian angel. But this was probably just as well, since the man would have disappeared if someone else had turned up. Still, she decided to pause for a moment before she went back to the office building, just to torture Bella a bit, make her pace the floor and worry over Thóra's fate. She was going to find Matthew and finish her glass of wine in the lounge before going back to bed. She did not need to search long; he and the doctor came running to the vestibule while she was still pulling off her coverall.

'What's wrong?' Matthew hurried over and took hold of her shoulder to steady her when she stumbled trying to get out of the second trouser leg. 'Did something happen?' He looked in astonishment at her dress but said nothing. The last time he had seen her in it, they were at the theatre.

'Well, not exactly. I met Igimaq, the hunter the woman told us about. He came here to tell us to leave.'

'What?' Matthew seemed furious. 'What were

220

you doing out there?'

'I was coming over to warn you. The floodlights went on and we saw a man outside. He was walking in this direction and I thought maybe you were asleep.' Suddenly she realized what a bad idea this had been. Maybe Oddný Hildur had made precisely the same mistake when she disappeared. The floodlight system hadn't been operational at the time, but she could very well have seen the man despite that and followed him out into the cold. 'Anyway, nothing happened. He was very cryptic and it was impossible to get anything useful out of him. We need one of the locals to speak to him for us.'

'Are you out of your mind, just rushing out there like that? Especially when you'd just seen a stranger outside?' He was nearly shouting.

'I'm very sorry, and I know it was ridiculous,' she said as apologetically as possible, 'but I still managed to talk to him. That was worth something, since we're not going to get to visit him by snowmobile.' Thóra hung up her coverall. 'He pretty much confirmed that Bjarki and Dóri are dead, as well as Oddný Hildur.'

'What do you mean by "pretty much confirmed"?' asked Finnbogi.

'He said that our friends would not return. I can't interpret that in any other way.'

'Was he involved in their deaths?' Matthew was clearly still annoyed about Thóra's impulsive trip outside. And no doubt his anger was fuelled by the fact that he and Finnbogi had sat by the window and peered through a crack in the curtain when the floodlight came on, but had seen nothing. It hadn't crossed their minds to go outside to see what was

221

up. Doubtless it irritated him that, for once, she had proven to be more resourceful than him.

'Maybe,' she replied. 'I have absolutely no idea.' They moved into the lounge, where she told them everything she could recall of her conversation with Igimaq. Neither man understood his statement about marks. They guessed that he had meant some sort of signs or symbols. Natural phenomena that in a primitive understanding could be considered omens of hidden danger. After drinking the remainder of the Opal schnapps Thóra returned to the office building, now accompanied by Matthew. When they entered the meeting room Bella was not pacing the floor fretfully, as Thóra had hoped, but snoring under her duvet.

Chapter 20

22 March 2008

Oqqapia sighed in resignation as she surveyed the kitchen. There were no clean glasses or dishes. The stack in the washing-up bowl had become so tall that it was no longer possible to wash what one needed to use at any particular time without running the risk of all the crockery crashing to the floor. She couldn't afford to replace the dishes, so she had recently resorted to wiping off the glasses and dishes as they were needed, using a ragged old dishcloth that was hardly any cleaner than they were. It wasn't even as if she could wash up even if she did pull herself together. The village had no running water, which meant that she had to fill the house's tank before she could do anything about it. Long ago the authorities had drilled for water in the village, but they hadn't thought to lay pipes to the houses. If the villagers wanted access to water, they had to fetch it, drawing it from a pump in a little pumphouse into various-sized tanks. In their household it was Naruana's job, but he'd been unusually lazy lately and in that kind of mood he was useless. Oqqapia was completely different, perhaps because she couldn't allow herself not to care. Her job wasn't much to speak of, but it was still important. Every three days she took on the task of emptying all the village houses' indoor latrines into the sea. She made many trips with the foul-smelling buckets down to the beach, and although her burden was lighter on the way back she wasn't able to carry more than two buckets at a time. When she started this job three years ago she made numerous attempts to carry four buckets at once but quickly discovered that this was unworkable as too much splashed up out of them along the way. Therefore, she had no choice but to make more trips with fewer buckets, and if she missed a shift she soon heard about it. The same people that had a go at her the few times it happened never complimented her when everything went according to schedule. She wished there were other work to be had, but the villagers knew that no one was waiting anxiously to take over from her and were thus careful not to keep her informed about other jobs that occasionally came up.

Oqqapia wasn't about to add carrying water to the tank to her latrine duties. Naruana would have to do his own job. If she went and fetched the water for him he would take it for granted, and before

223

she knew it it would be her job and he would be left with no responsibilities. So she had to settle for staring queasily at a juice carton before drinking from its spout. A sour smell rose from the frayed cardboard every time she raised it to her lips. The contents were still all right but the instant before the liquid entered her mouth was difficult. If there were just one clean glass.

Naruana appeared in the doorway. His black hair was dirty and hadn't been cut for ages, and although his bare shoulders were still well-muscled they didn't come close to looking like they had when she saw him undress for the first time. It was painfully clear that life had been tough on them both, and it wasn't finished with them yet. She had removed the mirror from over the bathroom sink a long time ago. It was bad enough to wake up feeling as if death had settled into her guts, without having to look at herself to boot. But that was a temporary respite. She could see herself, and how things had turned out for her, reflected in Naruana.

'Give me a sip.' Naruana held out his hand and took the half-empty carton. He raised it to his lips and drained it, then put it down on the kitchen table, adding it to the pile of empty beer cans. 'Are we all out?' He didn't need to explain what he meant; they were too similar.

Oqqapia nodded. 'You drank the last can last night.' She'd searched the house high and low for a beer, without success. In fact she couldn't recall which of them had drunk the last one, but she supposed it had been him. That's how it always was and how it always would be. He took priority, even though she contributed more to the household. For instance, they'd bought the beer with the

224

money she'd received from the foreign woman. If they hadn't used it, yesterday evening would have been pretty miserable; of course it had been dull anyway, beer or no beer, but that was another story. Alcohol numbed her feelings and made life bearable. When everything came good there would finally be no reason to drink. But when would that be and what would it take for it to happen? Two years ago she, like other villagers, had thought that better days were ahead with the arrival of the mine they'd heard was going to be dug in the vicinity. Finally she, and the others, would have more than an occasional half a day's work, and life would regain its purpose. Wake up, work and sleep. That was better than wake up, drink and sleep. She still remembered the disappointment all the villagers had felt when it turned out that the mine would be in a place they had been taught to avoid and with which it was forbidden to tamper. The numbness that consumed everyone and everything in the wake of this discovery was awful, actually worse than life had been before the future appeared to hold some promise.

'You shouldn't have talked to that woman.' Naruana could say that now, but he hadn't complained when she came home with money. He had run immediately to Kajoq, who ran the village shop—if it could be called a shop. One never knew whether a product would be available since goods were supplied only twice a year, in spring and autumn. Fresh foods weren't available except for a few weeks a year, but Kajoq never failed in one respect: there was always plenty of beer and liquor. She couldn't recall him ever running short there. 'You shouldn't have talked to her.' Naruana was repeating himself, like the old men who sat on the pier and went on about the same things day in and day out.

'I didn't tell her anything. Just suggested that she talk to your dad.' Oqqapia knew this would cause him pain. Every piece of news concerning his father seemed to hurt him, no matter how insignificant. Despite this, she saw no reason not to mention him. She'd learned from one of the teachers who had lived in the village for a time when she was a child always to tell the truth, but also that unspoken words were sometimes just as misleading as outright lies. But what should one include in the telling, and what was better left out? Still, she did what she could to live by this maxim, despite the fact that many other virtues she had once held in high esteem had long since departed.

'Why on earth did you say that? Why don't you just invite her round here as well?' Naruana turned away from the open refrigerator towards her. He was even angrier than before, but for other reasons now than just the lack of Coke or juice to be found there.

Now Oqqapia was in trouble, and her cheeks reddened slightly. Should she take this opportunity and tell him that she had actually promised the woman that she could use their phone to call, or should she not? She hadn't technically invited her to visit, so she could deny that accusation in good conscience. She decided not to mention it even though she knew this was perhaps not entirely honest. Maybe the woman wouldn't come, and if she did appear Naruana might not even be at home. It was just as likely that he would be down at the pier or visiting someone who might have beer to

226

spare. 'Come on. You were happy enough about it yesterday.'

'I'm never happy. You should know that.' He slammed the refrigerator door, causing the jars of jam and other food in it, most of it gone off, to clatter. That was another thing that had been neglected, besides the washing up: clearing out the refrigerator. 'I just want to be left alone by that lot and you're stirring things up by talking to them. If no one says anything they'll just leave and everything will carry on as usual.'

Neither said anything further. Everything carrying on as usual meant two things: futile drunkenness for them, and contempt from those villagers who hadn't gone down the same road as they had. These people were in the majority, more likely to be out and about and therefore more likely to pass one by on the street. The others—the ones who were in the same boat as the two of them—seldom left their own houses and slept late waiting for the hangover to pass so they could get up and start the vicious circle once again.

'I also told the woman about Usinna.' Oqqapia didn't know why she was mentioning this. If Naruana was sensitive about his father, the topic of his sister was even more explosive. He never brought it up unless he was so drunk that he was no longer in control of what he was saying, and then he would usually doze off soon after. Since Oqqapia generally did the same when she drank, she could rarely remember what had come out of his mouth. Yet she did recall some bits and pieces, so strange that she was sure she had misunderstood or misheard him. Some sort of gibberish about marks and ancestors that he couldn't let down, an awful

227

story about Usinna's fate that there was no way of confirming. Whether she misremembered or not, it was certainly true that the day after saying those strange things about Usinna Naruana had started talking about children, whether they should maybe just have one kid. He never mentioned this topic otherwise—they weren't a couple in any formal sense and neither of them was in any condition to raise children. At first she'd been flattered when he brought it up, but when she started to suspect that it was less than sincere she pressed him and discovered that his desire for a child wasn't connected with her at all. He simply needed offspring and she was the one who happened to be at hand. His sister's soul required that the family line be maintained and he alone was left to save it. Oqqapia had suffered a lot over the years but this hurt the most. The harsh reality that he couldn't care less about her. His sister was topmost in his mind, despite the fact that she had died long ago.

'What did you tell her?' Naruana remained standing by the closed refrigerator, his back to her. The long, slender muscles of his sinewy shoulders clenched and his breathing slowed.

'Nothing. I told her that Usinna had died there. Nothing else.' She wished she hadn't mentioned it. Perhaps she'd wanted to hurt him for choosing his sister over her. It was an incredibly stupid decision on her part, and hardly likely to change anything. His sister would never have done or said anything so hurtful; she was too perfect for that. For a moment Oqqapia considered pointing out to him that his sister had been too perfect for life in the village and would have been the last person to stick to old traditions if she were alive. If their fates had

228

been reversed, she would never have had children just to guarantee the return of his soul. Usinna had been a few years older than Oqqapia, but she still remembered her quite well. It was impossible to forget her. Her grace and spirit were apparent to everyone. She had gone abroad to study when Oqqapia was a teenager and returned several years later, even more elegant than before, but now the light that seemed to shine from her had an added cosmopolitan aura. Perhaps it wasn't surprising that Naruana wanted to ensure her reincarnation.

'Don't you dare even speak her name, you fucking whore.' He turned around and punched the refrigerator door with all his might. A large dent appeared on the scratched surface.

Oqqapia said nothing. She hadn't been raised by a violent, drunkard mother without learning a few lessons. In moments like these it was wiser not to stand up for oneself. But he had called her a whore. And this was her home, however unglamorous it was. She wasn't such a whore that he couldn't live under her roof or drink the beer that she'd procured by giving out some insignificant information. On that basis, he was the whore, not her. She had never sunk to the depths like him; she had simply been born at the bottom of society and stayed there. As a little girl she would never have dreamed that Naruana, the son of the great Igimaq, would later live under the same roof as her, the daughter of the village slut and a good-for-nothing father who had passed out drunk outside one winter and frozen to death. She did not remember him, but her mother and various others who enjoyed reproaching her for her heritage reminded her constantly of his wretchedness. The only thing that

229

Oqqapia could thank him for was having been man enough to build the house in which she now lived. Like a large proportion of the houses in the village, the material for the house had been donated by the Danes, who provided it to those Greenlanders who wished to build themselves homes. If people did so, and lived in the house for several years, they then gained ownership of it; so Oqqapia had inherited something from her parents besides a bad taste in her mouth. The only people who had shown her any kindness were the teachers who came rather irregularly throughout her childhood to see to the education of the village children. She remembered them all fondly. The departure of each one had caused her the same feeling of disappointment as the broken promise of a good job with the mining company. They had never called her a whore or other bad names. They told her that she was just as good as anyone else, and some had even said that God and his Son loved her no less than the others, however wretched her parents.

She suddenly felt the same as she had in her youth, when in all innocence she had believed it when people said that she was no less worthy than others. It was true, after all, and this furious jackass in front of her was living proof of that. His family had good people in it on both sides, yet he had ended up the same as her. His mother was in the same position, and although his father didn't drink his reputation had diminished in the eyes of the villagers. No, he was the one who had fallen furthest, not her. For her, the only way was up. Her heart swelled with indignant anger at everyone and everything, not least herself. Her life was in her own hands and she could still save herself from

230

destruction. She still had all her own teeth, so she wasn't as unfortunate as her mother had been at her age, and her body, despite everything, was still strong and fit. Maybe the God her teachers had spoken of had held a protective hand over her after all, made sure that she had the opportunity to change if only she could find the desire to do so. She stood up.

'You're one to talk. I never did anything to your sister.' She decided to look for the book that the man from the alcoholism charity had left behind. Although she'd never been much of a reader, it couldn't have been thrown away, any more than any of the other rubbish that had come into the house. She looked at him and saw a waste of space, just like her mother had been. 'Pity the same can't be said about you.' She spat out the words that she knew would cut him to the bone. 'When you're half asleep and rambling on about it, you're always whining that it was you who treated Usinna worst of all in the end.'

He screamed like an animal and jumped towards her. Just before his fist struck her face she recalled her deceased mother and thought how little she missed her.

*   *   *

Thóra finished washing her face with the lukewarm water that Matthew had apportioned to her. In the morning he had gone and filled a large pot with snow, heated it and split the water between them. In the absence of a shower this was better than nothing, and after Thóra had dried herself she felt much better. She dressed in the finest outfit she

231

could find in her suitcase, a felt tunic top and skirt that she could wear over leggings, which she hoped would serve as thermal underwear. She was relieved when she saw that she'd been right about Matthew's baggage. He had run out of casual outfits and had started wearing formal shirts beneath a fleece jacket with suit trousers. They stuck out like a sore thumb in comparison with the others, but that was just too bad; they all had other things to think about at the moment besides Thóra and Matthew's fashion blunders. It wouldn't be as noticeable if she could find a smaller coverall to put on over her outfit. They were going to go straight to the village in the hope of making a phone call.

Everyone was sitting in the cafeteria but Bella, who, like Thóra, was taking plenty of time over her makeshift bath. Friðrikka was also absent, but that came as no surprise to Thóra, since she was standing firm and refusing to set foot in the accommodation block. She was adamant about remaining behind in the office building when Thóra and Bella came over. No one looked very enthusiastic about their breakfast, which had become increasingly sad with each day that passed. It had taken the edge off their appetites knowing that there was a body in the kitchen freezer, so close to the dining hall. Thóra took a seat but made do with a cup of coffee and a dry biscuit. Her preferred option would have been to starve herself until they left, but that was inadvisable in the light of how cold it was outside. The doctor had been strictly supervising their food intake, and since it was thanks to him that they hadn't put anything in their mouths that predated their arrival at the camp, Thóra felt it best to follow his advice. If he

232

hadn't been so insistent, they would all have eaten something from the freezer.

'When are we leaving?' Thóra broke her biscuit in half and dipped it into her cup.

'As soon as we can.' Matthew had finished eating and was itching to get going. 'Just the two of us. We thought it best that as many people as possible remain here, to make sure no one goes into the freezer. They'll keep watch on each other, so to speak.'

Thóra smiled to herself. It was more likely that those who remained behind would make a pact to all look in the freezer together—apart from Friðrikka, of course. Thóra was sure that she herself would succumb to the temptation. What was horrifying could also be extremely fascinating. The other possibility was that they all go down to the village, but that wouldn't work. The more of them that went, the smaller the likelihood of them being allowed to use the phone. This must not look like an invasion of the village. She stuck the final piece of biscuit in her mouth and mumbled: 'I'm ready.'

At the coat rack she tried to find the smallest coverall available. Behind one huge one she found another that fitted her quite well, and she put it on. When she held it up in front of her to stick her feet into the trouser legs she noticed what was written on the collar: *Oddný H.* Thóra hesitated, but common sense quickly won out. What difference would it make if she wore Oddný Hildur's clothes? It could hardly matter. She pulled herself together and put on the coverall. But before leaving she had to steel herself. In her mind there was no doubt that Oddný Hildur was dead and it was strangely uncomfortable to wear a dead person's clothing.

233

To her knowledge she'd never done so before. She could not avoid the thought that perhaps the trouser legs would take control and lead her against her will to where the owner of the coverall lay. In her mind's eye she saw her own frozen body alone and abandoned out on the ice, staring with glazed eyes up into the dim morning sky in the hope of seeing a falling star, so that she could wish to be found and brought home to rest in peace under Icelandic soil. 'Is everything all right?' Matthew stood with his hand on the doorknob.

'Yes, I was just a bit distracted.' What was wrong with her? As if clothing could bring her messages from the other side!

It wasn't until she was on the way out that she felt the notebook in the coverall's large side pocket.

Chapter 21

22 March 2008

The breakfast was actually not bad, but Arnar had no appetite. He had never found breakfast to be the most important meal of the day as general wisdom often proclaimed, and it was enough of an effort to eat lunch and dinner. Yet he did know that he needed to eat. That way he could maybe overcome the feeling of gloom that was overwhelming him. He stirred his yoghurt distractedly.

Suddenly the sad woman from the night before was standing beside him, holding a tray and asking whether she could sit down. Arnar said yes and then watched in surprise as she chose the chair next

234

to him, even though there were plenty of free seats at the table. At first the woman stared silently at her tray, but then she lifted her cup in her scrawny hands and sipped her coffee. She took it black. 'I can't stand toast.' The woman took another sip. 'It reminds me of a hotel. Hotels remind me of bars and bars remind me of alcohol.'

Arnar did not make the connection. However, he couldn't recall ever having had breakfast at a hotel, so it could very well be that hotels only had toast on offer. 'Is it your first time here?'

'Yes.' The woman put down her cup and started scratching the back of her hand. The skin there was red and irritated but her expression did not alter and she appeared to feel no pain.

'I've been admitted several times.' Arnar fished his spoon out of his yoghurt and put it on his tray. That was enough stirring. Although he still wasn't hungry, the company cheered him up somewhat. He hadn't realized how lonely he'd been recently. 'You feel better little by little. About a minute longer each day.' He smiled flatly at the woman, who was staring at her tray again. 'There are 1,440 minutes in a day so you should be feeling good all day and all night in about four years.'

'Fantastic.' There was no joy in the woman's voice, nor anger or bitterness. She was perfectly lifeless.

'Do you have children?' Arnar asked the question as gently and warmly as possible for fear of causing the woman even further distress.

'No.' The woman must have realized that her replies were too curt, because she hurriedly added: 'You can't drink during pregnancy. At least not in peace.' She raked at the back of her hand even

235

more fervently. 'My husband didn't think that was a good enough reason not to increase the world population.' She added hurriedly: 'My *ex*-husband.'

'Oh.' Arnar hadn't thought about that. Naturally, alcohol passed from the mother to the foetus during pregnancy. How many mothers were there in the cafeteria who had drunk while carrying children? The thought of being hungover inside another individual and unable to have even a painkiller was more than he could handle. 'You can still have a child later if you want to. Unlike me.'

'You can't know that.' The back of the woman's hand had become swollen from her scratching. Suddenly she stopped and placed both hands in her lap. 'What do you do?'

'I'm an engineer.' Arnar decided not to try to make his job sound more impressive by saying that he worked overseas. Neither of them was in the mood to try to outdo the other, fortunately. In this place the conversation most often centred on who had been the hardest drinker, and the stories were, almost without exception, saturated with regret.

'Bridges and stuff like that?' The woman seemed happy to have something other than their troubles to talk about.

Arnar smiled for the first time in many days and immediately felt better. 'Most engineers end their professional careers without having ever worked at anything connected with bridges. I work for a contractor.'

'Wow. I'm unemployed. I'm actually a massage therapist but I was fired from my job at the gym after I fell asleep on top of a client on the table.'

'I can't believe they fired you for something so trivial!' Arnar smiled at her, and this time she

236

noticed and smiled back. Her smile was crooked and fleeting. It had been even longer since she had smiled.

'I know, right?' She took another sip of coffee, then put down her cup and stared into it. She seemed unsure of whether she wanted to allow herself to feel better by chatting with Arnar. He felt the same; it seemed much easier to plunge into depression. Then he could allow himself to do nothing, either mentally or physically, and right now that prospect was extremely attractive. It was much harder to rise up out of it. The woman glanced at him. 'There was such a strong scent from the massage oils that they masked the smell of the booze. How about you? Did you drink at work?'

Arnar shook his head. 'No. I'd been dry for around two years. However, I did used to when I worked for the Highways Agency in the old days, but no one ever noticed. I worked alone so much.' The feeling of sadness returned. Was there anything more wretched than having been drunk in a crowded workplace without anyone noticing?

'Great. I should have studied engineering. Then I could have postponed my detox by several years. Being fired was the last straw. It doesn't mean much being an alcoholic if you can't afford to drink. I've never been able to drink grain alcohol or anything like that, I find it disgusting, so this was an expensive hobby for me. Actually, hobby isn't the right word; I became a professional.'

'I can relate to that.' If this were utopia and everything were free, Arnar could quite easily contemplate drinking his whole life. He had no sense of ambition and his job was not important to him. In fact he did not understand *why* he worked,

237

or why he did anything at all, come to think of it. And yet. He was too much of a weakling to kill himself, so it was just as well to have something to do with this life he'd been given.

'I'd like to be a lighthouse keeper. They don't need to do anything and no one ever visits them. I could use my wages to buy all the white wine I needed and sit up in the tower and count the circles the light made.' The woman looked up at Arnar again. 'And you?'

'I don't know. No matter what I do, I'll always be me. If I could be someone else I'd be willing to try a few things.'

'You're stuck with yourself and I'm stuck with myself, just the way we are.' She sighed quietly. She would perk up when she'd been here longer, thought Arnar, but it would take time. The first stretch of treatment was always the worst. That's when you started waking up to how you had treated yourself and others. The woman sipped her coffee again. 'You're not so bad, so I don't know why you're complaining.'

Even though she had played down the compliment and said it in a monotone, Arnar felt himself cheer up at hearing these words from an unfamiliar woman. He wasn't used to people speaking to him that way. Ever since primary school he'd been teased, insulted and bullied, and if people expressed their opinions of him while he was in earshot it still always hurt his feelings. 'Thanks.' The yoghurt did not look any more appetizing than before, but suddenly Arnar was able to face the idea of eating a piece of bread. 'Thank you for sitting with me. Yesterday the walls of my room were my only companions.'

238

The woman turned in her chair and looked at Arnar. 'Are you going to join this AA thing?'

'I'm already a member of AA,' replied Arnar. 'Maybe not its most active member, but still.'

'And have you gone through the twelve stages they were talking about in the lecture?'

They were forced to listen to so many lectures that they all ran together in Arnar's mind. He didn't quite know which lecture she meant but understood that she meant steps, not stages. The twelve fucking steps. 'Yes, I have.' He didn't feel up to saying more and suddenly wanted to shut himself up alone back in his room.

'Is it very difficult?' The hesitation in the woman's voice suggested that she desperately wanted to throw herself wholeheartedly into the programme, even though she might not say so outright. Doubtless she feared that she would fail and call yet another disappointment down on her head. It was better to act as if she didn't care.

Arnar didn't know how to answer. Praise the system and encourage her or tell her to take it slowly and not rush into anything? 'It takes effort. But you should talk to a counsellor about it. Not me.' He stood up. He couldn't talk about this any more. Not with her. Not with anyone. He'd already done enough bad things and caused enough damage.

The woman remained sitting at the table, surprised and hurt. As Arnar pushed his chair back and walked away, he saw that she'd resumed scratching the swollen back of her hand.

*   *   *

239

The car moved slowly over the snow-covered ground. The speed was certainly to Thóra's liking. She was terrified of driving on ice and highly doubted Matthew's own abilities in such conditions. Still, she trusted him at the wheel much more than she would herself. Her fear would override her common sense as soon as the car started skidding. The stretch ahead was straight, with a gradual incline, so she relaxed her grip on the ceiling handle slightly and with her other hand flipped the pages of the little notebook that she'd found in the pocket of Oddný Hildur's coverall. 'This appears mainly to have to do with geology,' she said, turning the page. 'At least, I hardly understand any of the endless figures and diagrams.'

'Maybe Friðrikka can go over the text.' Matthew didn't take his eyes off the road as he spoke, but instead squinted to shield them from the sun as it reflected off the broad expanse of snow.

'Yes, that's probably a wise idea—there's some stuff here that doesn't seem to be connected to rock strata and that kind of thing, but it's impossible for me to make the distinction.' She continued turning the pages. 'For example, here are a bunch of phone numbers that could be related to the project, or to something totally different.' Most of the numbers appeared to be Icelandic, although one of them was longer than the others. 'What do phone numbers in Greenland start with?'

'299, as I recall.' Matthew took one hand off the steering wheel and fumbled at the compartment between the seats. It was closed and he was unable to open it without looking down. 'Can you check whether there are any sunglasses in there or in the glove compartment?'

'There is one Greenlandic number in her book.' Thóra looked in both compartments and found some yellow plastic sunglasses, which she handed to Matthew. 'They're incredibly ugly but they're all I can find.'

Matthew put them on and looked completely content. 'These are those really good snow glasses,' he said, obviously not caring at all how he looked in them. He relaxed his shoulders. 'The Greenlandic number probably has something to do with the helicopter or the airport. If I worked here I'd want to have those numbers at hand.'

Thóra read him the number. 'Do you recognize it at all? You called the helicopter service, didn't you?'

'I don't recognize it, which doesn't say much. I have a number in my wallet if you can get it out of my pocket.'

Thóra found the wallet and after a bit of searching through a number of business cards and credit card receipts she pulled out the right slip of paper. 'It's not the same number,' she said.

'They could easily have other numbers besides this one.' Matthew slowed down and took a wide turn. They approached the village slowly but surely. 'It could also be the number of the hotel in Kulusuk, or a hospital, or anything.'

'Maybe.' Thóra said nothing as she tried to imagine what Greenlandic number Oddný Hildur would have wanted to keep handy. She couldn't think of any. She thumbed through the book again but spotted nothing new. The only thing that caught her attention apart from the phone numbers were the words *Usinna* and *blood tests*; after the latter was a question mark. Both appeared on the same

241

page. Obviously you wouldn't expect to read *blood tests* in the notebook of a geologist, but there it was nonetheless. Thóra had no idea what it signified. 'I wonder what "Usinna" is?' she mused. 'It has a capital "U", so it could be a name. Do you recognize it?'

'No, I don't,' Matthew replied. 'I don't even know what nationality it is or whether it's a woman's or a man's name. It could be Greenlandic.'

'It sounds like a woman's name, since it ends in "a".' Thóra closed the book. 'If it's a name. It could also be a place name.'

'Do you know the name of the woman who's letting us make our phone call? I think we're almost there.'

'Oh. I didn't ask her. Maybe her name is Usinna. Who knows?'

Matthew sighed and looked at Thóra. 'What will you do if her husband or a child answers the door? Say, *May I make a phone call? The woman who lives here said that I could.*'

Thóra ignored this. It was typical of Matthew to be worried about small details. This was why they got along so well; she was in the habit of getting on with things and he preferred to stay in one place. She just smiled at his grumbling. 'Something like that. Don't worry, she'll answer the door. I can't imagine she has kids. I hope not, anyway; she seems to have enough to deal with on her own. If she has a husband, then I'll simply explain everything.'

They drove up a hill, behind which the little village spread out. As before, it seemed devoid of any human presence, but down at the pier men could be seen moving about. Thóra spotted the house where she thought the woman lived. As with

242

the other houses, there was no sign of life. They drove calmly down the slope; so slowly, in fact, that they might as well have been walking. When they reached level ground Matthew sped up slightly and they stared through the windscreen in search of lights or any other sign that someone was home. There was no sign of activity, and the curtains were drawn. 'Maybe she's asleep?'

'Then we'll just wake her by knocking.' Matthew undid his seatbelt. 'Or her husband and children.' He smiled at Thóra and opened the car door. 'There's only one way to find out.' They both jumped when a snowmobile suddenly started up and came flying out of the yard of the adjacent house. At the wheel sat a man who did not even glance in their direction. Behind him sat a little girl who just managed to reach around his waist with her short arms by pressing tightly against his back. Her face was turned towards them and she stared at Thóra and Matthew with two pitch-black eyes. On her face was a large scar which stretched from one eye down to her chin. The girl made no attempt to hide the ugly mark that covered her chubby cheek. It was a sign of the revulsion that the place awakened in Thóra that she found something unpleasant about the girl's gaze, and she was thankful for the din of the engine that drowned out all other sounds. She wasn't sure she wanted to hear the words that the child's mouth was forming.

They watched silently as the snowmobile disappeared around a corner. Thóra slammed the car door shut and drew a deep breath. The strange girl had rattled her and she kicked herself for failing to have asked the woman her name. She wasn't as happy about the situation now. The

243

paint had started to peel from the door and the knob hung loosely, reminding her of a withered flower. The soft creaking of one of the loose corrugated iron plates covering the house gave her the creeps. She could not avoid the thought that this dilapidated house had sucked the vitality from the woman. 'Oh, God,' said Thóra as they stood on the wooden landing before the door. She looked at Matthew to assure herself that he was actually still there, and knocked.

Nothing happened. After a moment Matthew knocked harder, using his fist. The orange skis propped against the outside wall shook at the blows. After a moment they heard footsteps inside. They approached, then fell silent. Shortly afterwards they heard a man's voice say something that neither of them understood. Thóra called out 'Hello,' in return. Nothing was heard from within, but the doorknob moved and the door opened enough for the man inside to see them. They caught a glimpse of half his face.

'What?' he said gruffly in Danish.

'Is the lady at home?' Thóra ignored how clumsy this sounded. She should have put more work into learning Danish at school.

'The lady?' The Greenlander did not open the door any wider. 'What lady?'

This is when it would have been useful to know the woman's name, thought Thóra.

'Usinna,' she tried.

The man's reaction caught Thóra and Matthew completely off-guard.

Chapter 22

22 March 2008

Thóra half expected the sofa to break beneath hers and Matthew's combined weight. That would have been the icing on the cake as far as their visit was concerned; Thóra still hadn't regained her composure at the reception they'd been given. The man had completely lost it when he heard the name "Usinna" and had shouted himself hoarse. The only thing that seemed to prevent him from lashing out at her with his fists was Matthew standing next to her. Although the man appeared to be in decent shape, he was a head shorter than the German. Instead he vented his anger on the door and doorframe and continued pouring abuse over them. Naturally, Thóra did not understand any of what he said, but it was clear that he was calling them some rather unpleasant names and was not overjoyed at their arrival. He turned several times to shout back into the house, probably to share his joy with the poor woman living there. In the end Matthew had enough, and he shouted back, ordering the Greenlander to shut his mouth for a moment. In German. At that the man abruptly shut up and stormed back in. He left the door open and although Thóra wanted more than anything to run to the car, she forced herself to peek in through the doorway and ask courteously whether they could make a phone call. No reply. Thóra tried calling the name Usinna, which she now believed to be the name of the woman there, and in a flash the

245

young woman came running to the door. She waved her hands to silence Thóra and her worried look convinced Thóra not to dare say anything else.

The woman's face was swollen and blood oozed from the corner of her mouth. Her lower lip was twice as large as when they had last met and when she got to the door she cradled one of her upper arms in the other hand. She was wearing faded old sweatpants and a tatty polyester jumper, so well-worn that the pattern was nearly gone. When Thóra repeated her request to be allowed to make a phone call the woman refused to let them in and said it was a bad time. However, barely had she uttered the words before a door could be heard slamming somewhere in the house. At that the woman's attitude changed abruptly and she invited them in. She explained that her housemate had left by the back door, so they could call if they did it quickly. She then showed them into the sitting room, where they took seats on the shabby sofa. There was a phone on a little side-table next to it.

'What happened to you?' Thóra asked the woman, who sat opposite her on a plastic folding chair. This had also seen better days. 'Did that man hurt you?'

'It just happens. I'll get over it.' The woman pressed her bare toes into the fur of the polar bear pelt on the floor in front of her.

'What is your name, can I ask?' Thóra had left it to Matthew to try to reach the police. They would certainly speak English, and he could not hold a conversation with the woman in Danish.

'Oqqapia.' The woman released her grip on her injured arm and straightened up. It was as if she suddenly realized what an abject picture she

246

presented and wanted to put on a better face.

Thóra introduced herself and Matthew and thanked her again for letting them in. 'I don't know what we would have done if you hadn't helped us. We've brought money to pay you for your assistance.'

'No thank you.' The woman seemed serious. 'I don't want the money. It just makes matters worse.'

'Oh, I see.' Thóra didn't know what she could offer the woman instead and felt slightly embarrassed. She decided to start with something harmless and asked the woman about the little girl she'd seen outside on the snowmobile.

'She's special.' Oqqapia rubbed her hands together and appeared very nervous about their presence in her sitting room. 'She was injured, which is why she looks that way. She adores that snowmobile and her father always has to take her with him if he goes somewhere on it. Still, she's an incredibly good girl even though she's mutilated, the poor little thing.' She said the last bit with enormous affection and appeared to be regaining her composure.

Thóra seized the opportunity and changed the subject.

'What does Usinna mean? Isn't it a name?' Judging by the reaction of the house's inhabitants it was most likely a profanity or some sort of term of abuse. Perhaps Oddný Hildur had written it in her notebook to remind herself never to say it.

Oqqapia looked over her shoulder once more as if she expected the man to sneak up behind her. 'It *is* a name. A woman's name.'

Thóra had at least been right about that. 'Why was the man who came to the door so angry when I

247

used it? I thought it might have been your name.'

The pink tip of the woman's tongue appeared at the bloody corner of her mouth and she ran it over her swollen lip. 'You shouldn't have mentioned her by name. Naruana is very sensitive about her and besides that he was already angry. You've come at the worst possible time.'

'Is this Naruana your husband?' Thóra hoped that he wasn't. 'He looks to me like a rather unsuitable life partner,' she added hesitantly.

The woman smiled flatly, just enough for the light to catch her white front teeth. Between them were dark streaks of blood. 'We're not married. He just lives here.' She thrust out her jaw and moved it from side to side as if to check whether it was broken at all. 'He doesn't usually act like that. As I said, you two came at a bad time.'

Thóra decided not to make any objection to this. She knew neither this woman nor her circumstances and would most likely never see her again. Who was she to think she could judge her and give her advice? Did she intend to give her a helping hand if she needed one? No, she was an adult and it was unnecessary for Thóra to point out to her that this was perhaps not the most desirable relationship in the world. 'You might consider getting away from him,' was all she said before changing the subject. 'Why does the name Usinna make him so upset?'

The woman was silent for a moment as she stared awkwardly into Thóra's eyes. Then she began to speak, rather determinedly, although her voice trembled slightly. 'His sister was named Usinna. She died several years ago and he took it very badly.'

'I understand.' What on earth was the name

248

of the dead woman doing in Oddný Hildur's notebook? Out of the corner of her eye Thóra watched Matthew try for the fourth time to dial what he thought was the phone number of the police. He still hadn't managed to reach anyone. 'When did she die?'

'It was almost five years ago.'

'And he still hasn't come to terms with it?' Thóra found this rather odd. She didn't know any siblings who were so close that one would take years and years to get over the death of the other. 'Did she die very young?' There was no way to determine the age of the man who had met them at the door. He could be anywhere from twenty-five to fifty.

'No, she was older than him. She died when she was twenty-something. Almost thirty.'

Matthew hung up and handed Thóra the slip of paper. 'Are you able to ask her whether there's something wrong with this number? I can't reach anyone.' Thóra asked and the woman checked the number. She handed it back to Thóra, saying that as far as she could tell there was nothing wrong with it. However, it was sometimes difficult to get a good connection and he should just keep trying. Matthew then asked Thóra to ask whether it were conceivable that the phone had been disconnected. The woman reddened a little at this question but then said that the authorities paid a fixed telephone service fee and that the phone was fine. Matthew continued trying.

Thóra turned back to what they had been discussing before Matthew interrupted. 'How did this woman die? Did she need blood, or did she have a blood disease?' It crossed Thóra's mind that the words 'blood test' in Oddný Hildur's notebook

249

were perhaps connected to Usinna. Perhaps she had needed blood tests, but transportation problems had prevented her from being treated in time. With this in mind, it was possible that Naruana blamed foreigners for his sister's death, although Thóra found that difficult to believe.

Oqqapia frowned, bewildered, and the facial movement appeared to cause her pain. She grabbed her jaw and stroked her swollen skin. 'She didn't die because of anything to do with blood. She just went missing.'

Thóra thought for a moment. 'Where did she go missing?'

'In your area. She went there despite being warned not to. I would never go there.'

'And then what? She went and just didn't come back? Did no one search for her?'

'She left in the morning and when she didn't return in the evening it was clear that there was no hope of her returning the next day. It was pointless to look for her although Naruana and his father did try. She was gone.'

'Doesn't anyone find it odd that people keep disappearing around here?' Thóra was dumbfounded. What was going on? She didn't know enough about the environment in these parts to imagine the main dangers people faced. She thought of avalanches and polar bears, but both were things it would have been easy to discuss in simple terms, instead of going on about the area being 'cursed' or 'evil'.

Thóra's question clearly irritated Oqqapia. 'Of course we do. That's why we don't go there and we try to warn others not to. That was the first thing I learned as a small child.'

'I didn't mean everyone who lives here, I meant the police and other authorities. Don't they make enquiries when people disappear?'

The woman shook her head and gave Thóra a puzzled look. 'How would they hear about it?'

At the other end of the sofa Matthew sighed and took a break from his attempts to contact the police. It was perhaps not surprising that people round here were disinclined to report missing persons.

'So was the death of this woman never reported?' Thóra asked.

'I don't know. Maybe. I didn't live with Naruana at the time.' She licked her lips again but the blood had stopped flowing. Perhaps the memory of the violence was starting to heal as well. 'We got together after all of this had happened. He was on the street and I had inherited this house from my mother.' She saw from Thóra's expression that she didn't think much of the arrangement, and added: 'He sometimes works down at the dock and comes home with seals and fish.'

This man would have to contribute a lot more to the household if Thóra were to allow him to even so much as rent her garage, but this perhaps more than anything else shed light on their different circumstances. 'How many people have disappeared up there?'

'Not many. I don't remember anyone else but Usinna and then your people. We're careful to keep away from the place, so there's never any activity there. Tourists hardly ever come here.'

'What about the daughter of the hunter that you told me about. This Igimaq?' Every wrinkle in the man's face was engraved on Thóra's mind; eyes

251

that were so brown they were nearly black, and his maimed hand. Usually she had a lot of difficulty remembering people's faces.

'Usinna was Igimaq's daughter. Naruana is his son.'

So they were one and the same person. 'What do you think is going on? Do you believe that the souls of the people who died of starvation all those years ago are killing others?' That couldn't be it. The bank's performance bond wouldn't be saved by an explanation like that.

'Yes, I do. It's an evil place, but exactly what happens I don't know, nor do I want to. Maybe the spirits drag people into the rock or transform them into animals. Those kinds of things happen here. Maybe not in your country, but they do here.'

'I think there is a different, more down-to-earth explanation.' Thóra wished that Matthew could understand them. He would certainly be less irritable about the phone if he could follow the discussion. She felt for him and knew that she would personally have started beating the receiver on the arm of the sofa in anger if she were in his shoes. 'How did Usinna end up going to the area if it's instilled in everyone from childhood to avoid it? And what was she actually doing there?'

'She had probably forgotten it was dangerous. She moved away from here as a teenager, went to school in Nuuk, and from there to Copenhagen for college. She was really clever.'

'So she was just visiting?'

'She didn't come often—maybe once a year. She was fond of the village and the people here even though everyone knew that she would never move back again. When she went missing, she was doing

252

some kind of research related to the mine. I think it was in biology.'

Usinna had been doing research in this locally notorious area? Thóra tried to ask her questions carefully for fear of belittling the folklore in which Oqqapia seemed to believe. 'Was she studying polar bears or something else that could have led her to the forbidden area?'

Oqqapia shook her head and looked indignantly at Thóra. 'No, she was studying births here in the village and another village farther north of here.'

'Births?' There were hardly many of those out on the snowbanks around the work site. 'Human births?' Thóra's Danish wasn't good enough for her to know what words were used for animal litters. It could well be that the research had involved seals or other mammals.

'Yes. No boys have been born here for many, many years. She wanted to find out why.'

Thóra thought this over for a moment. It suddenly occurred to her that they had only seen girls out and about in the village. Of course it could have been a coincidence, but she found no reason to doubt the woman's statement. 'Did Usinna have a theory about the reasons?'

'No doubt, but I don't know what it was.' The woman stared at her lap. 'I'm not going to have children, so I don't really care what the explanation is.'

Matthew slammed down the receiver and turned to Thóra. 'Do you have the notebook? I'm going to try the number in there.' Thóra pulled the book from the pocket of her coverall, which lay partly on the sofa. They hadn't been invited to take them off; nevertheless Thóra had unzipped hers and

253

pulled off the top part. Matthew lifted the receiver and dialled the number. He suddenly smiled victoriously. 'It works. It's engaged, though.'

'Who is he calling?' Oqqapia had been watching them but hadn't understood what they'd said to each other. Thóra reached for the open notebook and handed it to the woman. She pointed to the number and asked whether she recognized it. Oqqapia did not reply immediately, then asked, suspiciously: 'Where did you get this number?'

'It's the notebook belonging to the woman who went missing. Do you recognize the number?' Thóra took the book back and handed it to Matthew once more, so that he could keep trying.

'Yes.' The woman's trust in Thóra seemed to evaporate before her eyes. 'It's my number.'

'Still busy,' said Matthew, who had cheered up quite remarkably.

'That's not surprising. You're calling the same number that you're phoning from.'

Matthew was dumbfounded. 'You're kidding.' He hung up, closed his eyes and leaned back his head. Then he appeared to recover and wrote the number from the notebook on the slip of paper containing the number of the police. When he had finished he picked up the receiver again and kept trying to reach the authorities.

Thóra couldn't help but smile at him, but instead of responding she turned back to Oqqapia. 'How did your number find its way into this book? Did you meet her, perhaps?'

'Maybe. I don't know.' Oqqapia looked sheepish and avoided Thóra's gaze as she spoke. 'I don't even know what she looked like. The one who went missing.'

254

'So you met a woman from the camp?' Thóra tried to suppress the irritation that suddenly washed over her. The sofa was uncomfortable and her legs were boiling hot in the coverall. Her patience with Oqqapia's vague responses was at an end as well.

'Yes, but I can't remember what she was called. I only met her once.' Oqqapia's face brightened. 'I remember the name of the man who brought her here. He can probably tell you who she was.'

'Man? What man?'

'The AA man. Arnar.' The woman pronounced the name incredibly well considering that she knew no Icelandic. 'He often visited Naruana. He was going to help him stop drinking. He brought books and pamphlets that were supposed to make it easier. Once a woman came with him, maybe the one who disappeared. It was maybe six months ago? They didn't just talk about alcohol, because their conversation was partly about Usinna, I remember. I'm not quite sure how she came up but I remember that the woman had asked about a girl who was on board an ambulance flight. She wanted to know how she was doing, and from that the conversation led on to the subject of only girls being born here. The woman said she was planning to have children herself; maybe she thought that she would be infected by this strange phenomenon. No one wants just girls. Not Greenlanders, and obviously not strangers either.'

Thóra felt it likely that Oddný Hildur would have been concerned about more than just the gender of the foetus. If Thóra were planning to have another child she was sure she'd be interested in anything unusual about births in her immediate vicinity. 'And Naruana discussed his sister with those two without losing it like he did with us?'

'Naruana considered this Arnar to be his friend. He enjoyed his visits and he trusted him. I think he wanted to spend time with Arnar, even if he had no plans to stop drinking. He just felt comfortable talking to him, since he was friendly and seemed not to judge us for our lifestyle.' She shifted in her seat and took a folded piece of paper from her back pocket. 'I'm still thinking of trying it. I want to make something of myself, like Usinna did. I'm sure I could do it if I stopped drinking. I'm clever too.' She looked at the brochure as if it contained a magic spell that would change everything. Thóra couldn't help but hope this were the case. Oqqapia looked from the brochure to Thóra and seemed to notice the doubt in her eyes. 'I can learn, absolutely. I've looked at Usinna's books and I understand a lot in them.'

Thóra spoke slowly, although her excitement was growing; finally things were starting to become clear. 'Of course you can learn. If you know how to read and you can retain information, then all roads are open to you.' She was careful about what she said next. 'Which books are you talking about? Did Usinna leave behind something connected to her research?'

'Yes, not here, but Naruana brought them with him when he moved in. He also brought all kinds of junk that he had at his mother's.' She pointed at the polar bear pelt on the floor. 'He shot this polar bear when he was just twelve years old. He would have been a great hunter if he hadn't—' Her words died out.

'Finally!' Matthew stood up from the couch triumphantly. 'It's ringing!' He clamped the phone

256

against his ear with his shoulder and stuck the slip of paper with the numbers on back into his wallet.

Thóra was happy for him but didn't want to miss the opportunity to go over Usinna's research files if they were part of the book collection the woman was describing. There was only a small chance that they contained any information about the area, but she could always hope. 'May I perhaps see these books? And did she leave behind any notes?'

Chapter 23

22 March 2008

Thóra found it incredibly cold in the office building but Friðrikka had told her that it took the electric heating system more time than the hot water supply to heat the buildings when the temperature dropped so abruptly outside. Thóra hoped that they would be gone before it grew warm inside, and now she wrapped a far-too-large fleece jacket more tightly around her. She had borrowed it from the back of a chair in one of the offices, first checking carefully to see whom it belonged to. She was disgusted at the thought of wearing any more clothing from people who were almost certainly dead. It wasn't cold enough for that.

'When are they coming, then?' They were all gathered in the meeting room, where Friðrikka sat at a window, staring out. 'It shouldn't take them this long to get here from Angmagssalik in an emergency. You'd think they would have priority access to the helicopter.' Like the others, Thóra was impatient for the police to arrive, but unlike the others, she made no attempt to disguise the fact. After Matthew had managed to contact a policeman who spoke decent English he had been ordered to go back to the camp and gather the team in the office building in order to ensure the minimum possible disturbance of the scene. They were to wait there. That had been more than three hours ago.

'It takes them some time to prepare for departure.' Matthew had grown tired of Friðrikka's endless grumbling about how late it was and how the weather could change at any moment.

'What will we eat if they don't come today? All the food is over on the other side of the site,' scowled Bella. 'I'm not going to starve on top of everything else.'

'Then I'll go over and get us something to eat.' Matthew sat at the meeting table and watched Finnbogi examine Usinna's files, which Thóra had managed to prise from Oqqapia earlier in the day. At first he and Thóra had tried to go over the data themselves, but gave up quickly on the biology and asked the doctor to take over. Bella would photocopy the documents later, since Thóra had promised on her honour that they would be returned at the first opportunity. Oqqapia did not want Naruana to discover that she had let the files leave the house and the longer Thóra had the box, the more likely he was to notice that it was gone.

'But we can't go to the kitchen; the police have prohibited it. You said so yourself.' Friðrikka's voice was on the verge of cracking as she glanced back from the window to Matthew.

He sighed. 'Everything's going to be fine. They'll

258

be here before you know it.' Friðrikka opened her mouth as if to object, but Thóra decided to pre-empt her. 'Tell me, Friðrikka. How is it that you never mentioned that Arnar had acquaintances in the village? You insisted you hadn't had any interaction with the villagers besides the kind of brief contact that we've experienced on this trip.' She looked accusingly at Eyjólfur, who was absorbed in his laptop. 'And that goes for you, too.'

Eyjólfur was first to reply. Friðrikka, looking ashamed, said nothing. 'I knew nothing about it, so there's no need to tell me off. I didn't see him with anyone from the village, and I never heard him mention anyone. If he was meeting the natives, it didn't happen while I was here.' He stared at the back of Friðrikka's neck; she had turned to the window again, her cheeks bright red. 'She was here a lot more than I was.'

'What do you have to say for yourself, Friðrikka? Why did you never mention this?' Thóra was not about to drop it.

Friðrikka spun around. 'I just didn't realise it mattered. If I remember correctly you asked whether any Greenlanders had worked here, which they certainly did not.' She sniffed loudly, and Thóra hoped another crying fit wasn't on the way. 'To my knowledge he went to the village several times, on Sundays, but he didn't tell me much about it and he never mentioned that he had any particular friends there. I think he was trying to start an AA group. I never went with him and I don't know any more about it.' Then she brightened, as if a light had been switched on in her head. 'Of course, you can ask him yourself when we return to Iceland.'

259

'What about your friend, Oddný Hildur? Did she ever tell you that she'd gone with him down to the village?'

Friðrikka furrowed her brow. Her whole face had reddened and it almost looked as if she'd used red eye-shadow on her pale eyebrows. 'What?'

Thóra repeated herself, but she was wondering whether there could possibly be another woman. If neither Oddný Hildur nor Friðrikka had gone with Arnar to visit Naruana, there weren't any others to choose from as they were the only women listed on the staff organizational chart. 'Could she have gone without you being aware of it?'

Friðrikka seemed uncertain. 'Well, I sincerely doubt it, but I wasn't with her every single Sunday. For example, I was ill for several days and she might very well have gone to the village. However, I clearly remember that she never said a single word about it to me.'

'Isn't that strange,' said Thóra heatedly. 'You would have thought new topics of conversation would have been welcome around here.'

Alvar cleared his throat to remind them of his presence. Reserved as he was, he tended to blend into the surroundings. 'Is there anything to drink over here? I'm pretty thirsty.'

Finnbogi looked up from his reading. 'You're not drinking anything from here. Everything in the little refrigerator is old, and it would be too risky. You'll just have to get yourself a handful of snow.'

It clearly wasn't the oddest suggestion Alvar had ever heard, because he stood up without complaint and left the room.

'Is there really nothing else available?' asked Bella. 'I'm dying of thirst too, but I didn't realize until he started talking about it.' She snorted. 'I'm not about to eat a handful of snow, though.'

'Then you'll just have to stay thirsty,' said Finnbogi, without looking at her. He had re-immersed himself in his reading. Then he slammed the book shut and pushed his reading glasses up onto his head. They sat better there, since one of the arms was damaged, making them sit crookedly on his nose. He turned to Matthew. 'Will you come and discuss something with me in the hallway? There's more privacy there.' Friðrikka and Bella had clearly started to get on other people's nerves too, thought Thóra as she followed the men out of the room.

'I don't know how much to say in everyone's earshot,' said Finnbogi after shutting the door and leading them a way down the corridor. 'But I feel it's inadvisable to talk about anything out of the ordinary with Friðrikka. I think she may be losing it.'

'Did you find anything in the files?' Thóra hugged herself. It was even colder in the empty corridor than the meeting room.

'I'm not completely finished but I think I've got most of it. Some of it is actually beyond my level, which I'm surprised by, so I've been poring over every detail. This Usinna wasn't doing research for some secondary school or undergraduate programme. At least, it appears more theoretically demanding than that.'

'Is it connected to this area somehow?' Thóra was impatient and wanted to stop him before he started outlining the technical aspects of the study.

'Yes and no. The research is based on the theory that particular manmade toxins in the diet affect

261

the gender of foetuses. These toxins are persistent organic pollutants that do not degrade in nature, so they accumulate in the food chain and more often than not wind up in the sea. They are found in more plentiful quantities the higher they go in the sea's food chain, so they occur in the greatest quantity at its surface. They include substances like the pesticide DDT; PCB, which is used in coolants; fire-retardant chemicals, and other chemicals that affect the endocrine system. It has long been known that seals and polar bears have a high level of these toxins in their systems—a million times higher than in plankton, for example. Their meat is the main subsistence food in the Inuit diet, therefore it's not too surprising that the Inuits are the most impacted by this pollution.'

'It's pretty ironic, given that there can't be people that pollute the environment *less*.' Thóra had never read about any of what the doctor was telling them, since she was hardly a news addict—she made do with skimming the headlines.

The doctor appeared angered by her comment. 'Yes, it is. It's thought that if the toxins are present in excessive amounts during the first weeks of pregnancy they can be carried to the foetus through the mother's blood. There they imitate the hormones controlling the child's gender and prevent the creation of boys. Figures on the gender ratios of newborns in the Arctic support this theory. Among the Inuits in Russia and in northern Greenland it's not uncommon for two girls to be born for every boy. In some villages no boys are born—as appears to be the case here in these parts.'

Matthew's expression suggested that he found

262

this rather disagreeable. 'What do you mean about the hormones controlling gender? Is it like a sex change in the womb?'

'No, not exactly. During the first weeks of development male and female foetuses are identical. The genitals, for example, are formed from the same cells, so this makes sense. Even without these pollutants, historically more girls are born than boys. The difference is very small, but it's increasing throughout the world. I found an article there saying that since 1970, around 250,000 fewer boys than girls are being born each year in Japan and the US. No one has been able to explain this development, but these pollutants might be involved. Of course they cause much more damage to the natural environment than just these gender changes, but in a hunting culture in which the men provide the food it's extremely serious.'

'And elsewhere, too,' added Thóra. 'It's hardly desirable to disrupt the ratio of men to women in any community.'

'No, of course not,' said the doctor. 'But this is still just a theory, and this woman's research was trying to demonstrate that it could be substantiated.'

'Isn't a whole village where only girls are born pretty compelling evidence?' asked Matthew.

Finnbogi smiled patronizingly. 'That alone proves nothing about the relationship between *these substances* and the gender ratios. They could be caused by something completely different. Demonstrating it properly would require, among other things, the collection of blood samples from the girls' mothers, and that's one thing this woman was doing.'

This seemed a likely explanation for Oddný Hildur's entry about Usinna. *Blood tests.*

'Was she able to prove anything? Did she get the blood?' asked Thóra.

Finnbogi took a deep breath before continuing. 'I found a list with the names of the mothers, I think, and she'd put ticks against all of them. She'd probably got her samples, even though there are no results recorded there. She's hardly likely to have had the necessary equipment here to identify the substances in the blood. I don't know if she made several trips here and stored the samples elsewhere in the meantime, or whether they were still here when she disappeared. It actually doesn't matter. New samples can always be taken from the mothers.'

'So none of this is useful to us, is that what you're saying?' Thóra was slightly disappointed. Although the theory was interesting, it didn't look as if it would make a difference for the bank. 'Why did she come up here? She can't have thought she'd find any mothers.'

'I wasn't finished.' The doctor bristled impatiently. 'Usinna was going to try to find the bodies of the original inhabitants who died here at the beginning of last century, to demonstrate that the level of toxins in the blood of the locals had increased. The settlers were apparently interred in this area.'

Matthew and Thóra stared at the doctor. Matthew was the first to speak. 'Blood? Aren't those people just skeletons after all these years?'

The doctor shrugged, causing his glasses to slip back down his forehead. He grabbed them and returned them to their place. 'I found a printout

264

of e-mails sent between Usinna and her university supervisor, in which she says she had reason to believe that they hadn't managed to inter some of the original inhabitants of the village; they'd died in the middle of winter and had had to be buried in snowdrifts. Judging by the e-mails, Usinna seems to have known where these temporary graves were, without providing any further information on their location. I take this to mean that these bodies had been put on ice, so to speak, with the intention of finding them permanent resting places in the spring. Usinna seems to have been of the view that these unfortunate settlers were never actually buried.'

'Spring never came.' Thóra recalled the story from the book in the cafeteria. 'At least, not for those who were supposed to take care of the burials, because they died too. According to the article part of the group was missing, among them an infant and its mother. Maybe Usinna hoped to find them.'

'There's one thing I don't understand.' Matthew had been listening carefully to the conversation. 'How could Usinna have thought she knew where they were buried, since everyone died? You told me, Thóra, that nothing more was heard from the settlers after that winter. I don't see how she can have had any idea that some of the bodies were buried in snow and ice in the first place, let alone known exactly where they were.'

Thóra did not know how to reply, nor did the doctor have any explanation for where Usinna might have got this information. 'In any case, I think we have an explanation for the bones that we found here in the office building,' said Finnbogi.

'That these are bones from the people who died here a hundred years ago?' This seemed more than likely to Thóra. 'They couldn't have yielded much blood.'

'No, but they seem to be from one individual. The snow cover has been diminishing over the last decade. What once lay deep in the ice is maybe coming to the surface now, or almost. That's why the bones appear to be younger than I thought. So the ice could easily be hiding other bodies that simply haven't surfaced yet. The photos you had of the hand might actually show another body that has lain all this time at a greater depth, and is therefore still frozen.'

'What does this mean?' Thóra suddenly sensed a headache that immediately started to intensify. Before long she would have to take painkillers, and would wash them down with a handful of snow if she had to. 'If this whole place is crawling with the corpses of the original settlers, you can hardly justify allowing construction work to go ahead while they're being dug up.'

Matthew's face brightened. 'Of course. Aren't they counted as antiquities?'

Thóra wasn't quite sure, but thought they probably were. 'Hopefully. I think this provides us with good grounds for negotiating for a postponement with Arctic Mining.' She was relieved, but had to remind herself that this proposition was far from certain. 'We just have to hope that if the area is gone over with a fine-tooth comb, Oddný Hildur and the two drillers will be found. I doubt the employees of Berg Technology will return unless that happens. If they refuse to return, all the postponements in the world won't

266

help. The project will never be completed if there's no one to work on it.'

'I would be most intrigued to be allowed to examine the man in the freezer again,' said Finnbogi. 'I only caught a fleeting glimpse of him. After the police come we'll have no further opportunity and it's uncertain whether we'll gain the information that you need for your case.'

'Information?' Matthew looked wary, and Thóra didn't blame him. Was the doctor manipulating the situation for his own needs, masking his medical curiosity with concern for the interests of the bank and the project? 'What information could we need about this body that we can't get from the police?'

The doctor must have sensed their suspicion. 'There was more in Usinna's files than what I've just described. For example, there were instructions on how to protect against bird flu.' The doctor paused and gave them a meaningful look. 'I don't want to overinterpret this, but it did cross my mind that perhaps the two drillers had contracted it. To my knowledge no cases have been diagnosed this far north, but it could still have happened. Maybe the man in the freezer also died of bird flu. I just want to look at him and see whether I can find anything pointing to the cause of his death. Greenland has a peculiar history when it comes to epidemics, because all the settlements are so isolated. As recently as 1962 a third of the population was badly infected by measles, which had never before reached the largest portion of the country. So there could be a common disease that's showing up in this area for the first time. I don't actually know which disease it could be, but bird flu would wreak havoc on the population here.

267

You only have to remember the Spanish Flu, which some even believe *was* bird flu: it killed 100 million people throughout the world at the end of the First World War. As it happens, it didn't reach here, but I can imagine the consequences if it had.'

'That may well be, but bird flu didn't kill the drillers,' said Thóra resolutely. 'Firstly, where are their bodies, if they died of a disease? And secondly, there are no birds here. At least, none that I've seen.'

'They could have eaten infected poultry.' The doctor turned to Matthew. 'Let's go and take a look. It doesn't matter, we've already been in there, so we can hardly do any more damage than has been caused already.'

Matthew gave in. But when the plastic cover was pulled from the body in the freezer, it was clear that bird flu wasn't the cause of death. He had such a large hole in his chest that they could see right through it to the blue-tiled floor.

Chapter 24

22 March 2008

The hotel in Kulusuk would never be listed among the finest in the world, but it was clean and tidy and, most importantly, it had a shower. Thóra hoped the hot water wasn't too expensive, because it was impossible for her to drag herself away from the jet. The soap foamed on the enamelled shower floor as Thóra tried to scrub off the imaginary film that had seemed to cover her entire body. To her

268

it felt as though the revulsion she'd experienced at the work site had clung to her and refused to leave. If she could just wash it off, she could also wipe away the memory of the hole in the body of that poor man, lying in a freezer at the ends of the earth. She knew it was just an illusion caused by fatigue and hunger but that didn't stop her from scouring her body over and over again. Finally she had no energy for more; she put down the soap and stood with her eyes closed, letting the water play over her. However, she couldn't stay there under the shower until they were permitted to leave the country, so in the end Thóra composed herself and turned off the water. She wrapped herself in a large towel, her body steaming wherever her bare flesh showed. She quickly got goosebumps from the cool air flowing in through the bathroom window, which thankfully she had left open, otherwise she would be in a sauna now. As she rubbed most of the water from her hair she looked into the bedroom and saw Matthew lying asleep on the turned-down bed. So that was the reason he hadn't come to see what was taking her so long in the shower. It was late in the evening and the hour they had been given to rest before coming down to the dining room for supper was long past. Not that supper was really the right word—midnight snack was more like it. The day seemed as if it would never end, and they had either forgotten or not had time to eat in the afternoon. Since returning to the office building from the freezer so much had happened that details like food were neglected.

The police had turned up about an hour after Thóra, Matthew and Finnbogi returned from their scientific expedition to the freezer. Thóra had been so shocked to see what was beneath the plastic that she'd had to lie down in the meeting room when they got there. Now she regretted not having waited outside as Matthew had advised her to do while they inspected the corpse. The hole through the body had been so surreal that it took her a long time to accept what she saw over Matthew and Finnbogi's shoulders. The wound was relatively clean and the edges not all ragged as she would have thought would be the case with such an injury. Strangely, it was the fact that the hole was so clean that made it so horrendous; the man was like a cartoon character who had been shot through with a cannonball, except that there was nothing funny about it. Thóra wasn't alone in finding it all rather unpleasant; not a trace of a smile appeared on the lips of the policemen who came from Angmagssalik.

As Thóra dressed in a skirt and elegant blouse, which she hoped would be all right since they were in a hotel, she recalled how the policemen had questioned them. Five of them came on the same helicopter that had transported the group to the area, and the helicopter was made to wait. Two of them were pilots, the others police officers: two Greenlanders and the third a Dane. One of the Greenlanders questioned Thóra and although he had been extremely courteous, Thóra could have done without going through this particular experience. She'd been present at interrogations several times before, but always in the role of duty solicitor. Actually it was interesting to be interrogated, although she probably would not appreciate it until some time had passed. She had behaved precisely like most of her clients, getting over-excited and trying too eagerly to assist them and prove that she'd done nothing wrong. Throughout the questioning she was wholly convinced that the police officer suspected her of having murdered the man in the freezer, and of being responsible for both the bones in the office and the disappearance of the three Icelanders. All because she felt guilty for having re-entered the freezer against their instructions. Thóra had trusted herself completely to avoid answering if asked what they'd done after phoning the police, but she was worried about Finnbogi. Matthew would never admit their minor transgression, but she knew the doctor well enough to guess how he would react under such pressure.

In the end Thóra had recalled her own advice to those whom she assisted in such circumstances— answer only what is asked. Moreover, she had added nothing, and simply stared at the desk between her and the officer after replying to his questions. On the table lay several of the objects that they had found on the drilling rig, which Matthew had handed over as soon as the police appeared. Thóra had asked the policeman if he had any idea whether they were connected to the case, and the man had shrugged and told her that they were obviously old relics and it was unlikely to be relevant. For example, he told her, pointing to the bone with the two drilled holes and the leather strap, these were the goggles hunters used to wear to protect their eyes against snowblindness. No one used them now, as they were much clumsier than modern snow goggles. Thóra could understand that; she would have to have been blinded in both eyes by the snow before she wore a contraption like

271

that. After the questioning she felt greatly relieved as she returned to the meeting room, where they had been told to wait. She had neither been questioned about what they had done while waiting for the police nor about how many times they had gone into the freezer. The questions mainly concerned what business they had there, what they had learned and why they hadn't made contact with the police until that morning.

Thóra had explained that the telephone connection had been out and that the Greenlandic police had been informed about the situation before she and her colleagues set off on their trip, but had not seen fit to come to the work camp, to which the man replied that they had more important things to deal with than searching for missing persons in the mountains; these cases were not usually their business, though they did officially register them. Thóra and her colleagues, however, should have got in touch with them when they found the human bones in the office. Then it would have been clear to everyone that this case was about more than a few Icelanders getting lost in a snowstorm. Thóra had justified their decision by saying that the bones hadn't seemed that significant, since everyone could see that they were ancient. They had thus thought it sufficient to notify the police about them after making phone contact, and that is what they had done. Moreover, she had said triumphantly, they had left the bones more or less undisturbed so as not to spoil the police investigation. The Greenlander had then looked at Thóra as if she were an idiot and told her that the bones were far from ancient. Although they still needed to be examined by a specialist, it was clear that the individual to whom they belonged was from this generation. Thóra had been flabbergasted and asked why he thought this; the police officer informed her that there were two dental implants in the woman's lower jaw. So it was out of the question that this skull was from a past generation. Thóra's only response to this information was: 'Oh.' Dr Finnbogi was apparently not quite as smart as he pretended to be. Or in any case, he had completely missed the false teeth.

Thinking back on it, she recalled that Finnbogi had focused on the skull itself and for the most part neglected the lower jaw. His determination of the gender of the individual had mattered more than its teeth. If what the policeman said was true, it was still possible that the bones belonged to Oddný Hildur. Maybe the doctor had simply been wrong about their age. Thóra recalled that he had based his opinion on how clean the bones were, but it was conceivable that external factors had caused the corpse to decompose faster than usual. She doubted this, however. Oddný Hildur had disappeared earlier that winter and it was unlikely that the temperature had ever climbed above freezing since then. Maybe wild animals had picked clean the bones, but then the jawbone would likely not have been found with the skull, as Dr Finnbogi had said. In any case, one thing was certain: if these were the bones of Oddný Hildur, the employees of Berg Technology were a bunch of weirdos. Thóra had decided not to ask Friðrikka whether her friend had had any crowns, fearing that the question would cause the woman to break down completely. It was a miracle that Friðrikka had pretty much held it together while the police performed their

273

duties; Thóra had doubted she'd bear up under interrogation. And when it came to it she'd actually felt the same about Eyjólfur; the young man had paced the floor of the meeting room while waiting his turn, muttering that he knew nothing about this and shouldn't have come. Throughout all this, the fluorescent light kept on flickering. None of it, however, seemed to disturb Bella. She even appeared to be rather looking forward to her turn. Thóra was thankful that they had told the others they were only going to fetch water from the cafeteria, since she could rely on Bella to tell the police everything just to get her boss into trouble.

Now Matthew stirred slightly as he sensed Thóra's presence. 'What time is it? I'm dying of hunger.'

Thóra sat on the edge of the bed and patted his belly. 'It's late. We missed supper.'

Matthew opened one eye. 'Are you kidding?' Thóra shook her head. Matthew shut his eye again and rearranged his pillow. 'Then I'll just die here.'

'There must be something available. It's not as if we can pop over to the café next door and have a hot dog. The hotel must have sandwiches or something.' Thóra poked him in the ribs. 'Come on, let's check it out, have a snack and then go to sleep. Or to bed, anyway. You won't regret it.'

'Sounds good.' Matthew sat up. 'Can I shower?'

'Sorry. I think I've used up all the hot water on the east coast of Greenland. Maybe in the whole country.' Thóra stood up. Her entire body and soul were feeling much more refreshed. 'We won't be long, and then you can hop in the shower afterwards.' She knew he'd been craving a bath for days. 'We'll be really quick. I promise.'

*   *   *

The food wasn't all that good, but Matthew and Thóra were so hungry that they gulped it down as if they hadn't seen anything edible for days. The dining room had been empty so they'd thrown themselves on the mercy of the bartender, who had his hands full serving drinks to Alvar, Bella and Eyjólfur. The young man very helpfully offered to check whether there was anything to eat in the kitchen. He returned with five pots of yoghurt, a banana, a loaf of bread and some slices of ham. He apologised that there were no leftovers remaining from supper, but Thóra thought this was fair enough under the circumstances.

After Thóra had scraped the last bit of yoghurt from her second pot and only the end crust was left of the bread, she suddenly found she was craving alcohol. 'Let's go over to the bar, I need a drink.'

'What about my shower?' Matthew was still finishing his third bowl of yoghurt. 'I have to wash. I'm starting to disgust myself.' He looked towards the bar where their three colleagues were sitting. 'You go ahead while I go up and shower. I'll come back down when I'm finished. You'll be one glass ahead of me but I'll catch up.' He put down his teaspoon and stood up. 'I'll be in much better shape once I'm clean.'

Thóra went over and sat next to Eyjólfur. Bella was between him and Alvar, and Thóra was glad not to be too close to the latter. He looked like he was brooding, and was downing beer at impressive speed. 'You're looking very lovely,' said Eyjólfur, glancing appreciatively at Thóra's legs as she lifted

275

herself onto the high stool. 'I'd forgotten there was other clothing besides trousers.'

Thóra did not appreciate his drawing attention to her outfit. She ordered a glass of white wine. 'Aren't you all tired?' she asked. 'I can't remember ever having felt so exhausted.'

'Then you haven't lived much,' muttered Alvar, without looking at her. He was staring straight ahead at the bottles of alcohol on the shelves behind the bar, apparently hypnotized by the gleam of the glass.

'Was that meant to be an insult?' said Eyjólfur. He nudged Thóra with his elbow. 'Aren't you going to fight back?'

'Oh, I can't be bothered.' Thóra had no interest in bickering with a foul-tempered drunk in some bar in Greenland. 'Do you recall whether Oddný Hildur had two dental crowns in her lower jaw?'

'Are you kidding?' Eyjólfur put down his glass. He could see Thóra's question had been sincere. 'No, but I didn't really ever have a close look at her teeth.'

'Would you be able to tell?' Bella interrupted, yawning. 'I mean, you can often see someone's top teeth, but not always the bottom ones.'

Of course, thought Thóra, dental implants were more noticeable when people smiled and revealed the gums above them. In fact she remembered having been at a club in Ibiza when she was younger, where the UV lighting used on the dance floor had made it advisable for people with porcelain crowns to smile as little as possible. 'You never went with her to a club or anything like that?'

Eyjólfur laughed. 'Me at a club with Oddný Hildur? Christ, no. I never saw her outside of work.' His smile vanished. 'What sort of question is that, anyway? Did they find some teeth?'

'No, no. I'm just curious.' The white wine was ice-cold and was going down very easily. It was a shame there wasn't any decent food to have with it. 'Where are Friðrikka and Finnbogi?' She wanted to drop the subject of the teeth with him, but also to find out whether she would get a chance to ask Friðrikka about them. She'd have to be more subtle than she'd been just now, though, so Friðrikka wouldn't read anything into the question.

'The doctor was going to go to bed, but Friðrikka went for a walk.' Alvar emptied a nearly half-full glass in one go and ordered another beer. Thóra was willing to bet that it was his fifth or sixth in a row. He was talking up a storm, compared to how quiet he was normally.

'A walk?' asked Thóra in surprise. 'It's the middle of the night. Is it even possible to take walks here? And why hasn't she come back?'

Eyjólfur leaned round on the bar to look Alvar in the face. 'You spoke to her—what time did she leave?'

Alvar seemed upset at having to take part in the conversation just when the bartender had poured him a brand new beer. 'Not that long ago. Half an hour, an hour. She just wanted to have a stroll in the area around the hotel. There's a full moon and the sky is clear, so she's hardly in any danger.' He spoke in a rush, gulping at his beer as soon as he'd finished. Half the liquid in the glass disappeared into him.

'Aren't you on the rescue squad?' said Bella scornfully. 'I wouldn't call you if I got lost.'

'And I wouldn't search for you if you did.' Alvar

277

slammed the glass down on the bar. It looked like he really wanted to storm off in a huff, but that would have meant leaving the bar. So he just sat there stiffly. Bella was unconcerned. 'Maybe she came back without us noticing.' She drew a finger down her damp glass, leaving a broad streak on its slippery surface.

'Maybe.' Eyjólfur seemed sceptical. 'God, I'm dying to get online. There's no wireless or DSL connection in the rooms but the girl in reception pointed me to a computer with an Internet connection in the lobby. This is the longest I've been offline since the Internet was invented, I think.'

'Were you even born then?' Thóra sipped her wine. She was looking forward to Matthew's return; the conversation at the bar could only improve once he joined in. She carried on before Eyjólfur could defend himself. 'Did you definitely make a copy of the entire computer system?'

'Yes, and the contents of most of the PCs. It'll be almost like sitting in the office building at the camp except that you'll have a view of something other than snow while you go over the data.' Eyjólfur looked up at the ceiling. 'I can't wait to get home. Shouldn't we just ignore this travel ban and take the next plane out of here? The cops are still at the site, so who's going to stop us? It's not as if we've done anything wrong.'

'It isn't the most popular airport in the world. I'm sure the police have let their colleagues there know that we aren't allowed to leave the country.' Thóra smiled at him. 'Otherwise I'd be there like a shot too.'

The bartender suddenly stopped washing glasses

278

in the sink behind the raised bar and looked towards reception. The four guests fell silent and turned to follow his gaze. They heard a door shut and a moment later Friðrikka appeared in the doorway, her cheeks flushed from the cold. She walked over to them and as she drew nearer they felt a cold draught. 'I thought you'd all be asleep.'

'And we thought you were lost.' Eyjólfur lifted his glass and toasted her. 'I see that the search parties are just as motivated as they were when Oddný Hildur disappeared.'

Friðrikka pulled off her gloves and stuck them in her jacket pocket. 'When were you going to start the search, tomorrow morning?' she said. 'Or tomorrow night, even?'

'People are hardly considered lost after half an hour or an hour.' Alvar drew out each word. It seemed all that beer was starting to have an effect. 'We would probably have gone to look for you before going to bed.'

Thóra saw from Friðrikka's expression that this conversation was heading for trouble and she tapped on Eyjólfur's back, since he had turned around on his stool so as not to miss anything. 'Where is that computer?'

'Are you leaving?' Eyjólfur seemed frustrated. 'The fun is just getting started.' He pointed towards reception. 'It's out the front there.' He gave her an inquisitive look. 'Are you a blogger?'

Thóra almost laughed. If she had had any spare time outside of work and her home, she would take naps, not blog. 'No, I was going to send my son an e-mail. It was so late when we arrived that I couldn't phone home. I don't have a blog.'

'Okay. It just crossed my mind. Blogs can be

279

pretty cool. Some of Berg Technology's employees kept them, with news from the work site and personal stuff. I helped to set some of them up. Bjarki and Dóri's was fucking genius. Homemade videos and stuff like that that's really funny if you know them.' He stopped, recalling that the men were probably dead, and hurriedly gave them the website address.

'Tell Matthew where I am when he comes down.' Thóra took her glass and gave Eyjólfur a parting pat on the shoulder. Friðrikka stood awkwardly at the bar, obviously debating whether to stay or go, then as Thóra left the bar she decided to sit in her newly vacated chair.

The computer in the lobby was old and the connection slow, but Thóra managed to get into her e-mail and send Gylfi a message saying that she hoped to be home soon. She didn't mention the body or the bones, though it probably wouldn't have hurt to do so. After sending the message she tried to get onto the drillers' blog. Despite the wavering and flickering on the screen at every touch of the mouse Thóra became completely absorbed in the site, until Matthew laid his hand on her shoulder and asked how it was going. She could smell his aftershave, with an undertone of soap, and longed to go back with him to their room. But first she had to show him what she'd found on the blog.

Unfortunately, it couldn't wait.

Chapter 25

22 March 2008

The fourth step would be difficult this time. In his previous attempts to dry out Arnar had found this stage on his road to recovery fairly easy. But now things were different. 'We made a searching and fearless moral inventory of ourselves,' the step stated. Now he had to account for a far more serious issue than having defaulted on debts, disappointed his parents, betrayed his friends and colleagues and let his addiction negatively affect his work. To whom could he entrust this? God? Arnar was not convinced He existed. Yet he had accepted that there was some power that was superior to him, since it was impossible for him to become healthy again without believing that. Suddenly the thought struck him that perhaps there was no benevolent God in the universe, only evil. If so, Arnar had joined forces with the Devil and could have no hope of salvation, either in this life or in whatever might come after death.

He had once slaved his way through Dante's *Divine Comedy*. Although he hadn't understood the work thoroughly—or its strange title—it had had a great effect on him. Many of the poet's images of life after death were still embedded in his mind; for example, the fate of false prophets. They had offended God by pretending to be able to foresee the future and their heads were turned in reverse; in addition to this they wept so much that they were blinded by their own tears. Arnar had admittedly never been guilty of that, but he felt he knew exactly where he would end up in Dante's Hell. Until now he had thought it certain that he would be placed deep in the Seventh Circle of Hell, reserved for those guilty of sodomy; there he would wander a burning desert, trying unsuccessfully to protect himself from fire that rained from the sky. Now he realised he would end up even lower: in the Ninth Circle. This place was intended for those who had betrayed those closest to them. Arnar could not recall precisely how this circle was organised but he did remember that the souls there were trapped in a frozen lake; how much of their bodies was free of the ice depended upon whom they had betrayed.

As a mortal sinner he therefore had only two choices: fire or ice. At a glance he would prefer fire; though he trembled at the thought of either eternal cold or a sea of flames, at least in the latter he wouldn't be as lonely as he'd be in the frozen lake, where no one could speak and the souls could only gaze helplessly at the other wretches stuck in the gleaming ice. *Comedy* was a strange name for a poem that was mostly so devoid of joy. Moreover, Arnar had trouble tallying this description of hell with Jesus' having sacrificed himself on the cross for the sins of mankind. If Dante's description had any truth to it, it would mean Christ's sacrificial death had been for nothing. Perhaps the poet had felt like Arnar when he wrote the poem, certain that the sun would never rise again.

No, Arnar could think of no one to whom he could entrust this. In terms of who would be chosen to help him through the steps, it changed nothing. He detested himself when he thought about this, and he couldn't bear the thought of seeing that same disgust kindled in the eyes of someone else. He had painted himself into a corner; if he did not account for himself he would be unable to free himself from the claws of Bacchus. The memory of what he had done would eat at him from within and tear down his flimsy defences against his addiction. There were two choices remaining to him, both of them bad: to come clean and reap contempt and condemnation, or to go grovelling back to alcohol like a dog in the dirt. Whichever he chose, the reckoning or the bottle, it was clear he had many more sleepless nights to come. Once again the best solution seemed to be to kill himself, like a man. This gave him a third choice of location in Dante's Hell: in the middle of the Seventh Circle, where he would become a thorn bush fed upon by Harpies, winged beings with the heads of maidens.

Arnar laughed out loud in his dark, lonely room. What was wrong with him? Did he really think that he would gain peace of mind by contemplating an old poem; free himself from guilt over his treachery and lust for revenge? He emitted a dry and mirthless laugh, turned on his side and adjusted his pillow. How far could one go in the name of revenge? Were there any unwritten rules or ethical guidelines he had missed finding out about? Hardly. Right now he could think of two proverbs in connection with revenge. One was in line with what he had done—an eye for an eye and a tooth for a tooth—but the other was entirely the opposite; to turn the other cheek. The former had its origin in mankind's first attempts to codify laws in writing, with the Hammurabi Code, while the latter was from the New Testament. Nearly 2,000 years separated these two approaches and another 2,000 had passed without any new options being provided. It must be high time to invent a new phrase. It was hard to tell how it would be worded, but Arnar suspected that his actions would nonetheless have contravened it.

Maybe everything had worked out and there would be no repercussions. The men had not necessarily met their maker. They'd always had options, though Arnar couldn't see what they might have been. Unless God had intervened. Arnar relaxed a little. If God existed, saving the men was in His hands. Just as Arnar could have shown them mercy but chose not to do so. In that case, how could the Lord of Hosts judge him for exactly the same thing? Maybe there had been mitigating circumstances—what if he had been hurt by the men's insults and bullying and therefore couldn't help himself? Weren't people sometimes acquitted because they rebelled against their persecutors? He needed to keep firmly in mind how his life had been ruined and make sure to emphasize that. Maybe then people would show him understanding and judge him leniently, even come to the conclusion that they would have done exactly the same in his shoes. Maybe. Maybe not. The words of the reader at the AA meeting earlier that evening echoed in his mind. *You have no hope of recovery while you carry around your old sins. They will burden you with constant guilt and eventually you will give in to the cunning prompting of your addiction to have a drink. Account for yourself with full sincerity and you will feel how your burdens become lighter and life becomes simpler and more manageable. But your sincerity and honesty must be one hundred per cent. Not ninety-nine. One hundred per cent. Otherwise,*

284

this only works for short periods of time.

Arnar knew that the man was right. One hundred per cent, not ninety-nine. So there was nothing he could do. In fact, he was in the same boat as Bjarki and Dóri. God had to come to his rescue. That is, if God existed and wasn't too busy. The night would be long, just like other nights in the future.

Outside snowflakes fell lightly to the ground as if they didn't really feel like doing so. Was it snowing in Greenland now? If so, wouldn't Bjarki and Dóri's bodies soon be entirely buried? Hopefully gone forever, but at least until the spring. What would happen then? How would Arnar feel if a child came across their remains? He had to do something. But it could wait. Maybe until spring. Then he would have time to adapt his story to gain a little sympathy.

*   *   *

'Can you believe this?' Thóra leaned back in her chair. 'And then they put it on the Internet like it's just another silly film.'

Matthew didn't appear as shocked as she was. 'Maybe it wasn't as nasty as it looked. What led up to it? Sometimes the build-up reveals more than the event itself. And what happened afterwards?'

Thóra frowned at him. 'How can anything that was done either before or after make this any better?' She reached for the mouse and replayed the video. As they watched the scene a third time, Thóra felt as if she were as guilty as the pranksters. On the screen the image moved down the familiar corridor of the Berg office building in Greenland. The man holding the camera giggled and whispered to someone who was apparently following him. Thóra struggled to distinguish the words but thought that he whispered: *Do you think he'll start crying?* This was followed by the uncontrollable giggling of his companions. Next the men started singing 'Happy Birthday', and their singing sounded false to Thóra. The camera stopped outside one of the doors in the corridor, which appeared to be closed, and as the singing grew louder the camera zoomed in on the door's name-plate, on which stood the words *Arnar Jóhannesson—Engineer*. A hand appeared in the frame as the cameraman knocked hard on the door, then opened it almost immediately. Inside a man sat in a chair at a desk. At first his face displayed pleasant surprise, which quickly changed to suspicion.

The singing stopped and the man was handed a white shoebox tied with a large ribbon. The ribbon was made of yellow plastic and printed with a warning about underground cables. 'What is this?'

'A birthday present, or course! Isn't it your birthday today?' The two men outside the frame giggled again, now even more nastily than before. 'Aren't you going to open it?'

'No, thank you.' The man handed back the shoebox. 'I remember what I got from you last year.'

'Oh man, come on. We just didn't remember that you'd stopped drinking. Most people would be very happy to get a bottle of schnapps.'

'Yes, yes. Probably.' The man shook the box at the camera in an attempt to return it. 'Take this and get out of here with that camera. I need to work.'

'Come on. Open it. We went to a lot of trouble to get it for you.' He wasn't laughing any more. 'Open your present, man.'

The man looked into the camera, and the brutally honest lens captured the moment of his surrender. 'What is this?' The anxiety in his voice was clear, but he received no answer. He stared into the camera for a moment longer before violently tearing off the plastic ribbon. He was clearly upset about giving in to them, but was unable to toss the box at them and throw them out. It was as if this were inevitable; if he didn't open the box now it would turn up again at the supper table, in the lounge or somewhere else. Thóra frowned; it must have been horrible to be in this man's shoes in this kind of workplace. Before he took the lid off Arnar looked up nervously. Then he threw it on the floor with a quick flip of his hand and looked into the box. Thóra would have preferred to fast forward through the rest of it, but she forced herself to watch it again. The man cried out and looked at the others in bewilderment. 'What is wrong with you two?' His voice cracked.

'What?' The cameraman's simulated surprise fooled no one and Thóra supposed that the expression on his face was just as false. 'Aren't you happy? We went to a lot of trouble to get it.'

'Get out of here.' The man didn't throw down the shoebox, as he'd done with the lid, but let it lie in his arms and simply stared down at it as he spoke. 'This is even lower than I would have believed you two could go.'

'What?' His voice was falsely incredulous. 'Haven't you been trying to get this for a long, long time? You can stop now. We've done it for you.'

The other man crowed: 'Happy Birthday!' The giggling began again.

'Get out.' The man was still staring into the box. 'You're disgusting.' The camera zoomed in to reveal the box's contents. It had been filled with paper from the paper shredder and in the centre of the pile was a tiny sparrow.

'Now you can stop trying to lure it to you with breadcrumbs. Be happy.'

'I wasn't trying to lure it. I was feeding it. To keep it alive.' The man looked up and now anger radiated from his face. 'It's obviously too much to ask, expecting imbeciles like you to notice that there aren't any birds here. It ended up here and simply needed to be fed until the spring. Then it would have survived.'

'My dear man, don't be so sentimental.' The men snickered and now the camera was turned towards them. They were similar despite not looking at all the same, and to Thóra's eye they were the incarnation of boorishness—schoolyard bullies, all grown up. One of them was starting to lose his hair but tried to make up for it with his beard, which was ragged and discoloured. The other was dirty blond and could have seriously used a haircut. He was chubbier than his balding partner, but they were both wearing dark blue fleece jackets marked *Berg Technology*, which they should have thrown into the washing machine long ago. They jeered and made faces into the camera, repeating 'Happy Birthday!' before shutting it off.

Thóra turned to Matthew. 'What utter, utter bastards.'

'Yes, they don't seem to be particularly nice people, judging by this video.' Matthew was always cautious, so Thóra didn't push him for a stronger reaction. 'I assume that these are Bjarki and Dóri,

288

the drillers, the ones we're searching for, along with other things.'

'Yes, and I'm on the verge of believing that the world is better off without them. I want to show you something else on this page.' She scrolled down. 'Total nonsense, and most of it seriously nasty. I'd bet my right arm that if the bones in the drawers are Oddný Hildur's, then these men were involved in cleaning the flesh from them. I'm certain they wouldn't have thought anything of it.'

'Have you watched all these clips?' said Matthew as she scrolled from one media player window to the next.

'Yes.' Thóra let go of the mouse. On the screen was yet another clip waiting for her to click on 'play'. 'This is typical of the rest: the two of them thinking they're funny. I don't know who shot the video, or whether they set up the camera to record automatically. Usually only one of them is in the frame at a time.' On the screen the men sat and smoked cigars with great enthusiasm. The joke was based on the decision to allow all the workers to decide for themselves whether smoking would be allowed in their individual offices. The corridor would be a smoke-free zone, and the smokers' room as well, since its function was now obsolete. Speculation on what it could now be used for took over and the lameness of the humour increased exponentially.

'I don't understand half of what they're saying but it seems fairly innocent.' Matthew yawned. 'Shouldn't we just go to bed? We might very well have to wake up early tomorrow morning if the police have got anywhere in their investigation.' Thóra stopped the video. 'I doubt they've found

289

anything. We were there for days and we didn't make much progress.'

'They have better equipment than us. They can detect blood and handle everything that we didn't want to touch. And you never know, they might have sent additional personnel from the crime lab, and even sniffer dogs. I know that's what I would do if I were conducting the investigation on behalf of the police.'

Thóra sighed. 'Let me cling on to the hope that I'll get to sleep in tomorrow. Please.'

Matthew bent closer to the computer. 'What is this?' He pointed at the clip that had been stopped on the screen. 'Is this a part of the joke?'

Thóra also moved closer to see what he meant. The two men were frozen in strange positions, one with his eyes closed and his cigar raised, the other reaching for the ashtray, revealing dark sweat stains in his armpits. However, it wasn't either of the men that had drawn Matthew's attention, but something in the dark window behind them. 'Is it possible to enlarge this?' Matthew had got as close as he could without blocking the screen in front of Thóra. 'That looks like some kind of weird figure outside the window.'

Thóra peered at the image. 'Oh? I don't see anything.' She squinted to try to get a better look. 'Oh yes. Is that a mask or a helmet?'

'Maybe a snowmobile helmet.' Matthew pointed at the area directly above the vague figure. 'There's something else. He seems to be dragging something along the window.' He looked at Thóra and hurriedly added: 'Or she. There's no way to tell.'

Thóra tilted her head back a little and looked at the date of the clip. 'This was made on the same day that Oddný Hildur disappeared.' She set the clip in motion again and they watched the strange being move quickly past the window and out of sight. Whatever it had been dragging behind it left an irregular dark streak on the windowpane. 'Could this be related to her disappearance? If it's not an employee, then it's possible that it might have been someone who wished to do them harm.'

'Isn't that rather far-fetched?' Matthew straightened up as the clip finished. 'It's probably something related to the joke, or an employee of Berg.'

'We can find out.' Thóra stood up. 'It would be best to have Friðrikka and Eyjólfur look at it. Since it was uploaded on the same day that Oddný Hildur disappeared, they would both have been on site, and I'm guessing that everyone followed this blog.'

'Everyone but Arnar,' said Matthew. 'He would hardly have been waiting with bated breath for the next entry.'

'No, hardly. We have to speak to him. It seems to me that if he tells us what could get him to return to work, it would be child's play to persuade the other workers to do the same.'

Chapter 26

22 March 2008

Friðrikka and Eyjólfur watched the video without a word until the very end, when the figure appeared outside the window. 'What was that?' said Eyjólfur.

'We were hoping you could tell us,' said Thóra.

291

They were all grouped together in front of the computer. Alvar and Bella were standing at the back but tried to peek over the others' shoulders. 'Haven't you seen the video before? It looks as if it was made the day that Oddný Hildur disappeared.'

'I vaguely remember it but I don't think I watched it all the way to the end.' Eyjólfur rubbed his forehead as if to reactivate his memory. 'If I remember correctly this came in an e-mail from either Bjarki or Dóri, but it was sent just before supper so I didn't open it until the next day. There was so much going on because of Oddný Hildur's disappearance that I only looked at it for a second. At least, if I did watch the whole video I didn't notice that thing in the window. And I didn't feel inclined to watch the clip on their blog because I don't look at every single post.'

'How about you?' Matthew turned to Friðrikka. 'Do you recognize this?'

'No. Like Eyjólfur said, I had other things to think about when I got the e-mail. And I didn't even open it when I saw it was just more of their nonsense. They were always putting up some rubbish or other and I was in no mood for their childish humour. I certainly remember receiving the e-mail, because it struck me how inappropriate their jokes could be at times.'

'Well, obviously they didn't know what was around the corner when they sent this out,' said Eyjólfur sharply. 'It would have been different if they had sent it out the next day, when we'd discovered that Oddný Hildur was gone.'

Thóra interrupted in order to prevent yet another argument between Eyjólfur and Friðrikka. 'But do you have any idea of what this is in the window? Is

it one of you who worked there, or an outsider?'
She added quickly: 'What I mean is, do you
remember the video being discussed the day after it
was sent; maybe someone mentioned having taken
part in the joke?'

They both shook their heads. 'We didn't talk
about it,' said Friðrikka, 'and I sincerely doubt that
any others were in on it. It was always just the two
of them.'

Eyjólfur seemed put out that Friðrikka was
doing the talking. 'None of us was at the window
and the smokers' room was a long way from any
paths. You'd only be approaching that window if
you specifically wanted to look in, for some reason.
Actually, you can't see the person very clearly
but I would be very surprised if it was one of us.
We appreciated the heat indoors too much to be
messing around outside in the cold. Also, it looks as
if this person has something weird on his head and
covering his face and that doesn't fit either. I mean,
why would any of us do that?'

'I don't know. Maybe to scare the men?' Thóra
rewound the video slightly and stopped it at the
point where the figure had gone and the streak was
left behind on the windowpane. 'Do you remember
maybe seeing this streak on the window?'

Both Friðrikka and Eyjólfur moved closer. 'No,
not when Oddný Hildur disappeared.' Eyjólfur
straightened up. 'Bjarki said he'd found dried
blood on the window, but that was a bit later. Of
course we would have wanted to take a look at it
if it had been connected with her disappearance.
He noticed it when he went into the room to smoke
and thought it had been made by a bird that had
flown into the window. He was asking us whether

293

we'd heard some sort of thud. I can't remember exactly when that happened but it wasn't while we were searching. That was when we spent the least amount of time in the office building.'

'So that streak could well be the same one that appeared in the video,' said Matthew. 'If you weren't in the office building much, the smokers' room would have been empty. And if the window is far from the paths between the buildings, as you were saying, then the streak couldn't have been seen except from inside.'

Friðrikka paled. 'Do you think that it's blood from Oddný Hildur?'

'Hardly, if the e-mail was sent before supper. Wasn't she with you at supper?' As far as Thóra could recall, Oddný Hildur had last been observed when she ate with the others. After that she'd either gone to her apartment or over to the office building and never been seen again.

'Yes, but I couldn't say whether the e-mail had come by then. It could just as well have gone out later in the evening. Sometimes people went over to the office building to work or surf the Internet in the evenings.' Eyjólfur sat down at the computer and brought up some information about the video, including when it was created. 'If you want, I can ask someone at my company to look at this and check whether the image can be sharpened. Then maybe we can see better what it is.'

'Who would do that? We don't really want to draw attention to this,' said Matthew.

'We've got dozens of programmers working for us and they're not in the habit of running to the media with the work assigned to them.' Eyjólfur shrugged. 'It was just an idea; it would cost something,

294

naturally, and it's not one hundred per cent certain that it would work.'

Thóra looked at Matthew. 'Doesn't that sound like a good idea?' Matthew agreed.

'No problem, I'll get someone on it tomorrow.' Eyjólfur turned back to the screen and the information that he'd brought up about the video. 'It was indeed made the day that Oddný Hildur disappeared, but before supper.' He closed the window on the screen. 'So this couldn't be her blood unless someone was able to change the settings on the video camera to make it look as if it were an older file.'

'That sounds like a stretch.' Thóra couldn't see why anyone would bother. It wasn't as if this was spectacular evidence and if the intention was to cover up a foul deed it would be peculiar to smear the woman's blood on the window.

'What about the blood? Was it from a bird?' Friðrikka was becoming more and more agitated. 'And if not from a bird, then from whom? That's no bird in the video. Maybe this person killed someone else. A villager or something, and then ambushed Oddný Hildur.'

'We shouldn't let our imaginations run away with us,' Matthew said soothingly to her. 'What we've seen is entirely unclear and there's no reason for us to imagine the worst. It's still most likely that Oddný Hildur got lost and that this clip has nothing to do with her disappearance. The natural environment at the work camp poses considerably more danger than anyone living there. By which I mean both you and the locals.'

'I've always said that they were involved in this somehow. This is definitely one of them.' Friðrikka pointed to the screen and her finger trembled. 'What do we know of the strange reasons they might have for smearing blood everywhere? It could be anything. Maybe even a sacrifice, or something.'

'The Inuits don't offer sacrifices. In these kinds of cultures and communities people can't afford to waste food or anything else on such nonsense.' Alvar swayed slightly as he stood next to Bella, causing him to bump into her shoulder. She shoved him back irritably, making him rock on his feet even more. 'This doesn't have anything to do with sacrifices.'

Matthew cleared his throat. 'How about you all go back to the bar and we postpone this discussion until tomorrow. We won't come to any conclusions now and there's no need for us to lose ourselves completely in speculation that has no basis in reality.'

'You can refuse to discuss this as much as you want.' Friðrikka was the only one who seemed to be completely sober, apart from Matthew. 'It doesn't change the fact that until Oddný Hildur is discovered and an explanation found for what happened to her, I will continue to express my opinions. You can't forbid me from doing so.' She looked as if she were going to storm off.

'How is it,' asked Thóra, who had had enough of her fellow travellers, 'that on the blog we saw another video that appears to have been created only to make fun of Arnar? Was Oddný Hildur really the only one who stuck up for him? Did the rest of you find that kind of behaviour acceptable?'

'No, of course not.' Eyjólfur looked into her eyes. 'I wasn't there much, otherwise I might have done

296

something. At least, I think I would.'

Or not. Thóra turned to Friðrikka but decided not to waste time asking her about it a second time. She was sure she would receive the same answer. 'Could Oddný Hildur have had two dental implants in her lower jaw?'

The unexpectedness of the question seemed to disarm Friðrikka enough to make her reply quite mildly. Or perhaps she was just glad not to have to justify the blind eye she had turned to the harassment. 'No. Definitely not. She had really nice teeth.'

Matthew looked at Thóra and raised his eyebrows. Then who did the bones belong to? They weren't from any of the employees of Berg Technology and it was out of the question that the original villagers who had starved to death had been decades ahead of their contemporaries in dentistry. Perhaps they had been purchased online after all. Hopefully the police would find the answer. 'Do you think the employees can be convinced to return to work at the camp?' Thóra was almost afraid to hear the answer. 'Supposing the police find explanations for the disappearance of Oddný Hildur and the drillers, would the crew be satisfied? You must have spoken to them. Especially you, Eyjólfur.'

The young man apparently had some difficulty making up his mind about whether he would be betraying the confidence of his colleagues by talking about them. Finally he spoke, but slowly, seeming to weigh up every word. 'Of course, it depends what comes out of the investigation. If the findings are that all three of them vanished or died because of something that can be easily explained

297

and sorted out, it's likely that they'd return. Jobs like these are hard to come by, and people get used to having high wages.' He had started speaking faster now. 'If, however, it turns out that something horrible happened to them, then I don't know what will happen. Most people value their own hides more than money in the bank. I'm sure the other employees scheduled to arrive in the summer aren't thinking much about these issues, though; they'll be laying the runway and doing other construction jobs necessary for the mine.'

'Why didn't they start sooner?' Alvar had moved away from Bella a bit and could now sway around as much as he wanted. 'You'd have thought it would be wiser to have the airport ready for use immediately, for the transportation of raw materials and things like that. Not to mention the added security it provides in case something serious happens.'

'That wasn't possible,' said Friðrikka sullenly. 'First we had to get the results from the core samples so that we could situate the mine in an appropriate place. What use would it be having an airport here if the mine was in a completely different location?'

Alvar's drunken brain did its best to process the information. 'Yes, but . . .' He said nothing more, and instead just went bright red. For the first time Thóra felt sorry for the man, and she wondered what his idea of a nice evening might be. What sort of company made him feel comfortable, and what topics of conversation interested him? Probably stories about lost ptarmigan hunters. It would hardly surprise Thóra if their investigation turned up one of those.

*   *   *

It seemed to Igimaq that the policemen were finally starting to go to bed, though several lights were still on in the camp. He hadn't noticed any movement for a long time and the only sound that could be heard was the buzz of the electrical generators. He was still at some distance from the buildings because he did not want to set off the floodlights, but sounds carried well in the calm night air and he had heard the murmur of men's voices while some of them were still up and about, without being able to distinguish what they said. But even if the men had gone to bed it did not change the fact that tomorrow was a new day and they would start up again. They had arrived in two groups: first came five men, but after the people who had been in the camp over the previous few days were evacuated, three others joined the five, this time with dogs. They were not sled dogs, and the hunter had trouble understanding what purpose they were supposed to serve. They didn't appear to be pets, as were common in the cities, but rather working animals, although it wasn't clear to him what they were capable of. They were short-haired and their ears too long and thin to be able to endure the weather for long periods, which was likely to be why they had been taken inside and hadn't come out since. Igimaq was glad he had left his huskies sufficiently far away. They wouldn't have let strange dogs waltz around without at least letting them know who was top dog in these parts.

Unlike his dogs, who were never in doubt as to how to react to new circumstances, Igimaq

299

was stumped. What should he do? This is what happened when you trusted others. When he had first heard of the plans for the mine, his friend Sikki had promised him that the prohibited area would only be driven over—no work would be carried out there. Igimaq had believed him, despite the old familiar look in his eyes that suggested he was not telling the truth. When the camp started to be built on the outskirts of the area he had spoken again to Sikki and again been promised that it would be all right; he would tell those who came that they should not wander any further north, but instead keep themselves south of the camp. Again he had seen that look—nevertheless, Igimaq had chosen to believe what Sikki said rather than what his own eyes told him. Now the story had repeated itself a third time and although Igimaq should not have let himself be fooled, it was too late. There would be no turning back.

Had Igimaq dealt with this the first time he was lied to, things might have turned out differently. But just like his countrymen of the same generation, it simply ran contrary to his character and upbringing to argue or get worked up. It was an ancient custom; those who lived together in small groups could not afford discord, meaning that those who raised their voices or bickered with each other were looked down on. The only way to express one's disapproval was to remain silent, because words spoken in anger had a way of snowballing, intensifying and provoking hostility that would eventually put the survival of the entire community at risk. The Greenlandic language was thus free of invective and Igimaq was not about to start swearing in Danish. He should have pushed

300

the issue with Sikki, forced him to explain how he intended to keep the workers out of the area, even though such a discussion would have been against his upbringing.

He had also been taught to have immeasurable respect for his ancestors, and from them he had inherited the responsibility of keeping the area free of human activity. He and Sikki, his old friend. And now they had both failed. Igimaq could not lay all the blame on Sikki.

He tried to imagine what would happen next. He knew little about the police, since they were seldom seen in these parts. Through the years various things had happened that the police would undoubtedly have wanted to investigate, but the villagers were better suited to dealing with their own problems, evaluating them and determining guilt and innocence. And, most importantly, deciding on punishment for the guilty. More often than not it was enough for the offender to live with the shame of having done wrong, but Igimaq remembered one instance from his youth when a man who had murdered his son in a brutal manner and showed no remorse had been exiled from the area. News of him reached the village intermittently and it was always in the same vein: he was thrown out of one settlement after another when people found out who he was. Finally no further news came of him and people said that he had died alone out in the wilderness. The police would never have dealt with the situation like this, but this solution was the only correct one. The man had no more business being in prison than any other Greenlander. Greenlanders were not to be locked up; that was just plain wrong. Igimaq would go

301

crazy if he were denied the chance to breathe the cold, outside air and his eyes would go blind if they were deprived of the stimulation that the endless expanse of land granted him.

No, the police had no business here, even though the fact that four of them appeared to be his countrymen. They were doubtless more Danish than Greenlandic, probably from the west coast, and unfamiliar with the situation of the inhabitants on this side of the ice cap. None of them would understand Igimaq, or anyone else who knew the history of the place, and it was little use trying to explain it to them. They might even be the lowest form of Greenlanders: those who did not speak their own language, only Danish. Whether this was the case or not, these men would probably twist everything around and interpret it all the wrong way. It was perhaps wisest for him to leave; take his dogs and move even further north. He could easily lose them. It wouldn't matter how hard they tried to find him; in the end they would give up. He had no trouble at all living far from any human settlement for months or even years at a time; he knew places that no one could reach except exceptionally experienced men on dogsleds. Snowmobiles were no match for these old vehicles when it came to long distances, and no one could assess situations in the same way as dogs. Igimaq himself would have ended up at the bottom of the sea long ago if he'd chosen to cross the ice on a motorized sled, because the dogs knew the ice and where it was sound. They heard cracks that the human ear could not distinguish and which could not be seen on the surface of the ice, but which were the predecessors of larger cracks that opened into the icy cold depths of the sea, and spared no one.

If he left, then he would never return; that much was clear. Igimaq had long intended to end his life in this way: pack up and travel north with his dogs and avoid human contact. He would try to see how long he could last, and suspected it would be quite a few years. As long as the dogs stayed alive he could too; once they started dying, things would look different. When he was young his grandfather had taught him that out on the ice sheets his dogs were the hunter's lifeline. Without them he wouldn't get across quickly enough to survive. The distances between sources of sustenance were too long for travellers on foot to make it. Igimaq had often heard the story of the Danish cartographers who ran out of food in north-east Greenland and resorted to eating their dogs. They ate them one by one and after the last dog was gone, so was all their hope, and they died out in the wilderness. Their native guide made it the farthest and the expedition's diary was found on his body, describing the men's hardships in detail. Igimaq's father had once taken him to visit a friend who knew how to read and allowed him to listen to excerpts from the diary, so that he would learn from the men's mistakes. It had worked, and now Igimaq would sooner die of starvation than think of eating his dogs.

No, he would go nowhere for the time being. He had to remain here and fulfil his obligation even though it wasn't clear to him how he ought to go about it. He stared up at the starry sky and tried to identify the animals that he was told people in other countries saw there. He failed to see any, but suddenly realized what he could do. He would have to fetch Usinna and get her out of there. He was not the only one who had been involved in her death and it was unclear whether Sikki and Naruana would find disappearing as easy as he would. Igimaq was a man, and he did not let others pay for his actions.

Chapter 27

23 March 2008

Outside it was dark and windy, but that didn't matter when it was warm and cosy inside the hotel. The breakfast was particularly good, especially in comparison to the hodgepodge that they had eaten over the last few mornings. Bella was the only one who complained about the conditions. She was extremely unhappy that there were only non-smoking rooms at the hotel. 'I mean, we're in Greenland. We can go out and kill the first thing we see and we can probably do everything we can think of inside this hotel, except for smoking. This is fucking lunacy.' She stood up dramatically, grabbed her black jumper and dashed outside.

'Has anyone heard from the police?' The doctor wiped his mouth on a white napkin and laid it over his plate. 'Will we receive permission to leave today?'

'No, because they're probably having the same problem as we did reaching the outside world. Unless they have satellite phones.' Thóra looked at the large clock hanging on the wall of the dining room. 'It's only just eight o'clock, so I doubt they've started doing anything.' Iceland was two hours ahead, which meant everyone there was at work. They could use the time to call people and make enquiries about the case, but of course they would have to proceed carefully. In general it was better to meet people face to face than speak to them on the phone; if the phone conversation went badly they might not have any further opportunity to extract information from the people they'd interviewed. 'What's this Arnar like?' she asked, directing her question at Friðrikka, who sat opposite her. 'How do you think he would take it if I called and asked him some questions? Maybe he could tell us something about these bones?'

'Maybe,' muttered Friðrikka into her cup. She took a sip and put it down carefully on the saucer. 'I haven't seen him since Oddný Hildur's disappearance, but we weren't close at all. He kept pretty much to himself.' The woman rubbed her freckled forehead and shut her eyes, as if she had a headache. Even her eyelids were freckled. 'He'll probably answer your questions if he can.'

'Where can I find his phone number?'

'I don't have a number for him.' Friðrikka took out an old Nokia mobile from the pocket of her fleece jacket. 'I'll see if I put anything into my phone book, but I doubt it. We didn't have mobile phones then, you see, and I didn't know Arnar well enough for us to keep in touch in Iceland. The only person that I spent any time with was Oddný Hildur.' She looked up from the phone and stuck it back in her pocket. 'No, I don't have anything.'

'What about you, Eyjólfur?'

The young man was in the middle of a yawn but he suppressed it abruptly and shook his head. 'No, I didn't know him and I've never even known where he lives. Just look him up in the yellow pages on the Internet.' Thóra had thought of that, but the name Arnar Jóhannesson was extremely common and she'd wanted to take a shorter route. Eyjólfur turned to Friðrikka and continued: 'Maybe your ex-husband has his number?' His voice was charged with nastiness. 'They probably have the same group of friends. They seemed chummy enough at the Annual Ball back in the day.'

Friðrikka did not reply, nor did she look up. No one besides Thóra understood any of this, since Friðrikka had entrusted Thóra with the secret of her husband's sexuality in private, and it was unlikely that she would have dropped hints about her husband to just anyone. Still, the story had presumably circulated among her co-workers while the divorce was taking place and Eyjólfur had clearly got wind of the reason for the divorce. Thóra narrowed her eyes at Eyjólfur. 'Well, how do we know that you aren't also a member of that group's inner circle? Either way, I'd have thought a young man like you would be less prejudiced about something like that.'

'Hey, I was just trying to help.' Eyjólfur didn't take offence at Thóra's insinuation. 'You don't have to worry about me. If you want we can go to my room and I'll prove it to you.' He winked at her.

Luckily, Matthew was engaged in close conversation with the doctor and didn't overhear this. 'Thanks, but no thanks.' At the same moment a young Greenlandic girl came to the table and offered them coffee refills. She had a warm, friendly smile and was very careful when filling their cups. 'What are you doing here? Going up on

306

the glacier?' She spoke good English with a Danish accent.

'We're here because of the mine near Kaanneq. We're on our way home to Iceland.' The young woman nodded curtly. Her smile had disappeared as soon as she heard the name of the village. 'Do you know the place?'

'I visited it many years ago—I was there one summer to help my aunt. I found it fun as a child but I'm not sure I'd want to live there now.' The woman shuffled her feet as she stood at the end of the table. 'Are things progressing well with the mine?' she asked. 'I've heard there'll be a lot of well-paid jobs there once it's finished.'

'It's still in its preparatory stages,' said Thóra. 'It'll be some time before the actual work there begins.' Finally, a talkative person who knew the area. She decided to pump the girl for information. 'There was a small delay but hopefully they'll be able to make up for the time lost. I understand some people are blaming the delays on the area they've chosen to work in. Doing any kind of work there seems to be frowned upon. Do you know anything about that?'

The young woman looked at Thóra and seemed to be in two minds. It was probably due to some language difficulty, because after a few moments of deliberation, she replied hesitantly: 'I was told not to go to the area when I lived there and naturally I heeded that advice. And I've often heard and read about the history of the settlement that was there before Kaanneq was built, as well as what happened to the inhabitants.' She resumed her friendly expression, causing three furrows that had appeared on her forehead to vanish. 'We've

307

always loved scary stories and that one certainly fits the bill. The fact that there are photographs to accompany it makes it even juicier. You do know the story, don't you?'

Thóra said yes. 'It's no secret, is it? I imagine everyone who goes to the village gets to hear it?'

'Yes, I suppose so. At least everyone in Tuku should know it.' She saw that Thóra did not understand what she meant. 'Tuku is what you call Eastern Greenland.'

This simply confirmed what Thóra already suspected. Everyone knew about it, so so what? If she wasn't able to demonstrate that external factors had in some way contributed to the project being halted, it meant little to pull old stories out of a hat. 'I understand that people have disappeared there,' said Thóra, trying not to imply that she was connected in some way with the disappearances. 'Have you heard that?'

'When I was there all those years ago, I was told that people who went there were in danger of going missing. This was followed by a story about a man who ignored everything he'd heard about the area and went there contrary to all warnings. He was never seen again. I don't remember any other examples, and I don't know when he was supposed to have vanished or anything else about him. It was just a story about a young hunter from the northernmost settlements who thought he was a big man but was forced to bow down to the spirits.'

'So it's spirits, not dangerous wild animals, or crevasses in the ice, or anything like that?' Thóra asked, although the answer was obvious.

'Oh, no, it's nothing like that. These are the spirits or souls of people who died there and can't get away.' The girl's expression did not change and she appeared completely unembarrassed about this explanation.

Somehow her face reminded Thóra of the young woman in the village who had allowed them to use her phone, except that this girl was younger and had followed another, straighter path in life. 'I was told there were some marks connected with the place. Have you ever heard of these?'

'Yes, the spirits mark the people that they intend to seize. I've never seen such a thing, just heard it said.'

'What are the marks like?' Thóra imagined a forehead branded with black, smoking crosses.

'Something involving the facial features. I was told that the blood abandons the body through the eyes, mouth and nose—even the ears. And that the people turn blue. After a person has lost all his blood he disappears into the ice to be with the others.' The girl placed the nearly full coffeepot on the table. 'It must be a horrible way to die. That's why the villagers are determined to keep people away from the area. They don't want this to happen to anyone. They're also obligated to those who died to enforce the ban.'

'How?' Now Thóra was expecting a story about ghosts who appeared to people in dreams. 'Didn't everyone die? How did they deliver the message about the ban?'

'They didn't all die. One escaped.'

'One escaped?' Thóra didn't remember this from the book she'd read.

'Yes, so I was told. He didn't escape completely, but he managed to get far enough south to come across other people. They thought he was a ghost

309

but they took him to someone in the village who declared him to be a living person. The two of them spoke and he supposedly told the angekkok—that's a kind of shaman—which area was to be avoided, and made him promise that he would see to it that no one went there. I don't know what else he said because only the chosen are allowed to hear it.'

'Who are the chosen? Special people, or everyone over a certain age?'

'No, no. Descendants of the shaman. His sons, and their sons after them. I think the most important hunter in the village was also involved. Later on the people there even moved farther north to be closer to the area, so that they could keep watch on it. That's how the village of Kaanneq came to be, from what I understand. They'd heard that there were plans to encourage people to spread out northward along the coast, and they wanted to be sure that no one settled where the spirits were. Because the more souls the dead can seize, the more powerful they become.'

'How do you know all of this? I've read a bit about it and I haven't found anything saying that any more was heard of the people who died. Of course I read a description of how a hunting party saw one or two of the villagers out on the ice, but they supposedly fled and were never seen again.'

'That was the same man; he was by himself. Then he disappeared after delivering his message. When this story was recorded there was a lot of secrecy around what the shaman had been told. People feared the revenge of the spirits if they talked about it. So outsiders were never told, nor was it spoken of publicly. Most people thought that it was connected with a Tupilak, that one of the original inhabitants of Kaanneq had created one in the spirit of vengeance but that it had turned against him: rebelled against its creator and then against everyone else there. In the old days you couldn't even think about them without running the risk of dying, let alone discuss them out loud, so that could also explain why no one wanted to talk about this.'

'A Tupilak?' Thóra suddenly remembered the little statue that they had found in the cab of the drilling rig. 'Are they those little scowling figures made of bone?'

'Yes, you can read about them here in the lobby. There's a display set up near the exit. Of course no one believes in them any longer but they're popular souvenirs. That's why the case seems different now; no one fears the Tupilak any more, so people aren't afraid to discuss the story with each other. Maybe what you read will be corrected later, I don't know. Here in Kulusuk no one has any particular interest in it; I just know the story because I've lived in Kaanneq. My mother wanted me to learn about the old-fashioned hunting culture. Kulusuk is quite old-fashioned enough for me, but it's still far more modern than Kaanneq. At least here we have tourists.'

Thóra smiled at the girl. It was the same everywhere: the older one got, the more charming one found more old-fashioned ways of life. Thóra's parents had made many attempts to send her to the countryside, determined that she would not grow up without having tried haymaking or feeding an orphaned lamb from a bottle. She was starting to feel this way herself, regretting that Sóley wasn't outside in all sorts of weather, playing with skipping ropes or hopscotch or cat's cradle. The old, vanishing way of life was more appealing than the new one taking over, not to mention whatever was waiting around the corner. Thóra thanked the girl, who left with the coffeepot. She decided to read the information about the Tupilak, since she needed to go down to the lobby anyway, to go online. Although old horror stories about magical monsters could hardly have anything to do with the case, she found it rather interesting.

Friðrikka had said nothing while Thóra was speaking to the girl, but had been listening carefully. She was pale and tired-looking and still seemed a little shaky after having discovered the corpse in the freezer. 'Do you think they'll find Oddný Hildur?' she said now. It was clear that she'd been startled by the story about souls who pulled people down into the ice. No one wanted to imagine a loved one in those circumstances, no matter how far-fetched a notion it seemed.

'Probably.' Thóra said this with great conviction, though she was far from certain. The woman could have died out in the open in any one of a million different places—or been put anywhere, if she had died by human hand. There must be animals out in the wild who would take advantage of such an easy meal, though at that moment Thóra could not think of any scavengers native to the area. She had no idea whether polar bears and other indigenous fauna ate only freshly killed prey, or whether everything was considered edible in times of hardship. Considering how little food there was, she assumed the latter. It was extremely likely that neither hide nor hair of the woman would ever be found.

'We've got to get her home and bury her. She

312

can't stay here.' Friðrikka was gazing at the multicoloured tablecloth.

'Aren't you forgetting Dóri and Bjarki?' Eyjólfur was sitting at the end of the table, staring out through the window at the choppy sea. 'Don't we need to find them too?'

Apparently these two couldn't agree on anything. If one of them said the sky was blue, the other would say green. 'Of course it also applies to them. It just came out that way.' Thóra couldn't believe she was starting the day by listening to more of their bickering. She looked back at the clock on the wall, irritated at the time difference. Her children had already gone to school by the time she'd woken up, so she would have to wait until later in the day to reach them by phone, and her longing to hear their voices had become almost unbearable. Little Orri could rarely be persuaded to come on the phone and talk to her, so she would have to wait until she came home to hear him. He only ever spoke to the television remote control, which he thought was a telephone. 'I think I'll go online and see if I can find Arnar's telephone number.' She removed the napkin from her lap and stood up. Now they could argue as much as they wanted.

*   *   *

The online yellow pages turned out to have ten Arnar Jóhannessons listed, and although many of them had middle names that didn't help Thóra at all. None of them was listed as being an engineer. She asked Matthew to try to dig up his number through the bank, and then went over to the exit to read about the Tupilak. The display had just a few

313

paragraphs of text and a photograph of a hideous creature that did not look anything like what they had found, but more like a rather bony dog carcass with the face of a man. According to the display this was a being that shamans created from various parts of dead animals, birds and human bones. It was further noted that the most powerful ones were made with bones from a child. The Tupilak was created in a secret place out in the wilderness, where the shaman bestowed life on the monster by allowing it to suck semen from his penis. Thóra shuddered slightly at that, but forced herself to continue. After this, the Tupilak was cast into the sea to seek out its victim and kill it. Of course there was a catch: the being was unpredictable and liable to turn on and attack its creator—or anyone else that it met—especially if the enemy was a more powerful shaman than the one who had sent it out. The Tupilak could also cause illness and decimate entire communities, either with epidemics or by killing individuals one by one. This would have fitted in very neatly with the story about the dead settlers of Kaanneq, thought Thóra. The display further revealed that the phenomenon inspired real fear in the natives of former times, even though now it was considered just an entertaining story for tourists; and that since no original Tupilaks had been preserved, at the turn of the twentieth century the locals had started creating things that they thought resembled the creature for the benefit of Europeans. It was uncertain whether the imitation resembled the original version that people feared so much, because the Tupilak was considered so dangerous that it was always destroyed after it had done its job. Or, as legend had it, sometimes it was

314

also buried in the ground or the ice.

Thóra went back over to Matthew. 'I think I have an explanation for the bone figurine we found in the cab of the drilling rig,' she said. 'It could be a Tupilak that the original villagers made and then buried. That would fit with the story the girl told us earlier.'

'Is that good or bad?' Matthew seemed somewhat distracted as he stabbed at the keyboard.

'Bad for the bank's case. It would be silly to refer to force majeure and then hold up a little statue made of bone. No matter how ugly it is.'

Matthew stopped typing. 'I don't think I'll be mentioning it, then.'

'The only thing I can think of is that it might be necessary for archaeological excavations to be conducted in the area. That way we'd buy ourselves a little time. If it is a Tupilak, then it's potentially the only specimen to have been preserved in its original form.'

Matthew suddenly looked interested. 'That would be better than nothing, at least.'

'Did you get an answer to your query about Arnar?' Thóra looked at the long list of unopened e-mail messages in Matthew's mailbox. Hers had looked the same the night before, but she had decided not to open them until she got home.

'Not yet—I was sending this. I also found the e-mail address of the director of Berg Technology and sent him an enquiry. He has to have some information about his employees. I asked him to name others in the group whom he considers might be able to help us, too, but he hasn't responded yet.'

'Is there no office that you can call?' Thóra took

her phone out of her pocket.

Berg Technology's phone was answered by a polite but firm woman who did not introduce herself, and Thóra spoke briefly to her to explain her business and its connection with the bank. When she had finished she asked for the phone number of Arnar Jóhannesson.

'That figures,' said Thóra when she hung up. 'We have to wait for a response from the director or your friends at the bank. Arnar is undergoing treatment at Vogur and it's not possible to reach him.'

'That's no good.' Matthew seemed to take this even worse than Thóra. 'It would have been nice to be able to explain the bones in the drawers to the police when they contact us again. I'm not sure we'll get out of here until that matter is settled.'

'But what about the man in the freezer? Even if we were to wheedle an answer out of someone about the bones, it doesn't seem very likely that people would be willing to discuss the discovery of the body with us over the phone.'

'Hopefully the police will conclude that the body was put there recently. I doubt it's been stored there for very long. It must have been put in the freezer after the group left the area.'

Thóra did not reply to this. What did she know? Whoever stored the human bones in the desk drawers could just as well have put the body in the freezer. Just then, a new message appeared in Matthew's inbox.

Chapter 28

23 March 2008

The e-mail was from the CEO of Berg, who was in the Azores. The man was obviously quite agitated, since the future of his company depended on reaching an agreement about the project with Arctic Mining. The message's content was quite confusing and didn't reveal much about how he planned to make up for the delays in Greenland, once his crew could be persuaded to go back to work there. He said that he had convinced two of the company's other drillers, who were finishing up a job elsewhere, to take over from Bjarki and Dóri; it was clear that he believed them to be dead. He expressed certainty that he could persuade the others to return to work if some explanation were found for what had happened at the work site, and hinted that Thóra and Matthew should come up with a story about how the men had gone for a hike in the mountains that had ended badly, thus providing a rational explanation for their disappearance. If that failed, they should send all the employees a strictly worded message that their wages would be docked and they would be prosecuted if they didn't go straight back to work. However, the conclusion of this strange message was a list of the telephone numbers and e-mail addresses of all the employees who now refused to return to Greenland. It was not a large group, and Thóra and Matthew divided the task between themselves, with her phoning them one by one and Matthew sending e-mails to

317

those she couldn't reach or who refused to speak to her.

'What a charming bunch of people—I don't think.' Thóra hung up on the fifth person on the list and watched as Matthew started typing him a follow-up e-mail. 'Anyone would think they'd all conspired to keep their mouths shut.'

'They might have got themselves a lawyer,' said Matthew, grinning at Thóra. 'That would be terrible.' Thóra made do with nudging Matthew lightly with her elbow. She felt that he rather deserved the chance to stand up for himself after yesterday evening. While attempting to find a news programme on the TV in their room he had, much to his satisfaction, come across a station in German. However, his happiness was subdued somewhat when he realized that all the programme consisted of was young women walking around stark naked, enthusiastically caressing their own bodies and chewing on pearl necklaces that for some reason they didn't seem inclined to take off. Thóra had teased Matthew about how peculiar the news from his homeland was, and flicked over to the channel at regular intervals to check whether there were any actual news updates.

She tried the two numbers that supposedly belonged to Arnar Jóhannesson; one was his home phone, which no one answered, and the other his mobile, but either it was switched off or there was no signal where he was. That came as no surprise; if the man was in rehab, he might have lost his phone on a drunken binge or handed it over when he checked in. Thóra wondered whether she should call Vogur Hospital and ask to speak to him, but decided to wait in the hope that one of the others

318

could be persuaded to open up. She continued down the list, which now had only two employees left on it. She was fairly optimistic that they would be more easily convinced to talk about things than the others she'd reached. One didn't answer, and as she tried the last one, Sigmundur Pétursson, she said to Matthew: 'Well, keep your fingers crossed.' It rang three times, then a husky male voice answered unenthusiastically. After introducing herself, Thóra said, 'I'd like to know whether you could possibly explain to me the provenance of the bones found in the office building. It's really important, as the police are on site searching for the missing people.' She added this last bit of information in the hope of keeping the man calm and avoiding hammering one more nail into the project's proverbial coffin. The employees would never return if they expected to run straight into the police. 'They need to rule out the possibility that the bones belong to Bjarki or Dóri, and it would speed things up if it were possible to explain how they ended up there.' This was much further than she'd got in her previous calls.

'The bones, yes.' Pétursson sounded serious. 'They're not Bjarki's or Dóri's. You can tell that to the policemen.'

'I doubt that will be enough for them,' said Thóra. 'I'll have to give them a more detailed explanation if the investigation is not to be delayed by an examination of the remains, which would in turn delay further searches for the missing persons.' This was a white lie; obviously the team who would conduct the examination of the bones was not the same one who was searching the area. 'So this could be very important for your co-workers: if they've made it to shelter somewhere they could still be alive.'

At first she heard only the man's heavy breathing, but then he spoke, slowly and determinedly, and Thóra did not doubt the validity of what he said.

'We found a grave. In the area we were supposed to clear to make a track for the drilling rig.'

'And were these bones inside the grave?' Thóra waved her hand between Matthew's face and the computer screen to draw his attention to the fact that the phone calls were finally producing results.

'Yes. They were buried, if you can call it that. They were lying in a kind of animal-skin bag beneath a pile of stones.'

'A cairn,' said Thóra. 'They'd been interred beneath a cairn. How come they weren't all broken into pieces, if they were lying underneath a pile of rocks?'

'They were small rocks, so I'd say that's not so weird. Maybe the bag protected them as well. I don't know.'

'Where was this exactly?' Maybe there would still be traces, which would help convince the police of the story's validity. 'Is it possible to find the place?'

Pétursson gave a joyless laugh. 'Yes, it's possible. But it's disappeared beneath the track. It was at the very end of it, right at the place where the drilling rig is now.'

Thóra wiped the image of the bag from her mind and focused on the conversation. 'What did you do with the bag? Do you know where it is?'

'It got thrown away. It was pretty disgusting, you know, since a corpse had decomposed in it. There were holes in it where foxes had probably got in, since the stones were piled a bit haphazardly and

320

there was enough space for a creature that size to squeeze through. Anyway, we threw the bag away.'

'Where?' Thóra couldn't imagine rubbish trucks driving around the work site, so it was likely that the bag was still where it had been thrown.

'We put all the rubbish into a large container next to the cafeteria, but it was taken from there and buried on a regular basis in a place set aside for the purpose. If I remember correctly the container was emptied after we threw away the bag.'

Perhaps there was still some hope regarding the fate of the bag, if it turned out to be important. Friðrikka and Eyjólfur should be able to point them to the spot where rubbish was buried, so she needn't waste any of this conversation getting a better description of its location. 'So it was just bones and nothing else—no clothing, nothing that might suggest the person's identity?'

'There was a hair that could have been from either a man or a woman. It was pitch-black and medium-length, not necessarily a woman's hair, but on the long side for a man. The colour seemed to indicate that it was a Greenlander's. There were also remains of clothing in the bag but they were in tatters, so it was difficult to say what gender they'd belonged to.'

'Did you check on whether this had anything to do with the villagers? Did you give them the opportunity to move the cairn?'

'Of course.' The man sounded surprised and even irritated at the question. 'We went down to the village and tried to find out more about it, but no one there would speak to us, as usual. We would never have removed the bones without making sure that we weren't offending someone by doing so. We never got any answers out of them, but at least we tried.'

Thóra could imagine that the Berg employees might have got annoyed that the locals would not listen to them, and taken their annoyance out on this derelict cairn. 'Couldn't you divert the track around it?'

'No, that was impossible. There are large flat rocks all around and there was no other way through them. The drilling rig could only go up and down very gentle slopes, so we were forced to sacrifice the cairn. It wasn't up to us to decide where to drill. It was the orders from the mining company that paid the bills. We saw no reason to get them involved in the matter. It would have got ridiculous.'

'Did everyone at the camp know about the discovery of the bones?' Thóra was taking something of a risk by asking this, since it implied that there was something unnatural about the whole situation.

'At first, only the people who found them. I was one of them. We thought initially that it was just a strange natural rock formation that a retreating glacier had left behind, but when we looked closer we caught a glimpse of something among the rocks and removed them to get a better look. If we hadn't seen it the bulldozer would have crushed it all in a second.'

'So you removed the bones and stored them in the desk drawers?' Thóra had trouble concealing her astonishment at these working methods. But of course she had never been in the situation of having a grave stand in the way of her performing her job.

'We removed them. That's right. It seemed better

than just throwing them out of the way of the track.' Pétursson said nothing more about the bones' new resting place in the office building.

'But why were they in different desks all over the place? You couldn't have put them together in one location?'

'The desk drawers don't lock, and we thought it would be weird to leave them lying around. Now I don't want to discuss it any further. Others will have to answer for how the situation was handled. If you've been there then presumably you know that there were no bones in my desk drawer.'

He was right, and Thóra decided not to press him any further for fear that he would slam the phone down on her. 'And you didn't find out anything about who they might have belonged to?'

'No. Although there was one other thing in the bag when we cut it open . . .' The man stopped. 'I'm sure the police will gain enough information if they ask around the village. The people there probably know exactly who it was. I'm sure the locals don't give the cops the cold shoulder the way they did with us.'

'What did you find?' Thóra didn't believe for a second that the locals were at all respectful or afraid of the authorities, or that they'd suddenly open up and start talking to them. If Pétursson knew something more it would have to be him who told her. 'Who knows, maybe this grave is nothing to do with the villagers? They avoid the area like the plague, so it's doubtful that they would take a dead friend there. So what you found could be important.' Thóra shut her eyes and said a silent prayer that the man would trust this reasoning.

'It was a necklace.'

'Can you describe it or tell me what happened to it?' It was possible it had lain under the bones that they'd left untouched in the desk drawers, if it wasn't that bulky.

'It was a kind of typical Inuit thing. Carved bone, except that it didn't hang from a leather strip, but a metal chain. It was silver-coloured but I don't know whether it was steel or something fancier. The metal hadn't corroded, anyway.' He hesitated, then went on. 'The strange thing was that when we opened the bag the chain wasn't around the person's neck as if they'd worn it like a necklace, but lying inside its pelvis. We were careful to cut the bag open gently, so the necklace couldn't have rolled there. I thought it might have been in the pocket of the garment that the deceased was wearing and had fallen down there when the clothing had rotted away, but my partner thought it had been in the corpse's stomach. But I mean, who swallows a necklace?'

'Where is it now?' asked Thóra.

'I don't know. It was hanging on the bulletin board by the coffee machine last time I saw it. Maybe it's still there? It was a seagull. Something unintelligible was scratched on the back of the pendant. Maybe the name of the person who inscribed it.'

'What did it say?' Thóra grabbed Matthew's pen and notebook from the table. Perhaps the police could figure it out.

'I don't remember exactly. It was written from wing to wing, "s"s and "n"s, some vowels. *Business*, *sinner*, something like that, but Greenlandic.' Thóra put the notebook and pen down again. She didn't need to write this down.

324

'Did the necklace say "Usinna"?'

'Yes, I guess so.' Pétursson paused. 'Do you think they're dead? Bjarki and Dóri?'

Thóra had to answer honestly. Anything else would be unfair. 'Yes, I'm pretty sure they are, unfortunately. We still haven't found anything to contradict the theory that they died of exposure. Lost in a snowstorm, probably.' She added this last bit so as not to kill any hope that the employees might be persuaded to return to work, without any litigation or wage docking.

'In the middle of the night? Not likely.'

'What do you mean? We don't know for certain when they disappeared, but it could hardly have been at night.'

The man was silent for a moment. 'You might not have heard this before, but several of us had missed phone calls from the work site one night when only Bjarki and Dóri were left there. The calls came in the middle of the night, which is why no one answered, and the phone number couldn't be reached the next day. Nothing was heard from them after that, so you can maybe understand why we weren't particularly excited about returning. Bjarki and Dóri were probably calling for help, not to inform us that they were going for a walk. I can't help wondering if things might have turned out differently if one of us had answered.'

*　　　*　　　*

Thóra sat at the small bar at one end of the dining room and tried again to call Gylfi. Her son had answered a short time ago but had asked her to call back later, since he was driving. For some reason

325

the sound of his voice made her feel rather sad; perhaps it was homesickness, perhaps it was seeing the lives of her children continue as if nothing had happened even though she was nowhere near them. But probably the main reason was that she felt death all around her in this place, pressing upon her as if it meant to trap her in a corner and then consume her. Now finally it had made its presence known when she discovered that the bones in the office building must be those of Usinna, the daughter of the strange hunter. It was too preposterous an idea that another woman had been buried with her necklace in precisely the same location where this young and apparently talented girl had her final resting place. However, this didn't fit with the information that they had gathered in the village. She was supposed to have wandered to the notorious area and disappeared, not been buried. This didn't necessarily mean she'd been murdered, but it was clear that someone had at least found her dead—if not worse. It was hard to tell who that might have been, or why that same person kept it secret—or whether the missing Icelanders rested in similar graves in the same area.

'Gylfi! Hi, it's Mum.' Her words echoed down the phone. 'Are you at home now?' Her heart glowed as she pictured her offspring, Gylfi—with little Orri in his arms—and Sóley.

'Yes. Listen, I was thinking . . .' Not a word about when she was coming home or how the trip had gone. 'Sigga and I are thinking about going to Spain this summer and a brochure from a travel agency came with *Fréttablaðið* this morning. Would you maybe want to lend us the money for the trip because we don't have any and then we would pay

326

you after we started working in the summer?' He spoke so rapidly that Thóra had to try her hardest to figure out what he was saying.

'Lend you money for a trip to Spain?' Thóra was slightly bewildered. She connected Spain with sun cream, bikinis and beer, and nothing was further from her right now.

'Yes, it's not expensive at all or anything. If you pay right away you get a discount too.' Gylfi paused expectantly.

'But what about work? How do you plan on finding a job if you're just going to leave straight away? Usually, temps have to be found to cover employees who go off on holiday, to Spain or anywhere else. Have you not thought about that at all?'

'Maybe it was like that when you were young. No one expects people just to stay in Iceland in the summer any more.' Thóra tried to look on the bright side. He hadn't said *all those years ago when you were young*.

'Can we talk about this when I get home?' Thóra stared at herself in the large mirror embedded in the surface of the bar. In the second that passed between seeing this person and realizing who it was, she discovered how other people saw her. A blonde, attractive but worried-looking woman who should frown less and try to dress more appropriately. Her bright, low-cut silk blouse didn't belong here.

'Yeah, but this offer is only valid for a few days. And the best trips will probably sell out immediately.' Gylfi didn't explain which trips those were and what distinguished a good trip to Spain from a bad one.

'Let me think about it, then we'll take a look

327

when I come home.' Thóra heard the front door of the hotel open on the floor below. She could easily have craned her neck over the edge of the landing to see who had come in, but she didn't feel like it. If they had to stay here much longer, she would definitely start taking a keen interest in people's comings and goings, but things hadn't got that bad yet. 'You need to think about Orri, too. I doubt he'd enjoy that kind of trip, sweetheart. He's far too little.' She added silently to herself: *And you're too young to take care of a small child abroad.*

'Ah, but we're not going to take him with us,' said Gylfi proudly, convinced that he'd trumped her. 'He'll be staying with you. Just the two of us will go.'

Thóra opened her mouth to speak but closed it again immediately. Up the stairs towards her was walking the Greenlandic police officer who'd questioned her at the work site. 'Gylfi, I'll have to call you a bit later, when I know when I'll be home.' She hung up and stood up from her high bar stool. The man looked anything but pleased as he came towards her and greeted her with a terse nod.

'Will you please gather your group and ask them to pack their things?' Thóra was filled with an unreal hope that they were about to be sent home. 'You need to come back with us to Kaanneq.'

It had been good to have something to think about other than suffocating darkness, isolation and the lack of a shower, but now those thoughts reappeared in a flash. Thóra looked at her loose three-quarter-length sleeves. If this blouse was inappropriate here at the hotel, it would be completely ridiculous at the camp. 'Can I get changed first?'

Chapter 29

23 March 2008

'I can't be here. I have to get home.' Just as she had before, Friðrikka was staring out of the meeting room window and mumbling to herself. The atmosphere in the group was tense and anxious. Outside it was dead calm, but worse weather was forecast. The pure white snow glittered in the gentle daylight, but as darkness began to descend the landscape displayed its true face: here the struggle for life was hard; the strongest survived and the weak were shown no mercy. 'They can't send me wherever they want. I'm an Icelander and I must be allowed to go home.'

Eyjólfur was sitting on the floor, leaning against the wall with his eyes closed. He was chewing gum energetically—apart from that one might have thought he was sleeping. Having to return to the work camp seemed to have hit him and Friðrikka the worst. The others hadn't exactly celebrated, but had accepted the news silently and had uncomplainingly packed up to leave. It's not like they'd had a choice. The police had informed them that a travel ban could be slapped on them at short notice if they looked likely to try to leave or to get a plane to come and pick them up. They would have the court order in their hands before any flight from Iceland could even touch down. The only sensible thing to do was comply with the police and try as best they could to answer the questions put to them. Thóra had spoken briefly to the group

329

and emphasized that the most important thing to remember was that they had nothing to hide; they hadn't been at the site when Usinna vanished or when her bones were found, nor had they been there when the drillers had disappeared. It would work in all their favours if Oddný Hildur's fate were explained as soon as possible, and in that respect the police investigation was their best hope. They would simply have to accept this as a temporary inconvenience. When it was over they could go home proud that they had done all they could to try to determine the fate of these four individuals. Thóra's speech was received as most speeches are: it convinced those who were in agreement already, but did little to inspire Eyjólfur and Friðrikka. Both of them were unhappy about having to go back out into the wilderness, he because he allegedly had other duties to attend to, and she because her nerves appeared unable to endure any more.

'I'm not entirely sure what we're doing here.' Alvar wiped a bead of sweat from his forehead. It was hot and stuffy in the meeting room and their attempts to turn down the radiator had produced no results. Outside it seemed to have warmed up a little, despite the poor forecast, but it seemed to take the building as long to adapt to rises in temperature as it did to drops. 'I could help with the search if they want. It'd give me something to do.' They had watched some of the men set out into the snow; they were wearing thick winter coveralls and had two dogs on leads. They were too far away for anyone to see who they were, but it was clear the group had expanded since the first three had arrived.

'I doubt they care about receiving any direct

330

assistance from us. They just want to talk to us,' said Thóra. 'Especially now they know who the bones in the drawers are likely to belong to.' She had told the police about her phone conversation with Sigmundur Pétursson, and had gone with them to the coffeemaker in search of the necklace. The bulletin board was where he had said it would be, but the necklace was gone. That made his story slightly more dubious, but the investigators appeared to be content with the information nonetheless, even though Thóra understood from them that since Usinna had never been reported lost or dead it wasn't a given that any of this was connected to her. Thóra gave them Pétursson's name and phone number, in case they needed further confirmation. She didn't actually understand why the police had chosen to bring them back to the area instead of just sending one or two officers to take statements from them at the hotel. Maybe something else had come to light that they wanted to explain to the group, or have the group show them. For instance, it was easier said than done to investigate the computer system. Thóra herself wouldn't have found much there without the assistance of Friðrikka and Eyjólfur, who knew the system like the backs of their hands.

'They've found something.' Finnbogi seemed to be speaking to himself rather than to the others as he leaned on the table and stared into his lap. 'They're acting differently to yesterday.'

Thóra agreed with this, and from the look on Matthew's face he did too. The policemen seemed much more serious, avoiding looking any of them in the eye and if they addressed them at all they did so in short sentences, stiffly polite. 'I should hope they have,' she said nonchalantly. 'They're not here for a holiday. With all these personnel, they must have come up with something. But it's in our interests that their investigation succeeds. We're all looking for the same answers, aren't we?' Christ, it would be good to get home and no longer have to constantly be the group's cheerleader.

There was a knock at the door and a Greenlandic policeman walked in. At first Thóra thought he had a gun, but then she realized it was a black radio attached to his belt. The radio crackled for a moment, but no voice was heard. 'I would like to speak to you two further.' The man pointed at Friðrikka and Eyjólfur. 'Am I right in thinking that you are employees here?'

Eyjólfur sighed but Friðrikka appeared not to have heard the man. 'Does this have to do with anything in particular?' asked Thóra. She did not trust them to help the investigation in their current states. 'Neither of them was at the place where the bones were found. Friðrikka had stopped working here by then, and Eyjólfur was only here occasionally. Besides that, they'd never been to Greenland until after Usinna died.' She hoped this was true. 'I'm just wondering whether this is something Matthew or I could help you with. Those two are rather tired.'

The policeman opened his mouth and appeared on the verge of bawling her out when his radio started crackling again. An unfamiliar name was called and the officer brought the radio up to his mouth. 'I'm here. Over.' The officer turned his back on the group. 'I'm not alone.' Through the static they heard someone say in Danish: 'I think you need to come. It's impossible to describe this. I'll

332

send someone for you.'

*   *   *

'There they are,' Matthew called from the window. He was speaking to Thóra, but naturally everyone heard him and tried to see what was going on. A car drove extremely slowly along the track to the camp and entered the parking area. Thóra thought it resembled a funeral procession, and judging by how quickly the policeman had left them it was entirely likely to be one. He had rushed out but come back in to the meeting room almost immediately to get the keys to Berg Technology's jeep, since there were too many people for one car. The jeep had then sped off. At least two hours had passed and everyone in the stuffy meeting room had been a bit bleary-eyed by the time he returned and informed them of what was going on.

The cars were parked outside the cafeteria, but their chrome bumpers and exhaust pipes could be seen from the meeting room, gleaming as they pumped their fumes into the cold, still air. 'I'm going out.' Thóra took Matthew by the arm. 'Come on. The man didn't say anything before he left about us being banned from getting fresh air.'

'He just forgot to say it,' said Friðrikka shrilly. 'We shouldn't go anywhere. What if they have body bags in the cars? I couldn't bear it.'

'Fine. Then you stay, but I'm out of here.' Thóra yanked determinedly on Matthew's arm. 'Come on.' After one final unsuccessful attempt to see into the cars through the window he followed her, but was clearly reluctant.

'They'll herd us back in as soon as they see us.

333

We're getting dressed for nothing. It's also blatantly obvious what we're doing. Who goes out into this weather without having urgent business?'

Thóra had already thought of this. 'Loan us some cigarettes, Bella. We'll just say we came out for a smoke.'

'Me too.' The doctor had become just as excited as Thóra. 'I'm coming with you.'

Bella held tight to her cigarette packet, just in case they tried to take it off her.

'Okay, okay. Let's go.' The more time they wasted standing there bickering, the more they would miss. In the end four of them went outside, while Eyjólfur and Alvar stayed inside with Friðrikka, who was still lecturing them about what a bad idea it was as Thóra shut the door behind them. They beat all speed records putting on their coveralls and snow boots and showed the same swiftness in lighting their cigarettes on the landing outside, before walking in the direction of the cars. Thóra didn't dare not smoke her cigarette properly, but it took all her willpower not to retch. She noticed that the doctor appeared to be having the same problem. Matthew, however, exhaled a grey cloud and beamed at her.

They stopped a short distance from the cars. From there they could see everything that was happening without running the risk that the police would herd them back inside. The police noticed the smokers but didn't appear too worried about them, since they were busy unloading one of the pickup trucks.

Thóra was relieved when she saw that it was a number of bags each too small to contain the body of an adult individual, though they seemed heavy.

334

The men were silent as they carried the grey bags into the cafeteria building. Their seriousness was compelling; the smokers all forgot to keep up the pretence of activity and even Bella's cigarette burned up slowly and evenly. Finally the last two bags were carried towards the house. One of the policemen was careless and slipped on a patch of ice. He landed on his tailbone with a great shout, but it was not concern for his possible injuries that made the four 'smokers' gasp. When the man dropped the bag, an arm rolled out of it.

'What the hell was that?' Bella hung her coverall on a hook that was already overloaded and the bulky orange garment ended up in a heap on the floor. She didn't bend down to pick it up, and no one made any comment. They had other things to think about.

'That was an arm. Without a doubt.' The doctor leaned up against the wall to kick off his boots. 'I don't know whose it was or where it came from, but it was an arm.'

'I don't think there are many candidates to whom it could have belonged,' said Thóra. 'It would be quite something if it *did* come from someone other than one of the people we're looking for.' She stepped from the floor up onto a wooden platform that remained dry while the floor was awash with melted snow. 'But what was in the rest of the bags? Did anyone count them?' No one had thought to do so.

'What should we tell the others?' Finnbogi held hesitantly on to the knob of the door to the corridor. 'I'm not sure Friðrikka will take this well.'

'We'll say nothing. Simply that we didn't see anything,' said Matthew. 'We'll find out soon

335

enough who this is and what happened and until then there's no need to upset her any further. I think an animal must have attacked someone. Under normal circumstances people's arms don't fall off.'

Thóra was silent, but she thought about the frightening video that was the main reason for their expedition from Iceland. She remembered how the splayed feet had jerked abnormally and how before the jerking there had been a whistle that ended with a dull thud. This had been followed each time by a splash of blood. She remembered clearly thinking that it looked as if either a corpse were being dismembered or someone were being killed, and now she had the feeling that it hadn't been a polar bear or a rogue walrus that had separated this arm from its body.

The landing outside creaked, the main door opened and in walked three policemen. The first was the Greenlander who Thóra was certain was directing the investigation. 'Well.' His manner was dry, which was nothing new, but now his voice was tempered with anger. 'I need to speak to each of you privately and then get one of you to come and identify some human remains. I understand that you've seen what's going on and I must express my disappointment that you didn't stay inside.'

'We wanted to have a cigarette. The smokers' room is too wet, from the snow that was in there when we arrived.' Matthew had sidestepped the policeman's accusation rather neatly, in Thóra's opinion. 'We had no idea what awaited us, or we'd have just smoked out of the window.'

It was impossible to tell whether the police officer believed him. 'Well, it can't be undone,' he said.

'I would simply ask that you don't waste any time trying to read anything into it.'

His last statement obviously went in one of Bella's ears and out the other, because she immediately piped up, 'Did a polar bear attack someone?'

The police officer stared coldly at her. 'No one has died here from a polar bear attack for seventeen years, and the last one happened by mistake. An old woman walked too close to a bear in a whiteout and it swiped at her, knocking off the top part of her head. The bear neither ate her nor tore off her limbs. She died in hospital from her head wounds. Polar bears don't attack people except under very unusual circumstances.' He turned to look at Finnbogi. 'You're a doctor, aren't you?' Finnbogi replied that he was. 'We were hoping to get your opinion on something we've found. No one can get here until tomorrow, weather permitting, and it would help us to get some confirmation on a few things.' He didn't elaborate any further.

'Of course. There's not much I can do here but you're welcome to take advantage of my expertise. However, we won't be able to do any autopsies. We don't have the equipment for a procedure like that.'

Thóra seized her opportunity while the policeman appeared to be in a talkative mood. 'Is this either of the men we're looking for?' She didn't know whether she was hoping for a positive or a negative response.

The police officer did not look at her or answer her question directly. 'We need one of you to come and identify . . .' He hesitated, but then added: 'It's more than one person. Probably two.'

That made things clearer. It had to be Bjarki

337

and Dóri.

*   *   *

Thóra and Matthew had a problem. They had successfully managed to behave as though everything were normal when they returned to the meeting room, as had Bella. Friðrikka, Alvar and Eyjólfur seemed to suspect nothing and had only asked once where the doctor was. They were told that he was going over to show the police where he had taken samples of water from, and that was all. None of them seemed to find that strange at all, so they had no idea yet that the investigation had reached a different level. However, this could change at any given moment, since it would fall to either Friðrikka or Eyjólfur to identify the remains if the doctor determined that they did belong to the drillers. This was where their dilemma lay. Which of the two would be better suited to the task? Eyjólfur seemed less stressed than Friðrikka; on the other hand, he appeared to be getting steadily more upset, while Friðrikka appeared to be recovering a little. Maybe it would be too much for him to see the dead men, whereas it might do her good. Friðrikka seemed less concerned about Bjarki and Dóri than about her friend Oddný Hildur, but the reverse was true for Eyjólfur. If the doctor concluded that these were the remains of a man and a woman, the choice would be simpler: Eyjólfur would have to go; but if it were two men, it would complicate matters somewhat. Thóra had read somewhere that it helped the bereaved to see their dead friend or relative; it was important for them in their coming to terms with death and in accepting what could not

338

be changed. Otherwise, they might have difficulty accepting what had happened, and moving through the grieving process. In this case neither Friðrikka nor Eyjólfur could be considered a close relative, but this advice could still apply. Perhaps identifying the remains would help Friðrikka to shut off her flood of tears and Eyjólfur to calm down. But it might also throw them completely off-balance. The corpse in the freezer had certainly agitated Friðrikka enough.

'Aren't we ever going to get out of here?' Eyjólfur was sitting on his haunches against the wall, beneath an erasable message board. Written on it were a few words connected with arrows that doubtless meant a great deal to those in the know, but to Thóra they were meaningless. 'I'm in deep shit if I can't get back to work soon. I heard we were supposed to go home on the 24th. And that's tomorrow.'

'Don't worry.' Thóra stood up and walked to the window. Personally she was going crazy hanging around like this. 'I'm sure they'll understand. It's not as though you're bunking off or pretending to be ill.' She glanced out of the corner of her eye at Bella, who caught a mysterious flu every month, especially on Mondays and Tuesdays. Bella acted as if she didn't notice and continued playing Solitaire at the table.

Dr Finnbogi walked into the room. It looked to Thóra as if he'd changed his clothes, and his hair appeared wet. He said hello to everyone but asked Thóra and Matthew to confer with him privately. Friðrikka watched them as they went off to the corridor, her expression suggesting that she had an inkling they were discussing something more sinister than water samples.

'It's two men.' Finnbogi ran his fingers through his hair and shut his eyes momentarily. 'I managed to put the parts together, more or less, although I could reassemble them more comprehensively if I was working in better conditions than on a bunch of cafeteria tables. As far as I could see, it was the two drillers. They weren't Greenlanders, at least.'

'Where were they found?' Matthew seemed alarmed, just like Thóra. While the men had been missing there had still been hope, albeit weak, that they were alive somewhere. Now that illusion was unsustainable.

'On a nearby island. It appears to be connected to the mainland, but that's because the water level has gone down in the surrounding bay. The dogs found a trail that led there. At first the search party thought they had caught the scent of something else there, but the body parts soon came to light from beneath the snow.'

'What scent?' asked Matthew. 'What else was there?'

'A lot of bones. Animal bones, not human, thankfully. Throughout the summer and autumn sled dogs are kept there, while there's no snow and ice. During those periods the dogs are just a burden and it's better to have them running free on an island than chained up in the village. They come through the summer in much better shape that way. Their owners throw them meat from boats once or twice a week, which explains all the bones. Apparently it's quite normal, since the police all appear to accept this explanation.'

'And were the men just found lying among these bones?' Thóra was still clinging to the idea that a

340

polar bear had killed the drillers.

'No, they'd been left by some rocks in the middle of the island. The police officer who assisted me said it was clear that the person who put them there had intended the dogs to erase all the evidence in the spring. They eat not just the flesh but all the bones too, when they're hungry enough, and dogs that are only fed about once a week must get terribly hungry as the week goes by. Not to mention the fact that these creatures are much more wolf than dog.'

'What about Oddný Hildur?' asked Matthew. 'Did they find any trace of her?'

Finnbogi shook his head. 'No. But it's not out of the question that she's there. Some parts of the men's bodies are still missing, so maybe she'll turn up when they go back and investigate the scene again.'

'Isn't it most likely that they fell prey to predators?' Thóra wished that this were the case; it would be easier for everyone to accept that conclusion, quite apart from the fact that it would strengthen the bank's position in its contractual negotiations with Arctic Mining. 'Maybe this place by the rocks was a kind of larder. I know many animals store food if they don't eat everything they catch.'

'No. Animals didn't kill these men.' The doctor seemed quite certain of this. 'They were cut to pieces by an edged weapon; the wounds were far too clean for them to have been torn apart. My gut feeling is that the video we saw shows the crime being committed. I can't for the life of me understand how someone could do such a thing.'

'And what does that mean? That someone

341

from the village killed them? There was no one else around here—not that we know of, anyway.' Matthew was obviously as stunned by this news as Thóra. His brow was deeply furrowed.

'No, I really don't think so. I doubt that the villagers killed the men.'

'Then who?' Thóra couldn't imagine who could have come here and found himself compelled to kill anyone who got in his way.

'No one. My theory is that they died from some kind of disease or poisoning. It'll be determined conclusively in the autopsy. There are no wounds visible on the whole body parts in places that could actually cause death. They didn't suffer head wounds, or knife wounds in the lungs or other organs, and there are no bullet wounds or anything that could have caused internal bleeding. Nor are there any signs that the men bled to death. On the other hand, I found specific marks that suggest a serious infection of their respiratory tracts and mucous membranes, but like everything else revealed by such a hurried examination, these findings may well differ from the ultimate conclusion.'

'Couldn't there have been fatal wounds in the places where the bodies were cut apart?' asked Matthew.

'In theory, but these cuts are all at joints, where people can't be fatally wounded, except when arteries are severed; but as I said, the men didn't bleed to death.'

'What disease could they have contracted?' Matthew edged away from the sink in the corner, mindful of what the doctor had said about Legionnaires' disease in the pipes.

342

'I'm not exactly sure, but whatever it was it killed the men surprisingly quickly. It is extremely rare for an infection to cause a victim to succumb to death in the short time that appears to have passed between the others abandoning the camp and these two departing this world. I'm wondering whether it might have been poison, or perhaps a very serious case of food poisoning.' He suddenly looked rather pleased with himself. 'I assume you're grateful to me now for having been so uncompromising about the food and drink here in the camp.'

'Yes, yes,' said Thóra, annoyed; now was hardly the time to pat himself on the back. 'But if bacteria or poison killed them, I don't understand how the bodies ended up dismembered out on an island where dogs are kept.'

'No, I have no idea about that, either. I just know that the bodies have been packed away and no one can come near them without putting on the appropriate protective clothing. We used masks and gloves that I'd brought with me in case something like this came up, but that won't be enough if this is a deadly disease. For example, I threw away my clothing, and made the police officer do the same. I'm hoping the extreme cold saved the people who gathered up the body parts out on the island. Still, they're being disinfected at the moment. If this was a virus, we've got serious problems. Of two evils, the lesser one would be for the men to have ingested poison accidentally.'

'How would that have happened? Could we have been infected?' Matthew moved even farther from the sink.

'No, I doubt it. Maybe the person who cut up the bodies, but I can't be absolutely certain.'

'Why not? Do you think he was wearing protective clothing?' Thóra couldn't imagine that the person carrying out his task so energetically in the video had been wearing a white coverall with a hood and plastic mask covering his face. His actions seemed too barbaric for that degree of premeditation.

'I imagine that person is already dead, if what killed the drillers is as deadly as everything seems to suggest. Maybe others have died as well, if he had a family or was in close physical contact with other people. But we would have heard about it, if that were the case. He would have been forced to detail his recent movements if he had admitted himself to a hospital somewhere, and although he would hardly have told anyone that he'd stopped in the wilderness to cut up a couple of bodies, he would have named the location in the hope of a quick diagnosis.' Finnbogi added hurriedly: 'But I should emphasize that I have nothing more to go on than an external inspection of a couple of dismembered bodies. Proper autopsies need to be performed on them and all sorts of samples tested before we know anything for certain.'

In other words, Thóra could stop worrying about whether Friðrikka or Eyjólfur would be better suited to identifying the remains. That wouldn't be happening. She also had enough to contend with, worrying about her own health and that of the others in the group. 'What about Oddný Hildur? Could she also have been infected by something and died there that night?'

'That could very well be the case,' replied the doctor. 'If so, it's imperative that we discover the mode of transmission. Enough time passed between the two events to make it clear that the disease is not transmitted between humans.'

'But the man in the freezer?' Matthew was still frowning. 'Did he also die from some kind of infection?'

'Funny you should ask, Matthew,' said Finnbogi, smug as ever. 'They did in fact allow me to examine him more closely, and although there is much to suggest that he died from that huge wound, there's some likelihood that he suffered the same kind of illness as the other two.' He shook his head thoughtfully. 'However, I discovered something quite alarming when I looked at him under better light.'

Thóra didn't think Finnbogi was just talking about the giant hole in the man's chest. 'What did you find out?'

'The man has been dead for years. Even decades.'

Chapter 30

23 March 2008

Igimaq stood as if petrified, staring into the forbidden area. It repulsed him to stay there for long, but the unrest in his mind prevented him from turning back. The dogs were all whining, each more loudly than the next. They could not understand why they'd been forced to stop in this place, where there was nothing. Only a black hole in the cliff-face where the heart of evil beat. Now it was clearly visible that it was a cave. It became more visible with each year that passed, though at first

345

only a very thin streak of black had distinguished it from the grey surrounding rock. This was the place that people had to be kept away from; the place that pulled anyone who came too close down into the abyss. The spirit would be dragged out of the body leaving behind an empty, hollow carcass, like the sea-conch shells Igimaq discarded after he'd sucked out the meat. But it was not the small cave that disturbed him most. He had seen it many times before and always made sure to keep himself at a suitable distance, like now. No, it was not the expanding opening in the cliff wall that made his heart ache and filled him with despair.

Usinna's cairn was gone. Where the low stone pile had been there was now a path that the snow was not able to hide completely. Tyre tracks were visible running up to it, indicating that someone had driven there only a short time ago. Tracks in loose snow, whether from animals, men or vehicles, were blown away like foam on the waves as soon as the breeze picked up, so the biting wind of the preceding days would have made all but the most recent tracks disappear. But it had been longer than that since the cairn had vanished. Igimaq jumped off the sled and took several steps in the direction where it had been. He did not need to rely on landmarks or locate the cairn in any other way. He simply knew where it had been and could never forget it. It was enough for him to see the low stones on both sides out of the corners of his eyes to come to precisely where Usinna had been laid to rest. He stopped there and stared down at his feet. When had this track been laid? He had been here several months earlier to ensure with his own eyes that the people in the camp kept themselves away

346

from this area. He had felt lighter after turning his sled around, not only because he was leaving a place where he felt bad, but also because of the false hope that it raised in his heart, that his lifelong friend Sikki had been true to his word. Igimaq had gone the way of other men—believing what he wanted to believe. Yet he also remembered having considered himself deserving of some honour, since the area was still devoid of human activity at that time; the vandalism he had committed on the equipment that had to be moved out of the dangerous area had perhaps frightened the people away.

The dogs' whining grew louder and to Igimaq it sounded as if it were accompanied by a different, human sound, the piteous weeping of tormented souls who had waited more than a man's lifetime to be freed from the clutches of the land. They wanted to soar with the birds of the sky, watch the land from above; not from within, where eternal darkness ruled like a winter's night in the farthest corner of the north, but worse, because down under the rock neither moonlight nor stars could mitigate the darkness and make it more tolerable. Maybe it had been the weeping of only one soul; the soul that was closer to his heart than any other. He was not certain, but he had to get away from here. The weeping sounded uncomfortably similar to the beseeching voice of his daughter when she had died here in the sight of her father and brother. The two of them had stood here, in this very same place, trying to ignore her pleas and not let her see that they were on the verge of giving in and extending a helping hand. Igimaq did not regret having stood by and observed from a safe distance, but when

347

Sikki had demanded his presence there he could not conceive of watching his own offspring die from a place of hiding. Of course he could have done it that way—there were enough crags here to hide behind—but his pride had prevented him from watching from out of sight. He was fulfilling his obligations to his ancestors and those who demanded revenge for their deaths. If Igimaq had lost his courage he would have brought an even worse fate upon himself and the village. He could not heal his daughter and sacrifice others. In any case, that would only have been a temporary respite. His daughter bore the mark, and for that she was killed. She would only have dragged him and Naruana to death with her. The message was clear: those upon whom death places his mark will die, and they must do so alone and uncomforted, because any who try to ease their passing will suffer the same fate. And Igimaq had no intention of dying here.

Now the dogs had fallen quiet in the still, frozen air, and Igimaq could hear every sound. The peace here was very different from the silence around his tent, more complex. The gift of being able to read the unknown was vanishing; just as the ice thinned, the knowledge that had been in this country for centuries was disappearing, and one day, when he and his generation had passed on, it would have melted away as completely as the ice. The silence encouraged him to get moving, not to hang about there any longer than necessary. It told him that the dogs awaited his command and were growing restless and suspicious of his intentions. They wanted to go farther out into the wilderness, run until nothing mattered but the horizon. Igimaq

348

breathed quickly through his nose and looked at the snow-covered track beneath his feet. He would find out later which had happened first, the removal of the cairn or the laying of the track—or whether it had happened at the same time. It didn't really matter. The damage had already been done. What could not happen had happened. Usinna was gone from the resting place that was supposed to have kept her until there was nothing left of her. The only tiny positive note was that the police had obviously had nothing to do with it. The evidence showed that the track was older than that. In fact only the people at the camp could have removed the cairn.

The hunter had to remedy this. Usinna had to have her final repose back here, in this place. It was not a question of his opinion—he had given his father his word, and that he could not betray. When, as a young man, he had sworn his oath, it had not occurred either to him or to his father that Igimaq's own child would end up violating the prohibitions of past generations and call down upon herself the eternal restlessness of her own soul, which would never find a refuge. Usinna was childless, like her brother. As things stood, it seemed unlikely that Naruana would do his duty in that regard, which meant Usinna's soul had scarcely any hope. Its only escape would be to settle in a newborn child fathered by her brother. Until that happened her bones would have to rest here in the vicinity of her soul, and also far from the living, to whom she could do many types of harm, even drag them to their death. Igimaq knew this well; wandering souls were to be feared and dreaded. They could not be stopped with a bullet, or even a

349

volley of them. What was already dead could not be killed again. Igimaq wasn't actually scared of death, nor did he understand those who said they wished to live longer than was natural. To create the conditions for a new life, you had to clear space, and it would soon be his turn. He accepted this completely, but nevertheless wanted to have some say in his own death. He wanted to die as he had lived, under the open sky with his rifle in his hand, in harmony with nature, which could strip him of his flesh after he drew his final breath. He did not want to die with his heart in his throat, fleeing something nameless as it snapped at his heels. That, he could not accept. He would have to bring Usinna back to this place. And he knew how he would go about it. If there was one thing the hunter was good at, it was trading, which he had done from a young age. The people in the camp would get the people they were searching for, or a clue to where they could be found, in exchange for Usinna's remains. Igimaq let his eyes wander to the entrance of the cave and stared for a moment at the black hole. It looked like the mouth of a monster that had been buried under snow and ice and was now trying to eat its way up from the cold, white hell. He turned on his heel and walked back to the sled. The dogs pricked up their ears and the harness tightened. Igimaq watched them stand up, one after the other, and although he knew they were looking forward to getting moving, he could not avoid the thought that they wanted to get away from there because of something that had crawled out of the cave as soon as he'd turned around and that was now creeping along the snow towards him. He didn't know what souls looked like, and he didn't want

350

to find out. And so he chose not to look back, but instead stared at the dogs and took increasingly larger strides towards them and the sled that could carry him away from here, as quickly and safely as possible.

* * *

'You hated her.' Friðrikka had moved away from the window and now sat at the table, leaning forwards over the tabletop, which was covered with circular coffee cup stains.

'What is wrong with you?' Eyjólfur was still sitting on the floor, his back against the wall, his legs stretched out. Their argument was brief but had progressed more quickly than usual from silly remarks to earnest conflict. 'I didn't hate her. You're nuts. I hardly knew her.' The young man stared at Friðrikka's back as if he would dearly love to throw something at her. 'Who are you to talk about hate? As far as I recall, you hated Arnar yourself! You can pretend all you want in front of this lot, but you hated his guts!'

'Shut your fucking mouth!' She nearly screamed the last word. 'Why should I have hated him? I felt sorry for him. You were awful to him.'

'Oh, shut up. I wasn't anything to anybody. You might not have joined in tormenting him, but you did nothing to help, just went along with it and laughed at everything, as long as Oddný Hildur didn't see. If she was nearby you made sure you didn't smile.'

'Shut up yourself! I never laughed. I might not have been as brave as Oddný Hildur, but I didn't encourage it. That's bullshit. And it's bullshit that

351

I hated Arnar, just like everything else that comes out of your mouth. What reason did I have to hate him? He never did anything to me.' Friðrikka turned abruptly and glared at Eyjólfur. 'No, if anybody hated anyone here, it was you guys. You hated Oddný Hildur for reporting you to the owner for harassment. I wasn't reported.'

'You hated Arnar because Oddný Hildur was disappointed by how you treated him.' Eyjólfur clenched his teeth and his jaw muscles bulged. This made his youthful face appear more mature and gave him the appearance of the adult that he would change into over time. 'And I wasn't reported either, just so we're both clear on that.'

Thóra yawned discreetly. Their bickering was dying down, as she had hoped it would when she had made the decision not to intervene. 'That's enough, you two,' she said, without much conviction.

'I can't just sit here and take this,' said Friðrikka, looking to Thóra for support. She obviously hoped to find an ally in another female. She was wrong.

'You started it, as far as I recall,' said Thóra as indifferently as before. She was hungry again and envied Matthew, who had managed to fall asleep sitting next to her. Finnbogi seemed about to follow his example.

'Yes, but . . .' Friðrikka appeared to give up the fight. She looked angrily at Thóra and flopped back over the table. 'Dóri and Bjarki hated Oddný Hildur. There's no question about it.'

'Jesus!' Eyjólfur's jaw had dropped. 'I can't believe you'd talk shit about people who aren't here to defend themselves. Mind you, that's just your style, so I don't know why I'm so surprised.'

Neither of them had been told about the discovery of the body parts and it didn't look like there would be any need to do so today, since they all seemed fated to hang around in this sainted meeting room forever.

'What difference does it make whether they're here or not?' Friðrikka got up again. The buzz of the fluorescent lights intensified and one of them started blinking—not exactly the best thing for calming frazzled nerves. 'They hated her for reporting them, and if she hadn't disappeared they would have switched their bullying to her. Don't try to deny it.'

'Christ.' Eyjólfur shook his head angrily. 'I'm not having that. How do you know what would have gone on if this, that or the other had happened?'

'That's enough of your bloody bickering. Listening to the two of you makes me want to puke.' Bella stood up and slammed her fist on the table. The Solitaire cards jumped and scattered. Eyjólfur and Friðrikka looked sheepishly at the furious secretary. 'Keep your fucking mouths shut if you can't talk to each other like normal people.' She flung herself dramatically back down into her chair and gathered the cards. Then she started another round of Solitaire as if nothing had happened.

Thóra smiled to herself, but her amusement was short-lived. How exactly would things end up if they had to stay here much longer? The police would doubtless find other deaths to investigate. She looked around and tried to imagine what it would have been like to work here. To be stuck with your co-workers for weeks, never to be able to get away, to have to be around them regardless of what mood

353

she was in. When you added conflict to the mix, as had obviously been the case here, it must have been a real trial. Maybe it was out of old habit that Eyjólfur and Friðrikka were always arguing. Maybe they knew no other pattern of communication.

Suddenly the floodlights came on outside. Thóra stood up and went to the window, more to have something different to do than out of any raging curiosity. The lights had been going on and off regularly due to the police driving in and out of the camp. What they were doing, Thóra didn't know, but she guessed they were still searching for the missing body parts. Although it was dark outside now, so perhaps it wasn't that, but either way something was going on; maybe they had business in the village, since they must at least have wanted to question the young woman and the hunter's son. And of course the hunter himself. Maybe they were looking for him everywhere. Thóra watched a car drive up to the cafeteria. As she had thought, it was the police.

'I'd do anything for a cup of coffee.' Alvar ran his finger around one of the stains on the tabletop. 'At the very least we should be able to have something to drink, seeing as how we can't even help out.'

Thóra turned to him. 'Shall I check and see whether we can get something from them?' She longed to get out of the room even for just a few minutes. The fresh air would rejuvenate her and help her survive the night. 'I'd really like a cup of coffee myself.' She was glad that Matthew and the doctor were sleeping, otherwise one of them would have gone. She walked slowly to the door so as not to wake them, and carefully opened it onto the corridor. There she drew a deep breath, happy

354

to be free of the room's stale air. But it wasn't until she went out onto the landing that her lungs got what they desired. She stood there for a few moments and enjoyed feeling the cold air stream into her. Then she set off, making sure not to walk too quickly, so she could relish her freedom for as long as possible. Her happiness was short-lived. When she walked around the corner of the building she was so startled that her stored-up energy vanished into the cold night. Up against the gable stood the hunter. Thóra would have missed him if he hadn't spoken softly to her as she walked past. He had positioned himself behind a snowdrift that had formed near the wall of the building. He had probably found his chance to sneak into the camp when the police car set off the floodlights.

The man was far from being invisible or looking like he'd be capable of disappearing into his surroundings, but he seemed in some unfathomable way to assimilate with them, so that anyone not focused solely on searching for him would never notice him. Perhaps it was because he was so completely motionless. 'The police are probably looking for you.' Thóra's voice was shrill with shock, but she could do nothing about it.

'We're all looking for something. I'm also looking—although not for myself.' The man did not seem to move a muscle. 'I'm looking for my daughter. The people here moved her and I have to know where she was laid to rest.'

Of everything that had happened in the camp this was the worst thing he could ask about. Thóra felt a lump in her throat. *Oh, you mean her—yes, she was moved from her grave into some desk drawers.* 'I don't have her.' She could think of nothing better

355

to say.

'I will trade with you. I know that you are looking for someone from here. You will have her in exchange. I know that you moved my daughter. You laid the track. I will trade with you.' The man seemed serious about this. He moved now, to adjust the rifle he held at his hip. Thóra hadn't noticed it earlier and the weapon made her even more uneasy.

'Do you have the woman who disappeared from the camp?' Thóra tried to imagine how long it would take the police to appear if she screamed with all her might. 'Is she alive?'

'No. Not any more.' The hunter's eyes narrowed. 'Nor is my daughter. So it is a fair trade.'

Thóra had to ask about one thing, even though the man had a rifle and help was far away. 'Did you cut the men up?'

The hunter's surprise seemed sincere. 'No. I do not understand what you mean. Will you trade with me or not?'

'I can't,' replied Thóra. 'The police have your daughter's bones.' She saw that the man was not pleased with this news. 'You will get them back, definitely, but it won't be immediately.'

'Then when?' A howl came from somewhere in the distance. First from one dog, but then others joined in. 'I must have them back.'

Thóra tried to think logically. 'I promise that you will get them back. It's just not possible right now. The police have the bones because they were found here. Her cairn ended up beneath the track that you mentioned and they had no other choice but to move them. They tried to consult the villagers, and if the villagers had agreed to talk to them the

356

bones would probably have been returned to you.' She took a deep breath. 'You've got to trust me and return the woman. It means a great deal to us, and she has a husband in Iceland who needs to know what happened.' She regretted this last statement. If the hunter had murdered the woman, it was ridiculous to talk about finding out what had happened to her. 'He has the right to stop hoping that she's still alive.'

'Hope is often better than certainty.' The hunter suddenly became alert. He seemed to hear something that escaped Thóra's notice. He looked at her and then nodded. 'It will be here behind the house in just a short time. Go back in and do not come out again until half an hour from now. Do not go to the police until I am gone, and do not tell them that I was here.' He saw that Thóra was struggling with these conditions. 'Otherwise it will not happen. And I need to have Usinna's bones as soon as possible.'

'Fine. Agreed.' Thóra felt her heart pound in her chest. 'I'm leaving. I'm leaving now.'

The man nodded again silently and when it looked as if he would say no more she turned on her heel and hurried back into the office building. She stood for a long time in the vestibule and tried to get her bearings. If she told her companions about this, the police would learn of the man's visit. Matthew was the only one she could trust with it. Her problem was not how to lighten her own burden, but how she could let the police know that Oddný Hildur had been found, and as soon as possible. She couldn't allow foxes or other creatures to get to the body while she waited for the police to come across it by accident behind the building.

357

They had already combed the whole area around the camp and it was unlikely that they would repeat the search without good reason. She took off her boots and made a decision—but she was not looking forward to it.

'No coffee?' Alvar stared at Thóra in surprise when she returned to the meeting room.

'Oh, I decided not to go.' Thóra had forgotten her original errand. 'I realized I really couldn't disturb them; they're probably doing something important and they'd just have been annoyed. It's not as though they've forgotten we're here, so someone's bound to come with food and drink for us soon.' She squeezed out a smile, took a seat next to Matthew—who was still snoring—and tried to act as if everything were normal.

Friðrikka and Eyjólfur both sat in grim silence as the minutes ticked past. A quarter of an hour later the radiator switched itself on again. Thóra jumped slightly in her seat, because she understood what was happening. Fortunately no one seemed to take much notice of her reaction, except for Bella, who raised her eyebrows before continuing with her game of Solitaire. When just over half an hour had passed, Thóra acted as if she had heard something unusual. 'What was that? Did you hear that?' She looked around, hoping her acting was not as awful as she felt it was.

'What?' Eyjólfur was the only one who appeared interested. Alvar had raised his head from his chest but otherwise his curiosity did not appear to be aroused. However, when Eyjólfur stood up, he did the same.

'It sounded to me as if it came from the corridor or behind the house.' Thóra stood up too. 'I'm going to go and see.' She yawned in the hope that her actions would appear more casual than they actually were. She went out into the corridor, followed by Eyjólfur and Alvar. Matthew and Finnbogi slept on, Bella was too preoccupied with her game of Solitaire to bother getting up, and Friðrikka was still sulking. Thóra pretended to look down the corridor in both directions but then walked straight into the open office across from the meeting room. She went to the window and looked out. Now her acting skills would truly be put to the test. Eyjólfur saved her at thc last minute when he pushed up next to her to see out.

'Hey!' He jumped back from the window. 'What the fuck . . .?'

Thóra stared in silence at the body of Oddný Hildur, which lay face down in the snow between the office building and the apartments. She was wearing a large, bright yellow coat, with a Russian fur hat and matching boots. 'Jesus,' said Thóra, her mouth dry. 'Who is that?' She looked from the woman to Eyjólfur, who stood by her side, his face pale. 'Is that Oddný Hildur?'

The young man shook his head. His adult expression was gone, and now he appeared even younger than he actually was. 'It's Arnar. What's going on here?'

Chapter 31

23 March 2008

Arnar couldn't decide whether he should go through with the follow-up treatment or go directly home from Vogur. He didn't want to do either; there was nothing waiting for him at home and at Staðarfell Treatment Centre his own wretchedness would constantly be reflected in the other patients. In any case, he knew what went on there and he didn't feel he needed it. If he remained dry it would be down to his own determination, not to whatever he did there.

'How are you feeling?' The therapist had come up behind him without his realizing it. He was too absorbed in his own thoughts. They seemed to be spinning in an endless circle from which it was impossible to break free. 'It's time to make the decision we discussed. I don't want to push you, but you'll be released shortly and there's no reason to leave it until the last minute. It's never a good idea to do it that way.' The man was kind, he would give him that, but it irritated Arnar that he spoke to him like a child.

'I know.' Arnar sat stock-still. He hated wearing dressing gown and pyjamas in the middle of the day, and if he stood up his absurd outfit was even more noticeable. 'I guess I'll just go home.'

'Do you think that's wise?' The man smiled warmly at Arnar, who had to look away. 'Many people think that they can utilize the experience from previous follow-up treatments and skip it, but it rarely works that way.'

An exit from the vicious circle suddenly opened up and Arnar made his choice. 'I'm going home. That's my final decision. It'll be fine.'

The therapist sat down opposite him. He made a point of looking deep into Arnar's eyes, as if to make contact with his innermost self. 'A phone call came for you today.'

Arnar's heart skipped a beat. The man said this so cautiously that it couldn't be anything good. What had he thought? That none of this would come to the surface and that life would continue on its merry way? Arnar blinked as he regained his composure, then stared back at the therapist as if he had just got something in his eye. 'And?' He took care not to show any sign of the tension that clutched at him.

'Nothing, really. The decision was made to wait a bit before letting you know, since there seems to be something serious going on. It's never good to tackle things like this when one is recovering.' The man cleared his throat nervously. 'I just wanted to tell you in the hope that it would get you to change your mind. You will need support and we can't give it to you if you go home. Nobody copes well with dramatic events post-treatment.'

More than anything Arnar wanted to prise more information out of the therapist by remaining silent, but he didn't want to take that chance. He had to know more. 'What phone call are you talking about? Who called?'

'A police officer in Greenland. And then an Icelandic lawyer called and said that she was also in Greenland and was extremely eager to speak to you. We generally block these kinds of calls, but it's different when the police are involved.' The man appeared to be trying to read Arnar's expression, without success. 'If the Icelandic authorities want to speak to our patients we have to permit it, even though it goes against our policy. This is the first time a foreign police force has wanted to speak to one of our patients, and we're exploring what options are available to us. We suggested that they contact their Icelandic colleagues if they deemed the case to be serious, but the officer who called didn't say whether they would try that. I didn't speak to the man personally, so I'm simply telling you what I've heard.'

'What was this woman's name and what did she want?' Arnar knew exactly what the police wanted but he had no idea what business the lawyer could have with him. Maybe times were so hard that this is what lawyers were having to resort to: identifying people in deep shit and offering them their assistance. 'She said it was related to your work. In Greenland. She wasn't with the police, neither the Greenlandic nor the Icelandic force.' The man looked at him, unable to hide his curiosity. 'Weren't you working there?'

'Yes.' Arnar would never discuss his problems here, but he needed to find out more about the woman. 'Did she leave her name and phone number?'

'As a matter of fact she did.' The therapist did not appear to be about to give him this information. 'I feel it inadvisable for you to make contact with anyone. Let these people figure things out for themselves and who knows, maybe it will turn out to be nothing and they'll solve it without you needing to get involved.' The man rocked in his

362

chair slightly. 'If you want to talk about it, I'm sworn to confidentiality.'

'No. But thanks anyway.' Arnar didn't want to appear ungrateful. The man did not mean him any harm; he was just curious, like everyone else. No doubt it made a change to have a patient who was entangled in a police investigation and had something to discuss apart from tragic drunken binges. 'This is probably some sort of misunderstanding on the part of the police. However, the woman might have something to do with work, so I've got to talk to her.' He would have bet his right arm that she was only connected with his job indirectly, and then solely through events at the work site. 'So I need to have that phone number.'

The therapist opened his mouth slightly and the pink tip of his tongue glistened. He seemed on the verge of pressing Arnar for more information, but then appeared to decide against it. 'It's on a slip of paper in reception. If you want to walk there with me, I'll get it.' They went together to the second floor. Arnar had to wait while the other man left the detox ward but he reappeared in a flash with a yellow Post-it note. He handed it to Arnar reluctantly. 'I strongly advise you to enrol in the follow-up treatment and let this wait. Remember that you're not well yet, by a long way.'

Arnar took the piece of paper wordlessly. Then he said goodbye and went back downstairs. He had some coins in his pocket from the time when he'd pretended to make a phone call to buy himself some space from his sponsor. He stuck a fifty-krónur piece into the coin slot and dialled the number of Thóra Gudmundsdóttir's mobile

363

phone. Although he had never heard of her, he thought it would be worthwhile to ask her what was happening. It could help him out to know if the police were now involved, as he would benefit from a little head start to think over his position before they questioned him. In order to gain it he would have to know what was up.

A familiar recorded message announced to him that the phone was out of range. Now it all depended on his making the phone call he had feared so much and hoped never to have to make.

* * *

The struggle for space at the window was so great that Thóra had to use all her strength to keep her place. She was standing in the best spot, in the middle, between Matthew and Dr Finnbogi. Friðrikka and Eyjólfur had taken places on either side of them and had to stretch to see out, while Bella and Alvar were forced to peek over the others' shoulders. The police force was working hard at photographing and measuring the body in the snow and investigating the area around it. The men had noticed their audience long ago, but apart from having tried twice to shoo them away with hand gestures, they left them alone.

'I don't understand this.' Eyjólfur sounded like a scratched record. He had repeated himself so often that Thóra had stopped counting. 'Arnar wasn't here. He went home with the others.'

'Couldn't he have come back to chop his co-workers into little pieces?' Bella exhaled gustily, and Thóra felt her warm breath on her ear. 'Weren't they the guys who harassed him?'

Eyjólfur seemed surprised that someone had been listening to what he said. 'No. I mean, yes, but it doesn't fit.'

'Maybe this is someone else,' suggested Alvar. 'He's lying on his stomach, so you can't see much. I don't get how you can be so sure who it is.'

'It couldn't be anyone else. He was the only one here who had a hat and boots like that.' Eyjólfur pointed at the furry knee-length moon boots the corpse was wearing. Presumably out of respect for the dead he said nothing, but everyone thought the same; the boots literally cried out to be made fun of. The matching hat was just as flamboyant.

The photographer squatted next to the body and a policeman hunched down beside him. He took off his thick gloves and put on latex ones, then used tongs to lift the bottom of the hat from the body's neck. The camera's flash blinded the audience in the window for a moment but they recovered quickly and saw what it covered.

'No disease killed that man.' The doctor was the only one who did not gasp when the large cut on the back of the corpse's neck was revealed. The hat's white fur lining was blackened by a large stain, and it was as if the rabbit hair had stuck or frozen fast to the wound, which lifted slightly along with the hat. It was difficult to determine whether the bits pulled between the head and the hat were human hair or fur from the lining, but Thóra prayed they were one of the two and not something even more disgusting.

Thóra heard Friðrikka's rapid breathing and cursed herself—and Matthew for good measure—for not having told her to wait at the table. Of course, Matthew had the excuse that he was woken with the news of the corpse behind the house, and

365

thus hadn't realized what was going on. Thóra, however, should have known better. She looked at Friðrikka, but couldn't see her face through the red hair that had fallen over her cheeks. Her head hung on her chest, but from the way she was shuddering it looked as if she had finally lost it. 'Friðrikka? Are you feeling OK? Maybe you should move away from the window and sit down. This could get even . . . worse.'

Suddenly Friðrikka's heavy sobs filled the office. She grabbed the curtains and tried to pull them shut. The rings on the curtain rod were stuck and only one of them gave in to her efforts, since she was pulling more downwards than to the side. 'Close the curtains. Close the curtains,' begged Friðrikka hoarsely. 'I can't watch this.'

'Then do as Thóra says and get away from the window. We want to watch,' said Bella, spying her chance to move to a better spot. Eyjólfur, who had leaned closer to the window, was now muttering repeatedly: 'Shit, shit, shit.'

'What's wrong?' Matthew grabbed the young man's shoulder and pulled him away from the window. 'It's not Arnar. His hair isn't that long, and it's blond.' Eyjólfur exhaled heavily—he seemed to have an endless supply of air in his lungs. Thóra remembered that the Greenlandic policeman had been very surprised when Thóra and Matthew had informed him that Arnar lay dead behind the office building, asking her to repeat the name and enquiring whether Berg might have two employees named Arnar Jóhannesson. When Thóra said no, the officer had replied that it seemed unlikely the body was Arnar's, since he had received information that the engineer was

366

undergoing treatment for alcoholism in Iceland, as Thóra had mentioned. He said he hadn't actually managed to talk to the man but had been assured nevertheless that he was there. Thóra had received a similar response when she'd called him from the hotel, after concluding her conversation with the final employee on her list, although the answer she'd received was more vague and did not actually confirm that Arnar was at Vogur Hospital.

Friðrikka gave a short scream, then sounded oddly calm when she whispered, 'It's Oddný Hildur,' before breaking into uncontrollable sobs.

ılı   *   *

'Please excuse the inconvenience, but unfortunately it was imperative that we detain you here in light of the circumstances.' The Greenlandic police officer who was leading the investigation addressed the group. 'I see no reason to keep you any longer, and you have been extremely helpful in keeping the investigation afloat as far as possible.' They had all been questioned and made to recount again and again the order in which things had happened.

'When can we leave?' Friðrikka had stopped crying now that several hours had passed since she had recognized the corpse in the snow. In the meantime they had been given food and drink, although Friðrikka hadn't been able to swallow a single morsel. The doctor had urged her to drink as much as she could since she was draining her body's water supply with her floods of tears, and fortunately she had heeded him, since she would be shedding more tears by the end of the meal. 'I can't bear to be here any longer.'

367

'I understand,' said the police officer almost gently, before continuing in an entirely more commanding tone. 'Unfortunately the helicopter can't fly in the dark, so you can't leave before dawn tomorrow. But the helicopter is here, and as soon as conditions are favourable you can leave.'

'Do you have any idea what happened? I mean, to the woman you just found. Oddný Hildur.' Eyjólfur was subdued and lethargic, and appeared distracted. It was as if this peculiar case had finally become too much for him. 'It looked to us as if she'd been in an accident.'

'I can't tell for certain at the moment but it appears that the woman received a head injury, perhaps more than one. Hopefully we'll figure it out.'

'Where was she?' asked Alvar. 'I mean, it's been several months since she disappeared and there's no way she was behind the building the whole time.' As usual, he blushed as he spoke. 'I'm a rescuer and I know a bit about these things.'

At first the police officer refrained from speaking, as if he were trying to contain his desire to say something inappropriate. Then he said, with a hint of sarcasm, 'I'll tell you. At first glance it appeared the woman had been dead for quite some time. You can stop worrying about the search you conducted for her. It's my understanding that although you did all you could to find her, things wouldn't have turned out any differently even if you had searched for longer or in larger groups.'

'So we could have saved her if we hadn't given up?' Friðrikka appeared to be completely disconnected from everything that was happening around her. 'I knew it. I always said that.' Eyjólfur started to say something in reply, but then decided against it. Even he felt sorry for her in this puffy-eyed, broken-down state. He pressed his lips shut and closed his eyes.

'You've misunderstood me, madam. You could not have done anything to save the life of your friend. I just wanted to point that out to you in the hope that maybe you would feel a little bit better. As difficult as it is.'

'Where did she come from?' Matthew acted as if he didn't notice when Thóra pinched him on the thigh. She had told him in private how the body had come to be behind the building and he had promised to keep quiet about it. 'I'm wondering where her body has been all this time.' Thóra felt relieved—the plan was working.

'We don't know,' replied the policeman. 'Probably outdoors, but somewhere sheltered from animals. She wasn't out on the island; we searched there today and it's out of the question that we missed her.'

'The most pressing question is obviously who you believe is responsible for the woman's death, if we presume that it wasn't an accident.' Like all of them, Finnbogi was looking tired, with bags starting to show beneath his eyes.

'It isn't possible to presume any such thing. But for the body to suddenly appear like this does raise certain suspicions.'

'It seems pretty unlikely that a person could receive a gash like that to their neck by falling, especially on level ground; and if she had stumbled on a mountainside or a steep slope you would think more injuries would be visible on her body, even in a snow-suit. It looked to me as if all her limbs

369

were as they should be, at least.' Thóra found the doctor's reasoning convincing.

'As I said, all of this will be revealed, and it's useless to be making guesses. If something unnatural occurred, we'll get to the bottom of it, and there's no need for you to spend time speculating about it.'

'Changing the subject, I have a question.' Thóra had to honour her promise about Usinna's remains. 'Will the bones that were found in the office definitely be returned to the family? It would be so sad if the woman were not allowed a permanent resting place.'

The police officer seemed not to find the question all that odd. 'Yes, that's almost certain. We have to confirm that the body is that particular woman and once that's done there'll be no reason to hold on to the bones. It shouldn't take very long to do, since I expect we'll be able to find her dentist, and then the x-rays should be sufficient to identify her. Things will be different if it turns out not to be her, however.'

'Let's hope that's not the case. We've had enough dead people.' Thóra leaned back in her chair.

'I would examine the bones thoroughly. I'm certain that this woman was killed, just like Oddný Hildur. And that the villagers are the culprits. I've always said that and I've always known it.' Friðrikka spoke without looking the policeman in the eye— perhaps because of his race. The officer did not seem to take it personally.

'We've already started questioning people from this area, especially those Arnar was in touch with, and we'll see what comes out of that. We'll find the guilty party; it will just take some time to clarify

370

who he is and what he did. Maybe he was just guilty of moving bodies from one place to another.'

'And of cutting them up,' added Matthew. 'Somebody took it upon himself to do that and I think it's fairly clear that none of us was involved.'

The policeman shrugged. 'It will all be explained. We have a lot of evidence, partly due to your initiative, and although much of it appears incomprehensible, these cases are usually solved when everything is put together and people start talking.' He didn't specify which people he meant. Instead, he clapped his hands and tried to smile good-naturedly, though the result looked more like a facial cramp. 'I'll have more mattresses brought over and you can decide whether you'll all sleep here in the meeting room or in different places, but I have locked the offices. If you want something to eat or drink it would be good for me to know about that now, but otherwise one of my men will be posted here tonight and he can help you if anything comes up.'

'What could come up?' As ever, it didn't take much to upset Friðrikka. She would doubtless worry about this until she fell asleep and unfortunately everyone near her would hear all about it.

The police officer spoke soothingly. 'Hopefully nothing, but in the unlikely event that it does, the officer will be on guard.'

'Are you implying that the person who did this will return?' Friðrikka would not be persuaded. She clutched at her chest and stared, terrified, at the police officer.

'Will you just shut up for once,' hissed Eyjólfur. Whether it was down to his words or to the policeman's obvious exhaustion, Friðrikka fell silent and wiped away the tears that still streamed down her cheeks.

When Thóra finally fell asleep Friðrikka was still weeping and her soft sobs, which had bothered Thóra for so long, had now started to have a soothing effect. It had been decided that Thóra and Matthew would move from the meeting room along with Friðrikka and sleep in the records storage room that was a bit further down the corridor. They thought it might be a bad idea to leave Friðrikka and Eyjólfur in the same room overnight.

When the sound of cars driving into the camp and the glare of the floodlights filled the room a short time later, Matthew was the only one still awake. Only the sound of heavy breathing came from Friðrikka's mattress. Matthew did not have the heart to wake Thóra and get her to come with him to see what was happening. Thus he was the only witness to the police dragging Naruana, the hunter's son, out of the car and over to the cafeteria.

Chapter 32

24 March 2008

'My God—is daylight never going to come?' Eyjólfur looked once more in the direction of the window. None of them had needed an alarm clock to wake up in the morning, since they were all desperate to go home. Thóra, Matthew and

Friðrikka had moved back into the meeting room with the others and waited with them for the sun to rise. A policeman brought them bread, yoghurt and a pot of coffee, which was emptied surprisingly quickly. After all the food was finished the wait began again and they took turns asking what time it was.

'Here it comes.' Alvar looked happy, but it was probably the thought of beer at the airport in Kulusuk that cheered him so much. 'You can see a big difference in the sky now from just a moment ago.'

Bella yawned. 'It's just as dark as it was before. Maybe time has stopped.'

'What nonsense. You need your eyesight checked if you can't see the difference,' spat Alvar, before turning back to the window again and staring up at the sky. It was indeed as plain as day that the darkness was slowly starting to vanish.

Friðrikka did not take part in the discussion about the colour of the sky. She was in a much better state than the night before. Admittedly, she wasn't laughing and joking, but she was a great deal calmer. Crying was said to be cathartic, and it seemed to have done Friðrikka some good at least. 'I can't believe we're finally going home.' She looked at Thóra, who was starting to slump in her chair. 'I only made arrangements for my cat until today. I haven't been able to call or send a message to my neighbour, so I would have been in deep trouble if we'd had to stay here any longer.' She looked embarrassed. 'I know a hungry cat is hardly a big deal compared to what we've seen here, but I'm still worried about it.'

'Bless you, of course you are.' Thóra smiled

encouragingly at her. She had worried about having the bawling woman sitting next to her on the flight home, but those worries seemed redundant now. 'If we always had to compare everything with the worst thing we can imagine we'd never get to the end of it, you can't ask that of anyone. Your cat will be happy to have you home.' Thóra decided not to mention her children, who had hopefully missed their mother just a little bit.

'I'm going to celebrate by going downtown and getting completely pissed.' Eyjólfur stopped chewing his fingernails and shook himself as if he felt a sudden chill. 'But first I'm going to take a two-hour shower.'

Although Thóra envied him in a way, her years of getting wasted downtown were behind her. She just wanted to see her children and pinch her grandson's chubby cheek, but once she'd done that she would certainly be ready for a two-hour shower. With Matthew, and without the influence of alcohol. Until then she would try to keep her wits about her. It would have been unrealistic to hope that they would find the three missing people alive in an igloo, waiting to rescued. Friðrikka was perhaps the only one who had allowed herself to believe that. But their trip hadn't been completely useless. As far as the bank was concerned, Thóra was quite content; the sudden deaths of the three employees, which appeared not to have had anything to do with Berg, were a big step towards a settlement with Arctic Mining. Thóra had already started writing a report for the bank but was finding it difficult to describe what had happened to the three employees without sounding like she was under the influence of illegal drugs. Bragi certainly wouldn't appreciate her efforts if the bank came to that same conclusion.

'The helicopter pilot has come out,' said Alvar, excited. 'It can't be long now.'

Thóra saved her document and shut her laptop. In any case, she couldn't finish the report; Matthew had told her about the arrival of the hunter's son in the police car during the night and it still remained to be seen what role he had played in the case. Unfortunately what did seem clear was that his role would be an ugly one. Thóra felt sorry for poor Oqqapia. Their relationship had seemed quite unhealthy to her, and it could not have been pleasant for the woman to see the man she lived with dragged out of their home in handcuffs. Hopefully she would manage to stop drinking and get her life back on track. Unfortunately, statistics were not on her side. The police had taken Usinna's files and books, the ones Oqqapia had lent them, promising to return them; Thóra hoped the delay in returning the box would not get Oqqapia into trouble.

Eyjólfur had got up and now stood next to Alvar, watching the helicopter pilot. 'What are we waiting for?' he said, turning around. 'Shouldn't we go out?'

'They'll come and get us when it's time,' replied Matthew. 'They still have to load the helicopter and there's no reason for us to wait out in the cold while they're doing that.'

'Are we taking Oddný Hildur's body with us?' asked Friðrikka in a weak voice. 'She needs to get home.'

Thóra was quick to reply. 'Almost certainly not today, but she'll be sent back to Iceland soon. They still need to investigate a few things before that can

375

happen.' She didn't want to use the word 'autopsy' for fear of upsetting Friðrikka. 'The same goes for Bjarki and Dóri. They'll be sent home so that they can be buried properly. You remember what the policeman said about the bones; they'll be returned to the family as quickly as possible. The same goes for Oddný Hildur and those two.'

There was a knock at the door and in peeked the young policeman who had stayed with them during the night. 'You can get ready to go. We estimate the helicopter will be ready to take off in just over half an hour.'

They didn't need to be told twice, and within the promised half hour they were all hurrying out to the helicopter. Their bags had been brought out and when Thóra's suitcase was thrown in rather roughly she suddenly felt overwhelmed by the longing to go home. She accepted Matthew's help in getting into the helicopter and in a few moments they were all in their seats with their belts fastened. However, they had to sit that way for some time. 'Don't tell me something's come up,' muttered Eyjólfur, craning to look out of the window in the hope of seeing some activity. 'If this helicopter doesn't take off soon, I'll go mad.'

He'd barely got the words out before the reason for the delay became clear. It wasn't because the bodies of Oddný Hildur or the drillers were being sent on the same flight; instead two policemen appeared in the cafeteria doorway, half dragging between them Naruana, the son of the hunter Igimaq. The man was in handcuffs and walked with his head bent, hiding his face. The chief investigator took his shoulders and directed him towards the helicopter, while his partner followed close on their heels. The two helicopter pilots ran to assist them, then got on board, put on their headphones and started going over their instruments while the policemen tried with some difficulty to strap the prisoner into his seat. Thóra and the others bore silent witness to the young man's unhappiness and desperation. They either had to shut their eyes or witness the man's hopeless attempts to escape, his crazed, bloodshot eyes and swollen face as he fought against the police tooth and nail. Then he collapsed without warning and surrendered control to them. The policemen exchanged cautious glances as they put the seatbelt around Naruana's waist.

Thóra took Friðrikka's gloved hand in hers as she stared at the back view of the man who had probably killed her friend. She leaned in close to Friðrikka and whispered in her ear so the others couldn't hear: 'Don't think about it. You'll be home soon, with your cat in your arms.' Friðrikka nodded vigorously and seemed to accept this. Thóra released her hands and hoped that they would reach their destination without World War Three breaking out on board the helicopter.

The propeller blades started rotating and after that no one spoke. Thóra watched Naruana in between looking out of the window at the harsh white landscape. She noticed that he turned his head several times to look out, and couldn't help but wonder what was going through his mind. Perhaps he knew he wouldn't see his home again for a very long time and wished to fix in his mind how the cliff belts highest up on the mountains tore through the snowy wastes, and how the endless ice cap reflected the light of the sun, which was still low in the sky.

The helicopter landed in Kulusuk. Thóra and her colleagues were greatly disappointed to discover no plane from the Icelandic airline waiting for them on the runway. They would have to wait at the airport or go to the hotel. They left the helicopter wearily and waited as the police took Naruana off. Then they followed the trio in the direction of the terminal. As before, the chief investigator steered the young man, who seemed to have given up any attempt to escape. He walked alongside the officers without protest, although his steps were heavy. In the doorway of the terminal he suddenly turned around and looked back at them all. Friðrikka stopped abruptly, causing Bella to run into her.

'I didn't kill anyone.' You didn't need to speak much Danish to understand Naruana's words. 'I didn't kill anyone,' he repeated, before being pulled roughly inside. The group remained standing outside, silently. Thóra didn't understand what the man hoped to achieve by telling them this; maybe he thought the group would get the authorities to release him. However, none of them wished to involve themselves in the man's case, even if they had been in any position to do so.

'What's wrong with him?' scowled Eyjólfur. 'Does he expect us to feel sorry for him?'

'I have to admit that I do now. This is a tragedy, no matter how you look at it. Maybe he thought he was pleasing the spirits that everyone fears so much.' Thóra entered the terminal without waiting for a response from Eyjólfur or Friðrikka, who might have taken this to mean that Thóra was insulting the memory of her dead friend. A police officer approached her as she entered and said they should sit down and wait for a moment while

378

he checked on their flight home. They sat in a row in the plastic seats fastened to the wall of the little waiting room. The police walked off with Naruana, who did not look around, but stared fixedly down at his feet.

'That's the worst duty free shop I've ever seen.' Bella pointed at the corner of the hall where the different types of alcohol, countable on the fingers of one hand, and cartons of four different types of cigarettes were arranged on the shelves. 'And I thought the duty free shop in Reykjavík was a joke.' Her comment lightened the rather oppressive atmosphere.

'Wouldn't it be a good idea to have a drink?' Alvar stood up and walked to the window where American chocolate and Greenlandic artworks were for sale. He cheerfully ordered a beer from a young Greenlandic girl and looked over at the group in the hope that others would follow his example. They did not respond. Alvar seemed slightly disgruntled as he paid; he walked back to his seat with the green Tuborg can in his hand and took a swig before sitting down. Thóra predicted that he would make another trip to the window in the blink of an eye. Her prediction was correct. In no mood for watching this idiot pickle himself again, she took out her mobile and called her son. He answered happily and informed her that all was quiet on the home front. Of course his dad was driving him crazy with his endless questions about what he was going to do after graduation, but since Gylfi still had two whole years of school to go after this one, he found the question more than premature. When you're eighteen years old every year is like an entire lifetime. Otherwise everything

379

was going fine except that, as a conscientious older brother, he felt that Sóley hadn't been encouraged enough to practise her violin. He didn't mind putting up with the screeching, and felt bad if she didn't keep it up. According to him it was his dad's new wife that had hampered Sóley's musical development, since she couldn't bear to be inside the house when the girl played. Thóra would have to deal with that when she came home. When Gylfi had sufficiently aired his concern for his sister's music lessons he quickly switched to the proposed trip to Spain and described in a long speech how important it was that they planned their trip early. From what Thóra could gather from this monologue, he and Sigga were missing the boat and the gates to the wide world outside Iceland were about to close for good. Thóra stuck to her guns and said that she would discuss this with him calmly when she came home.

She hung up but didn't have time to put away her mobile before it rang again immediately. She didn't recognize the number, but it seemed familiar. She hoped it wasn't the music school calling to complain about Sóley's performance, but it turned out to be Arnar Jóhannesson, calling from Vogur. Thóra stood and moved over to one of the furthest corners of the hall so that she could speak to him in private.

'I was told you were trying to reach me.' Arnar's speech was sad and slow; he sounded like a man who had suffered a shock but who would come to accept it. 'I'm not exactly sure who you are or why you want to talk to me, but . . .' He tailed off.

Thóra explained her position and the situation. She was in Kulusuk, on her way home after a trip

380

to Greenland to work on finding a solution to the bank's problems with Berg Technology. She deliberately gave nothing away about how the case was going. It was unwise to blurt out everything immediately, because then the man would have no reason to keep the conversation going. 'I wanted to speak to you because I was hoping you could help me with some questions that still haven't been answered. The case has been going well over the last few days, since the police arrived on the scene, but I've still got a few loose ends to tie up.'

'What are the police saying?' He didn't expand on this question or specify what aspect of the situation he was asking about.

'Naturally, the police aren't telling us much.' Thóra wanted to avoid upsetting Arnar for fear that he would hang up on her. 'They're in the middle of their investigation, and although it looks to me as if everything is going well for them, we don't know exactly what's happening.' It surprised her that the man hadn't begun by asking if they knew what had befallen his colleagues.

'Has someone been arrested?' Arnar spoke as ponderously as before, although now his voice seemed tinged with worry. She found this puzzling, since she'd expect him to be concerned by the idea that a culprit had *not* been identified. But perhaps she had simply misunderstood the tone of his question.

'Yes, it seems so. One of the villagers. Naruana, whom I understand you know. He appears to be partly, if not fully, responsible for what happened.'

'He hasn't hurt anyone.' Arnar paused. 'The police do realize that, don't they?' Now the man's voice had become childish, hopeful, reminding

381

Thóra of Sóley when she asked her mother about something obvious, searching for reassurance. *Mummy, the people in the plane crash will be all right, won't they?*

'Forgive me, but I have to ask. How much do you know about what happened here? You say he hasn't hurt anyone, but you haven't asked yet whether anyone was hurt in the first place.'

'I know a few things,' replied Arnar, apparently not as offended by the question as Thóra had feared. 'I called Naruana yesterday and he told me that the police were on the scene; that they'd come to his house to ask him and the woman living with him, Oqqapia, about various things. He told me everything that he gleaned from their questions, so I do know something about it.'

'So you're aware that Oddný Hildur, Bjarki and Dóri were found dead, and that she at least was murdered?'

Arnar said nothing, but then spoke up again. 'I didn't know that Oddný Hildur had been found or that there was any suspicion she'd been murdered. However, Naruana told me that the drillers had come up during the police questioning and that they were dead.' He was breathing rapidly.

'When exactly did you speak to him yesterday?' Thóra guessed that Oddný Hildur's body hadn't been found at the time. Naruana wouldn't have had any reason to keep that a secret from Arnar.

'It was after dinner, around eight thirty or nine.' Thóra subtracted the time difference between the two countries and saw that that fitted; Oddný Hildur's body hadn't been found until over an hour later. The police had then set off again to question Naruana and brought him back in handcuffs during

382

the night.

'Then was Naruana arrested for the murder of Oddný Hildur? That's bollocks; he didn't kill anyone. How the hell could they have thought that?' Arnar seemed agitated, desperate to convince Thóra of his friend's innocence, as Naruana himself had tried to do not long before.

'I know nothing about that, unfortunately. I'm unaware of what might have happened.' She slowed her breathing down to ensure she didn't lose control of the conversation. 'There's more. A body was found in the camp's walk-in freezer and bones were found in the office building; the bones seem to belong to Usinna, Naruana's sister. Maybe his arrest has more to do with them. Of course the body was very old, so maybe he had nothing to do with that. However, I understand that it's not known how his sister died, but that she was interred far from the settlement.'

'He hasn't killed anyone, and the police can't say he did. He's very sensitive and I doubt he's capable of defending himself properly. He could easily end up being convicted even though he's innocent.'

'Well, I don't know the man but I certainly agree that he's taking this badly. He travelled with us in the helicopter and it was difficult to see him in that state. He'll probably get help now that he's been brought to a larger community. I don't know if he's on his way to Angmagssalik or Nuuk, but they're hardly going to question him at the airport or in the hotel.'

'This is a total misunderstanding and it would probably be best if you were to tell the police that. For fuck's sake, Naruana is an alcoholic, he could never kill another person, let alone more than one. He already has enough of his own problems to deal with, without looking for new ones.' Arnar's words came out in a torrent, as if he were recounting everything he could think of that might help to defend his friend. 'He took his sister's death very badly and it's absolutely clear that he holds no responsibility for it. He had no say at all in where she was buried; that was up to his father, he chose the place. I know Naruana quite well, I was trying to help him overcome his addiction and he would be incapable of murder. He even had to stop hunting because it affected him so badly, and he had trouble staying on the wagon. And it's considerably more difficult to kill a man than it is to kill an animal for food.'

'I agree with you completely, but the police will need something a bit more concrete if your friend is to be saved. Hopefully he's perfectly innocent and is hoping that the truth will come out, even though he might have trouble defending himself.'

'But what if the truth doesn't come out?'

'I'm not familiar with the penal system here in Greenland but it seems likely that he'd receive a prison sentence. I couldn't say how long that would be. I suppose it would be something similar to the sentence in Iceland. Sixteen years or so.' Now it was time to turn the tables. Thóra had done too much answering and wanted to do more questioning. 'Why were Usinna's bones scattered around the offices and not kept in one spot? I've already heard one explanation for this, but I wasn't convinced.'

'That just shows you what things were like there,' replied Arnar. He seemed pleased that for the moment, attention was being directed away from Naruana's troubles. 'Nobody could work out what

384

to do with the bones after the villagers refused to speak to the people who went down there.'

'Why didn't you go and talk to Naruana or Oqqapia, since you knew them?'

'I didn't want the others in the camp to know that I was going down to the village on my days off. It wasn't any of their business. I also didn't know until I spoke to Naruana on the phone yesterday that they were his sister's bones. I didn't pay particular attention to them at the time and I wasn't involved in what happened to them, any more than I was with anything else there. I just assumed they were the bones of a man who had died long ago and that the villagers knew nothing about them. So I didn't waste much time thinking about them.'

'Then you don't know how the bones ended up in the drawers?'

'Yes, I do know, although I'd really rather forget it.' Arnar fell silent, but then continued when Thóra said nothing. 'I couldn't help noticing that most of the people in the office building had their eye on the skull and were bickering about who should be allowed to keep it. Should it be the man who first found the cairn, or the one who opened it, or the one who noticed the bag, and so on. It was disgusting to listen to, like most things that went on in that office. I was the only one who laid no claim to the bones, since I didn't want them. I found it all to be in extremely poor taste.'

'What about Friðrikka and Oddný Hildur? Did they try to claim the bones?'

'Oddný Hildur had vanished and Friðrikka had left. It was last January. In the end it was decided that the bones would be divided through a game of chance. A game of bingo, to be precise.'

'They played *bone bingo*?' Thóra exclaimed.

'It was supposed to be one of the activities for the Midwinter Feast, which was being planned at the time. The bingo game was to be the highlight of the evening, as far as I could tell. I didn't go, any more than I went to any of the other activities and events that passed for a social life there. I wasn't usually invited, but I wouldn't have been interested anyway.'

Thóra felt sorry for the man, but now was not the time to discuss the harassment he had experienced, or to sympathize with him. 'So the bingo game decided who got what?'

'Yes. The skull was the main prize, but the other bones were divided into several different lots. Not everyone won some. Far from it. Bjarki and Dóri, for example, didn't win any, and they were rather upset. They'd been the most excited about getting some, preferably the entire skeleton.'

'I understand.' Thóra felt rather lost in this strange conversation. At least now she had an explanation for the little note found lying under the skull, *G-57*. Was it that number that had granted the skull to its new owner? 'But if your friend didn't kill Oddný Hildur, then who did? Do you have any theories you'd like to share with me?'

'No.' Although the answer was curt, there was no anger in it. 'I've only just found out that this is a murder case—I honestly thought she'd got lost and died of exposure. Thinking about it, most if not all of the Berg employees could be suspects. Everyone except for me and Friðrikka, of course. Oddný Hildur was the only one who was decent to me, so as you can imagine I was absolutely beside myself when she disappeared. Of course the others were shocked but I don't know how deep their shock went. She'd fallen out of favour after drawing the CEO's attention to the way they treated me. That didn't make the men very happy, but instead of dropping it they started bullying Oddný Hildur as well. Idiots.'

'So the group found out that Oddný Hildur had complained?'

'Yes. Not from me, that's for certain. I guess the owner hadn't been very discreet about it, which is nothing new for him.'

Recalling the CEO's awkward e-mail to Oddný Hildur, Thóra could well imagine. 'Is it conceivable that someone was trying to play a prank on her in revenge, but that it got out of control and she died accidentally? Maybe the two drillers?'

Arnar thought it over. 'I don't know. It seems quite a stretch, but I'm damned if I know. Neither Bjarki, Dóri nor anyone else acted in a way that led me to suspect they might have done anything like that.'

Thóra tried not to feel too disappointed, but she had thought she'd get more out of him. 'Who knows, maybe it was just an accident, even though the circumstances are very peculiar.' She smiled ruefully and decided to tell Arnar what her clever theory had been. 'I got a little ahead of myself there. I was starting to imagine that the drillers killed her by mistake, regretted it when they were left alone at the camp and killed themselves. With poison.' However, her fantastic hypothesis did not explain how they wound up cut into pieces and dumped on an island.

'Yes, well, no. They didn't kill themselves.' Arnar cleared his throat. 'I killed them.'

Chapter 33

24 March 2008

After Thóra hung up she couldn't bring herself to stand up from her seat in the farthest corner of the hall. She needed to digest what Arnar had told her at the end of their conversation. It was entirely possible that the man had completely lost his mind and that his story was total fabrication, but she doubted it. He was far too serious for that, and his descriptions too precise. It also explained so much that it was difficult to imagine any other explanation.

Thóra signalled to Matthew to follow her a short distance away from the group and told him everything she had learned, adding that Arnar wanted the Greenlandic police to be informed of his involvement in the case. It took Matthew a little while to absorb the story too, and he had to ask numerous questions before he could fully grasp what had occurred. They were forced to converse in low voices in the little waiting room so that their colleagues wouldn't hear about any of this before the authorities did. The Greenlandic police were the only ones in any position to determine the validity of the story, and there could be grave consequences if the group went home with snippets of hearsay about such a serious matter.

It took them some time to convince the young policeman standing watch in the waiting room that they desperately needed to speak to his boss. The officer was supposed to ensure that none of the Icelanders left the terminal, and he obviously intended to carry out his task to the letter. In the end he saw that they would not give up and conceded to their demands. He said something incomprehensible into the radio and shortly afterwards they heard a car crunch to a stop in the gravel car park outside the terminal. The chief investigator strutted in and indicated that they should accompany him to the reception area. The others in the group watched in amazement, but none of them had asked yet what was going on. If they had, the answer would have been pretty succinct: *None of your business*. Dr Finnbogi did in fact call out after them and ask where they were going, but neither of them turned around or answered him.

They all sat down at a little table where Thóra informed the police officer what she wanted, choosing her words carefully so as to be taken seriously. She asked that the conversation take place in English, since she worried that her inexpert Danish could lead to misunderstandings.

'So Arnar Jóhannesson says that he killed the two drillers?' The policeman had pulled out a small notebook as soon as Thóra began speaking, and now he scribbled something in it as she continued her story. 'But not the woman—is that right?'

'Yes. He denies that, and he sounded very convincing. He thought she'd died of exposure. Just as everyone else seemed to believe.'

'All except for one person, I expect. It's almost certain that she was murdered. We're transporting her body to Nuuk for an autopsy, but we sent photos of her injuries to the coroner and his conclusion was that she'd been struck with some sort of blunt instrument. Possibly even a hammer.'

'Oh.' Thóra tried not to let this throw her off-course. Oddný Hildur's demise did not seem to be connected to those of Bjarki and Dóri, judging by what she'd learned from Arnar, so it was unnecessary to dwell on it now. So she began to tell the officer everything she knew about Arnar's dealings with the drillers and the harassment that had taken place at the isolated work camp. She had only mentioned it to him in passing before, since she hadn't realized how integral it was to the mystery of the drillers' fate.

'In other words, he lashed out in self-defence against their bullying and killed them?' The officer did not seem overly surprised at this explanation, since no one reason for committing murder was better than any other.

'Before I go on, I feel it's only right to mention that I'm not entirely sure he can be directly connected with the men's murder.' Thóra smiled, feeling her cheeks flush in embarrassment. 'In a legal sense, it's not entirely clear, although Icelandic law may prove me wrong. Morally, there is no question of his involvement, although it's difficult to know whether he has fully realized the consequences of his actions.'

'This is not a court of law. Tell me simply what the man told you, and then others will determine who should be blamed.'

'It has to do with the "bone bingo" at the Midwinter Feast that I told you about during questioning yesterday. Bjarki and Dóri, the men who were found on the island, tried hard to win the skull to use as a decoration in their office. When they missed out on the main prize they were very disappointed and complained about it constantly. According to Arnar, the others put the bones they'd won in their desk drawers while they waited for these two to calm down, since they'd all had enough of their grumbling and didn't want to provoke it by leaving the bones on display. Their disappointment probably explains what happened after the group left. It appears Bjarki and Dóri also found a body where they had been instructed to drill. They caught a glimpse of it beneath the ice at the mouth of a cave in the forbidden area and decided after a lot of head-scratching to dig it out and bring it to the camp to tease their co-workers, or even use it to make a whole skeleton that they could brag about to thc others. They also found several old artefacts that they hoped were of some value, and started by digging those out. Among other things they found the objects that we gave to you, including the little statue that they thought was a genuine Tupilak. They were understandably very excited, since no such object has been found preserved before. They knew the history of the area well enough and thought that the man in the ice was one of the original inhabitants of the village who died of hunger, and that the Tupilak in question had called down the curse on the settlement.'

'Did you hear this from Arnar?'

'Yes, and it's what Bjarki told him. I'll come to that.' Thóra went on with her story. 'They had a hard time freeing the man from the ice so they decided to use the drill. After breaking up the ice around the body by drilling and chopping at it, the body was still stuck, since they couldn't drill beneath it. That's when they got the idea of drilling through the body and pulling it out with the drill shaft.' Thóra hesitated. 'Since they wanted to keep the bones intact they were careful to position the drill so that it wouldn't damage the spine. That explains the hole penetrating one of the lungs.'

'Why not the stomach or the abdomen? Then they would have kept the ribcage intact.' The police officer asked the same question that Thóra had thought of. It was easier to accept the story by putting themselves in the shoes of these dimwits.

'They had to sacrifice some of the ribs to get a hold on the body, according to Arnar. If they had gone through the abdomen the drill would just have jerked straight out and not pulled the body free. The ribs gave them some grip. This at least explains the hole in the corpse in the freezer—because obviously this is the same man. They took him there while they were deciding what to do with him.'

The policeman's pen moved rapidly over the page and it quickly filled up. Before he turned to the next page he skimmed over what he had already written. 'And then what happened?'

'At first, nothing. They freed the corpse from the ice, brought it back with them and put it in the freezer. The next day Dóri felt a bit weak and two days later he was seriously ill. At first they thought it was just the flu and Dóri pumped himself full of painkillers, but he just got worse. Then Bjarki began to display the same symptoms, two days after Dóri first started feeling bad. He had begun to suspect that Dóri was seriously ill. He searched the Internet to try to find out what infectious diseases were going around but found nothing that fitted with their symptoms. In the end blood started pouring from Dóri's eyes, nose and mouth, and his face turned dark blue. So Bjarki dragged

392

him out of his apartment and over to their office. There, he put him in front of the video camera so that a doctor could see what was going on and give them some advice. It was late in the evening. Bjarki himself had a high fever and it didn't help matters when Dóri lost consciousness in front of the computer. So Bjarki didn't finish his filming, and he began to panic. He might have been delirious, but he apparently considered it possible that the Tupilak, or the curse that had been put on the area, was punishing them for tampering with the body. He left Dóri behind but the camera was connected to the computer, with everything set up for recording.'

'And how does Arnar know all of this? Was he there, after all?'

'No, Bjarki called him that night and told him everything I'm recounting to you right now, and doubtless other things that Arnar forgot to tell me about. Bjarki actually tried to call the emergency services in Iceland to get in touch with a doctor or the police, but the number doesn't work if you call it from a different country. So he started phoning his colleagues one by one, after giving up trying to contact friends and acquaintances. That fits with his other co-worker's story, which I've already told you. It had got late and the time difference wasn't in his favour, so no one answered. No one but Arnar. In some ways that was deeply ironic. In his despair, Bjarki forgot that Arnar wasn't exactly indebted to him; in his shock he described the situation to him and said that he thought Dóri was dying, and that he was too.' Thóra stopped, and the policeman looked up at her. 'That put Arnar's conscience to the test. And he decided to keep quiet and do

393

nothing.'

'Did they both die that night? Why didn't the man call someone in the morning when he realized that there was no help on the way from Arnar?'

'He couldn't; Arnar made sure of that. Instead of making an honest attempt to come to Bjarki's assistance as he had promised him, Arnar called his friend Naruana and asked him to go up to the camp, disconnect the satellite dishes and remove the keys from the cars and snowmobile. He told him that this was a well-deserved prank, but didn't let Naruana know his actual purpose. Naruana was quite drunk and didn't question anything; he simply went up to the camp and did as he was asked, and more. Instead of disconnecting the satellite dishes he tried his best to destroy them, and since he couldn't find the keys to the cars or the snowmobile he put sugar in the petrol tanks. In other words, in doing this Naruana became the reason—unwittingly—for the men not being able to get to a doctor to receive the help that might have saved their lives. Before Naruana did these things Arnar accessed the server via the remote connection and deleted all the images of the body in the ice, or so he believed, in order to throw those who would later want to know what had happened off the scent. He himself said that at the time he had been half-crazed with hatred and not thinking clearly.'

'I see.' The police officer looked up from his notebook at Thóra. 'And Arnar didn't have a change of heart straight afterwards, phone Naruana back and try to call him off? Sometimes people regret what they did in the heat of the moment and try to limit the damage they've caused.'

Thóra replied that she couldn't speak for the

man's actions; she could only relay what Arnar had told her. 'It may be relevant that as soon as he made his fateful decision he started drinking again. He said that he went to the liquor store the next morning and stocked up. The binge lasted until he enrolled in treatment. I would imagine his regret played a large part in his tumble off the wagon.'

'So. The men died.' The officer didn't mince his words.

'Dóri died first. He never regained consciousness and died in the office without Bjarki being able to drag him back to his apartment. Two days later Bjarki died.'

'I don't quite understand. How could anyone know that, since the men were disconnected from the outside world?'

'Bjarki told Naruana about it.' Thóra explained in more detail: 'The day that Dóri died Bjarki set off for the village in the hope of either finding assistance or phoning for it. He was very weak and clearly seriously ill, but he made it to his destination on skis. But his fortitude didn't pay off. None of the villagers would open their doors to him or listen to his cries for help. Only Naruana. He saw him from a distance on his way home from the pier and offered to take him back to the camp. The skis are probably still outside Naruana's house, if that would help your investigation.'

'Do we know why he did this? I'd have expected him to be the one most inclined to avoid the Icelanders, in light of the damage he'd done at the camp.'

'You'll have to ask him about that, but maybe he wanted to prevent Bjarki from speaking to anyone else. In any case, he took him back up to the camp on a snowmobile he borrowed from someone. He also probably lied to Bjarki about help being on its way. Naruana found Dóri dead in the office and realized that things were a lot more serious than Arnar had led him to believe. I understand that he thought he saw on Dóri's body, and on Bjarki's face, the same marks that had led his sister to her death. It frightened him. He was convinced that the curse on the area was manifesting itself again and he got out of there as quickly as possible. Bjarki had no strength to chase him and instead lay there alone and exhausted, and he seems to have died shortly afterwards. He was lying in the corridor near the coffee room.'

'What about the dismemberment of the bodies? How did that happen?'

Thóra's throat was dry from talking non-stop, but she continued. 'Naruana called Arnar after returning home and told him that one of the men was dead and the other was going the same way. Arnar, who was totally smashed at the time, asked him to dispose of the bodies, throw them out on the ice, take them somewhere where they would be eaten by animals or just do something so that they wouldn't be found. He hoped that people would think that Bjarki and Dóri had died of exposure, like Oddný Hildur.'

'And it's not really necessary to spell out what Naruana did,' said Matthew. He seemed to sense that Thóra had had enough of talking.

'No, you're right.' The policeman tried to determine what his next question should be. Apparently he wasn't finding this any easier to digest than Thóra had. 'But how did the video get made of Naruana cutting up the bodies, and what

396

was that singing in the background?'

Thóra shrugged. 'As I said, Bjarki was going to position Dóri in front of the webcam in the hope that a doctor would be able to diagnose him by looking at his symptoms. Whether that was a good idea or not, he was too weak to finish the task. When Naruana returned to the camp he brought along a helper. A child, in fact.'

'He brought a child with him to cut up corpses?' Matthew couldn't hide his disgust. Since Thóra had given him only an overview of Arnar's story, he hadn't been aware of this particular detail.

'He took along a girl who lived in the house next door. Again, I should say that I don't know what motivated him, and he will have to tell you himself. I just know what Arnar told me, that this girl had been in an accident and never recovered properly; she doesn't speak, for instance. Maybe that was the reason he took her along—she can't tell anyone about it. Anyway, it's so fucked up, I can't even imagine what he was thinking. But in any case, the girl must have messed with the webcam and either knew how to work it, which is doubtful, or started it by accident. Bjarki had already set it all up, so she would only have needed to press maybe one or two buttons. You can check it yourself, because we didn't touch the camera or anything else on the table. The original plan was to take the bodies out to the ice, as Arnar had suggested, but Naruana found his sister's necklace on the bulletin board that I showed you, and flew into a rage. He was convinced that she had arranged this from the other side and was provoking him. So he hacked the men to pieces. That way they couldn't do anything to him if they woke up while he was moving them.'

397

The policeman nodded. 'This is going to take some sorting out.' He looked up from his notes. 'What about Naruana's sister? If she died in a similar way to the drillers, it's possible they had the same disease. I think we should drop all the talk about a curse and spirits. What did Arnar say about it?'

'I simply didn't think to ask him about it. He actually told me that Oddný Hildur was specifically interested in Usinna, or rather, her research, because Oddný Hildur wanted to convince herself that she wasn't putting the health of her future children at risk by being there. He took her to visit Naruana and she got Naruana's phone number, so she could call him and see if he'd discovered anything of interest to her among his sister's things. Nothing came of it, because Oddný Hildur disappeared soon afterwards. I know that Usinna's research involved taking blood samples; maybe she found this same body and took blood from it.' Thóra didn't want to make something out of nothing, but surely this was connected to the drillers' illness in some way? She'd become a little unsure of what she'd told the officer and what she'd missed out, and there could very well have been some holes in her story. 'What I mean is that flesh, or bits of it, even blood, got onto the drill . . .' Thóra straightened up. 'And bits of lung. They must have got some of it on them. According to Arnar, Dóri stood next to the body and directed Bjarki on the drilling rig, and Dóri was the one who fell ill first. I suppose he could have breathed it in?' When she glanced at Matthew, he looked as though he felt that her theory made sense. 'I don't know whether viruses or bacteria can survive in such cold weather but I feel like it must be worth looking into it. Who knows, maybe Oddný Hildur was also infected and died from that, rather than from exposure.'

'Aren't you forgetting her head injuries? I'm no doctor, but those weren't caused by a virus. And besides, no one else appears to have been infected, even though many others have come near the body.' For the first time the police officer's expression had changed; he now looked worried.

'I wonder if we might not have already been infected? Dóri was bedridden the very next day, so hopefully it hasn't affected us. It would be a good idea to make arrangements for the corpses to be autopsied, though, on the understanding that the disease might be transmittable even if the body is frozen.'

The police officer smiled bleakly at Thóra. 'Don't worry. Everything is secure at the crime lab. However, I think it's advisable that you all undergo a medical examination before returning home.' Still looking at her, he continued, 'Did this Arnar give any explanation as to why he's telling us about all this now? He's had enough time to come clean.'

Thóra gazed back at him. 'He said he decided to sacrifice himself for Naruana. When the investigation is finished and he has taken responsibility for his part in the case, he intends to commit suicide. Not before then.'

Chapter 34

24 March 2008

Thóra still hated injections just as much as she had at primary school. The only difference was that nowadays she was better at hiding it. She was thankful that progress in medical equipment meant she could be sure that the doctor wouldn't have the same kind of giant-sized syringe that they had found in the drilling rig (and that had probably belonged to the long-gone doctor who had—in all likelihood—carried into the settlement the disease that killed all the original inhabitants). She exhaled heavily when the needle was withdrawn and all that remained was a little drop of blood that was gone shortly afterwards. She smiled happily but couldn't see the doctor's reaction, since his mouth and nose were hidden behind a mask. Thóra resisted the temptation to cough in his face. 'And when do I find out the results?' She pressed a cotton wool ball against the puncture wound made by the needle.

'We'll process it as speedily as possible, and as soon as we find out anything we'll let you know.' The man leaned forward in his chair and waited for Eyjólfur to come in and take Thóra's place. He took the vial holding her dark red blood, labelled it and placed it carefully in a small box.

Eyjólfur sat down. 'What if this is something serious and we've all been infected?' He rolled up his sleeve and laid his hand on the arm of the chair. 'Will we die?'

'Of course you'll die, like everyone else. However,

I doubt it will be anytime soon, or because of infection.' The doctor said nothing as he stuck the needle into Eyjólfur's arm, then: 'You're probably as fit as a fiddle, but this is a necessary preventative measure.' The face-mask and latex gloves suggested otherwise.

Friðrikka dropped her cotton wool ball into a small yellow plastic bucket where needles and other such things were thrown away. Thóra guessed that the red symbol on the bucket indicated that its contents might be infected, and needed to be destroyed under special conditions. Friðrikka turned to Dr Finnbogi as she rolled her sleeve back down. 'How do they know that this is the Spanish Flu?' Her voice was weak and although they were all alarmed, she was the only one who seemed unable to compose herself. The Greenlandic police force's announcement that the man in the freezer was suspected to have died of this pernicious epidemic had been made just a short time ago, although it had long been clear to everyone that something serious was going on. Soon after Thóra and Matthew's conversation with the policeman, the group was sent on foot in the direction of the hotel, but instead of going in through the familiar reception area they were led over to a row of buildings that resembled the work camp they had just left; these were the staff quarters for the airport in Kulusuk. They took seats on a sofa; Eyjólfur hurriedly turned on the television to try to find a news station in English. They stared at the television while waiting for further information. This soon became so tiresome that Thóra was on the verge of suggesting that they switch to the German porn channel for variety. Finally they were told that they would have to be ruled out as disease carriers before any decisions could be made concerning further travel on their part. By then they had watched the same news reports so many times that they had become immune to them. They were waiting for doctors from Angmagssalik, and so had to put up with several more rounds of the headline news. Then the doctors wished to consult with their colleagues at the hospital in Nuuk, since it was possible that a major epidemic was on the way. Now for the first time the group was seriously concerned, and their anxiety was not appeased when they were told that this looked like a case of Spanish Flu, and that it seemed likely to have killed both Bjarki and Dóri.

'They don't know for sure. They need to compare this virus with what they found recently in the grave of a woman who died of Spanish Flu in Alaska. She died around the same time as the settlers in Greenland, but was buried under a layer of permafrost. No sample of the virus has been found before, because the bodies of the victims decomposed in the ground. It is very unusual for a corpse to remain frozen for decades, as has happened here.' Finnbogi watched as the other doctor lightly tapped Alvar's inside arm. 'But the timing of the epidemic fits in perfectly with the period when the original inhabitants of the area died, and the symptoms match the description of the drillers' deaths. It's likely that the doctor or his guide infected the villagers when he made his survey trip there during that winter so long ago. In the isolation that characterized a place like this, and in fact still does, fertile ground is created for infectious diseases in the event that

402

they are brought in. In addition, the Spanish Flu was a deadly epidemic and could very well have decimated such a small and isolated settlement. Especially because the community's survival was based on hunting. When people become ill or are disabled, they can't provide for themselves. Some of the villagers died from the disease, others from starvation, so the story goes. Spanish Flu, unlike most other types of flu, affected the young and healthy rather than the elderly and little children.'

'I find it absolutely extraordinary'—Eyjólfur was still pressing cotton wool to his puncture wound—'that such an old disease can flare up again. As if we don't have enough new epidemics.'

'No one's saying it has "flared up".' Finnbogi looked askance at the other two doctors, but they were not even trying to follow the discussion. 'Although Bjarki and Dóri were infected, they came into a completely different type of contact with the man than we did. You might not all have seen the hole in the man's chest, but something happened when it was drilled through. The men got bodily fluids on them and even breathed them in.'

'But doesn't the man who cut up their bodies need to be examined as well?' asked Eyjólfur. 'The same thing must have happened to him, since he was probably covered in blood droplets, or something even more disgusting.'

'Not everyone becomes infected, but the man will certainly have to undergo the same sort of examination as us. If it's the young man who came with us in the helicopter, he's not ill, any more than we are. Those who were infected became ill very quickly, so he should be safe. The infected were at death's door after twenty-four hours, which may be one of the things that pointed the investigators towards this particular disease. The drillers didn't lie on their sickbeds for long.'

'And we were made to sit with him in the helicopter?' Friðrikka's voice had risen to a shrill high C again. 'We breathed the same air as him for almost an hour, didn't we? Who knows, maybe we were infected then, which is why we haven't become ill yet!'

'We shouldn't worry unnecessarily. We're still asymptomatic, and we'll probably remain that way,' said Finnbogi determinedly. 'I think we should talk about something more interesting and constructive; we're not going to change anything with foolish speculation.'

The group fell silent and remained that way as it tried to come up with another topic of conversation. 'Why do you think that guy killed Oddný Hildur? Is he completely mental, or do you think he raped her or something?' Eyjólfur got top marks for changing the subject, but a fail for the subject matter.

'She wasn't raped.' Friðrikka was nearly foaming at the mouth.

Eyjólfur turned to her, just as angry. 'I wasn't talking to you. What would you know about it?'

'Women aren't raped through their clothes. Her body was fully dressed, in case you managed to miss it.' Friðrikka was beginning to shout.

The Danish doctor turned round and raised his eyebrows, and Thóra cut them both off brusquely. She couldn't bear to think of the group being broken up and each of them shut in a separate room. Although the company wasn't at its most entertaining right then, time did pass faster when

404

something was happening besides them all staring out at the ice-bound bay below the town, no matter how beautiful it was. 'Settle down. We don't know Naruana killed Oddný Hildur. Maybe it was someone completely different. Stop yelling at each other and try to discuss something constructive instead.'

Thóra's words calmed Friðrikka and Eyjólfur down a bit but they still couldn't think of anything else to talk about. 'Who could have killed her if not one of the villagers? One of the employees at the camp?' asked Alvar. He had stood up and was now watching the final blood test, which was being carried out on Bella.

'It was someone from the village.' Friðrikka made this assertion like a stubborn child. 'Anything else is out of the question. None of us would have wanted to do her harm, even if she did complain to the boss.'

Eyjólfur ignored her. 'Maybe it was an outsider, but not someone from the village. Tourists who wandered into the area. A hiker, one of those fresh air freaks.'

'Excuse me, but I doubt this woman was killed by a "fresh air freak".' Thóra couldn't help but smile at his description.

'Why not? The weather was bad and visibility was poor; maybe he thought she was a polar bear. She was wearing Arnar's furry boots and hat.' Eyjólfur appeared determined to convince himself of his own hypothesis.

'Yes, that could be it,' blurted out Friðrikka, in agreement with Eyjólfur for the first time. 'The murderer will probably never be found, but that's a possible explanation. She could very well have looked like some kind of animal.'

'That explains it.' Eyjólfur surveyed the group smugly.

'No, come on, stop that.' Alvar clearly didn't appreciate the silence, or perhaps he thought it his duty to defend hikers. 'She was attacked from behind, and people don't try to sneak up on polar bears from behind. Nor are fresh air freaks, as you call them, prone to wandering about in a whiteout. They dig themselves down into the snow and wait for the storm to subside. They'd be even less inclined to start attacking polar bears under such circumstances.'

'Does anyone know why she was dressed like that?' Thóra hadn't had time to ponder this point.

'The weather was good that day and stayed that way into the early evening. Wouldn't she have been wrapped up well enough when she went over to the office? Maybe she needed something a little more protective. Arnar would hardly have made a big deal out of her borrowing some of his clothing.' Eyjólfur looked sad. 'Just think—if only she hadn't been wearing someone else's clothes she would never have been mistaken for a polar bear. Those were the only garments on site that would have made her look like an animal.'

Thóra bit her tongue, wondering if his dramatics were going to extend to singing a sad song in Oddný Hildur's memory. She allowed Alvar and Eyjólfur to continue debating the merits of the polar bear theory while she tried to get her thoughts in order. 'Isn't it more logical to assume that whoever came at Oddný Hildur from behind during the snowstorm actually thought she was Arnar?' Friðrikka, Alvar and Eyjólfur stopped arguing and looked in surprise at Thóra.

'What do you mean?' said Eyjólfur stupidly, but then quickly added: 'You mean the man intended to kill Arnar?'

'Yes. Isn't that more likely than your theory about the polar bear? Arnar wasn't short of enemies, and his popularity hardly increased when management were informed about the harassment.'

Alvar was quick to agree to this.

Eyjólfur frowned. 'I don't know. He wasn't so awful that people would have thought about killing him.' He looked awkwardly at Friðrikka in the hope of support. 'Right? It wasn't like that, was it?'

Friðrikka looked from him to her lap. 'No. Definitely not.' She abruptly fell silent. It was as if all the air had gone out of her.

Thóra moved over next to Matthew and waited for him to finish speaking to the Danish doctor, who was packing up his things. 'Do you still have the phone number for Oqqapia, Naruana's partner? I need to have a word with her.' Matthew found the slip of paper with the number on it, and Thóra stuck it in her pocket. While doing so she felt to make sure she had her mobile phone. Once she was certain she did, she asked the doctor whether she could go to the ladies'.

A young police officer followed her out into the corridor and informed her along the way that the toilet would need to be disinfected thoroughly after they left. Thóra thanked him for the information and shut the door behind her. She dialled the number and prayed silently that the woman was home. She was relieved when she heard her voice. 'Hi, Oqqapia, this is Thóra from Iceland. I visited you a short time ago with my friend, whose name is

407

Matthew.'

Oqqapia said she remembered her well. It sounded to Thóra as if she were completely sober. She seemed to be in a state of shock as she told Thóra the whole story of how Naruana had been arrested, and said that a group of men had come to the village to tell them that they'd possibly been infected with a serious disease. They were to remain in their homes while the investigators examined them, house by house. Thóra could hear clearly that she was frightened; the men had been wearing masks and strange outfits. It hadn't crossed Thóra's mind that perhaps all of the villagers had been infected by the hunter's son. 'Oqqapia, I've got to ask you to do me a favour that will probably help Naruana, and could even save his father as well.'

'Anything. I know Naruana hasn't killed anyone. He's even stopped hunting.'

'You've got to find Igimaq and ask him something for me. I suspect he has information that could help Naruana avoid a longer prison sentence than he deserves.' She was met only with silence. 'Oqqapia, this is extremely important. I'm not sure that Igimaq will tell the police anything—if they even find him. He's much more likely to talk to you, and if you explain things to him then maybe he can be persuaded to speak to them later.'

Oqqapia spoke up hesitantly. 'He doesn't want to talk to me. I've never met him but I'm quite sure he isn't happy with me as a daughter-in-law.'

'You're not unworthy of him, not at all. Igimaq realizes that, unless he's very stupid. But that's irrelevant. You simply need to make it clear to him that he can help his son. Him—and no one else.'

Thóra refrained from adding that it was possible even Igimaq couldn't help. She continued while the going was good; Oqqapia hadn't refused her request. 'You've got to go to him and ask how he knew where the woman's body could be found. Where was it lying? Did he see the person who killed her or does he know something that could explain who the murderer is?'

'Oh, I don't know. How can I reach him? I can't go anywhere.'

'You must be able to sneak away—borrow a snowmobile from your neighbours, if you have to. You've only been asked to stay there so you don't infect anyone else—if you've even been infected. Be careful not to cough or touch Igimaq. I actually think he's already come into contact with this disease and survived it, so he would be immune.' He must have touched the body of his daughter when he buried her under the cairn. Usinna had more than likely died of the same thing as the drillers, whether it was the Spanish Flu or something else.

In the end Oqqapia agreed to make an effort to find the old hunter and promised to call Thóra immediately when she returned home.

*　　　*　　　*

Four hours later, Thóra's phone rang. Since Thóra's first conversation with Oqqapia, Sóley had called twice; she had started really missing her mother. Thóra decided not to mention the disease, so as not to worry Sóley unduly. She spoke to her daughter about the cold in Greenland and the heaps and heaps of snow. Sóley immediately asked her mother

409

to convert the amount of snow into snowmen and Thóra guessed it would make one million and fourteen of them—just from the snow that she could see out of the window. The conversation she was having now with Oqqapia had a much more serious tone. She had made it out of the village on a snowmobile, as Thóra had suggested, without being followed.

'I found him. He was in his tent. The dogs didn't want to let me near the tent door and I'm sure they would have torn me to pieces and eaten me if they hadn't been tethered.'

'But he spoke to you, didn't he? How did he respond?'

'He found the woman's body where it was hidden beneath one of the buildings at the camp. He took it to a place where foxes couldn't get at it.'

'Beneath a building? Was it buried?'

'No, he said it was possible to crawl under all of the buildings and that the body had been shoved down there. All you needed to do to cover it was to shovel snow over it. At least until spring.'

'How did he know about it, then?'

'He saw the body when it was moved there. He'd been at the camp earlier in the evening in the hope of preventing the mining operation from expanding into the forbidden area. He tried some ancient magic, put on a mask and called upon the spirits of his ancestors with blood from a seal flipper to help him, but it didn't work. He waited there in the hope that something would change, but he didn't get his wish. However, he saw someone from the camp sitting in a car outside the office building, keeping a low profile. Igimaq wanted to know what was going on so he stopped and waited there. When the

410

woman came out of the office the car door opened, the person ran after her and hit her on the neck with a blunt instrument. A hammer or something like that. The wind had been blowing quite a bit and there was a storm, so Igimaq didn't have a clear view. He did insist, however, that it wasn't an accident.'

Thóra swallowed. 'Did he see the attacker well enough to be able to give a description?'

'Yes. The murderer stopped for a long time after turning the woman over, and then had a good look at her face. Igimaq thought that the woman would die of exposure there, but she suddenly seemed to pull herself together and started dragging the body towards the buildings; then she pushed it under one of them.'

'Did you say the *woman*? Do you mean the woman who was killed or the murderer?'

'The murderer. Igimaq said it was a woman.'

Thóra wasn't sure how to end their conversation. She glanced over at the subdued group gathered around the television. No one paid any attention to her. Except for Friðrikka. She stared into Thóra's eyes and had seemed to have taken in every word. Thóra thanked Oqqapia warmly and said the police would doubtless be getting in touch with her soon. She hung up without taking her eyes off Friðrikka, without so much as blinking. Apart from Oddný Hildur, there had only been one woman at the camp.

*   *   *

Friðrikka was a strange character. While they were at the camp she had been like a fragile little flower,

411

unable to cope with anything, but in the end she appeared strong and serene. Of course the tears flowed as before, yet she showed no sign at all of breaking down. Thóra had offered to assist her in the police interrogation, until another lawyer could be found. The search for one was already under way, so Thóra was only present when Friðrikka was first questioned.

Arnar Jóhannesson had poisoned Friðrikka's life so much that she was no longer in control of her own actions. She had difficulty explaining what had prompted the actual assault, whether she had intended to kill the man or just injure him. Thóra was quite sure that Friðrikka herself didn't know the answer. Her hatred had simply overwhelmed her. She blamed Arnar for her divorce and had done so for a long time. He had come to her and wanted to confess, since it was one of the steps in his twelve-step treatment programme. He told her that he'd had a relationship with her husband around the time that the man came out of the closet. They had met at Berg's Annual Ball, and Arnar had seen immediately that the man was pretending to be something he wasn't. He had been drunk, and hadn't had too many qualms about seducing the husband of his co-worker.

But after taking account of his life, it was clear to Arnar that he had betrayed a trust that under normal circumstances should have been worth more to him than one night's fun. Nothing had come of the relationship; nevertheless, after listening to Arnar ask for forgiveness, Friðrikka blamed him for the end of her marriage. Arnar hadn't been the first man in her husband's life, but when someone is hurting it is so tempting to find a

412

scapegoat for all the sorrow, disappointment and anger. Hence Friðrikka felt nothing but hatred towards Arnar, and when it appeared that her friendship with Oddný Hildur would be ruined because of him, it was the last straw.

They had argued bitterly over the harassment that Arnar was suffering. Oddný Hildur felt her friend simply turned a blind eye to the bullying, lacking the courage to condemn it. She just looked the other way and smiled at those who treated him the worst. Friðrikka hadn't entrusted anyone with the truth about what Arnar had done to her, so she was unable to defend herself against her friend's accusations. Her feeble objections did little more than pour oil on the fire. When she went to the office building she was thinking of taking revenge once and for all against the man who had destroyed her life twice. Arnar had said that he was going to work after supper, but Oddný Hildur hadn't told anyone that she was planning to do the same. Friðrikka stewed over her plans in her apartment but at some point, which she could not properly recall, she stood up, dressed, went to sit in the car outside the office building and waited for Arnar. She said that while waiting she'd felt as if she were in a trance; her mind had been completely empty. The die had been cast. She recalled seeing a sled dog sitting near the car, staring at her, but she'd been too upset to wonder why it was looking at her like that. She had seen the dog walk calmly round behind the building, and some time later the light had gone off in Arnar's office. Suddenly the entire workplace went dark. The front door opened. Friðrikka climbed out of the car and shut the door quietly behind her. She saw Arnar bend his head

413

down against the wind. He turned his face from the car, and so had no idea she was there. Until it was too late.

Friðrikka swung her rock hammer at the back of Arnar's neck. She didn't feel anything. Neither satisfaction nor fear. She felt nothing at the first blow. And she felt nothing at the second blow. Then she rolled Arnar over at her feet and discovered her mistake. Finally her emotions overwhelmed her. She fell to her knees and tried to shake her friend awake. She described in a low voice how it became clear to her that Oddný Hildur was dead and the tears that streamed from the glazed, staring eyes of her friend were merely melted snowflakes. Despair seized her. She decided to hide the body underneath her apartment building. That would give her a chance to assess the situation and decide what to do next. She shovelled away the snow, pushed the body beneath the building and pushed the snow back over it. The wind and snowfall would cover her tracks.

Circumstances allowed her to avoid having to cover up what she'd done, as everyone at the camp was convinced that Oddný Hildur had been lost in the storm. Search parties were sent out. Friðrikka's strange behaviour was ascribed to her concern for her lost friend. No one suspected that she had anything to do with it. The blood on the side of the building where the women's apartment was located had come from when she had leaned against the building as she struggled to dig away the snow, but even that evidence was not seriously examined. Nor did anyone comment on how she offered to search the camp area. She said that she had experienced her first major shock when she saw that the body

414

was gone. Then she'd started wondering whether she had maybe dreamt the whole thing; Oddný Hildur had actually gone missing and hadn't died of head injuries inflicted in a blind rage. She understood none of it and was constantly on the verge of a nervous breakdown. She decided to leave her job and again no one made any comments. Everyone just thought that she was feeling unwell after losing her best friend.

In fact, Friðrikka still seemed to be in two minds as to what had actually happened. She asked whether it were possible that the man who now claimed to have moved the body might even have killed Oddný Hildur. Her connection with reality was tenuous at best. She had even slunk out into the night once, to check one more time beneath the house to see if Oddný Hildur was perhaps still there. Doubt about what precisely had happened had gnawed at her ever since, and still did. She had reactivated the floodlight system when she was terrified that the person who had removed the body might return and attack her.

When the interrogation was finished and Thóra was hoping to rejoin the others, Friðrikka grabbed her arm frantically and asked what had become of her cat. The neighbours who had been looking after it hadn't been happy about having to carry on doing so and probably wouldn't take it. When Thóra reassured her that there was no shortage of good homes for a beautiful cat, Friðrikka gave her an imploring stare. Before Thóra sat a woman who had effectively banished herself from civilized society, and she doubted Friðrikka would now ever obtain what she desired so much, the friendship and love of another individual. Thóra would not

415

return home with a polar bear cub, but a cat would do just as well. 'I'll take your cat. My daughter will take good care of her.'

Epilogue

30 May 2008

Thóra hung up the phone and stared at the divorce papers that were waiting to be signed. A young couple had discovered too late that they didn't get on well enough, and like so many others in their shoes they now had nothing in common but debts. And as strange as it seemed, people were much more nitpicking about dividing their debts than their assets. But when all was said and done, couples applied for divorce because they couldn't imagine being in each other's presence any longer, so in the end, they came to an agreement. In the end, freedom from one's spouse was always a stronger impulse than anything else.

The trip to Greenland hadn't yielded the legal firm any other projects from the bank. Nevertheless an agreement had been reached with the mining company; Berg Technology was allowed to continue the project and the insurance money was left untouched. Thóra hoped that her report had played some part in the matter, but it was just as likely that things had been resolved at a political level, or that the temporary closure of the area for archaeological research at the cave had been the decisive factor. In any case, the mining company, contractors and the bank had reached agreements while individual employees were left with no idea what was going on, except that they had lost their co-workers under tragic circumstances. It was a great loss for such a small workplace: three dead

417

and two incapacitated, though one of them had of course already left the company. Fortunately there was no plan to start work again until the summer, so the employees were given time and space to recover in the company of family and friends. Hopefully the deepest wounds would be healed by the time work began again.

Thóra had experienced some minor inconveniences herself. The health authorities in Greenland had confiscated her large green suitcase and had it destroyed, along with everything in it, due to risk of infection. Of course this risk was small, but apparently they didn't want to take any chances. Her companions had had the same treatment. However, they, unlike her, had packed their bags while sober, which meant they lost mainly underwear, fleece jackets and the like. Now Thóra rued her many years of choosing classic work clothing that was likely to survive the whims of fashion. Like the others, the bank had paid her compensation, but Thóra hadn't been able to inform them that the contents of her luggage had been worth much more than that of her colleagues and had also had much more emotional value. Now that it was clear the bank would not be the source of further work, she regretted this deeply.

Friðrikka had been on the phone. Her voice sounded completely different to before and Thóra suspected that the woman was on drugs. She wanted to ask Thóra to help her ensure that she would be moved to Iceland when she was sentenced, so that she could serve her time in her home country. Friðrikka said that otherwise she would die; she couldn't stay in Greenland. She also asked about the cat, which Thóra assured her was being spoiled rotten. This at least seemed to make Friðrikka feel a bit better. However, Thóra said she needed to think over Friðrikka's request to defend her, though she would certainly lend her a helping hand. They had little else to talk about. Naturally, Friðrikka asked about Arnar's fate and Thóra was able to inform her that the engineer had officially confessed to everything that he had told her on the phone. A verdict was hanging over his head but it was impossible to say whether it would be suspended. Although Thóra did not mention it to Friðrikka, she had kept her eye on the obituaries recently and none had yet appeared suggesting that Arnar had killed himself. It could well be that he intended to wait until a verdict came from both courts in order to ensure that Naruana came out of it as well as he could, but the other possibility was that he had changed his mind or lost his courage. Thóra hoped that this was the case, but the determination in his voice when he'd told her of his plans had been so strong that in the end she doubted it.

Thóra knew less about the others; she hadn't heard from Alvar, Eyjólfur or Finnbogi since they'd parted ways at the airport in Reykjavík. Actually, she had gone to see the doctor about her final report, but that was all. When asked, she told Friðrikka that yes, Bella was fine, still working in reception at the legal firm, on top form and still intimidating clients and employees alike as only she could.

Thóra had only once given in to temptation and phoned Oqqapia. She didn't want to be connected to the woman any more than to everything else that had happened; all the signs indicated that the

419

poor woman's life would continue to be defined by sorrow, drinking and boredom. Thóra had enough disappointments in her own country without having to hunt them down across the borders. However, the telephone call had been surprisingly pleasant. Oqqapia had stuck to her word and got her life in order. She said it was difficult, but not counting a couple of small slip-ups she'd kept herself sober since the case had come to a head. She said that Naruana's difficulties had strengthened her, which had surprised her, but someone had to be ready to help him and his parents were in no position to do so. Like her, he had also put the cork in the bottle in the hope that this sign of progress would be taken into account when he was sentenced. Now they awaited the results together. The department of social services had sent alcohol counsellors to the village. It turned out that Naruana was also a teacher at the primary school, which had proved to be of priceless assistance to the couple in their struggle. Oqqapia stated with pride that Naruana had started hunting again, albeit only on a boat with others, but it was still a great improvement. At the end of their conversation Oqqapia had remembered to tell Thóra that Igimaq had now received his daughter's bones and that he was intending to lay them to rest once and for all. Examination of the remains had not revealed the cause of her death, but everything suggested that she had died of *that disease everyone's talking about*, as Oqqapia put it.

Before the phone call ended Thóra had asked the woman carefully whether Naruana had been able to give an explanation for why he'd taken the young girl with him to the camp when he went to remove the bodies. Oqqapia answered in the same nonchalant tone that she had used to describe the Spanish Flu. Apparently, the girl's parents had loaned Naruana their sled on the condition that he take her with him. Thóra didn't need to ask what sort of parents would let their child travel around on a snowmobile with a drunk. The answer was obvious: parents who were even drunker than the man who took their child. But some good had come out of it. The girl had been taken away for observation since she had been present at a bloodbath and it was possible that she was infected, and at the hospital in Nuuk it was decided that something could be done to repair her damaged face. Moreover, the fact that the girl had been humming provided hope that with the correct training and treatment, she would be able to regain her voice and the ability to speak. Thus her parents had been convinced to move to Nuuk in order to be able to continue looking after the child, and they had given the snowmobile to Oqqapia and Naruana in gratitude for their help in getting medical assistance for their daughter. Thóra did not presume to understand this gesture of appreciation, and settled for being pleased that not everyone was cast in the same mould. What mattered most was that all these people appeared to be slowly heading towards a better life. They could use it.

There was a knock at the door and in walked a prospective ex-husband in a divorce case. 'Hi, am I late?'

'No, you're right on time.' Thóra smiled. 'Have a seat. Everything's ready for you. Soon you'll be all by yourself.'

Igimaq looked out over the landscape. But when he turned his back on the cave, it spoiled the effect; what was the use of having beauty before his eyes when ugliness waited behind him? He held the bones of his daughter. He had wrapped them in an excellent sealskin that he himself had tanned many years ago and that he considered one of the most beautiful he had ever made. No one appreciated such things any longer and he had never let it out of his hands, but had saved it for a better time. Now that time had come. The skin would protect the bones from unnecessarily harsh conditions inside the cave until the end, when the land would melt and sink into the sea to the animals who would then have complete control. He and the dog would be long gone by then but that did not matter, at least not to anyone but the two of them.

The dog howled, wanting to get away from this cursed place. Igimaq had witnessed his daughter suffering and weeping, begging him to allow her to seek help at a settlement. But there had been no help to be had. When she'd entered the area, to her father's displeasure, they had clashed, and he'd still been furious at her when the marks began to appear and her skin began turning blue. She had already grown weak, and Igimaq had consulted with Sikki, who was absolutely certain about what should be done—it would not have been so black and white now, when the prospect of work seemed to cancel out all the ancient customs. Igimaq had not refused. He had dragged his desperately ill daughter back out to the area and forced Naruana to assist him, since in time his son would inherit the

422

obligation to his ancestors. Naruana had seemed to understand this at the time, but his swift decline after Usinna's fate had been sealed suggested that the decision had been ill-considered—with terrible consequences. Naruana had already been having problems with alcohol, and the terrible death of his sister had finally pushed him over the edge towards self-destruction. His mother had followed close on his heels, for the same reason. Igimaq almost understood them. Although Usinna's struggle with death had not been long, time passed slowly when you were forced to watch someone so close to your heart suffer so cruelly, turning blue in the face until blood poured from her mouth, eyes and nose. Her last breath formed a red bubble between her lips which did not burst until the wind blew a strand of black hair over her mouth. If he hadn't been so angry at her he might have comforted her or allowed Naruana to hold her hand, which was the last thing she had begged for. By the time he disposed of her body his anger had gone. He had planned to remove the necklace with her name on it, but saw that it was gone. It had been around her neck when he'd dragged her onto the sled with Naruana's help; it was a piece he had made for her when she was a little girl, and he knew very well that the fastenings were secure and that the chain hadn't broken. He also knew that Usinna had realized they were planning to leave her alone out in the wilderness, and he knew his daughter well enough to know what she had done with it. She had swallowed it so that her body might be identified later, if it were ever found. It was inconceivable that he would cut open his dead daughter's belly to retrieve the necklace—as inconceivable as allowing her to return home when she looked at him with bloody eyes and pleaded with him for the last time. The unquiet souls of the dead would never have allowed it. Naruana and Igimaq had only escaped themselves because of the strength of the souls' malicious excitement about the new young member for their tribe. In their greed, they forgot about father and son.

The men who came to investigate the cave had never experienced any of these things personally, nor had they listened to the souls that still dwelt inside even though their earthly remains were now in research institutes in Nuuk and farther afield. They had doubtless tried to draw attention to themselves while everything was being cleared out, wailed and screamed, but with no result. The ears of those who worked on freeing the remains from the ice only heard what floated at the surface, and ignored sounds that had their origins in the beyond. Yet these people heard the wind, even though no one knew where it came from or where it went; even though they could not put their hands around it.

Igimaq turned around. The mouth of the cave had been dug out and could be seen properly now for the first time in almost a hundred years. Summer was right around the corner; the ice on the ledge above the cave had melted and the icicles at its entrance resembled irregular, pointed teeth that glistened in the sun and dared him to look into the open mouth. It was a test; how would the great hunter defeat that which had no heartbeat to be stopped? Igimaq looked into the eyes of the dog, which howled again and turned its head in the direction they had come from. He had left the other dogs at home; they could not tolerate being in the vicinity of the cave and Igimaq could not allow their howling to disturb him. He knew that Naruana would look after them if he did not return; he and his son were back on speaking terms again, from time to time. Naruana was still not happy with what they had done to his sister, but he had stopped letting his conscience eat away at him from the inside. Igimaq hoped that the boy was finally starting to get a grip on life and would decide to marry Oqqapia and have children with her. Maybe then Usinna's soul would be saved, and if they were given the gift of a child, his own soul might also have some reason to hope.

The bones in his arms made their presence known again, clacking against each other in the sealskin bag. He arranged them as best he could but stopped when he heard the sound of faint crying coming from within the cave. He knew the voice very well even though it was softer than it had been in life. It was Usinna. Her soul called to him, and asked again why he hadn't reached out a helping hand. Death had clearly not eased her suffering. Now innumerable other voices joined in, all unhappy with their lot and demanding release.

The dog looked into Igimaq's eyes. It understood its master and knew that it was not bound to follow him any further. He would compel no one to join him on his final journey, because that journey had to be decided upon by men and beasts themselves. The dog looked away from Igimaq and stared into the black cave mouth. It was determined to go with him; its neck was arched and the hair stood up on its back. It took a step closer to the entrance and looked inquisitively at the hunter, who nodded his

425

head and set off. The closer they came to the cave the louder the voices within it grew. When they walked into the darkness the voices had reached an ear-shattering volume, and it seemed to Igimaq that they were looking forward to taking revenge for their cruel fate. Especially Usinna.

HO C9112
YTC 2/16
FORDHAM 4/19
3
WP 9/19